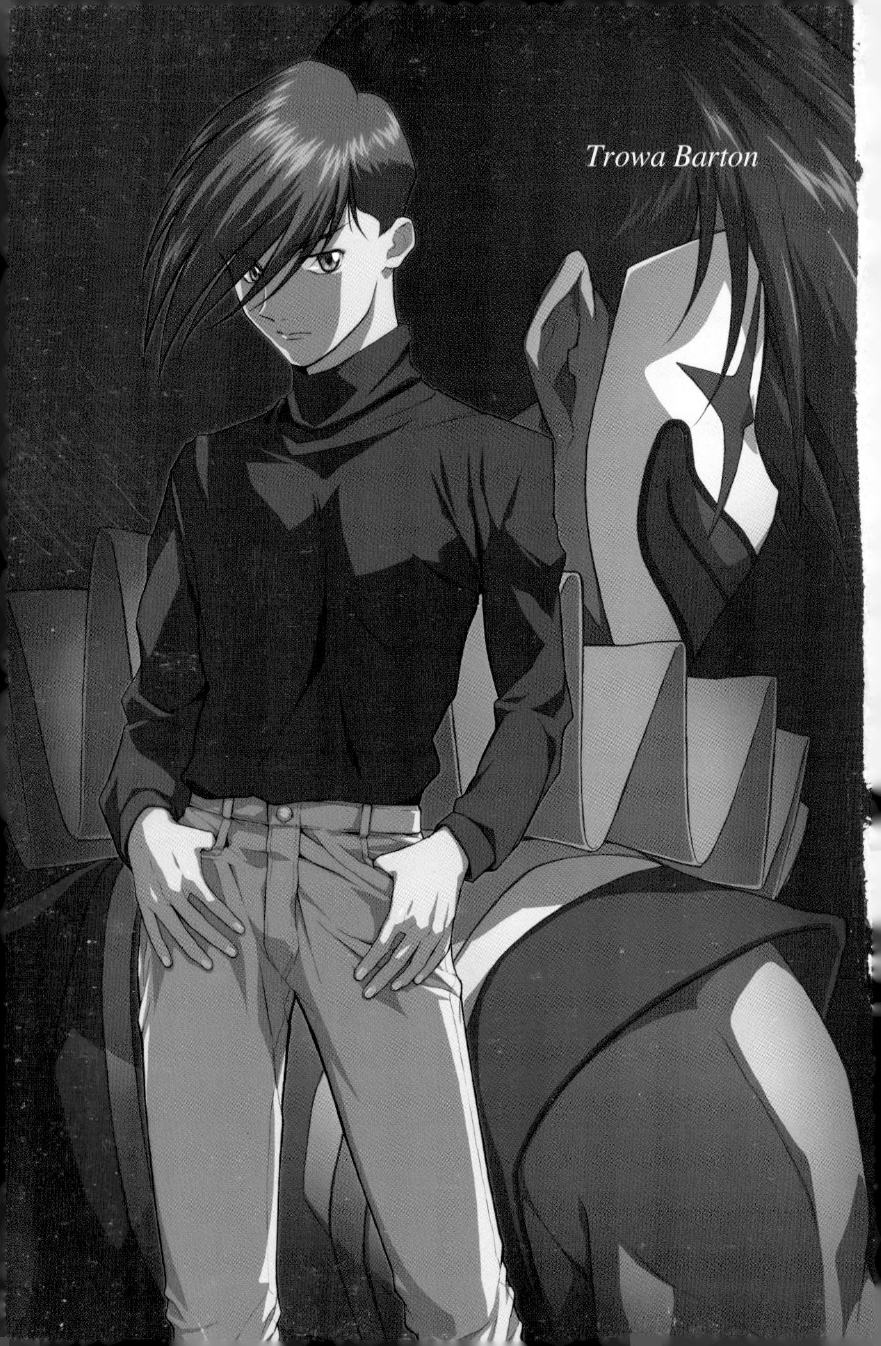
Trowa Barton

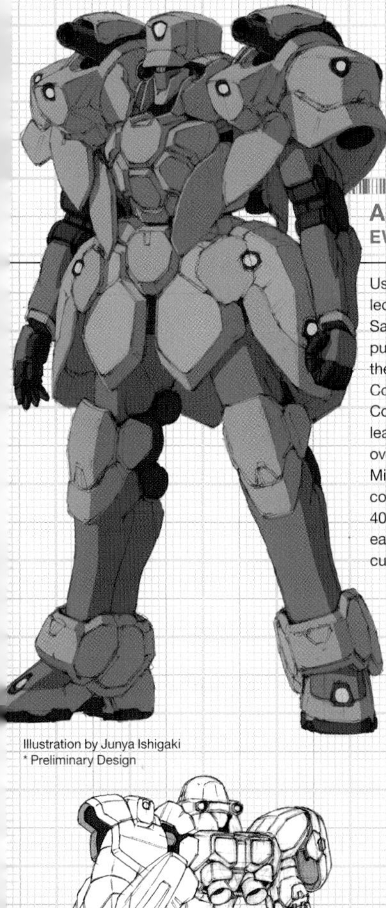

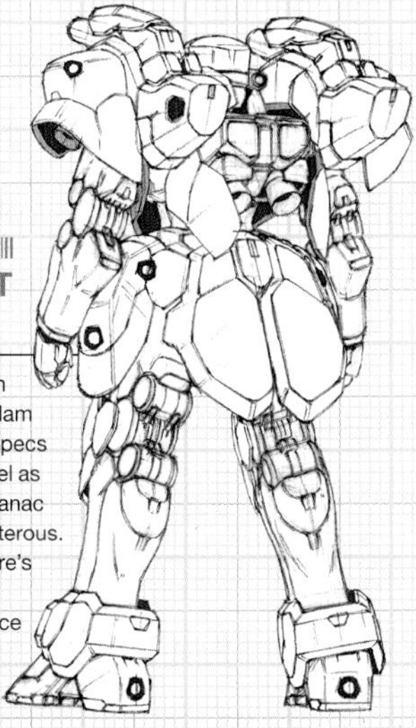

AHMAD UNIT
EW Version

Used by the MS team led by Quatre's Gundam Sandrock. Its basic specs put it at the same level as the Leo, but the Maganac Corps are highly dexterous. Combined with Quatre's leadership, they can overwhelm the Alliance Military in group combat. They have 40 units in total, and each unit is uniquely customized.

Illustration by Junya Ishigaki
* Preliminary Design

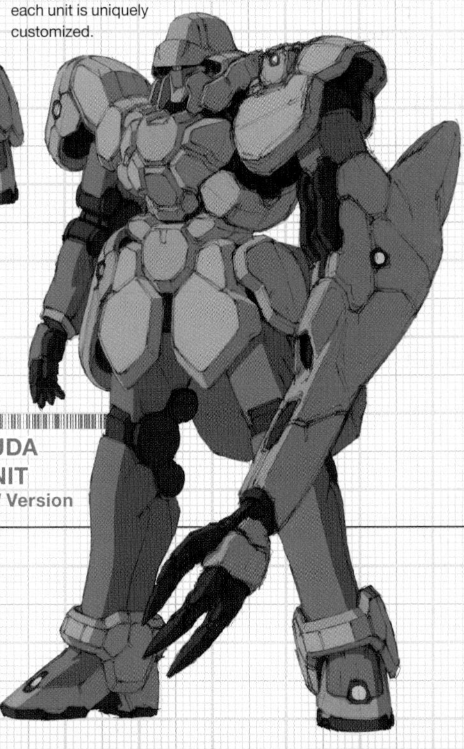

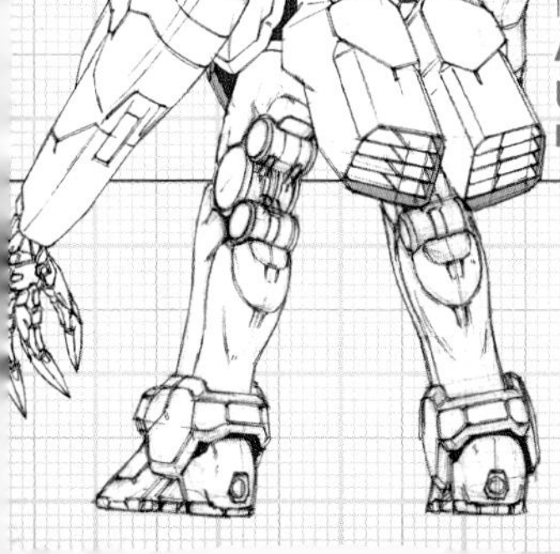

AUDA UNIT
EW Version

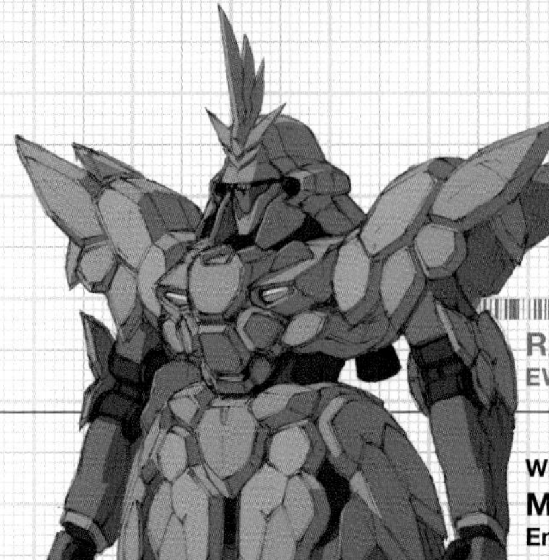

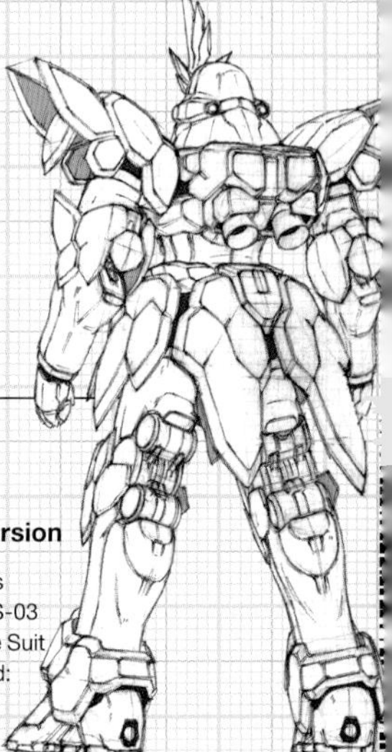

RASID UNIT
EW Version

WMS-03
MAGANAC
Endless Waltz Version

Pilot: Maganac Corps
Model Number: WMS-03
Classification: Mobile Suit
Height to Top of Head: 16.4 m
Body Weight: 7.4 t
Material: Titanium Alloy
Armaments: Beam Rifle x1, Heat Tomahawk x1, etc.

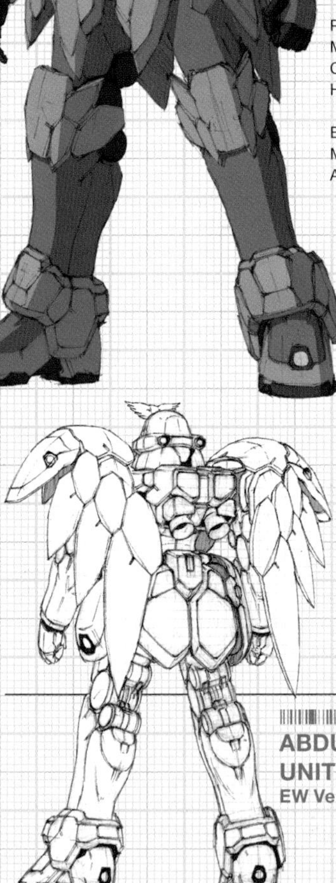

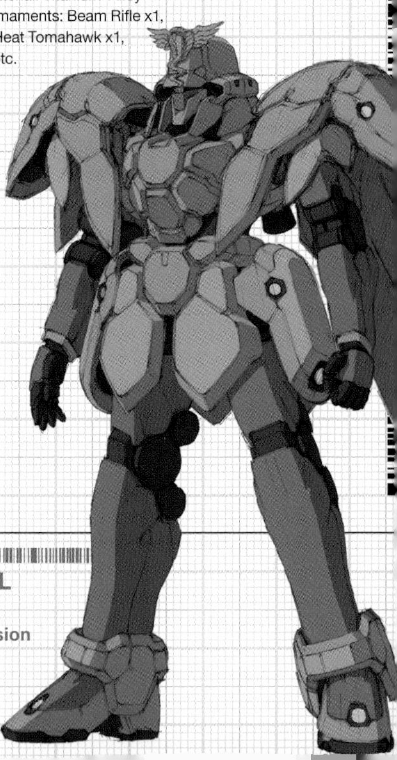

ABDUL UNIT
EW Version

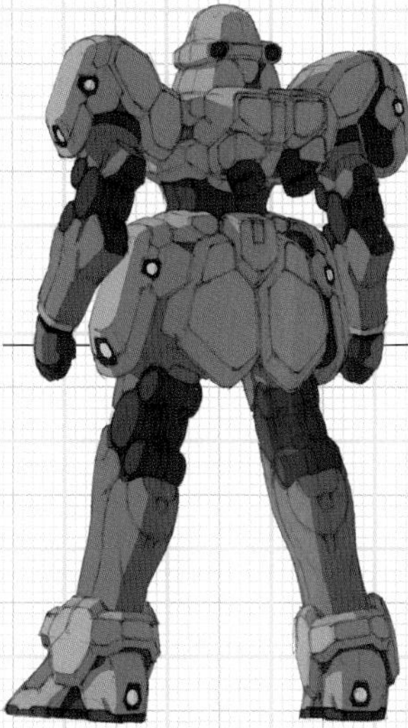

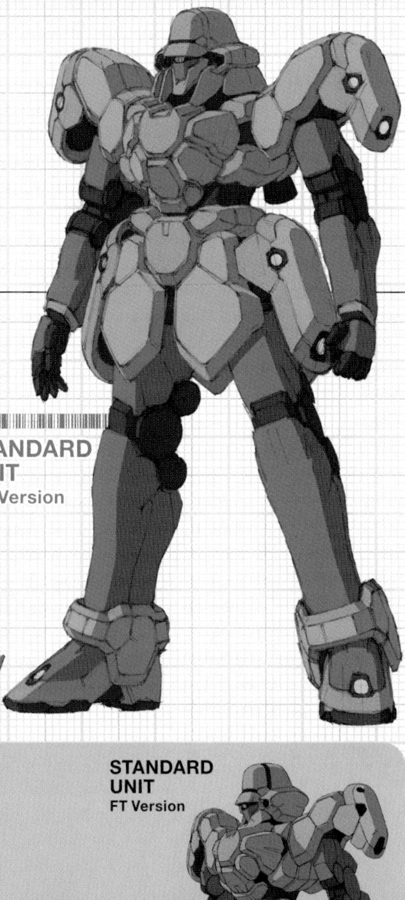

STANDARD UNIT
EW Version

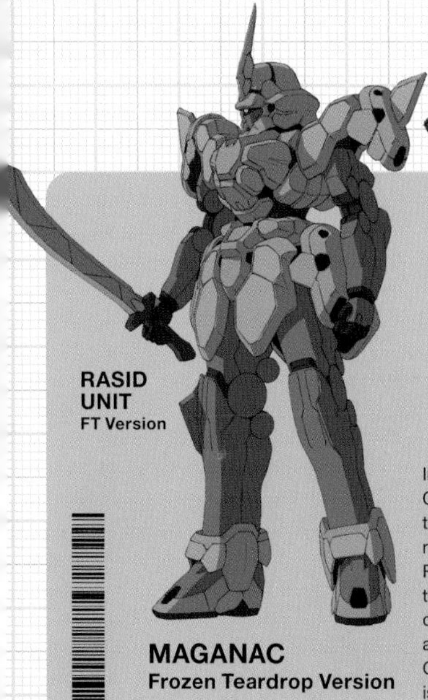

RASID UNIT
FT Version

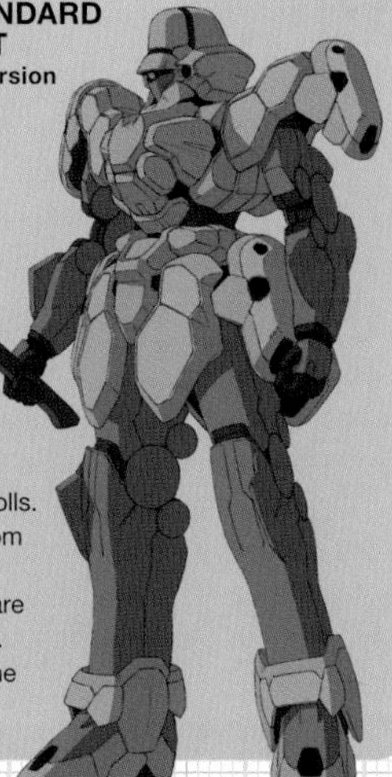

STANDARD UNIT
FT Version

MAGANAC
Frozen Teardrop Version

In the MC (Mars Century) timeline, the Maganac units reappear as Mobile Dolls. Remote-controlled from the Rasid unit, the 39 other Maganac units are all of the same design. Quatre's sister Cathrine is their controller.

Mobile Suit
GUNDAM WING
Endless Waltz
Glory of the Losers 3

Story

Katsuyuki Sumizawa

Art

Tomofumi Ogasawara

CONTENTS

XXXG-01D

GUNDAM DEATHSCYTHE ROUSETTE

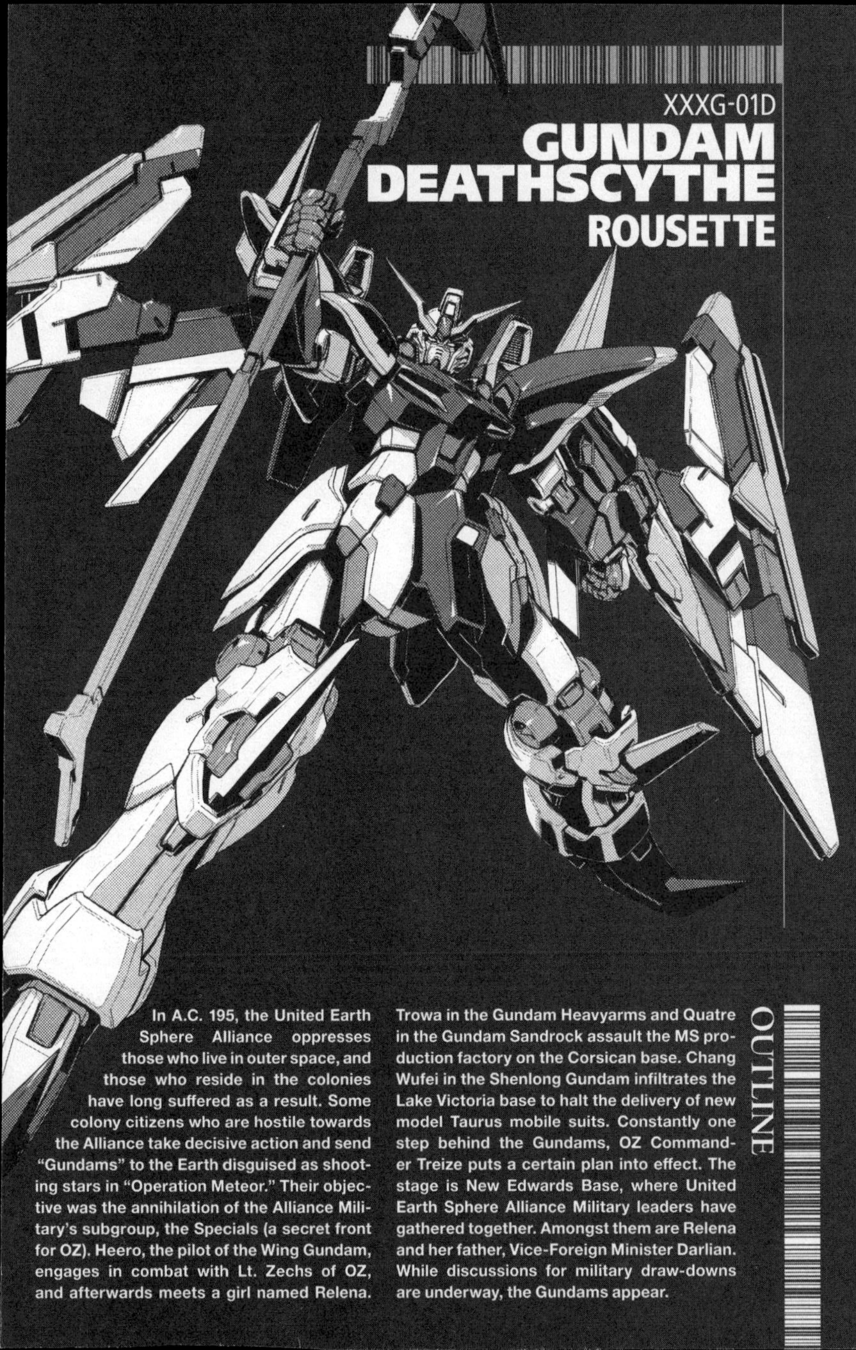

OUTLINE

In A.C. 195, the United Earth Sphere Alliance oppresses those who live in outer space, and those who reside in the colonies have long suffered as a result. Some colony citizens who are hostile towards the Alliance take decisive action and send "Gundams" to the Earth disguised as shooting stars in "Operation Meteor." Their objective was the annihilation of the Alliance Military's subgroup, the Specials (a secret front for OZ). Heero, the pilot of the Wing Gundam, engages in combat with Lt. Zechs of OZ, and afterwards meets a girl named Relena. Trowa in the Gundam Heavyarms and Quatre in the Gundam Sandrock assault the MS production factory on the Corsican base. Chang Wufei in the Shenlong Gundam infiltrates the Lake Victoria base to halt the delivery of new model Taurus mobile suits. Constantly one step behind the Gundams, OZ Commander Treize puts a certain plan into effect. The stage is New Edwards Base, where United Earth Sphere Alliance Military leaders have gathered together. Amongst them are Relena and her father, Vice-Foreign Minister Darlian. While discussions for military draw-downs are underway, the Gundams appear.

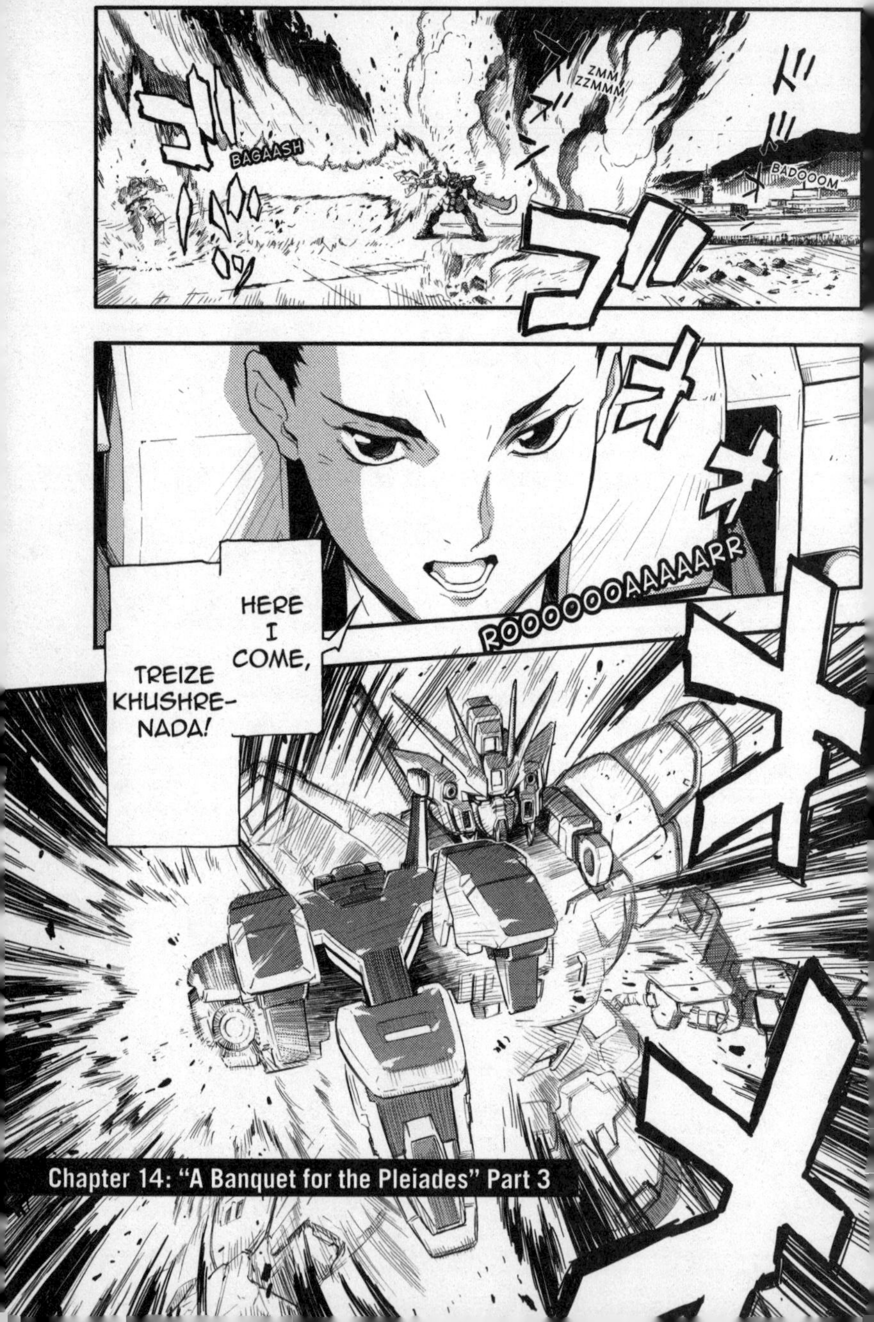
ZMM
ZZMMM
BADOOOM
BAGAASH
ROOOOOOAAAAAARR
HERE I COME, TREIZE KHUSHRE-NADA!

Chapter 14: “A Banquet for the Pleiades” Part 3

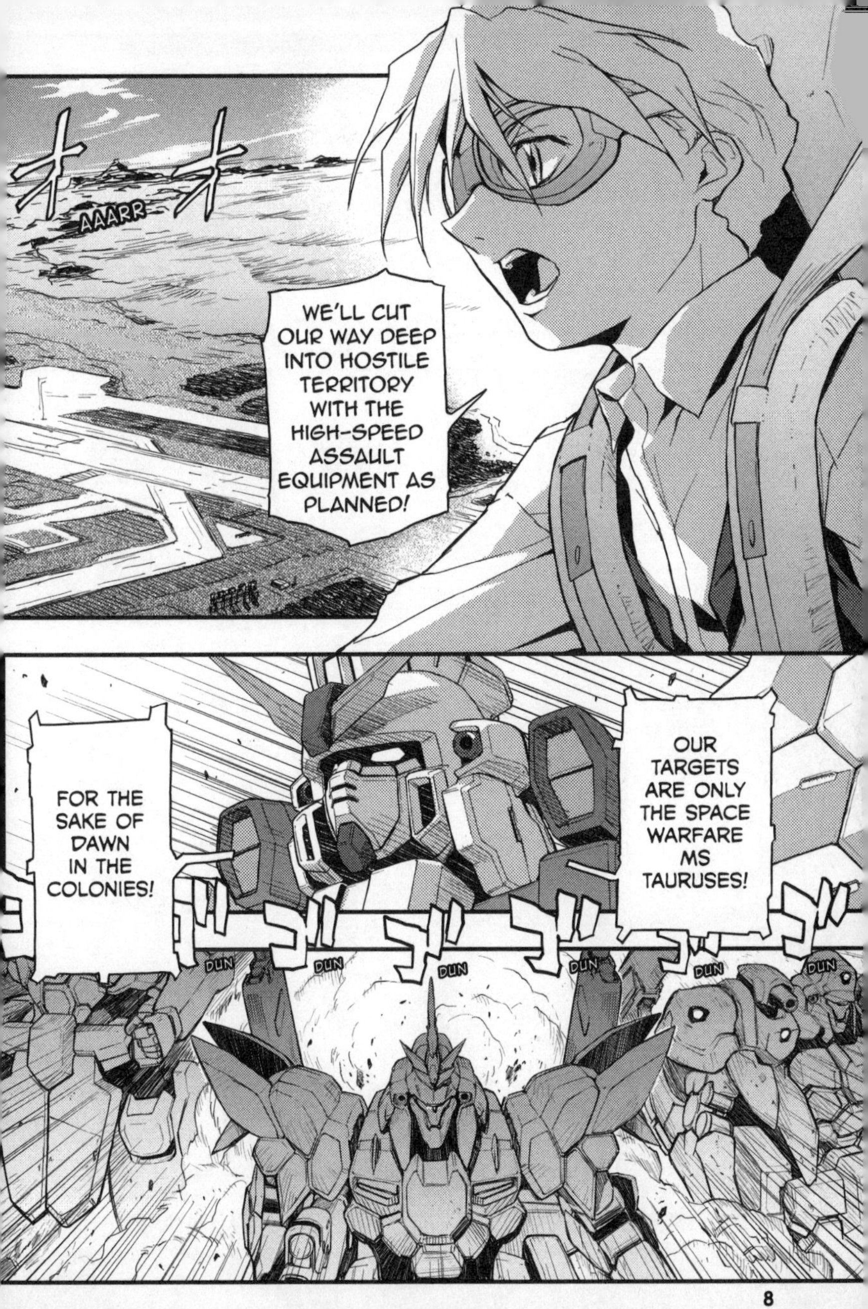
AAAARR
WE'LL CUT OUR WAY DEEP INTO HOSTILE TERRITORY WITH THE HIGH-SPEED ASSAULT EQUIPMENT AS PLANNED!
OUR TARGETS ARE ONLY THE SPACE WARFARE MS TAURUSES!
FOR THE SAKE OF DAWN IN THE COLONIES!
DUN
DUN
DUN
DUN
DUN
DUN

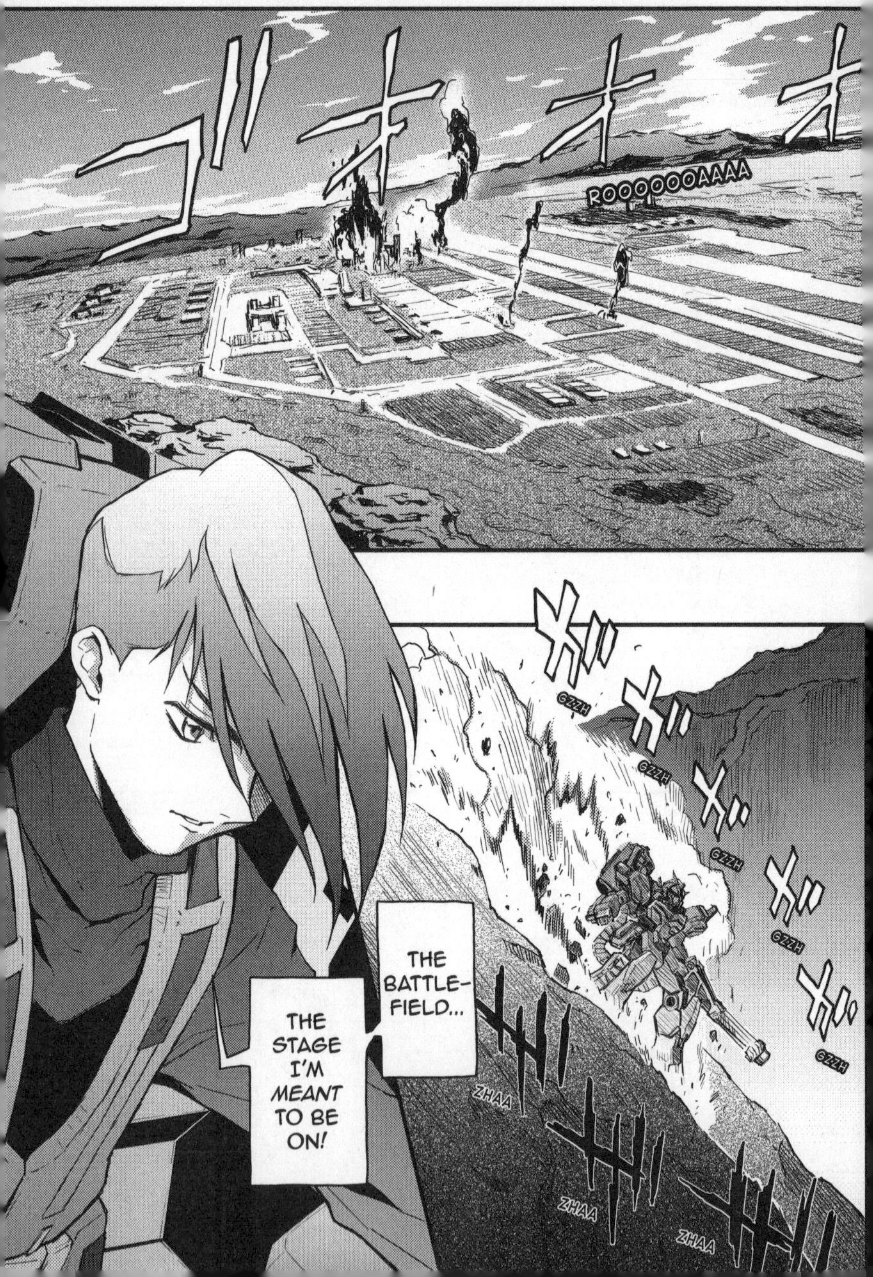

ROOOOOOAAAA
GZZH
GZZH
GZZH
GZZH
GZZH
THE BATTLE-FIELD...
THE STAGE I'M MEANT TO BE ON!
ZHAA
ZHAA
ZHAA

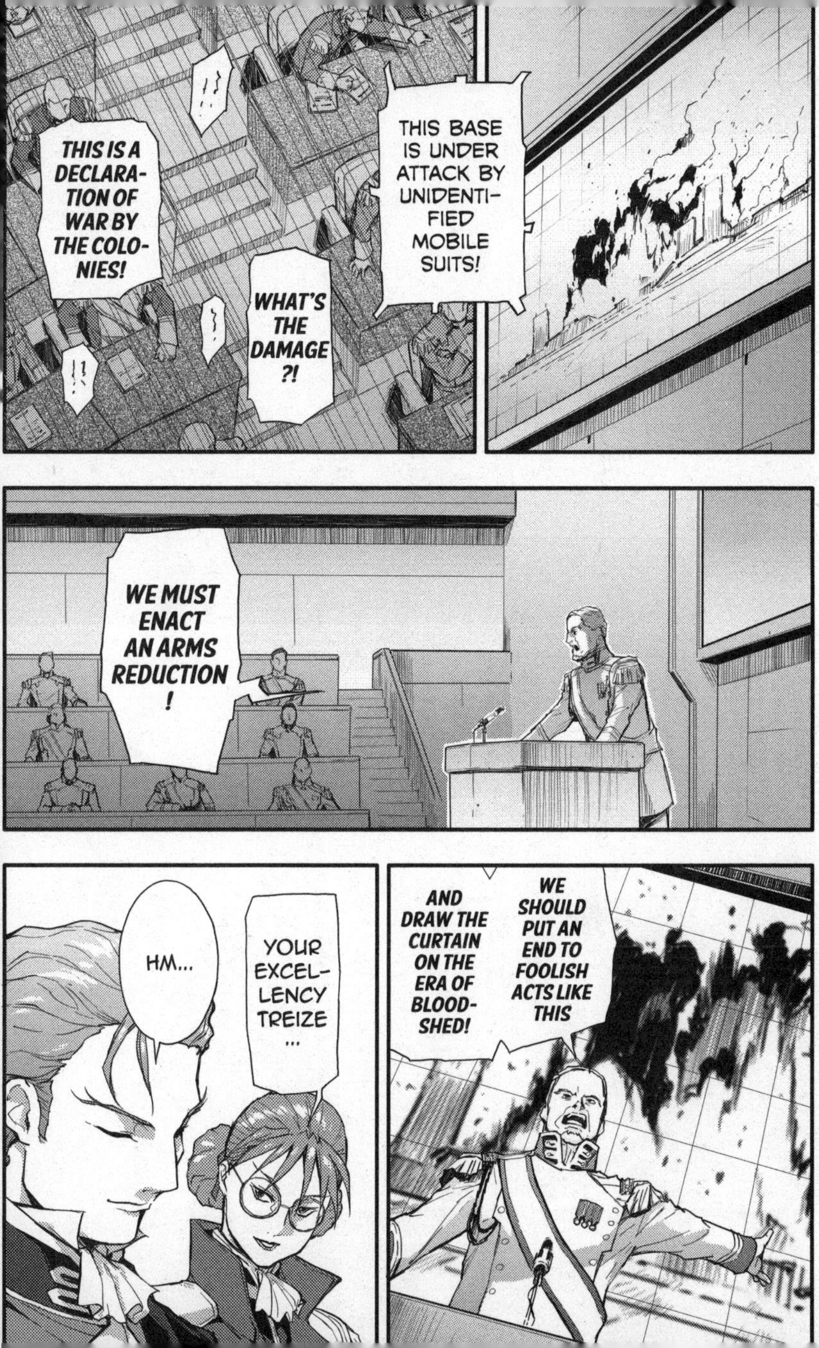
THIS BASE IS UNDER ATTACK BY UNIDENTIFIED MOBILE SUITS!
!?
WHAT'S THE DAMAGE?!
THIS IS A DECLARATION OF WAR BY THE COLONIES!
!?
!?
WE MUST ENACT AN ARMS REDUCTION!
WE SHOULD PUT AN END TO FOOLISH ACTS LIKE THIS
AND DRAW THE CURTAIN ON THE ERA OF BLOODSHED!
YOUR EXCELLENCY TREIZE...
HM...

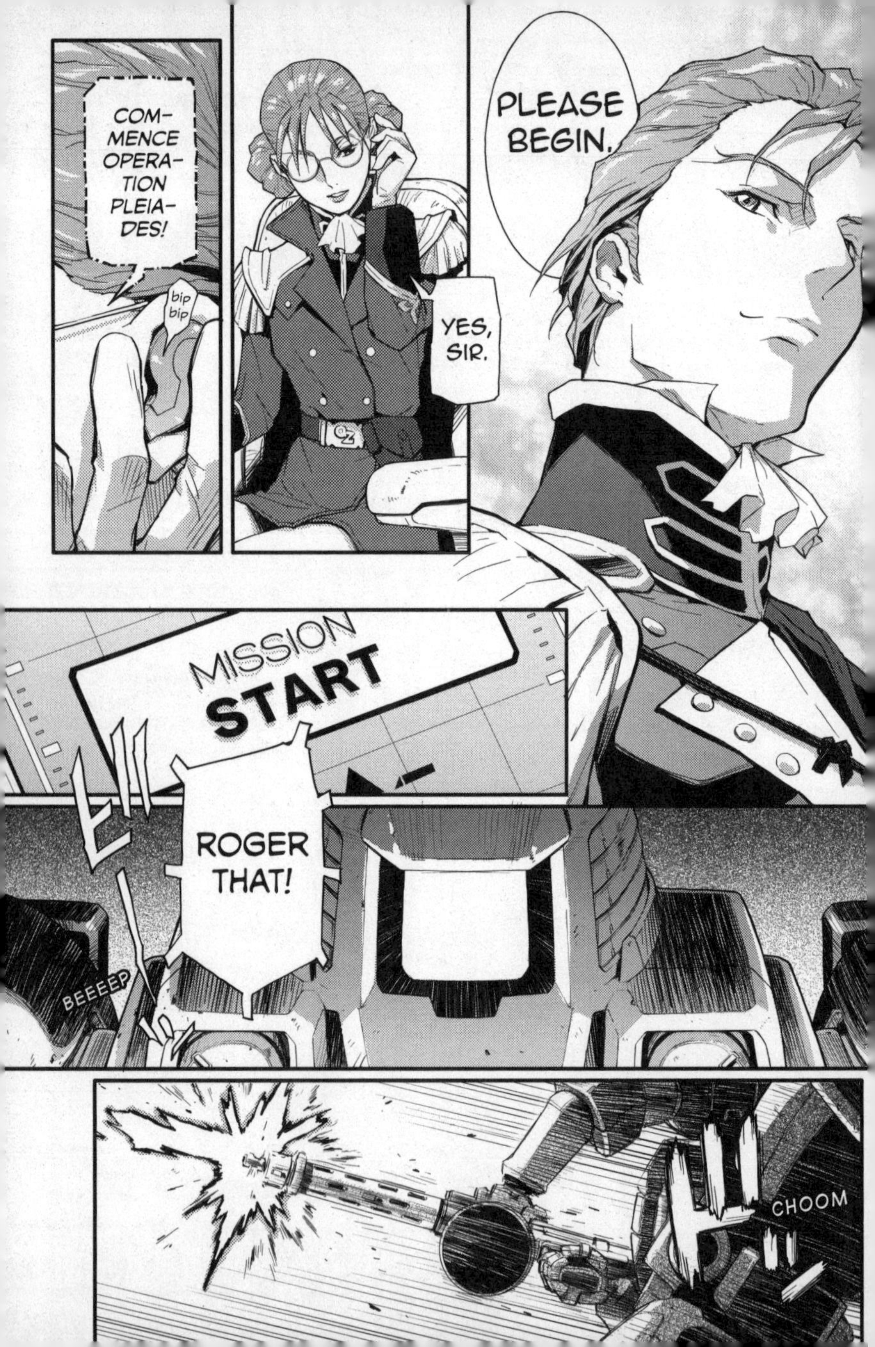
PLEASE BEGIN.
YES, SIR.
COM-MENCE OPERA-TION PLEIA-DES!
bip bip
MISSION START
ROGER THAT!
BEEEEP
CHOOM

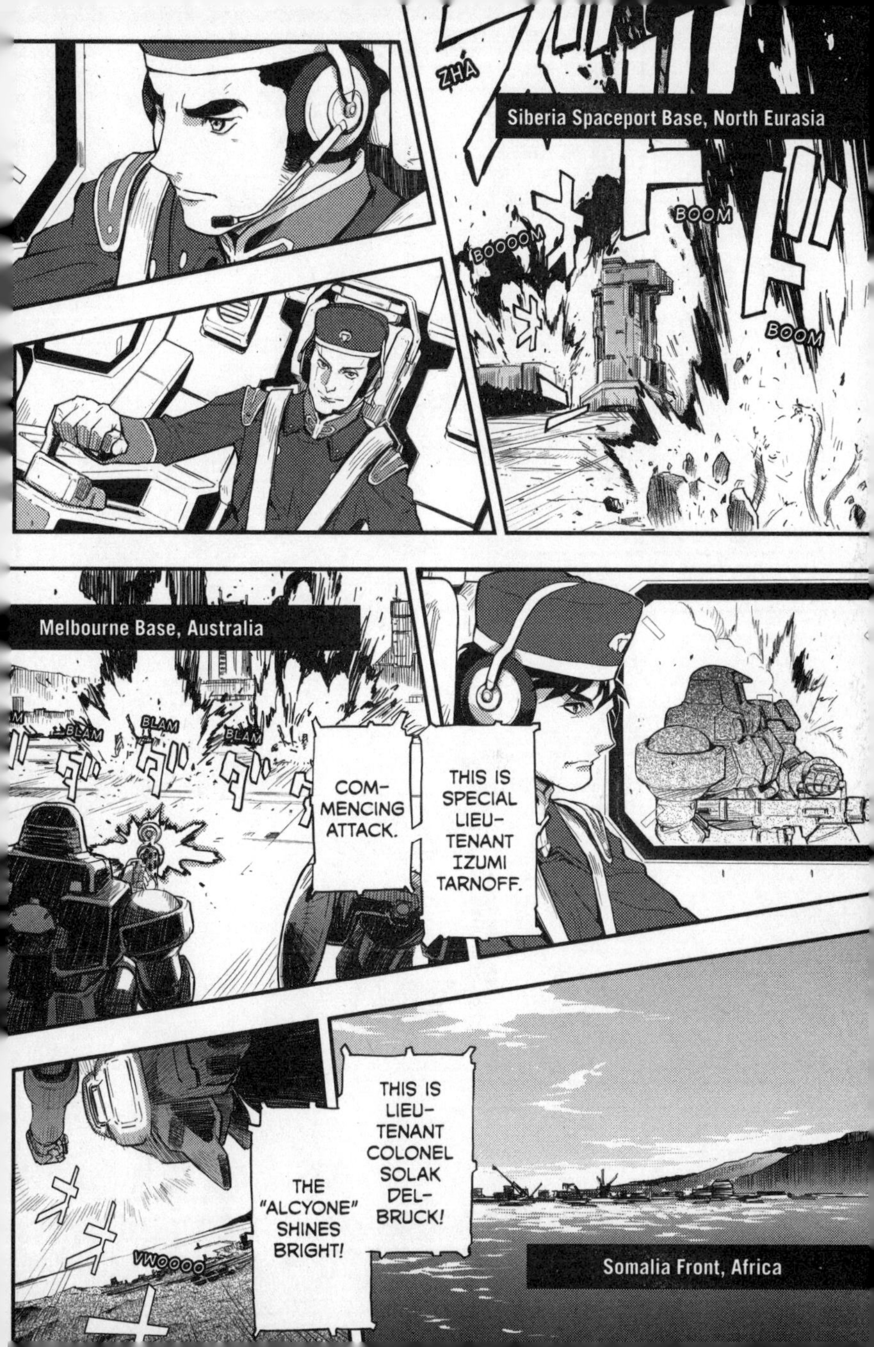
ZHA
Siberia Spaceport Base, North Eurasia
BOOM
BOOOOM
BOOM
THIS IS SPECIAL LIEU-TENANT IZUMI TARNOFF.
Melbourne Base, Australia
BLAM
BLAM
BLAM
COM-MENCING ATTACK.
Somalia Front, Africa
THIS IS LIEU-TENANT COLONEL SOLAK DEL-BRUCK!
THE "ALCYONE" SHINES BRIGHT!
VWOOOO

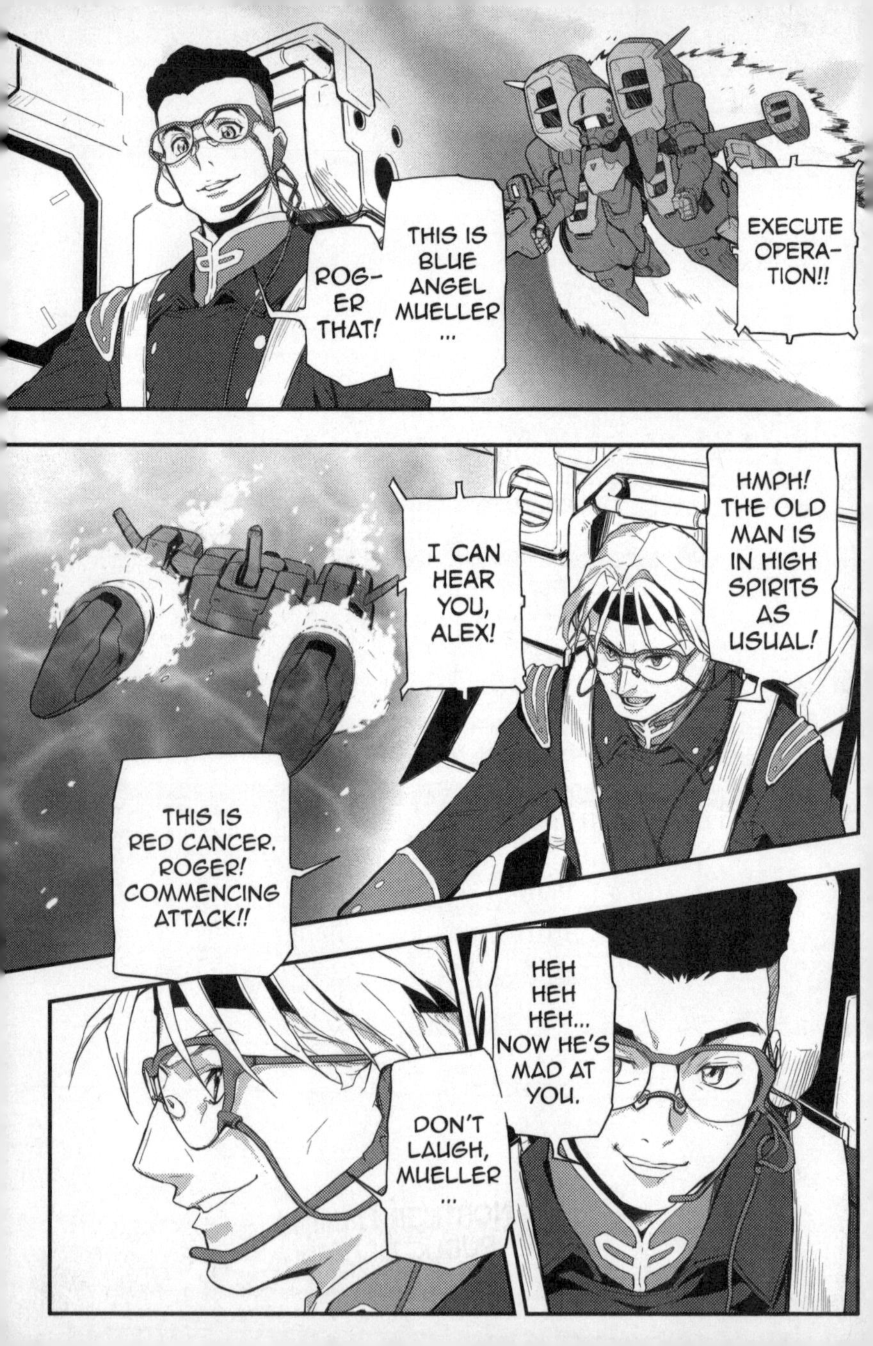
EXECUTE OPERATION!!
THIS IS BLUE ANGEL MUELLER ...
ROGER THAT!
HMPH! THE OLD MAN IS IN HIGH SPIRITS AS USUAL!
I CAN HEAR YOU, ALEX!
THIS IS RED CANCER. ROGER! COMMENCING ATTACK!!
HEH HEH HEH... NOW HE'S MAD AT YOU.
DON'T LAUGH, MUELLER ...

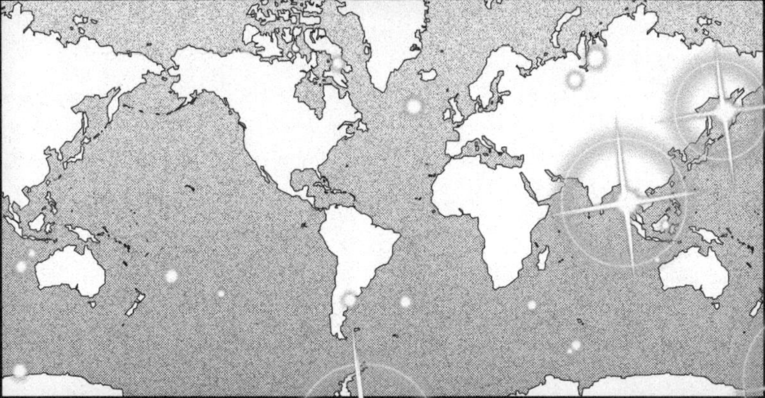

The mission was called "Operation Pleiades."
Its aim was to dismantle the United Earth Sphere
Alliance Military in one fell swoop.

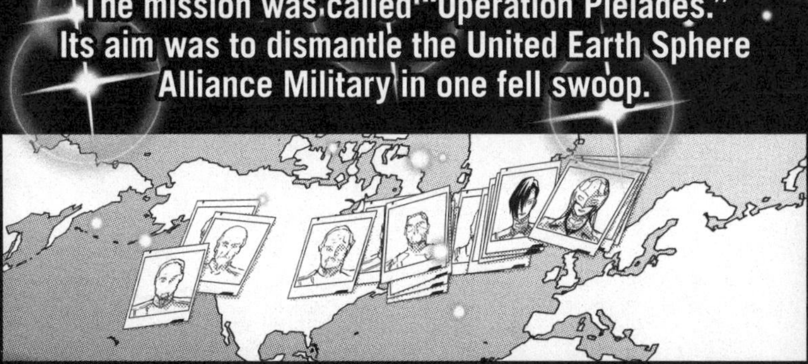

Crack OZ squads timed their all-out synchronized attacks for when the chain of command at principal military bases around the world was weakened due to the fact that key officers of the Alliance Military were gathered at New Edwards Base on the west coast of North America.

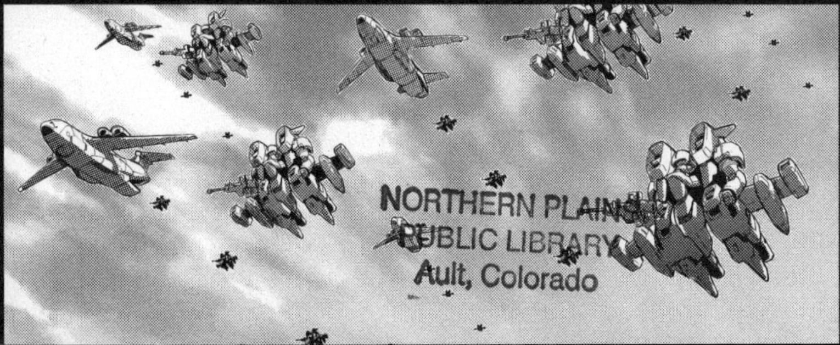

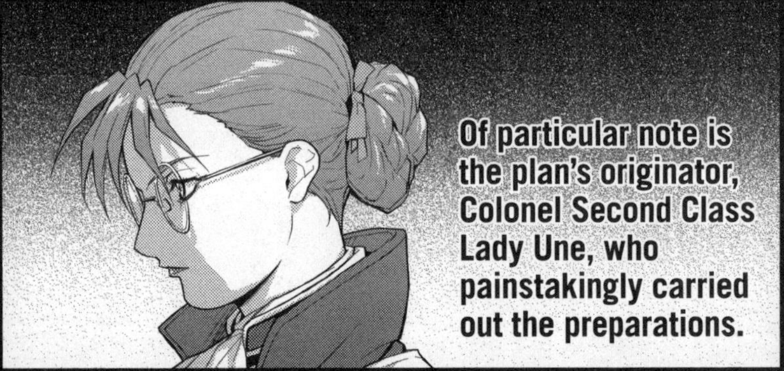
Of particular note is the plan's originator, Colonel Second Class Lady Une, who painstakingly carried out the preparations.

Further, luring together at New Edwards base the "Gundams," which would be wild cards during the operation's execution, was also considered a primary factor that would lead to the success of this operation.

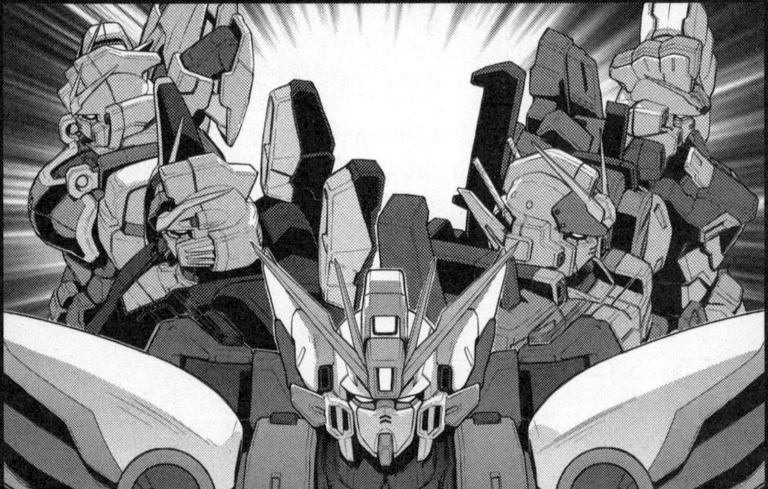

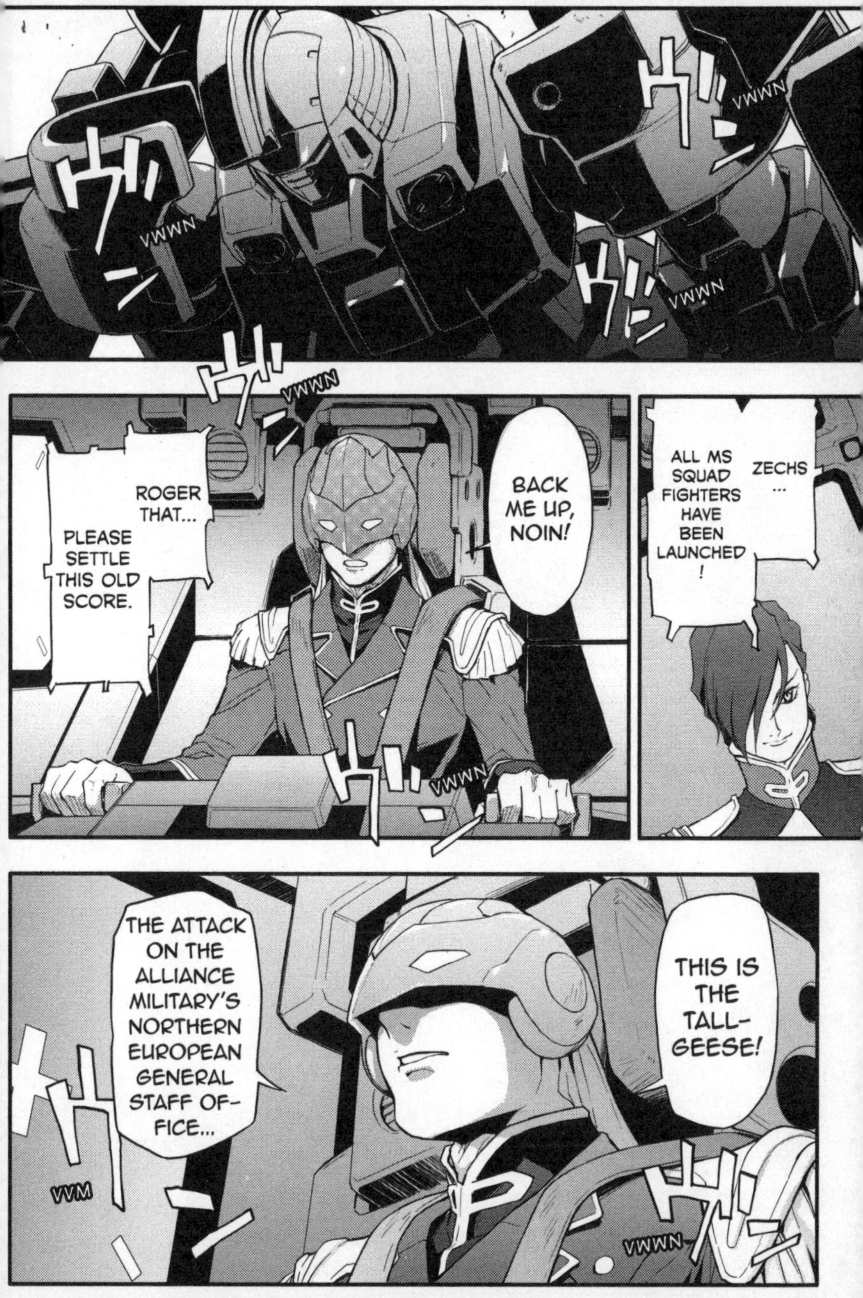
VWWN
VWWN
VWWN
ZECHS ...
ALL MS SQUAD FIGHTERS HAVE BEEN LAUNCHED!
VWWN
BACK ME UP, NOIN!
ROGER THAT...
PLEASE SETTLE THIS OLD SCORE.
VWWN
THIS IS THE TALL-GEESE!
THE ATTACK ON THE ALLIANCE MILITARY'S NORTHERN EUROPEAN GENERAL STAFF OF-FICE...
VWWN
VVM

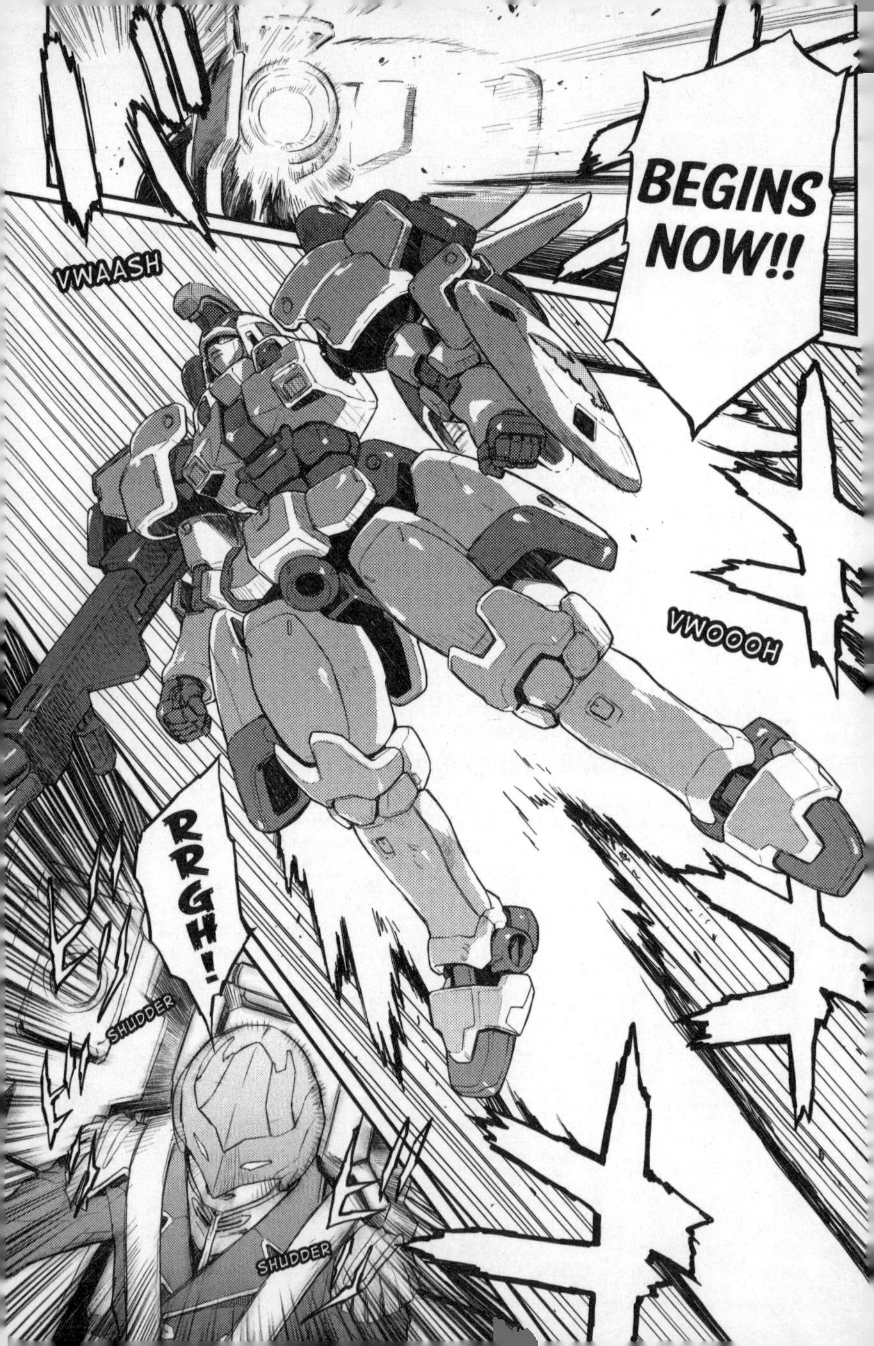
BEGINS NOW!!
VWAASH
VWOOOH
RRGH!!
SHUDDER
SHUDDER

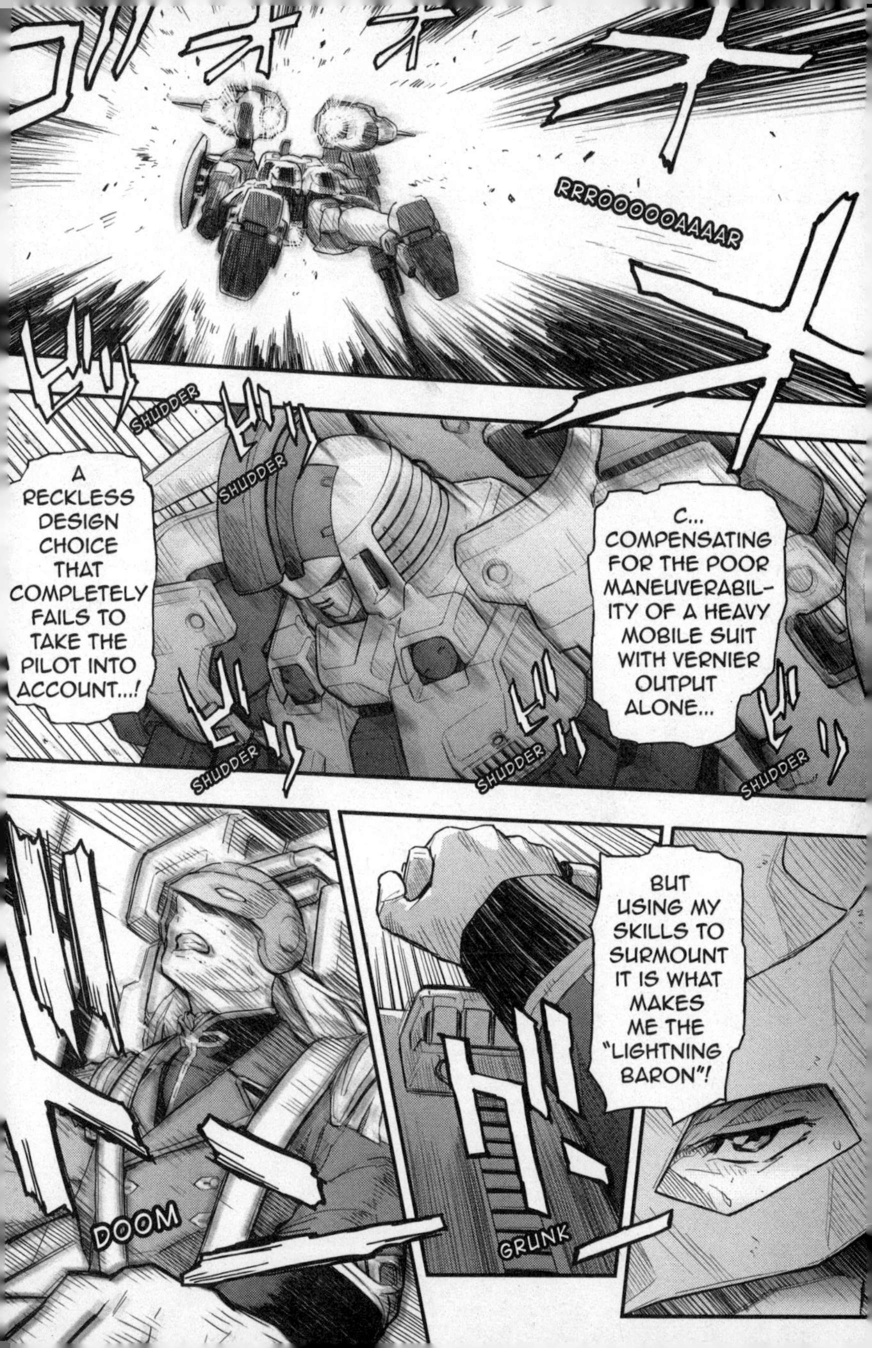
RRROOOOOOAAAAR
SHUDDER
SHUDDER
C... COMPENSATING FOR THE POOR MANEUVERABIL-ITY OF A HEAVY MOBILE SUIT WITH VERNIER OUTPUT ALONE...
A RECKLESS DESIGN CHOICE THAT COMPLETELY FAILS TO TAKE THE PILOT INTO ACCOUNT...!
SHUDDER
SHUDDER
SHUDDER
BUT USING MY SKILLS TO SURMOUNT IT IS WHAT MAKES ME THE "LIGHTNING BARON"!
GRUNK
DOOM

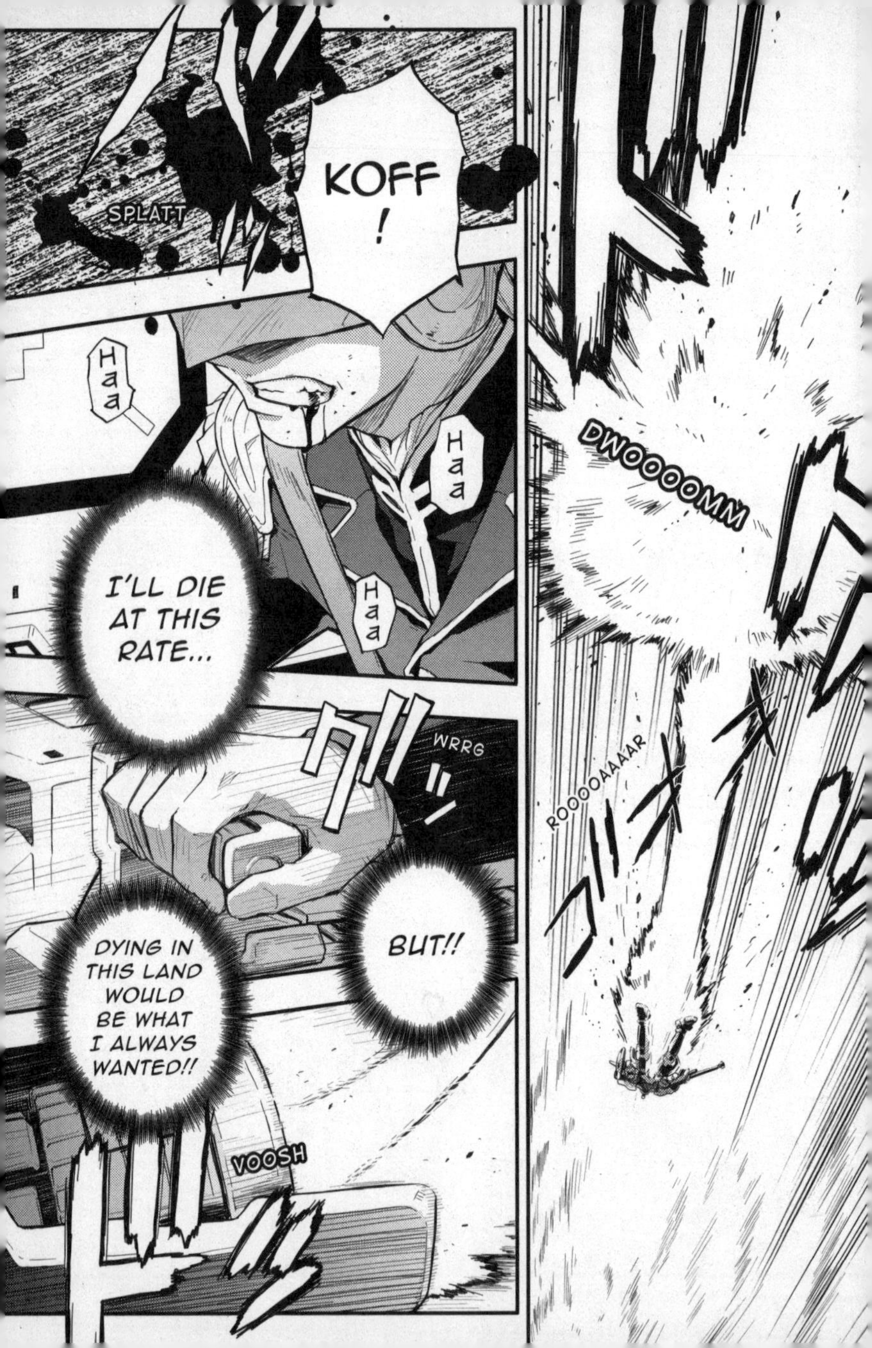
DWOOOOOMM
ROOOOAAAAR
KOFF!
SPLATT
Haa
Haa
Haa
I'LL DIE AT THIS RATE...
WRRG
BUT!!
DYING IN THIS LAND WOULD BE WHAT I ALWAYS WANTED!!
VOOSH

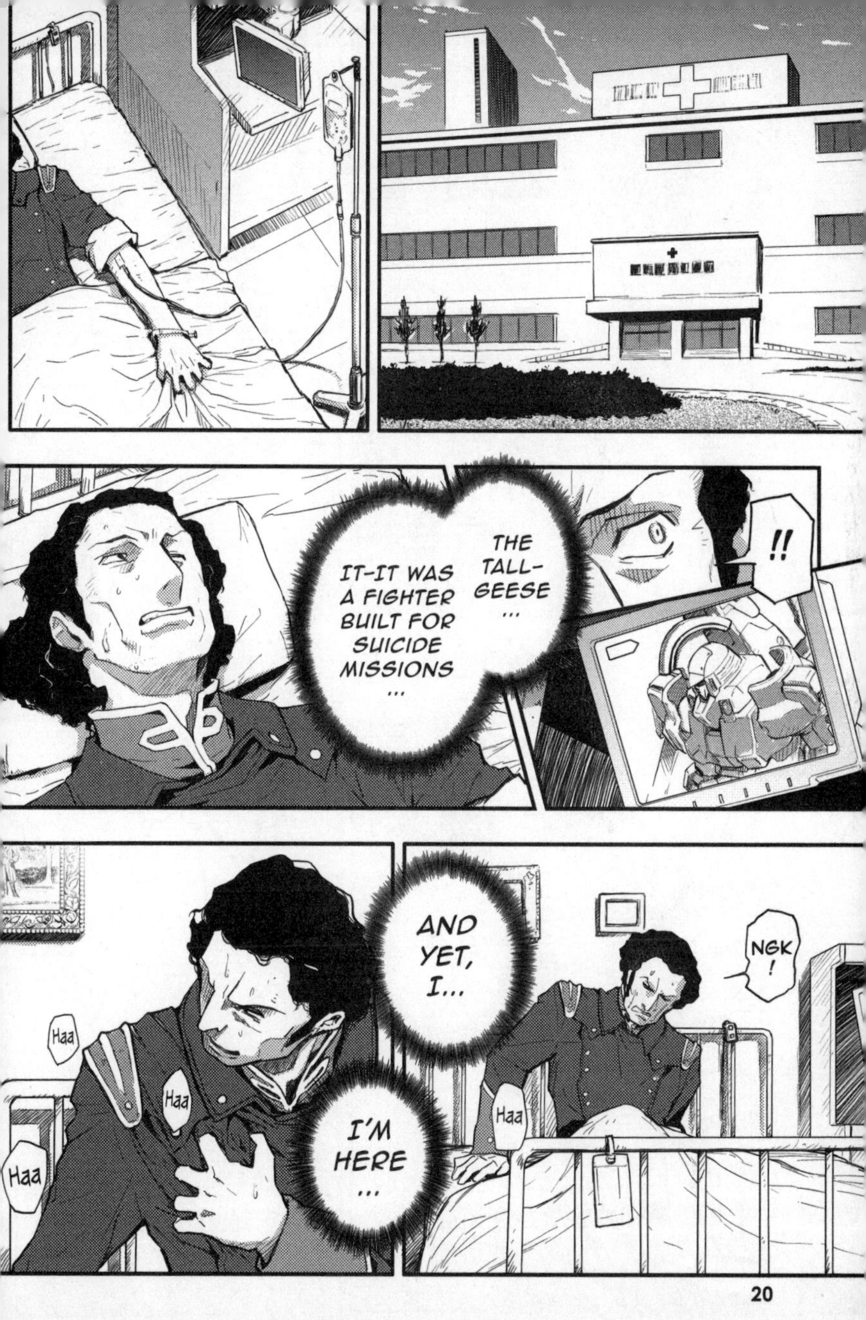
!!
THE TALL-GEESE ...
IT-IT WAS A FIGHTER BUILT FOR SUICIDE MISSIONS ...
NGK !
AND YET, I...
Haa
Haa
Haa
Haa
I'M HERE ...

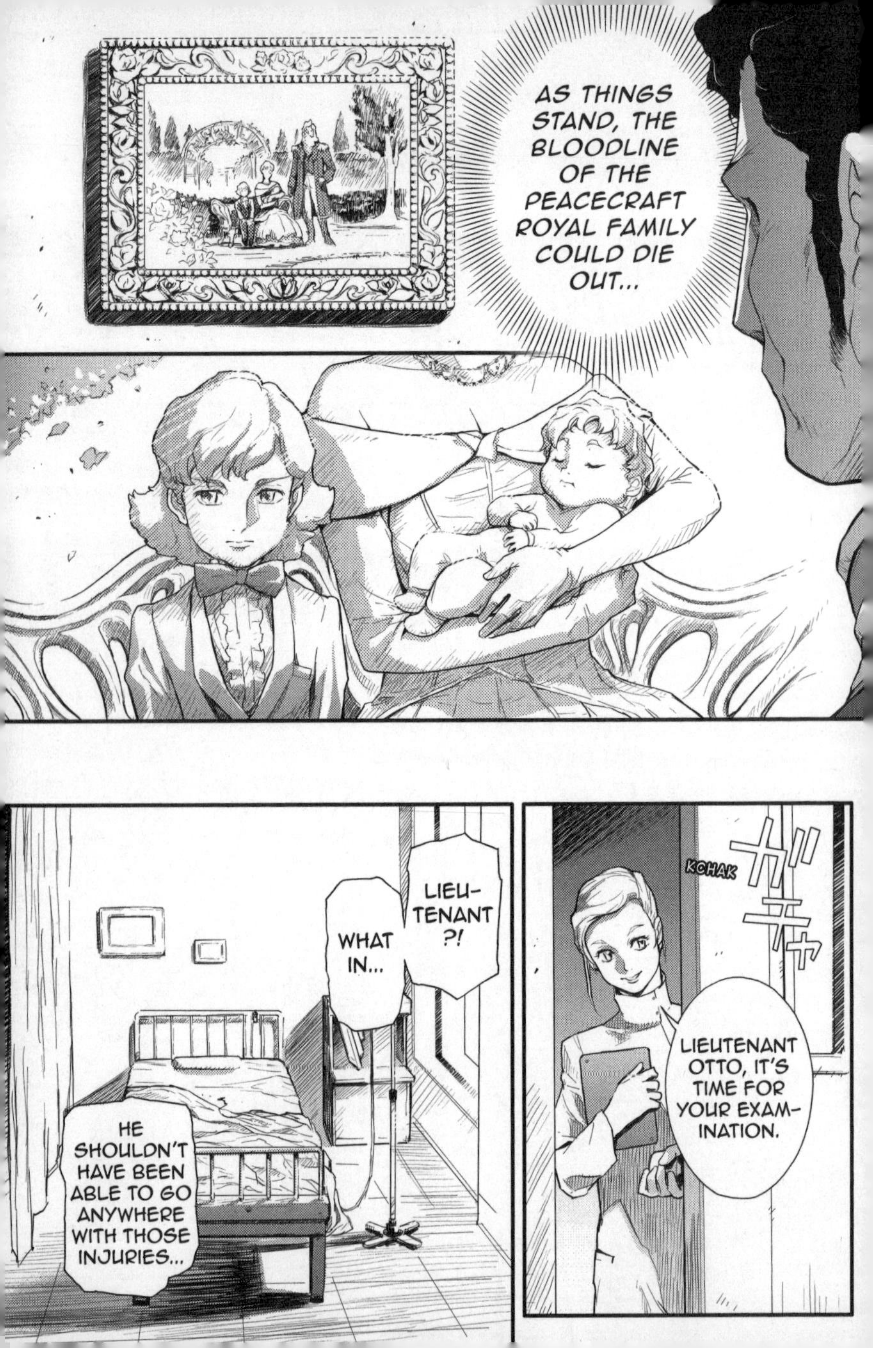

AS THINGS STAND, THE BLOODLINE OF THE PEACECRAFT ROYAL FAMILY COULD DIE OUT...
KCHAK
ガチャ
LIEUTENANT OTTO, IT'S TIME FOR YOUR EXAM-INATION.
LIEU-TENANT?!
WHAT IN...
HE SHOULDN'T HAVE BEEN ABLE TO GO ANYWHERE WITH THOSE INJURIES...

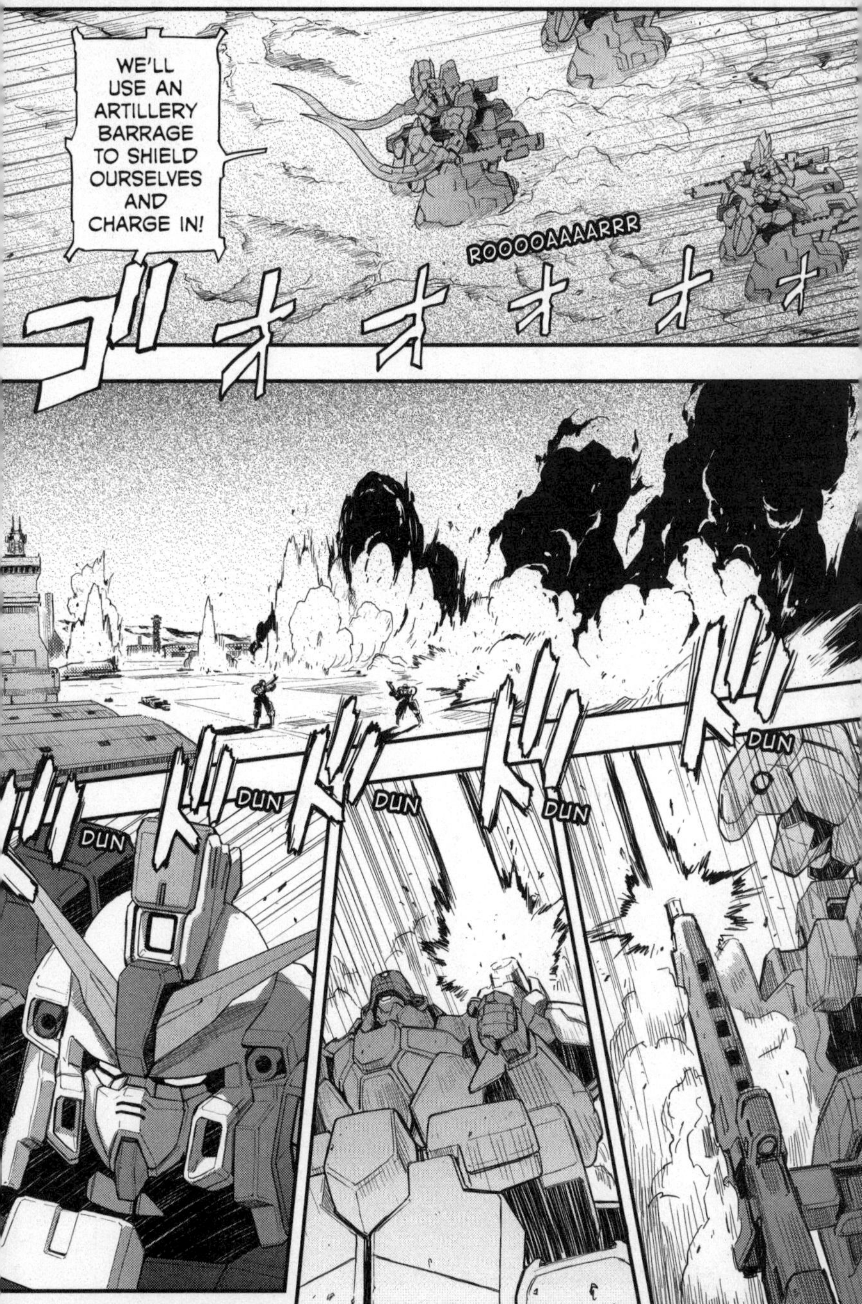
WE'LL USE AN ARTILLERY BARRAGE TO SHIELD OURSELVES AND CHARGE IN!
ROOOOAAAARRR
ゴオオオオオ
DUN
DUN
DUN
DUN
DUN
ドドドドド

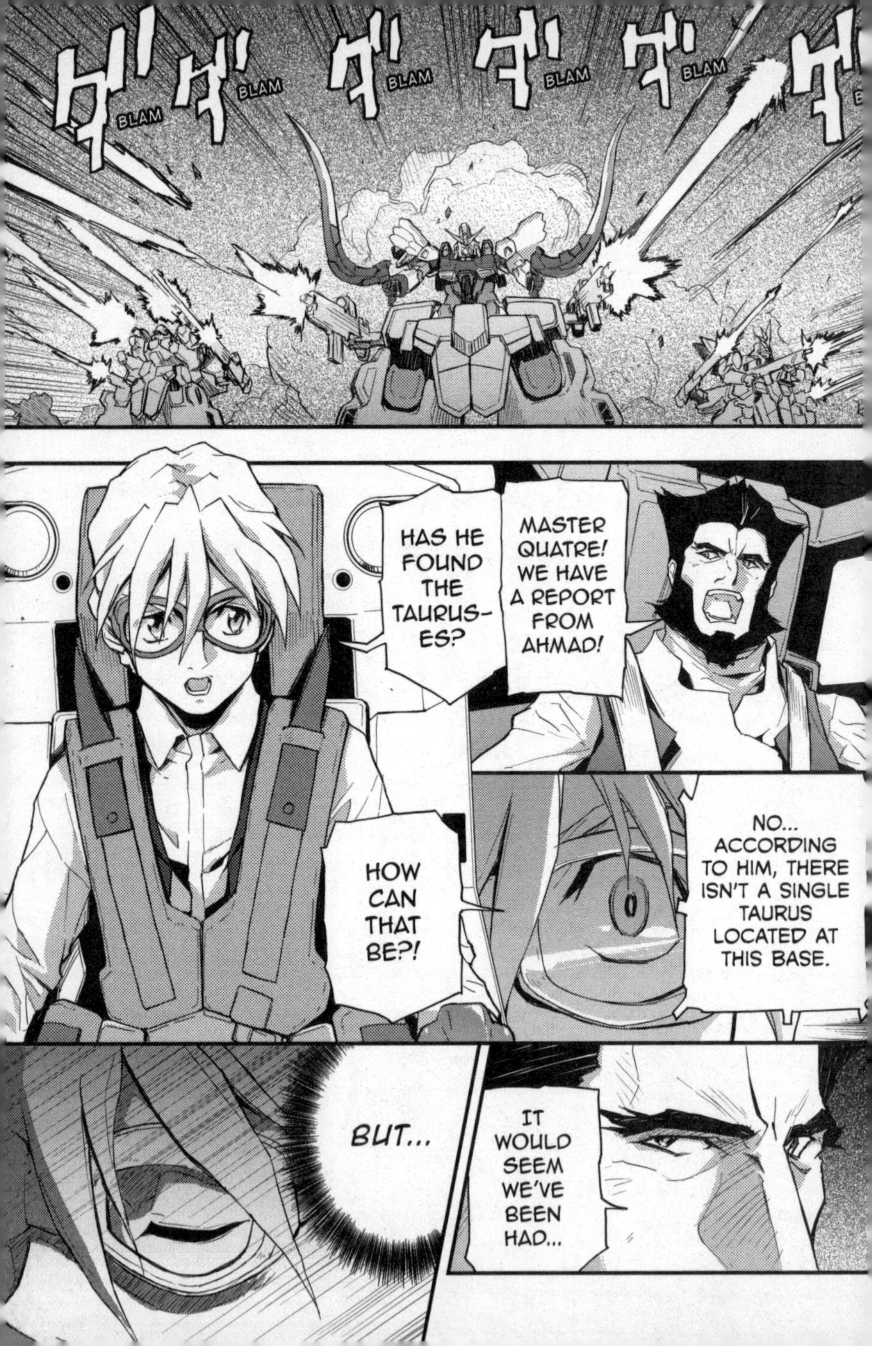

BLAM
BLAM
BLAM
BLAM
BLAM
MASTER QUATRE! WE HAVE A REPORT FROM AHMAD!
HAS HE FOUND THE TAURUS-ES?
NO... ACCORDING TO HIM, THERE ISN'T A SINGLE TAURUS LOCATED AT THIS BASE.
HOW CAN THAT BE?!
IT WOULD SEEM WE'VE BEEN HAD...
BUT...

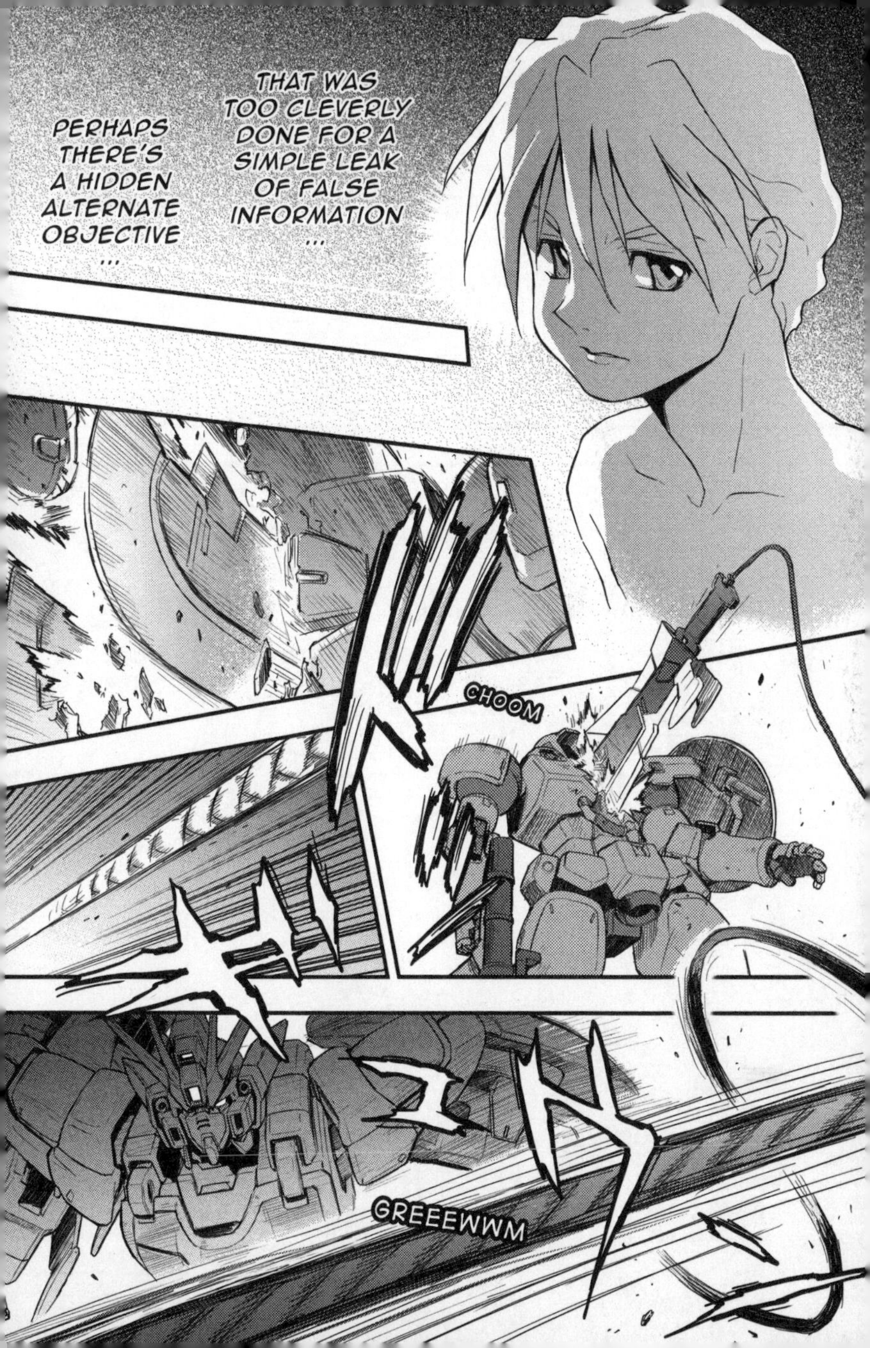
THAT WAS TOO CLEVERLY DONE FOR A SIMPLE LEAK OF FALSE INFORMATION ...
PERHAPS THERE'S A HIDDEN ALTERNATE OBJECTIVE ...
CHOOM
GREEEWWM

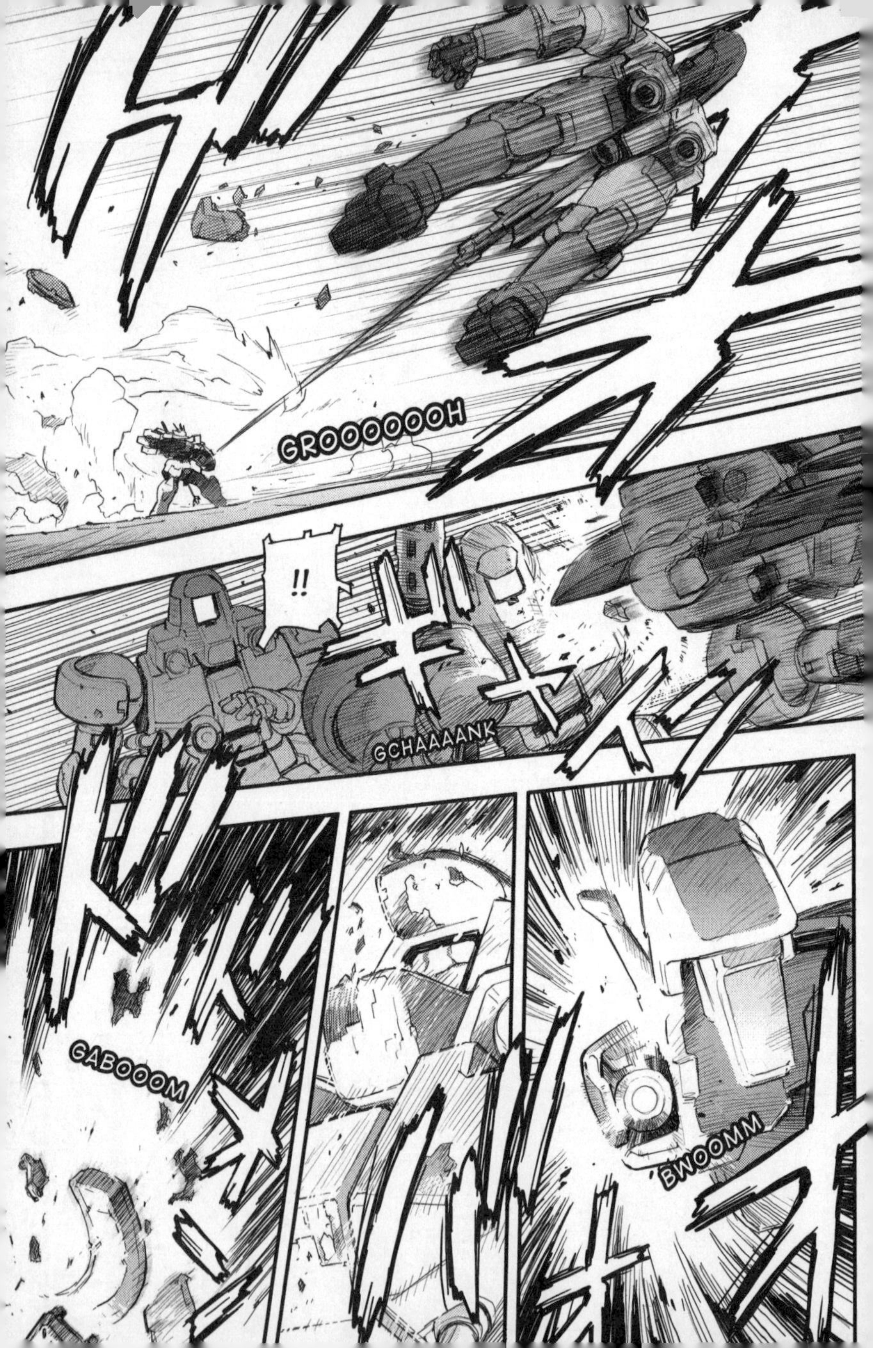
GROOOOOOOH
!!
GCHAAAANK
BWOOMM
GABOOOM

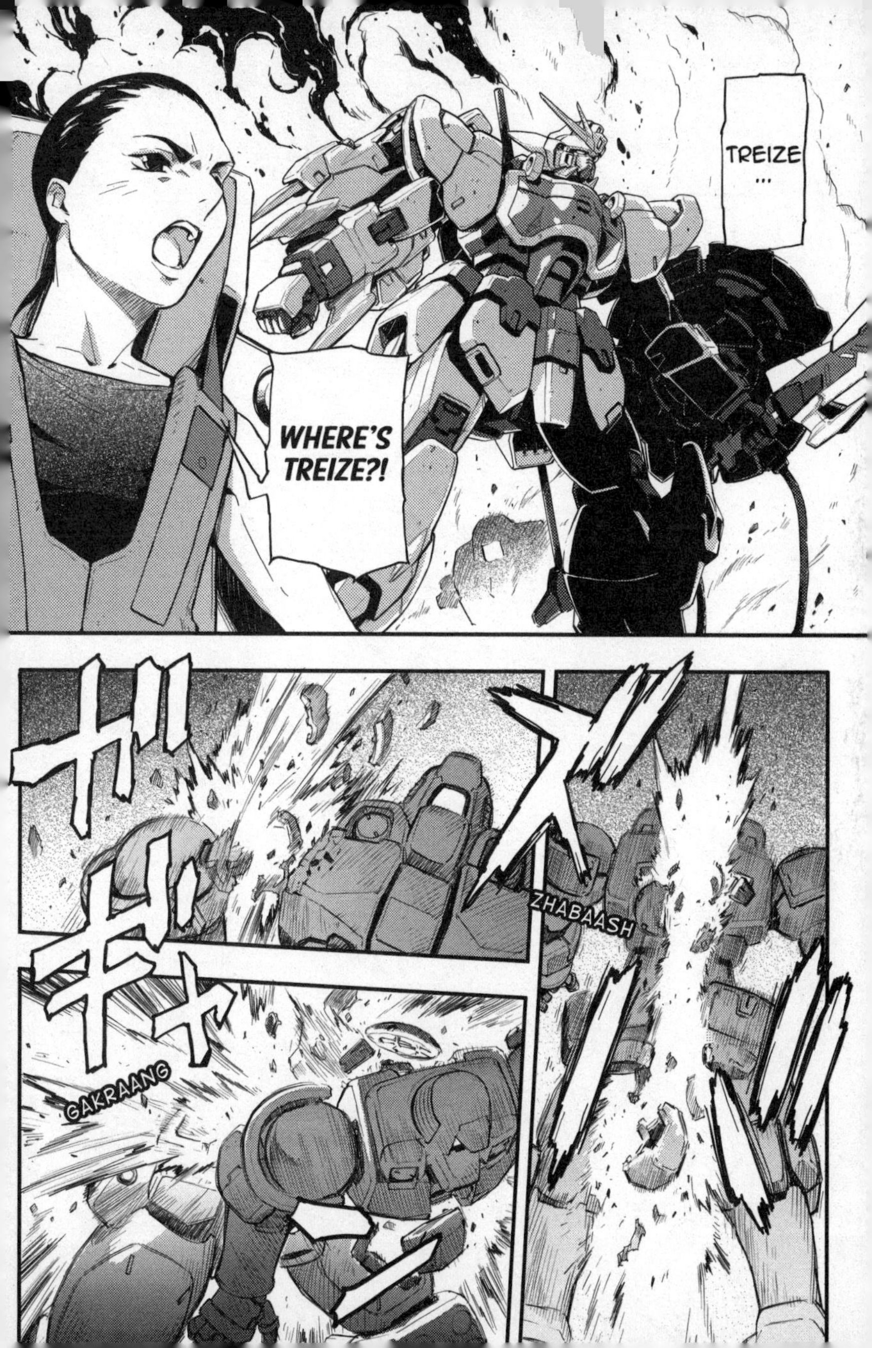
TREIZE ...
WHERE'S TREIZE?!
ZHABAASH
GAKRAANG

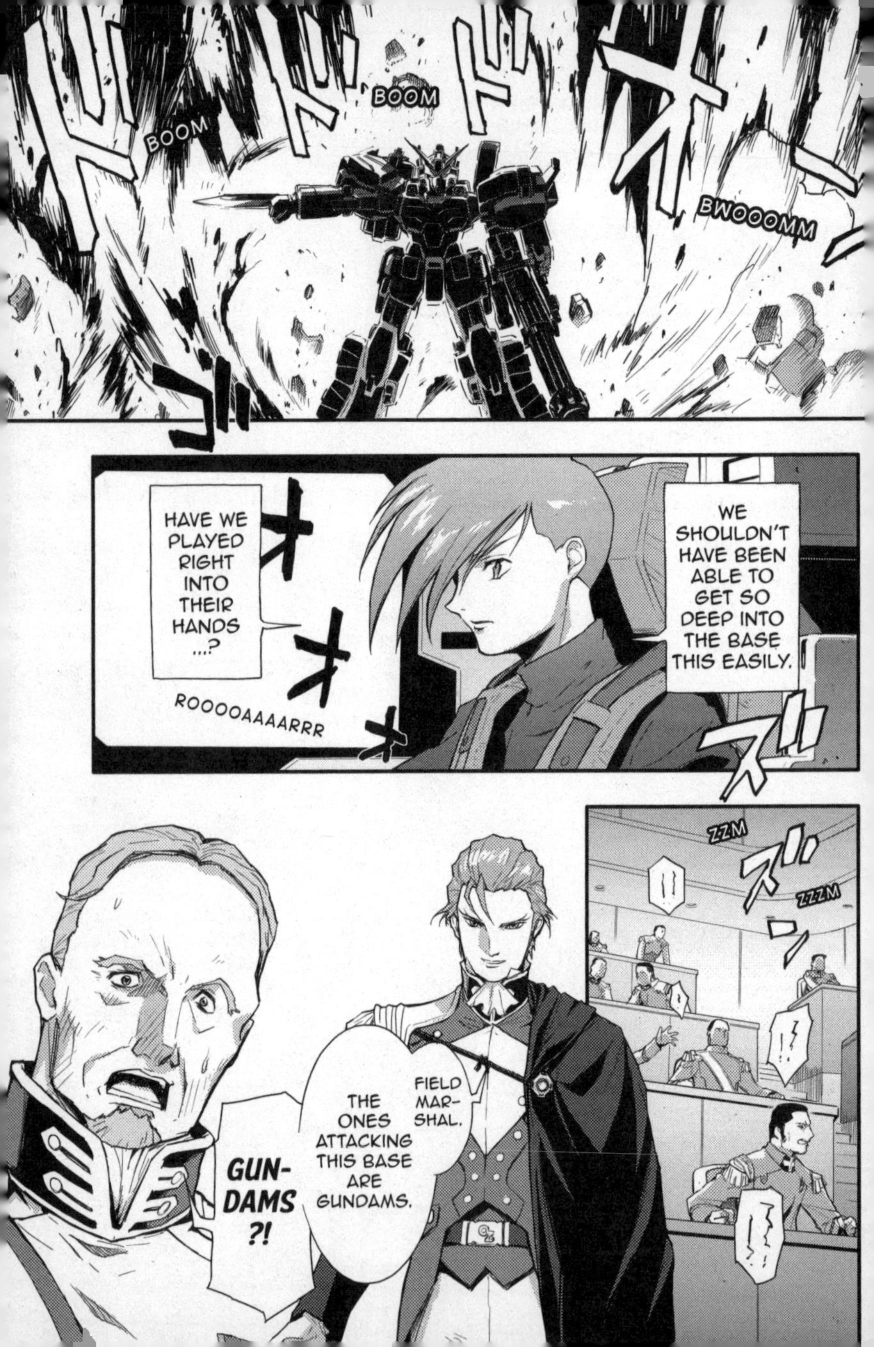
BWOOOOMM
BOOM
BOOM
WE SHOULDN'T HAVE BEEN ABLE TO GET SO DEEP INTO THE BASE THIS EASILY.
HAVE WE PLAYED RIGHT INTO THEIR HANDS ...?
ROOOOAAAARRR
ZZM
ZZZM
FIELD MARSHAL.
THE ONES ATTACKING THIS BASE ARE GUNDAMS.
GUNDAMS?!

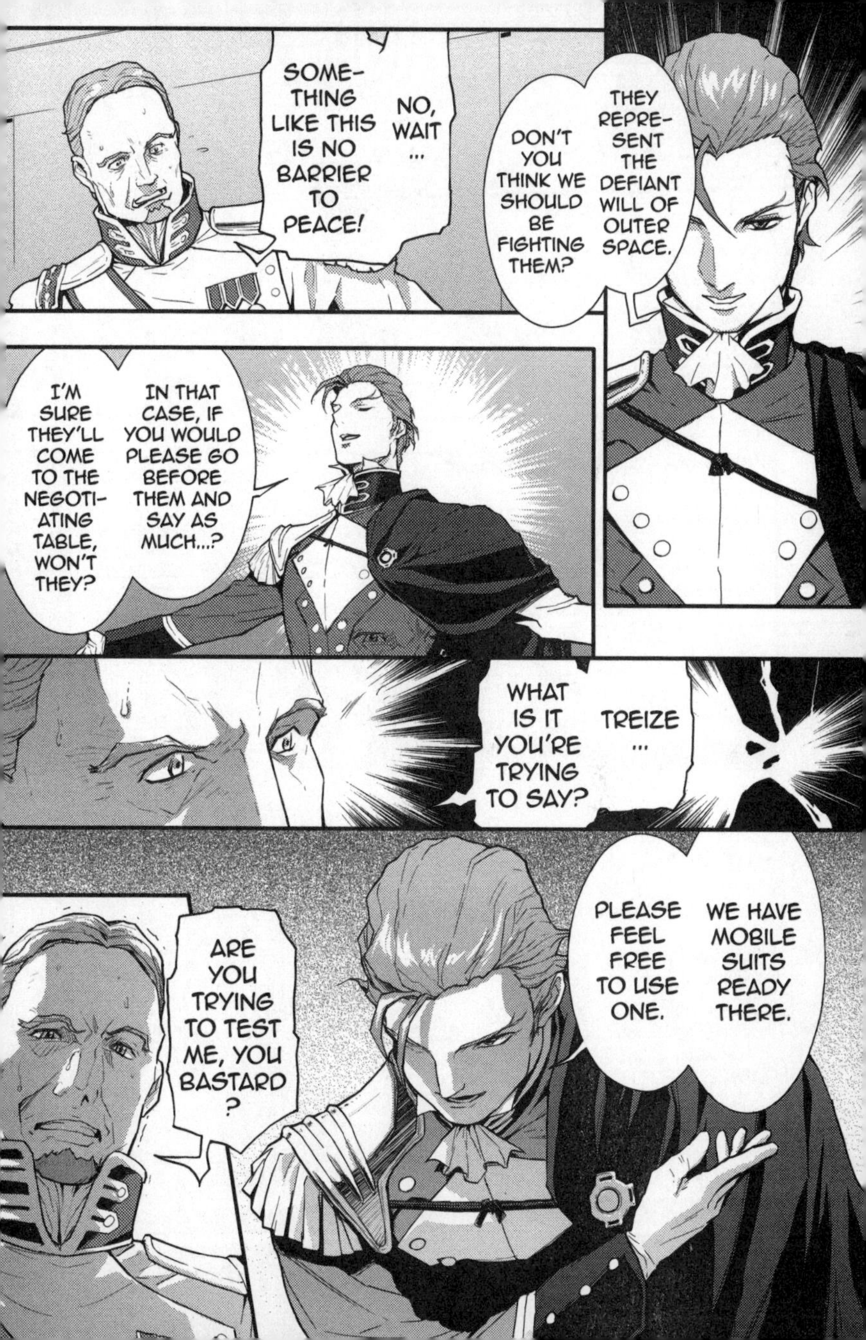
THEY REPRESENT THE DEFIANT WILL OF OUTER SPACE. DON'T YOU THINK WE SHOULD BE FIGHTING THEM?
NO, WAIT... SOMETHING LIKE THIS IS NO BARRIER TO PEACE!
IN THAT CASE, IF YOU WOULD PLEASE GO BEFORE THEM AND SAY AS MUCH...? I'M SURE THEY'LL COME TO THE NEGOTIATING TABLE, WON'T THEY?
TREIZE... WHAT IS IT YOU'RE TRYING TO SAY?
WE HAVE MOBILE SUITS READY THERE. PLEASE FEEL FREE TO USE ONE.
ARE YOU TRYING TO TEST ME, YOU BASTARD?

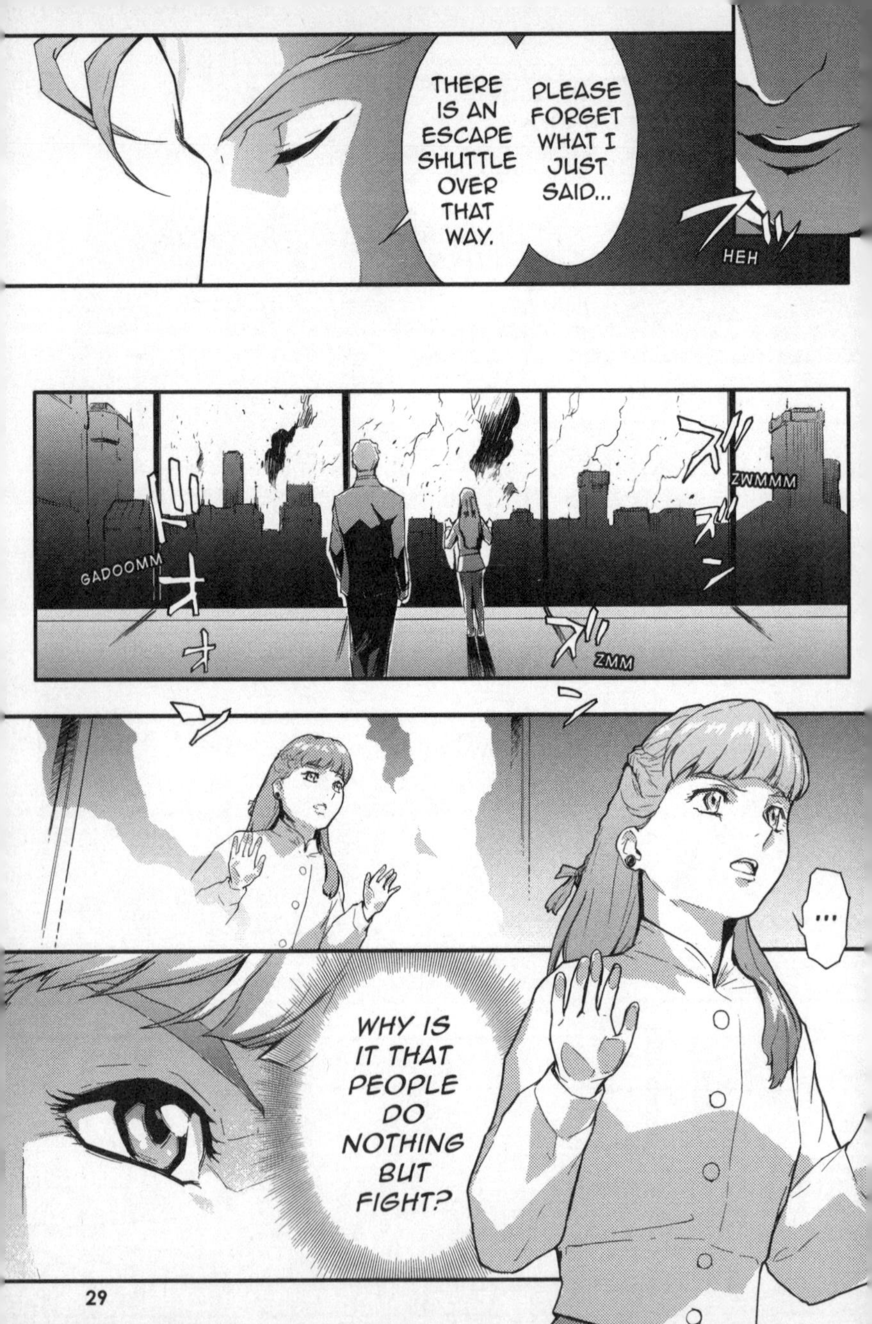
HEH
PLEASE FORGET WHAT I JUST SAID...
THERE IS AN ESCAPE SHUTTLE OVER THAT WAY.
ZWMMM
GADOOMM
ZMM
...
WHY IS IT THAT PEOPLE DO NOTHING BUT FIGHT?

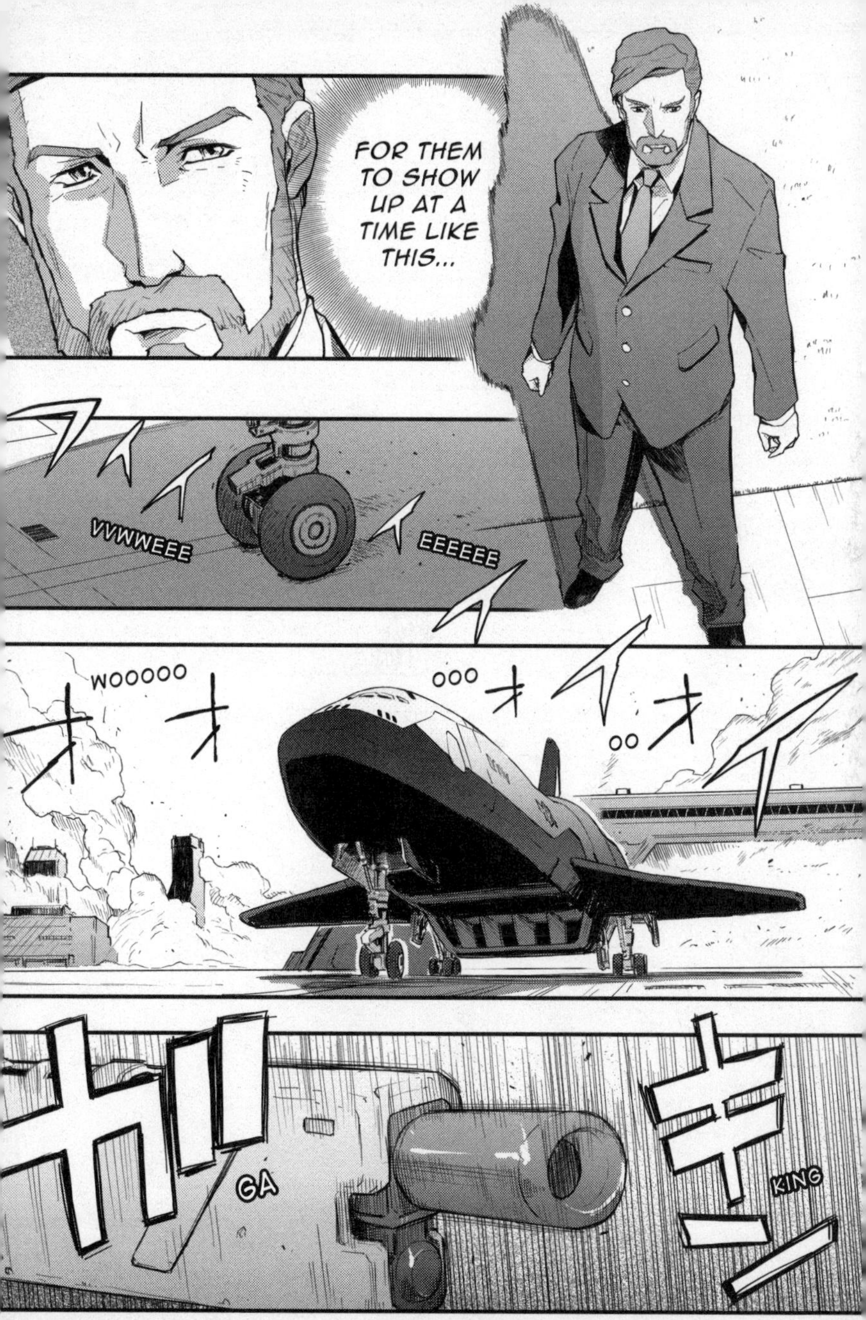

FOR THEM TO SHOW UP AT A TIME LIKE THIS...
VVWWEEE
EEEEEE
WOOOOO
OOO
OO
KING
GA

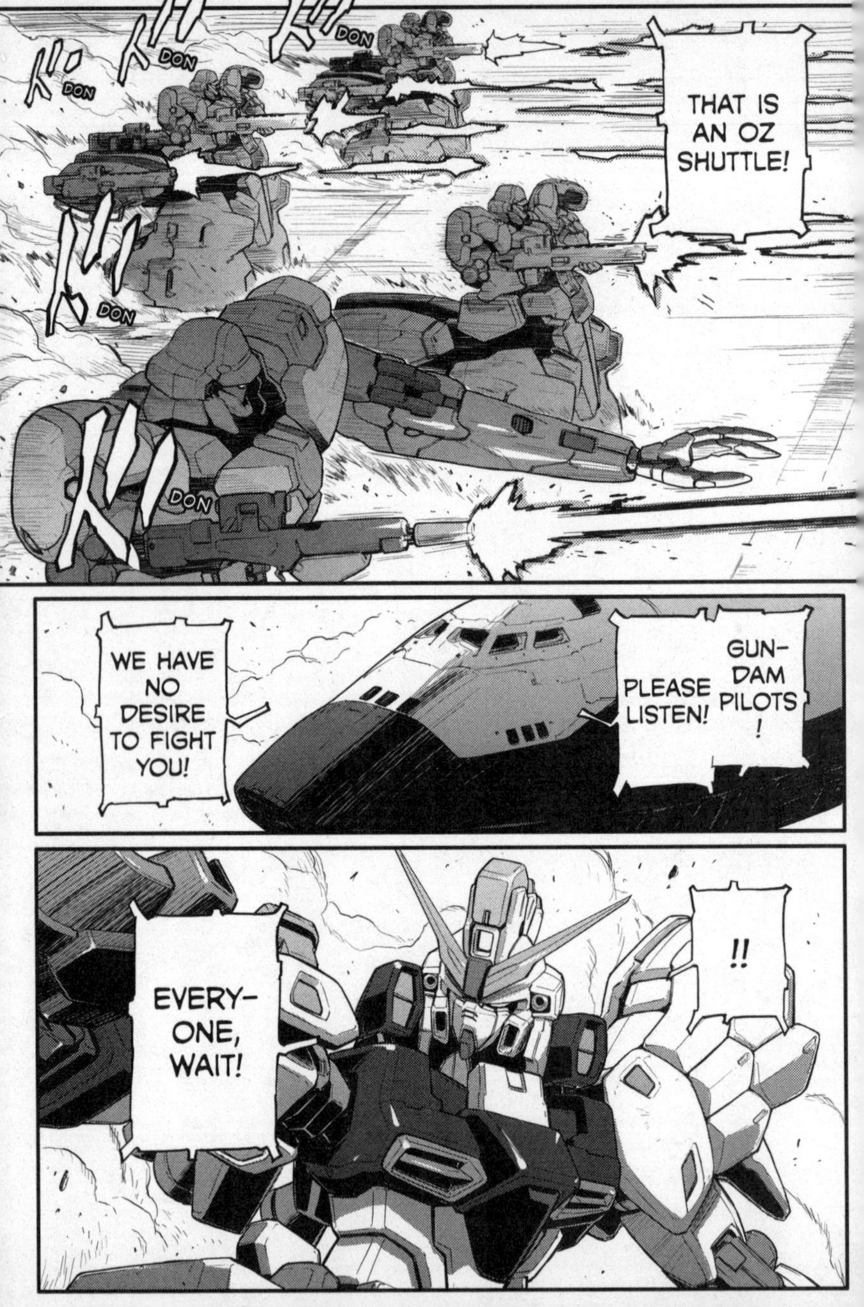
DON
DON
DON
DON
DON
THAT IS AN OZ SHUTTLE!
GUN-DAM PILOTS!
PLEASE LISTEN!
WE HAVE NO DESIRE TO FIGHT YOU!
!!
EVERY-ONE, WAIT!

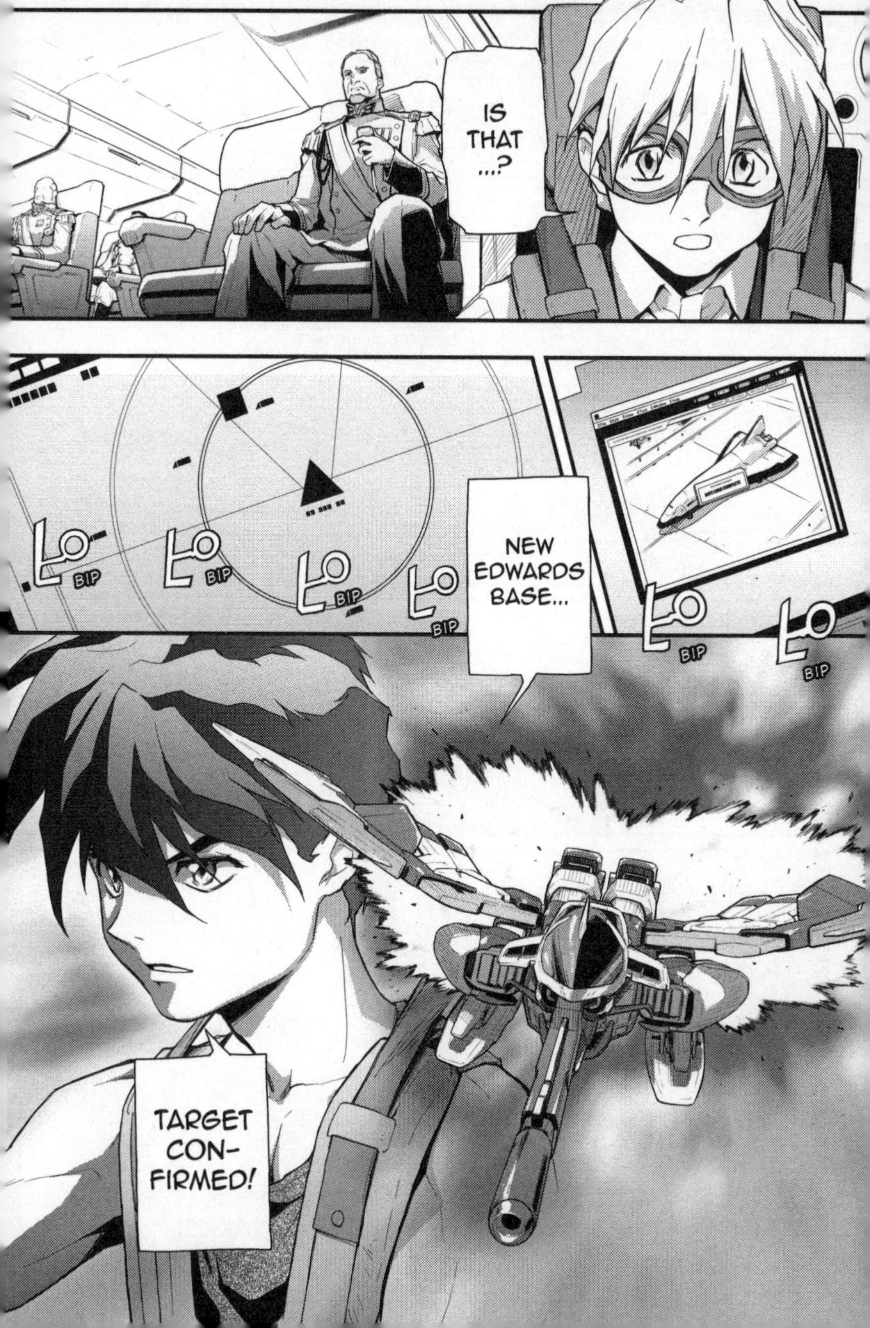
IS THAT ...?
ピ BIP
ピ BIP
ピ BIP
ピ BIP
ピ BIP
ピ BIP
NEW EDWARDS BASE...
TARGET CON- FIRMED!

Trowa *Barton*

SLEEVE NOTES:
Endless Waltz

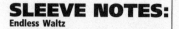

XXXG-01H
GUNDAM HEAVYARMS
Eagle Rigging

Additional armaments mounted for the Corsica Battle. Weapon containers are mounted on each shoulder with 12 container blocks on the front, rear, and sides of each. There are also additional missile pods on the legs. To compensate for decreased mobility due to the increase in weight from the added weapons, each is also equipped with a drive system.

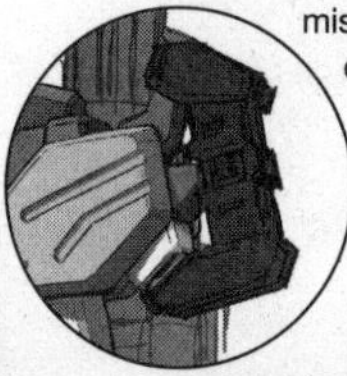

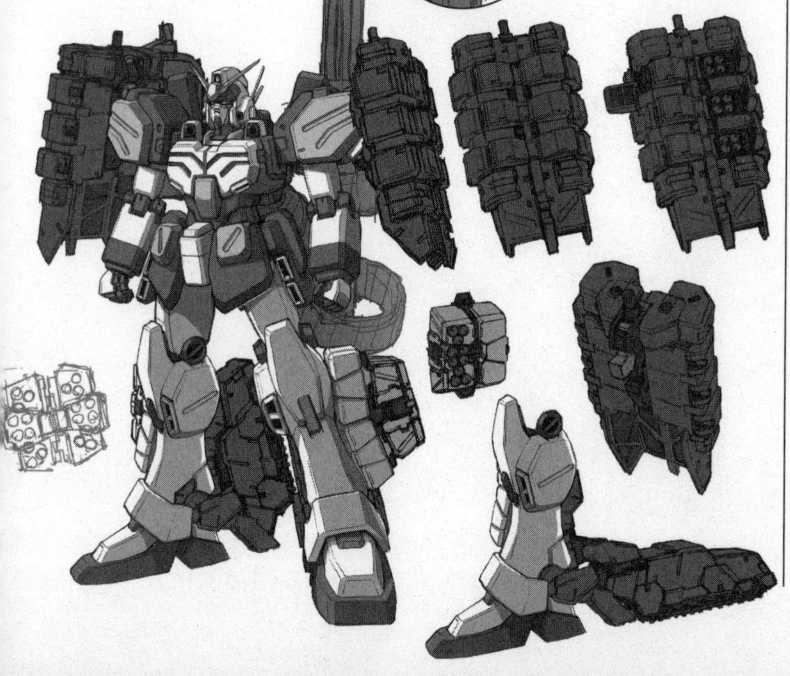

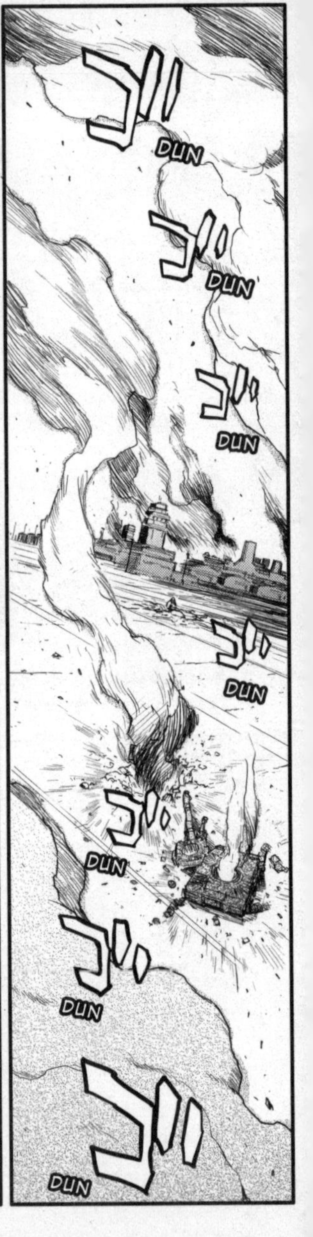
DUN
DUN
DUN
DUN
DUN
DUN
DUN

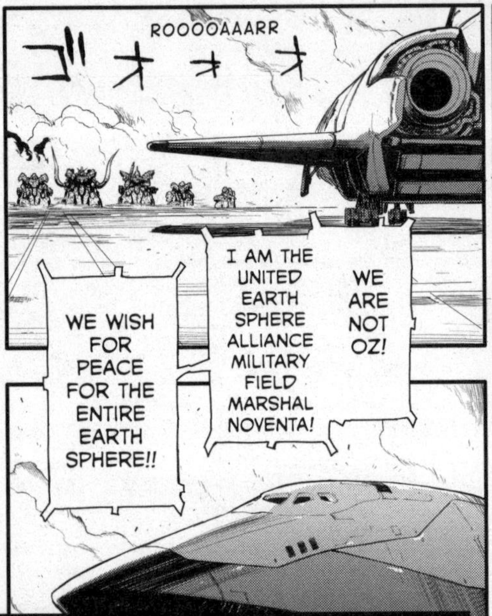
ゴオォオ
ROOOOAAARR
WE ARE NOT OZ!
I AM THE UNITED EARTH SPHERE ALLIANCE MILITARY FIELD MARSHAL NOVENTA!
WE WISH FOR PEACE FOR THE ENTIRE EARTH SPHERE!!

Chapter 15: "A Banquet for the Pleiades" Part 4

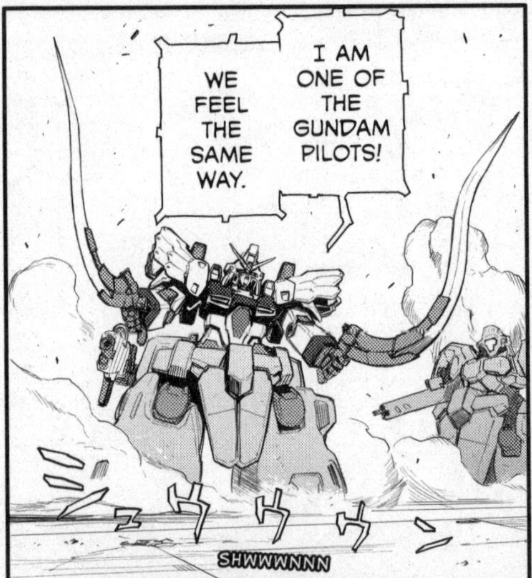
I AM ONE OF THE GUNDAM PILOTS!
WE FEEL THE SAME WAY.
SHWWWNNN

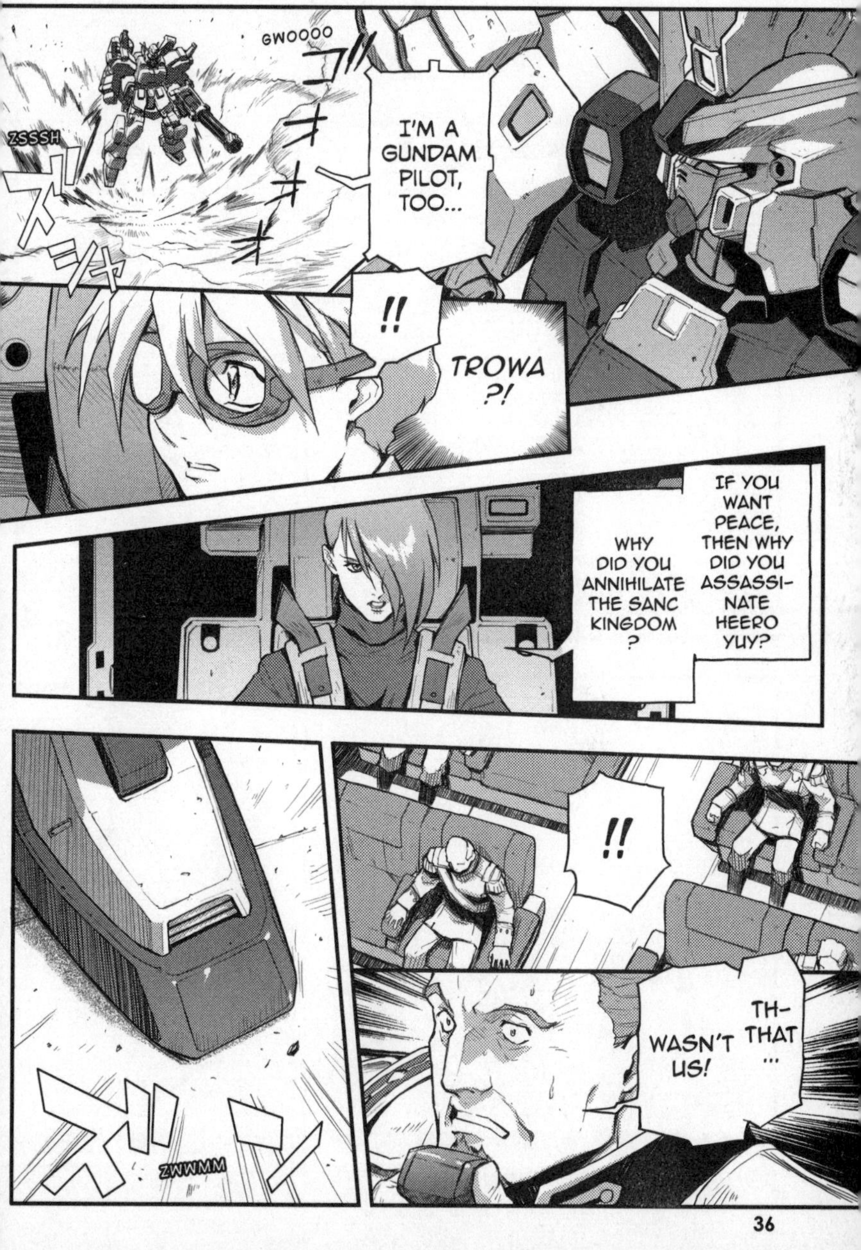
I'M A GUNDAM PILOT, TOO...
GWOOOO
ZSSSH
!!
TROWA ?!
IF YOU WANT PEACE, THEN WHY DID YOU ASSASSI- NATE HEERO YUY?
WHY DID YOU ANNIHILATE THE SANC KINGDOM ?
!!
TH- THAT ...
WASN'T US!
ZWWMM

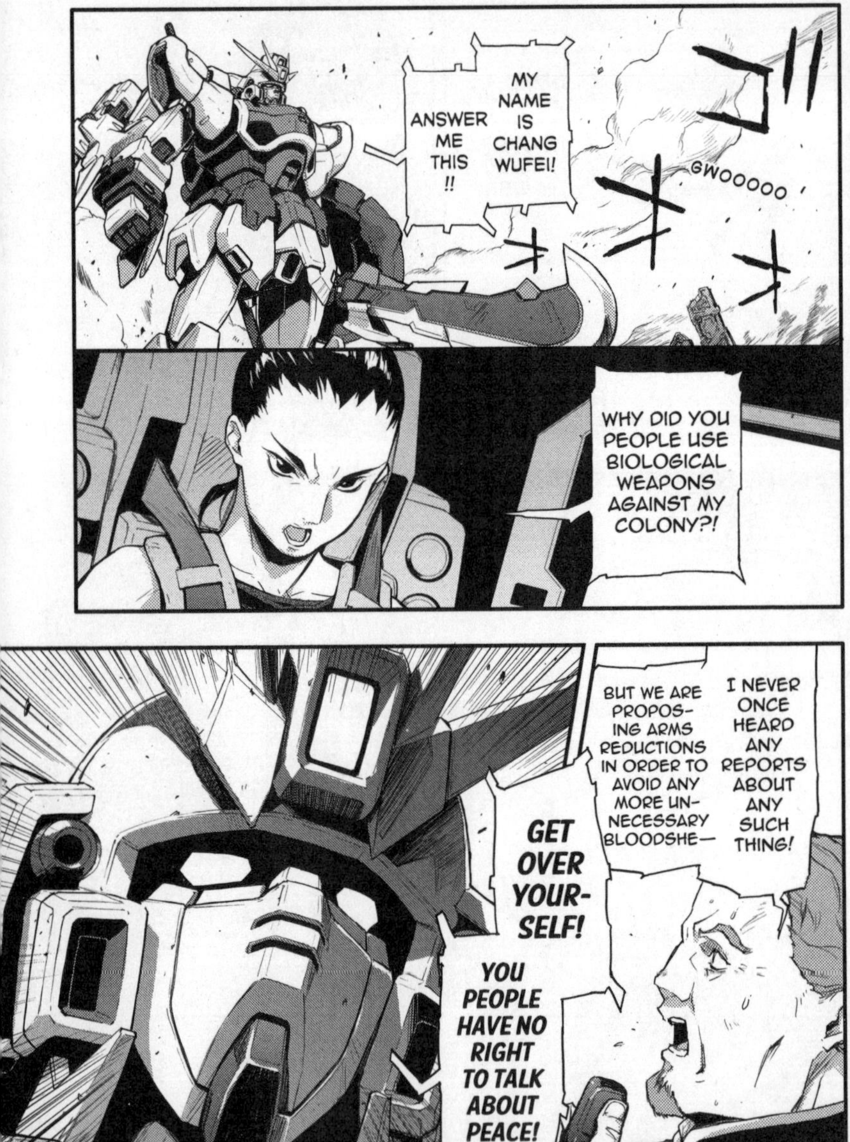
GWOOOOO
MY NAME IS CHANG WUFEI!
ANSWER ME THIS !!
WHY DID YOU PEOPLE USE BIOLOGICAL WEAPONS AGAINST MY COLONY?!
I NEVER ONCE HEARD ANY REPORTS ABOUT ANY SUCH THING!
BUT WE ARE PROPOSING ARMS REDUCTIONS IN ORDER TO AVOID ANY MORE UNNECESSARY BLOODSHE—
GET OVER YOURSELF!
YOU PEOPLE HAVE NO RIGHT TO TALK ABOUT PEACE!

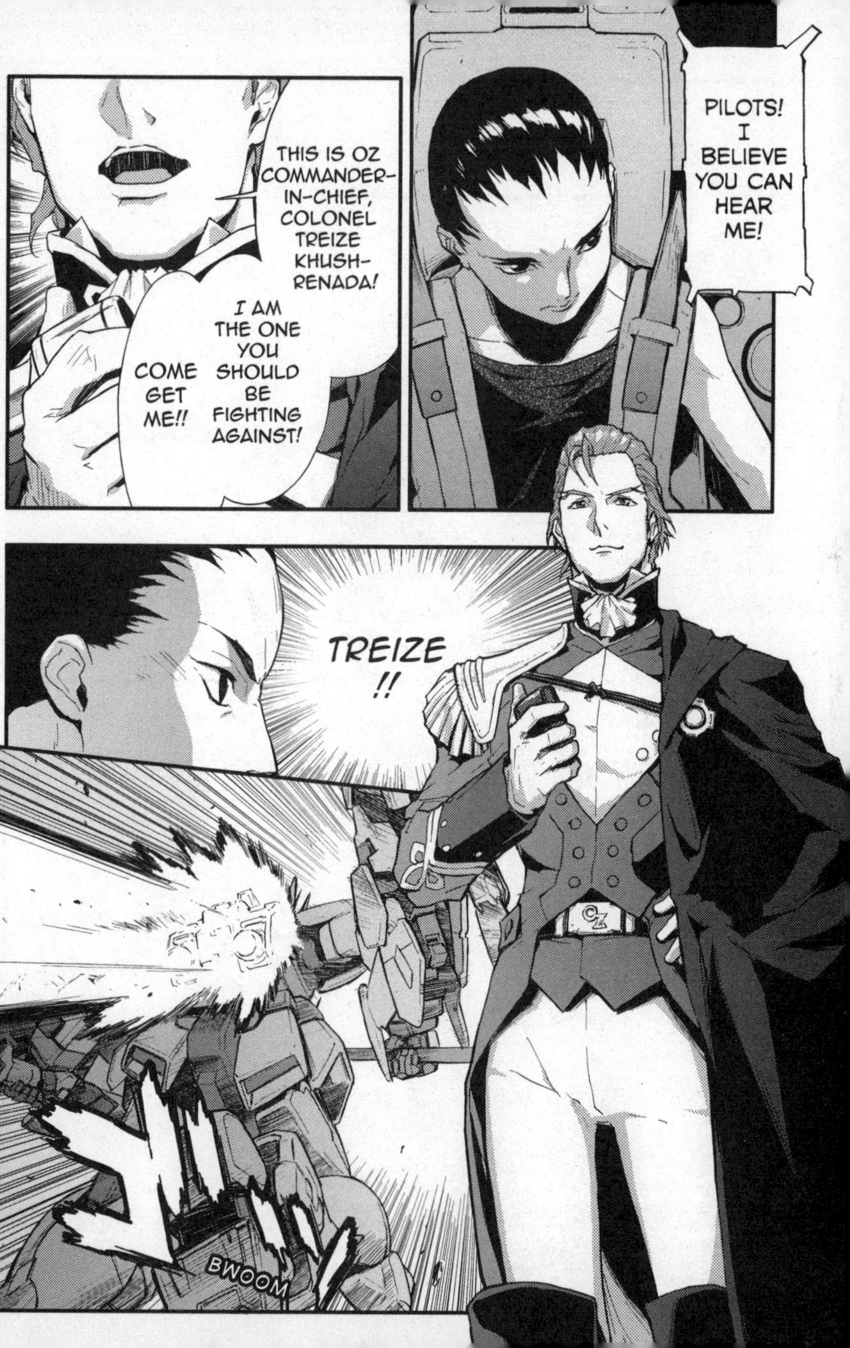
PILOTS! I BELIEVE YOU CAN HEAR ME!
THIS IS OZ COMMANDER-IN-CHIEF, COLONEL TREIZE KHUSH-RENADA!
I AM THE ONE YOU SHOULD BE FIGHTING AGAINST!
COME GET ME!!
TREIZE !!
BWOOM

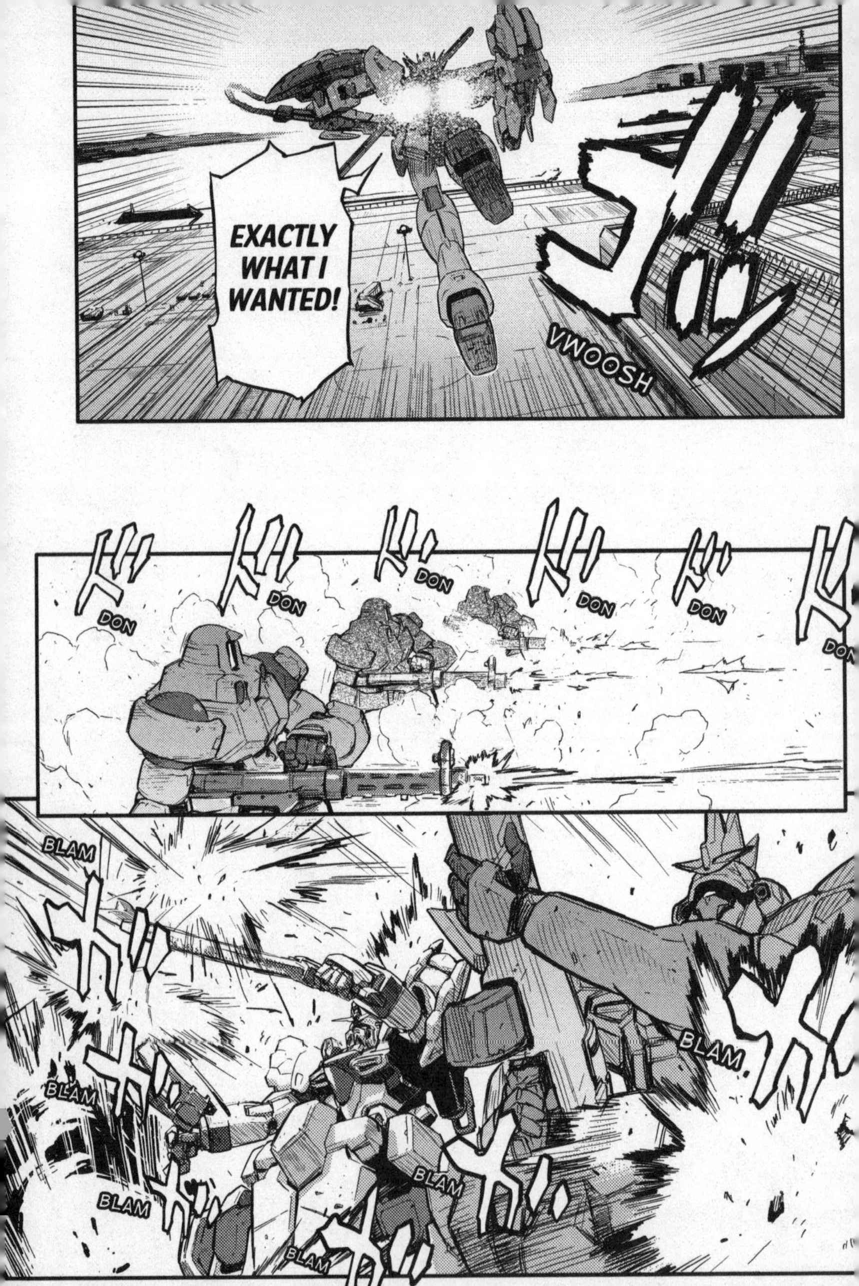
EXACTLY WHAT I WANTED!
VWOOSH
DON
DON
DON
DON
DON
DON
BLAM
BLAM
BLAM
BLAM
BLAM
BLAM

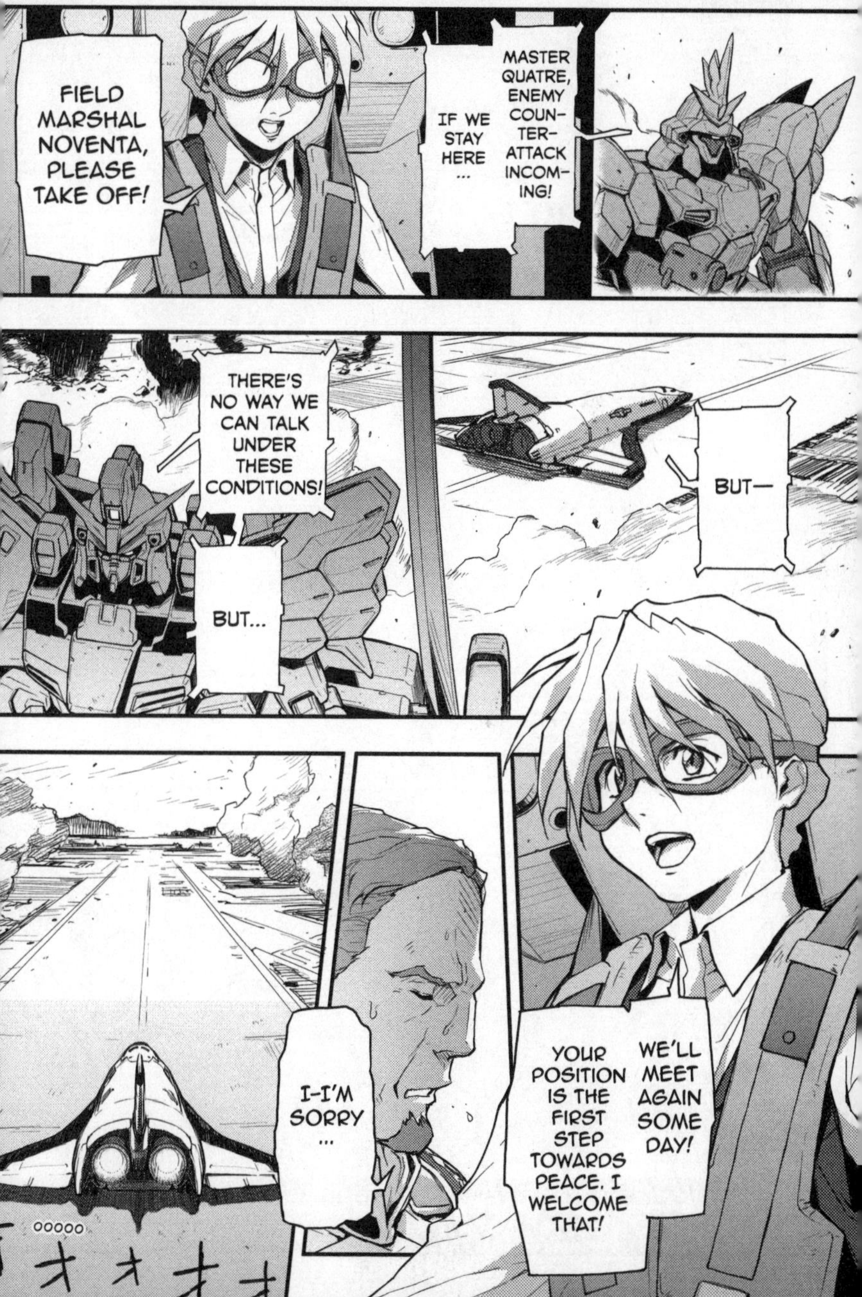
MASTER QUATRE, ENEMY COUNTER-ATTACK INCOMING!
IF WE STAY HERE ...
FIELD MARSHAL NOVENTA, PLEASE TAKE OFF!
BUT—
THERE'S NO WAY WE CAN TALK UNDER THESE CONDITIONS!
BUT...
WE'LL MEET AGAIN SOME DAY!
YOUR POSITION IS THE FIRST STEP TOWARDS PEACE. I WELCOME THAT!
I-I'M SORRY ...
OOOOO
オオオオ

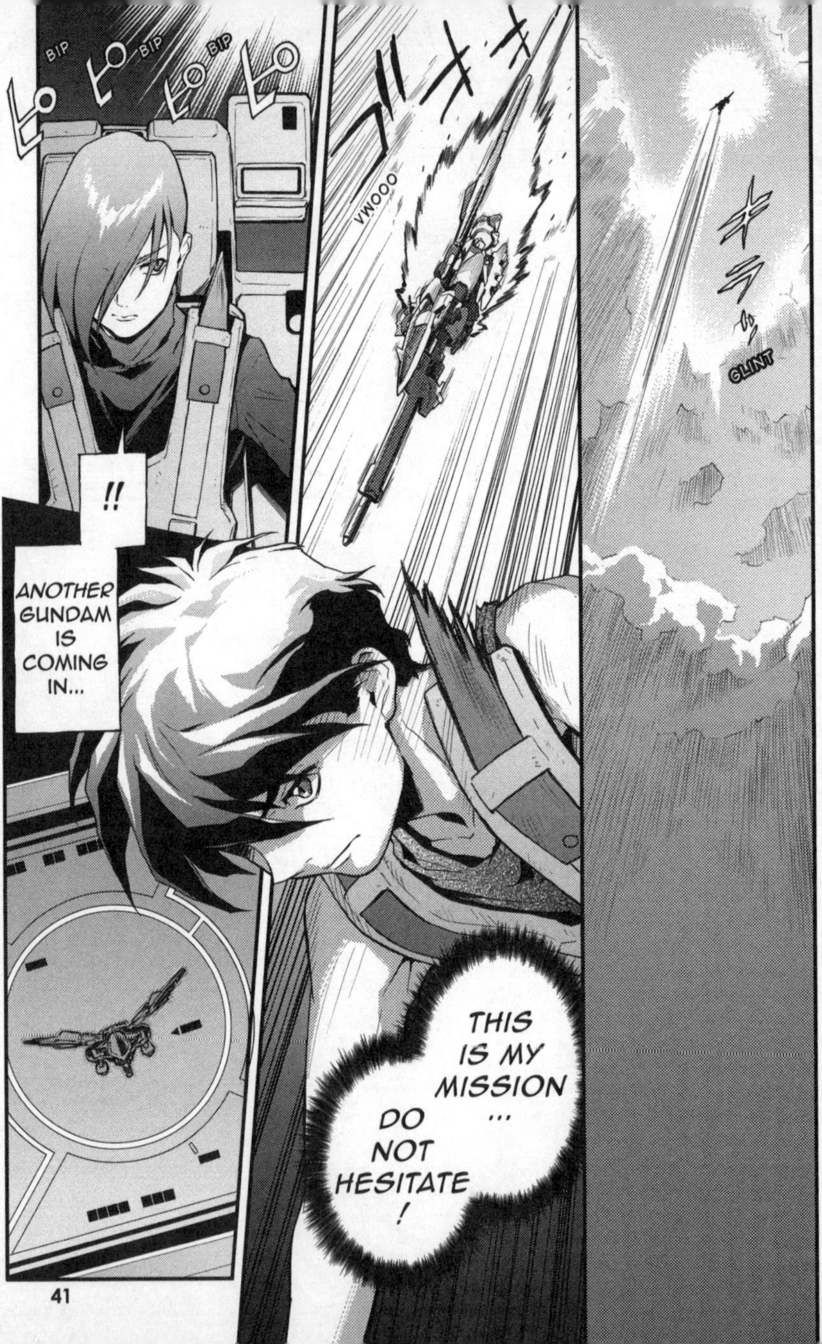
GLINT
VWOOO
BIP BIP BIP
!!
ANOTHER GUNDAM IS COMING IN...
THIS IS MY MISSION...
DO NOT HESITATE!

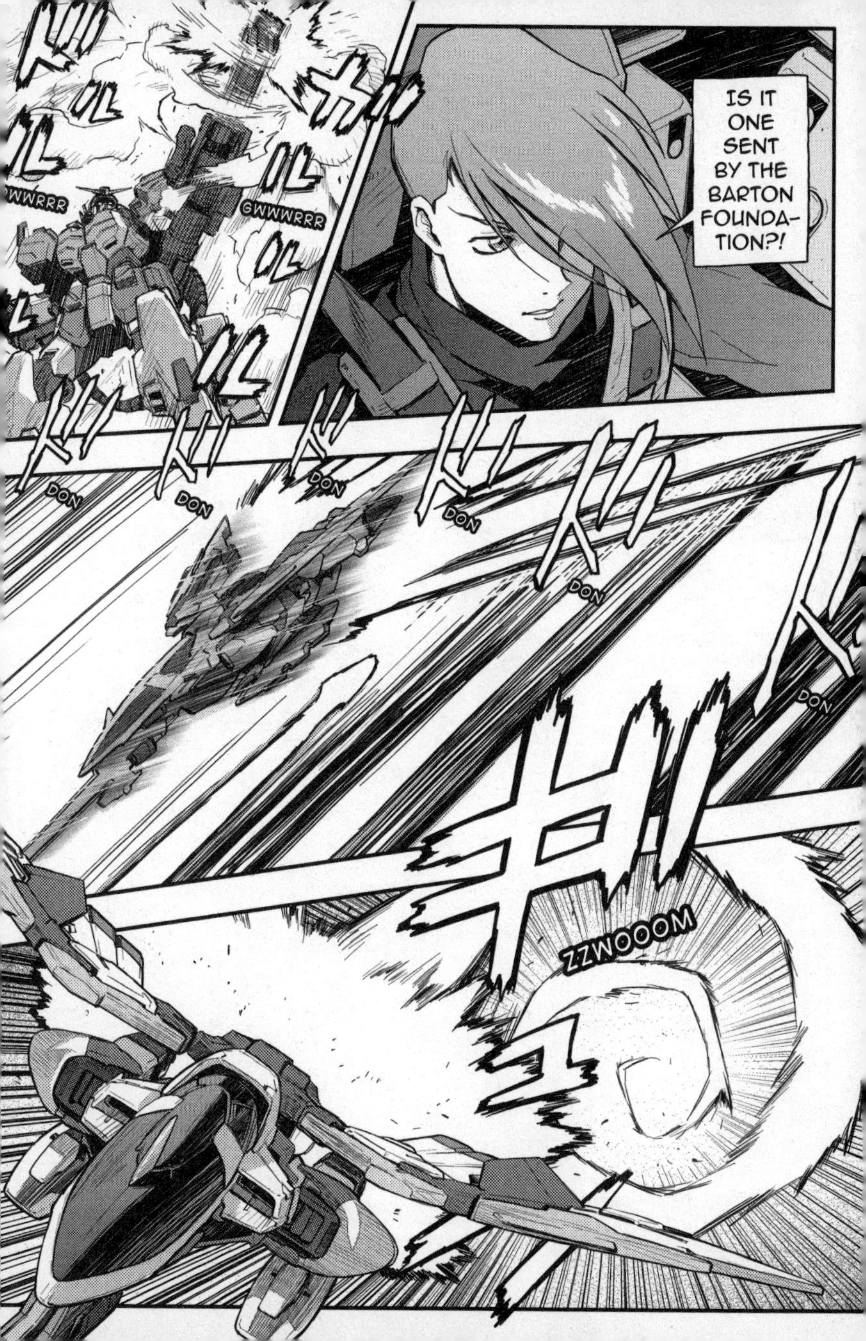
IS IT ONE SENT BY THE BARTON FOUNDATION?!
GWWWRRR
GWWWRRR
DON
DON
DON
DON
DON
DON
ZZWOOOM

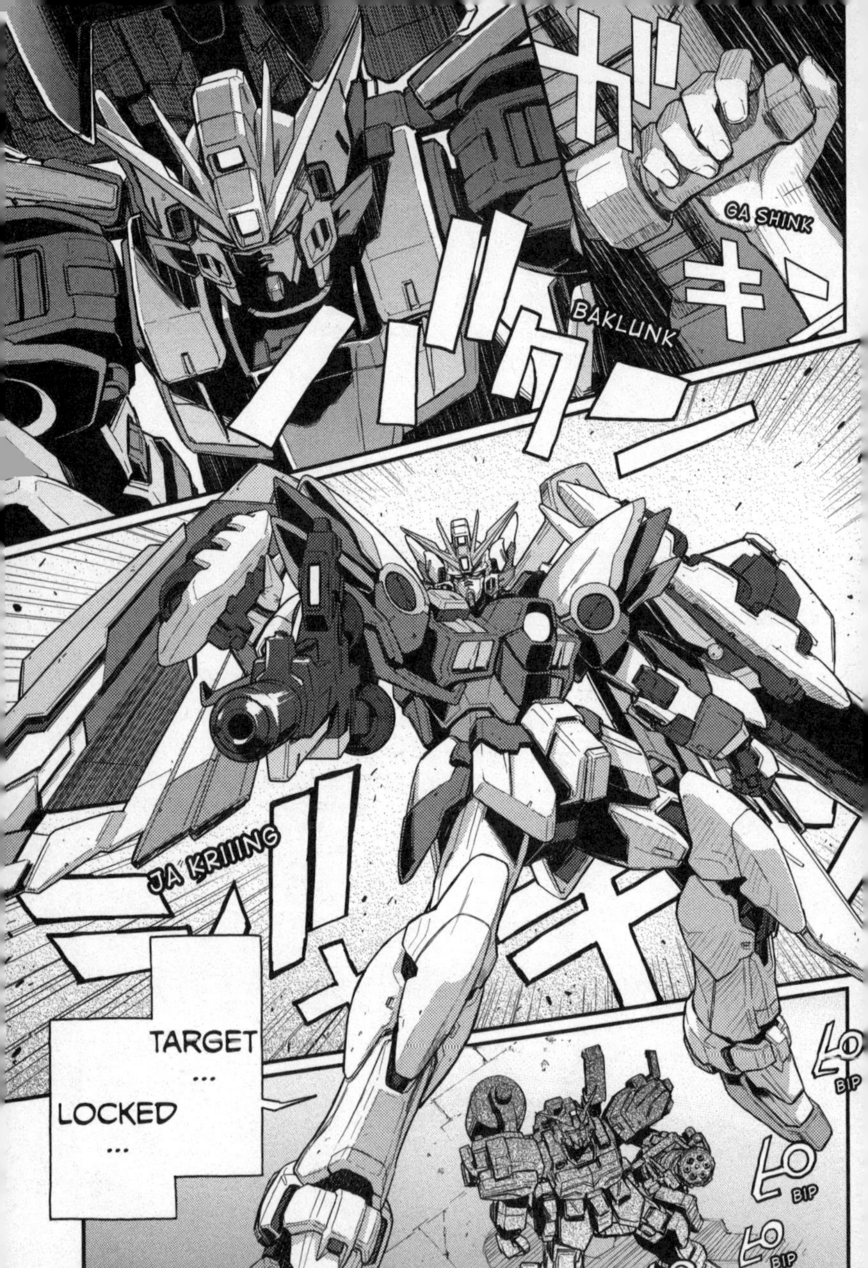
GA SHINK
BAKLUNK
JA KRIIING
TARGET ... LOCKED ...
BIP
BIP
BIP
BIP

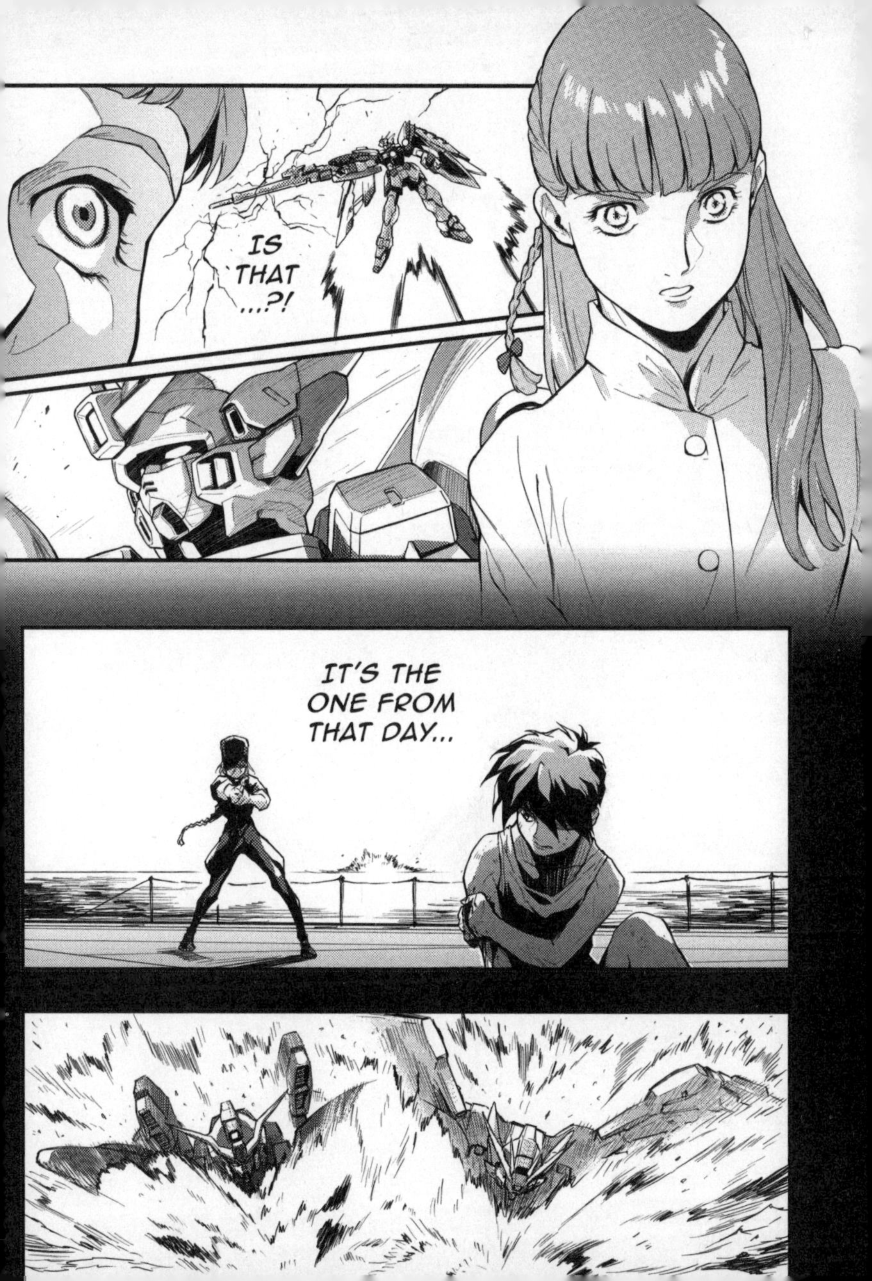
IS THAT ...?!
IT'S THE ONE FROM THAT DAY...

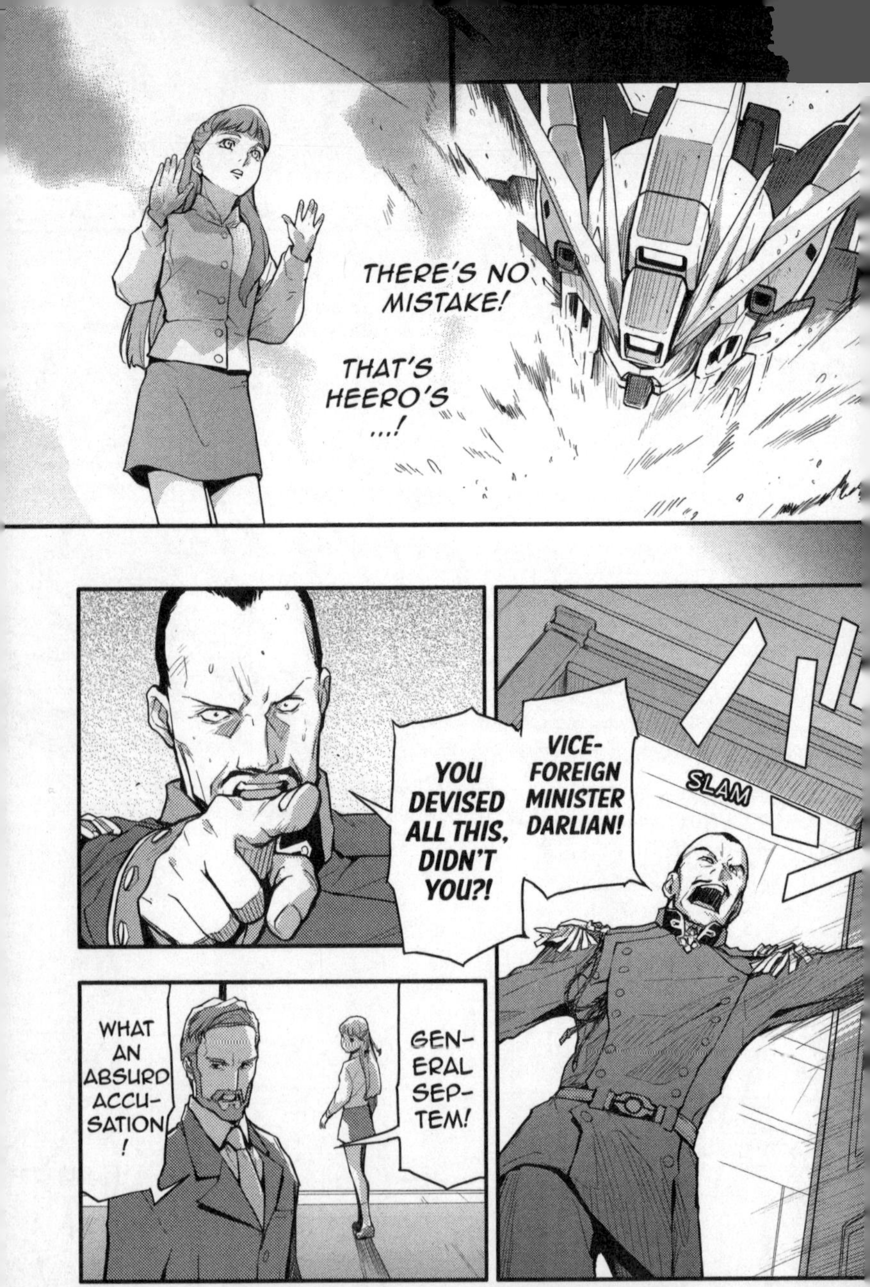
THERE'S NO MISTAKE!
THAT'S HEERO'S ...!
VICE-FOREIGN MINISTER DARLIAN!
SLAM
YOU DEVISED ALL THIS, DIDN'T YOU?!
GEN-ERAL SEP-TEM!
WHAT AN ABSURD ACCU-SATION!

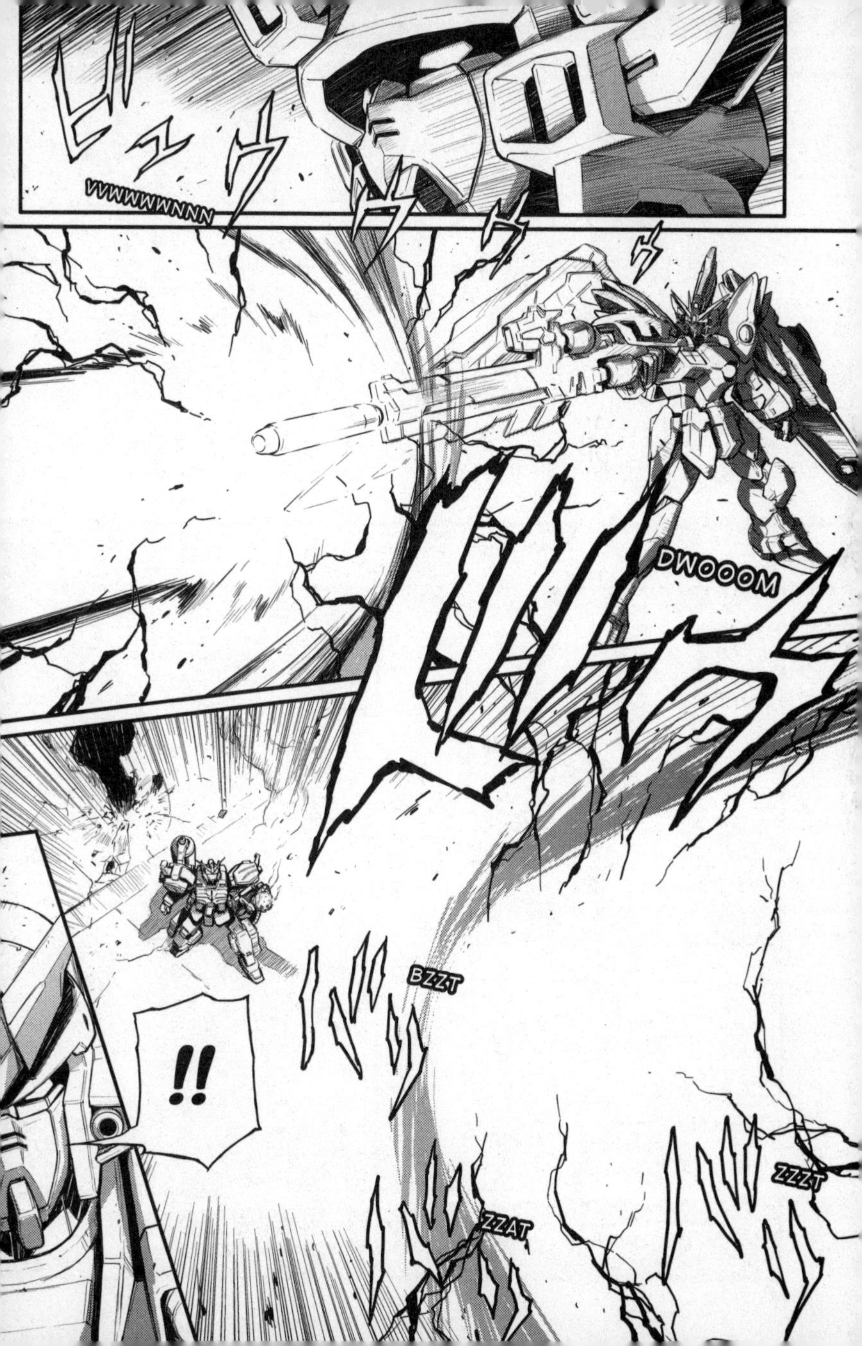
VVWWWWNNNN
DWOOOOM
BZZT
ZZZT
ZZAT
!!

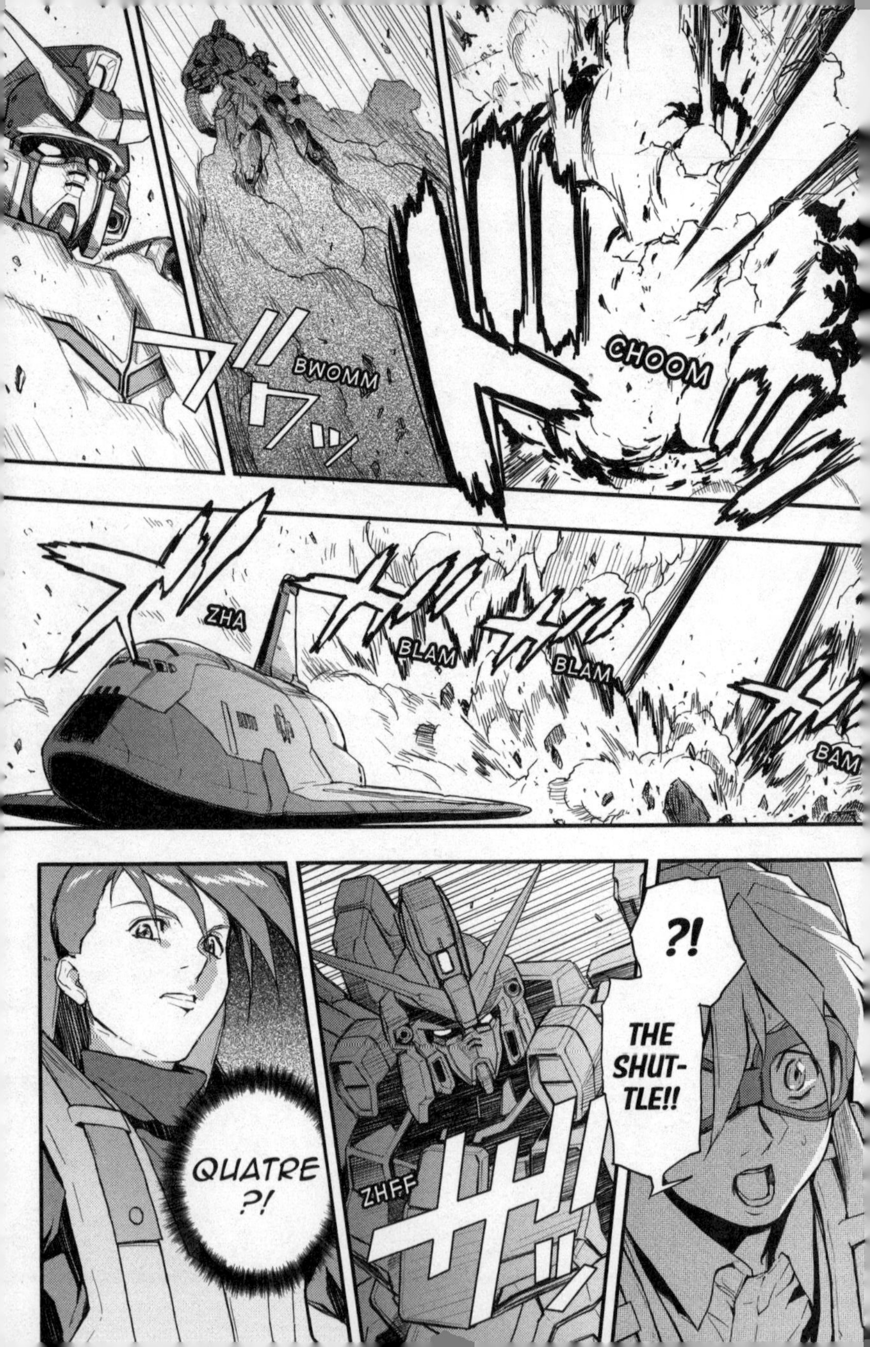
CHOOM
BWOMM
BAM
BLAM
BLAM
ZHA
?!
THE SHUT-TLE!!
ZHFF
QUATRE ?!

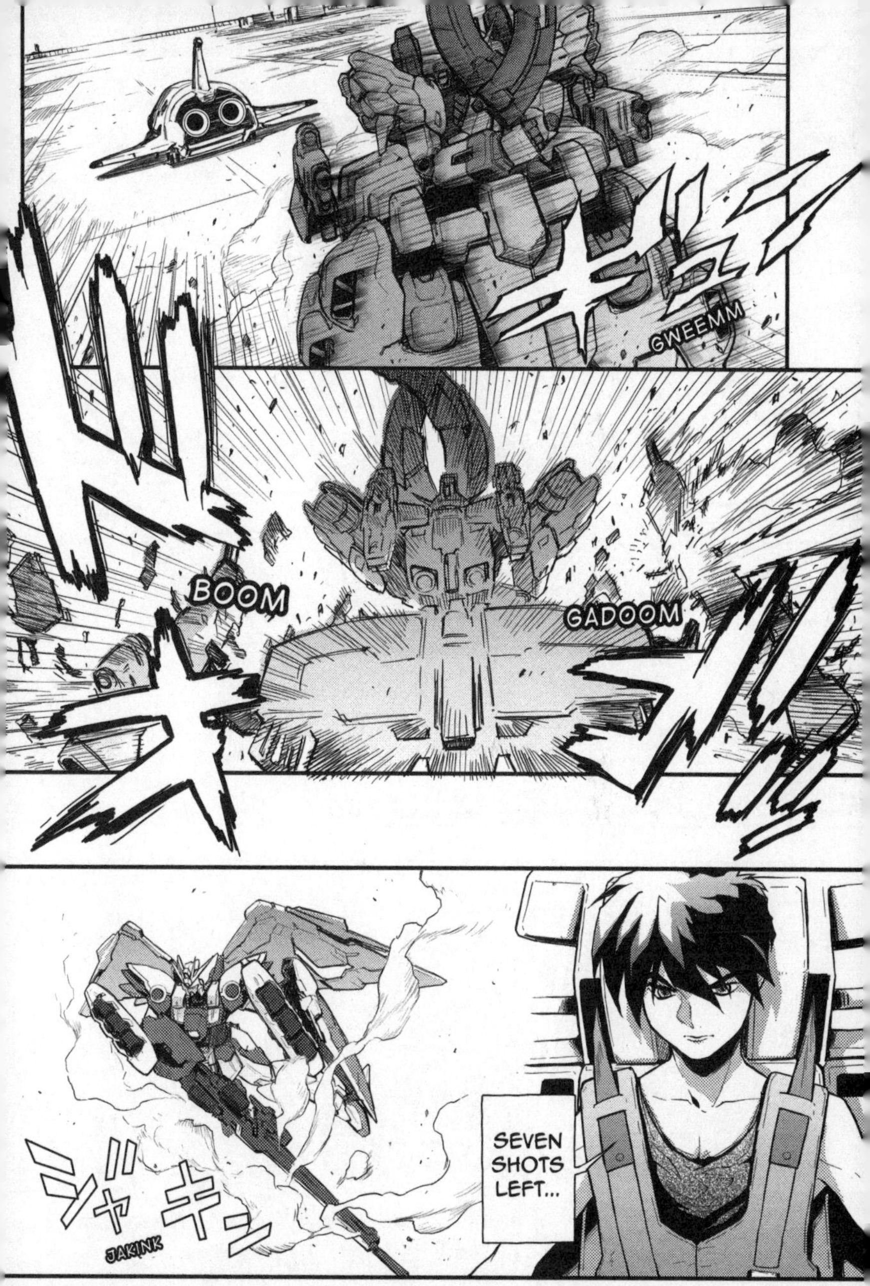
GWEEMM
GADOOM
BOOM
SEVEN SHOTS LEFT...
JAKINK

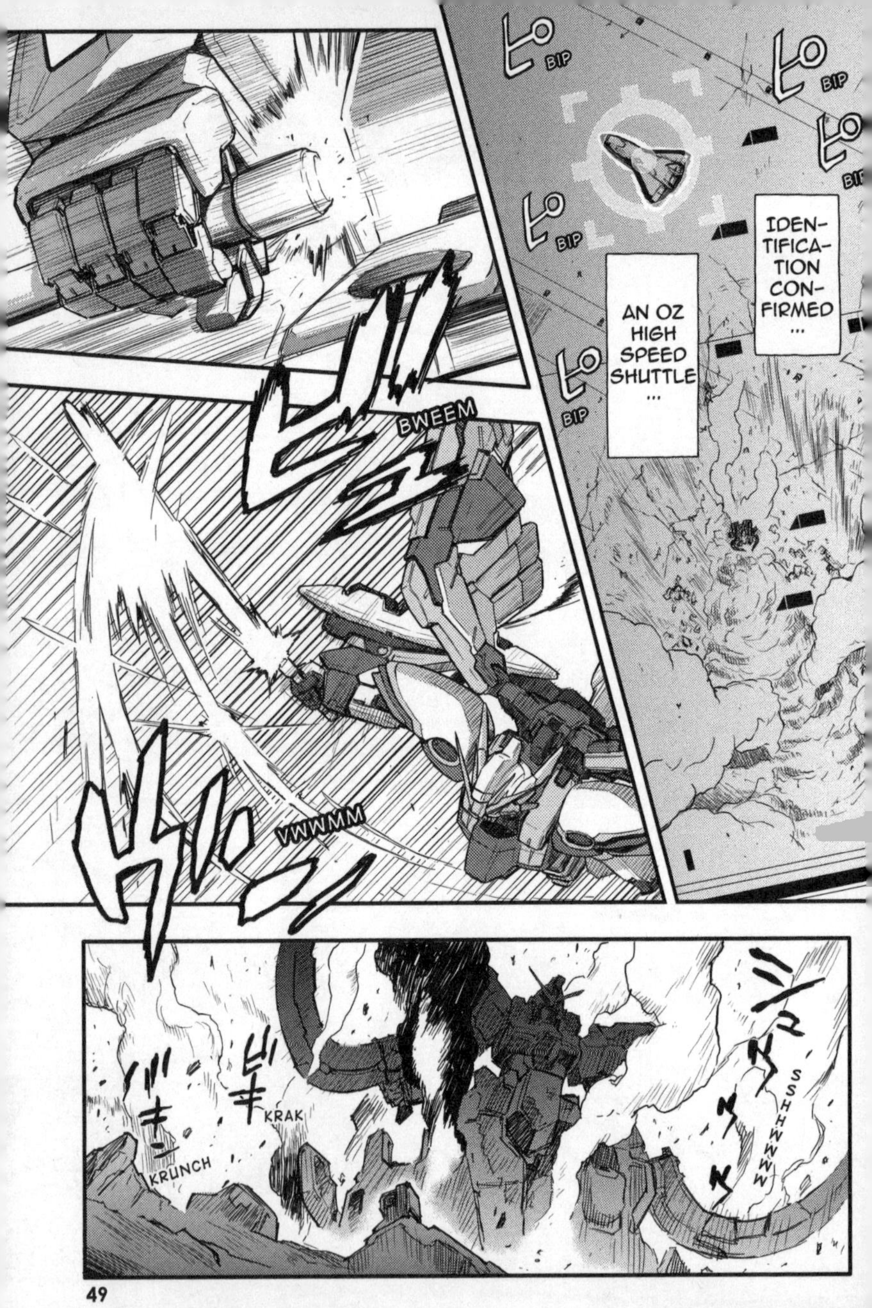
BIP
BIP
BIP
IDEN-TIFICA-TION CON-FIRMED ...
BIP
AN OZ HIGH SPEED SHUTTLE ...
BIP
BWEEM
VWWMM
SSHHWWWW
KRAK
KRUNCH

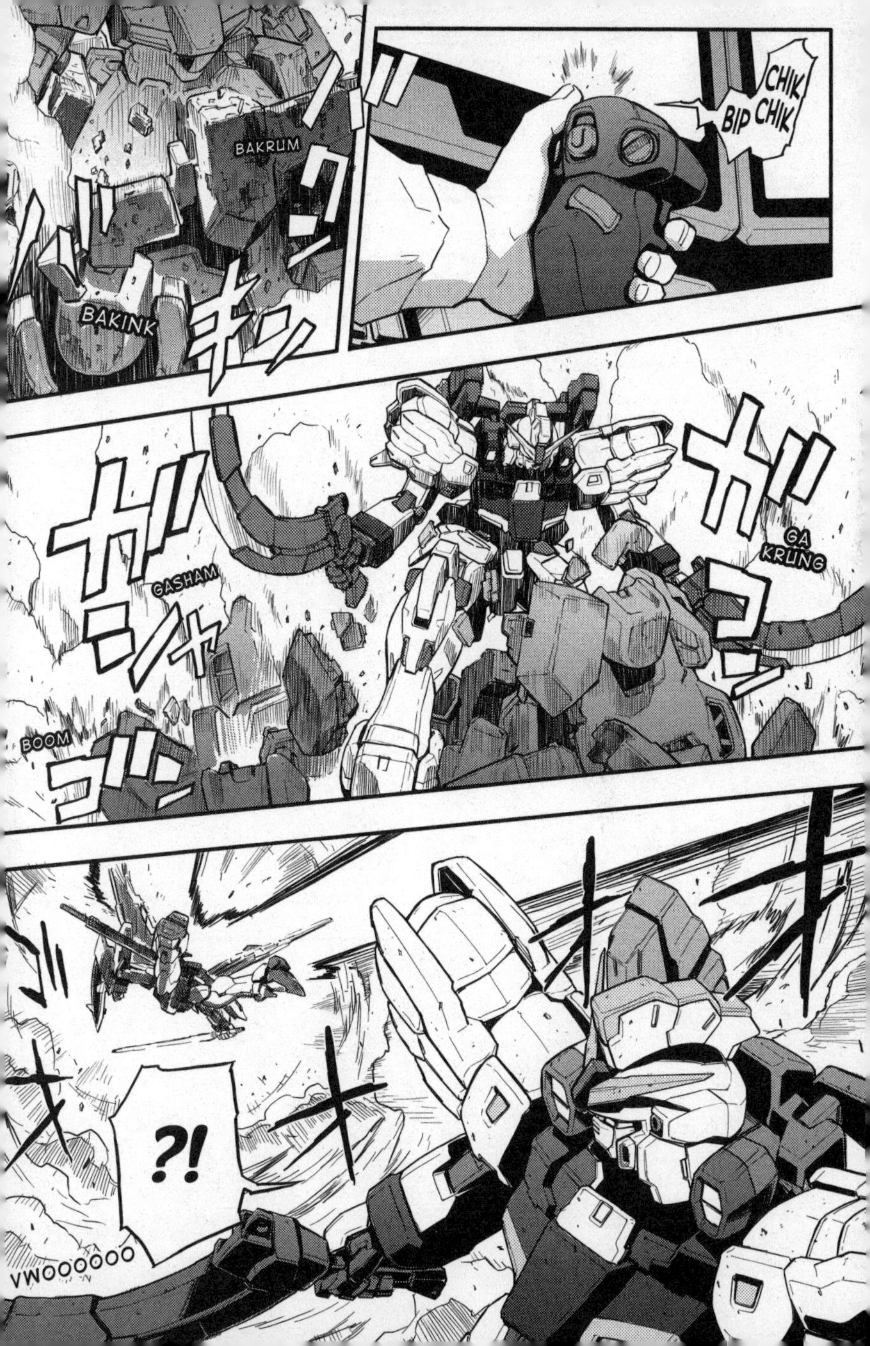
CHIK CHIK BIP
BAKRUM
BAKINK
GA KRUNG
GASHAM
BOOM
?!
VWOOOOOO

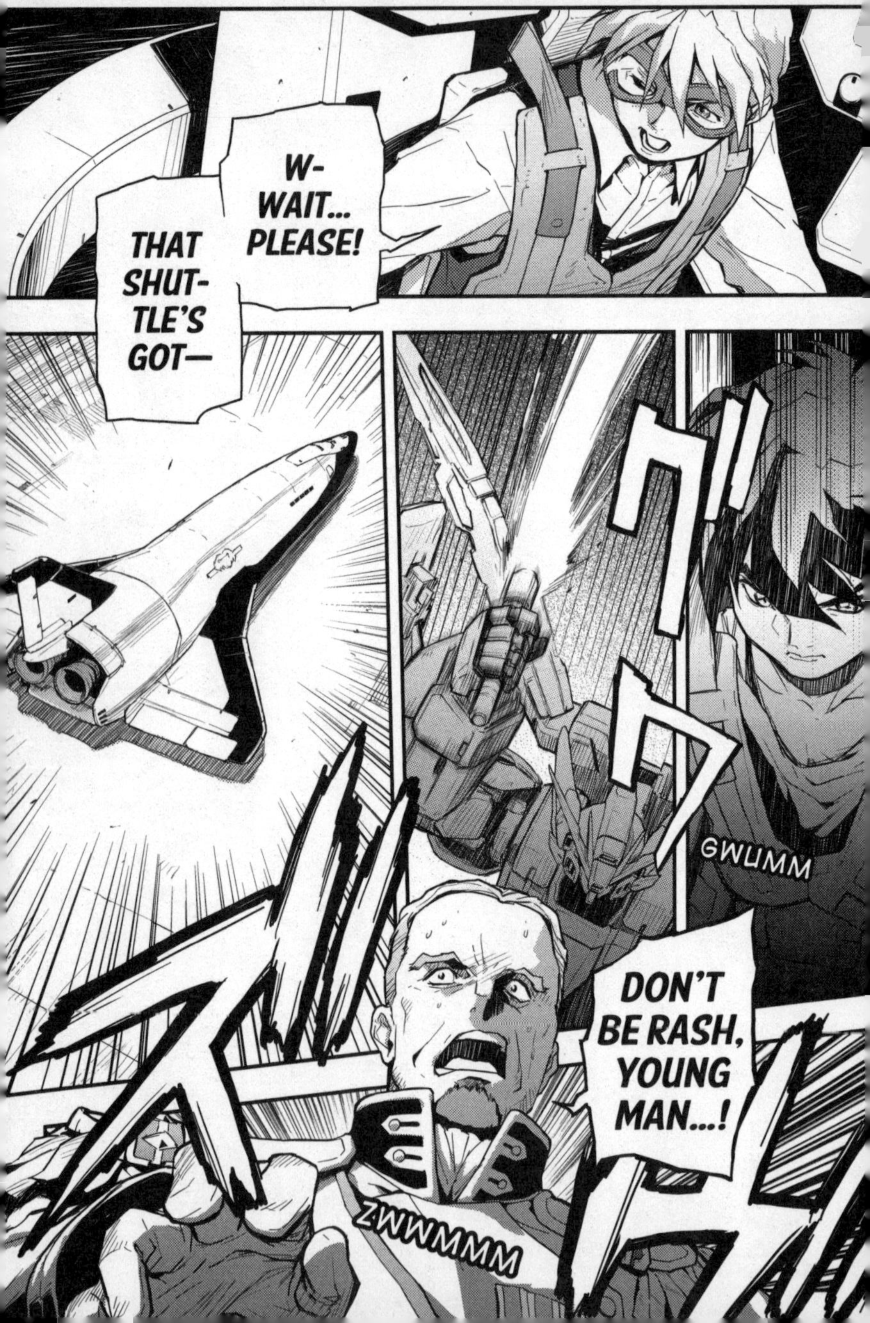
W-
WAIT...
PLEASE!
THAT SHUT-
TLE'S
GOT—
GWUMM
DON'T
BE RASH,
YOUNG
MAN...!
ZWWMMMM

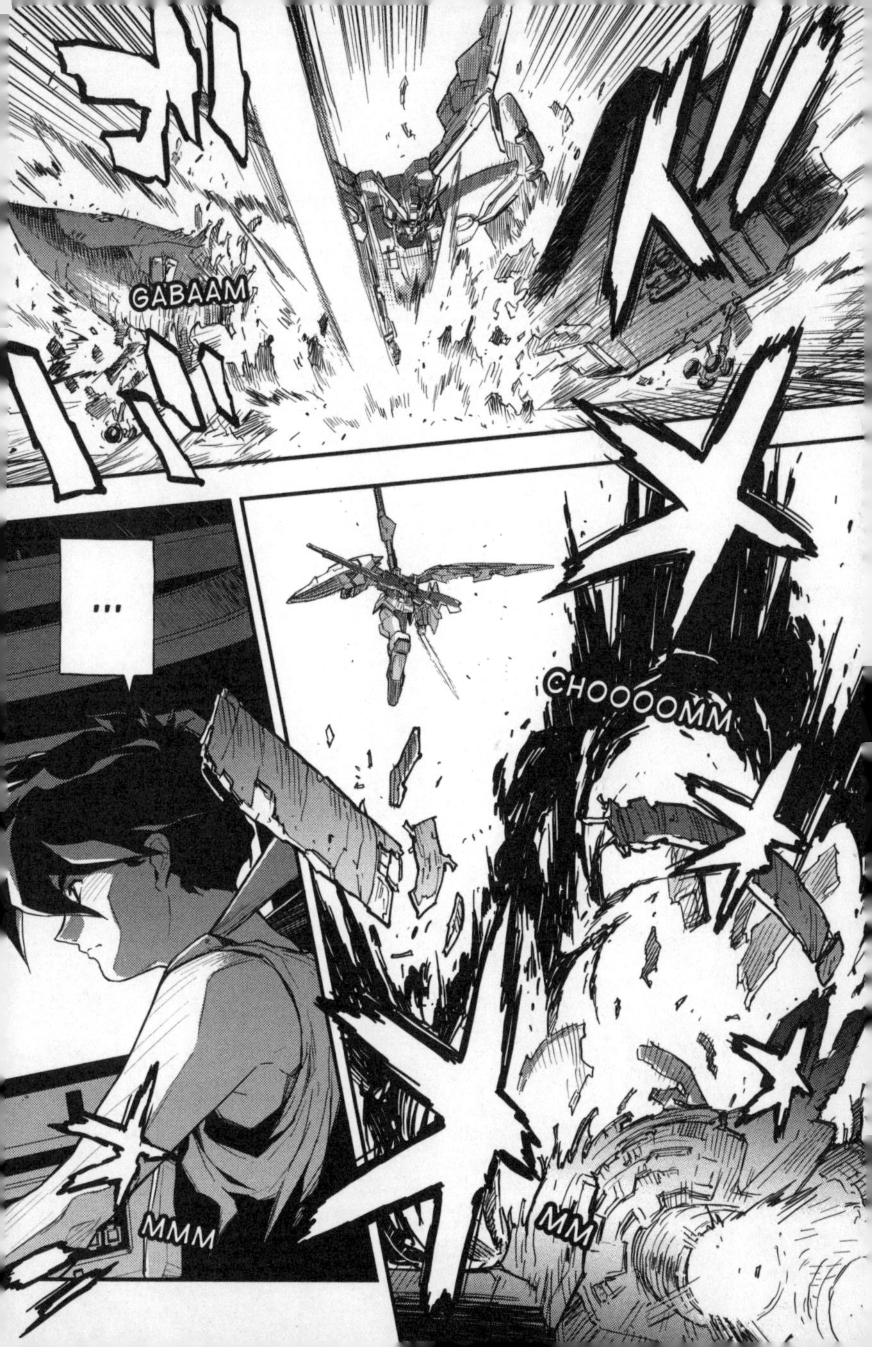
GABAAM
CHOOOOMM
MM
...
MMM

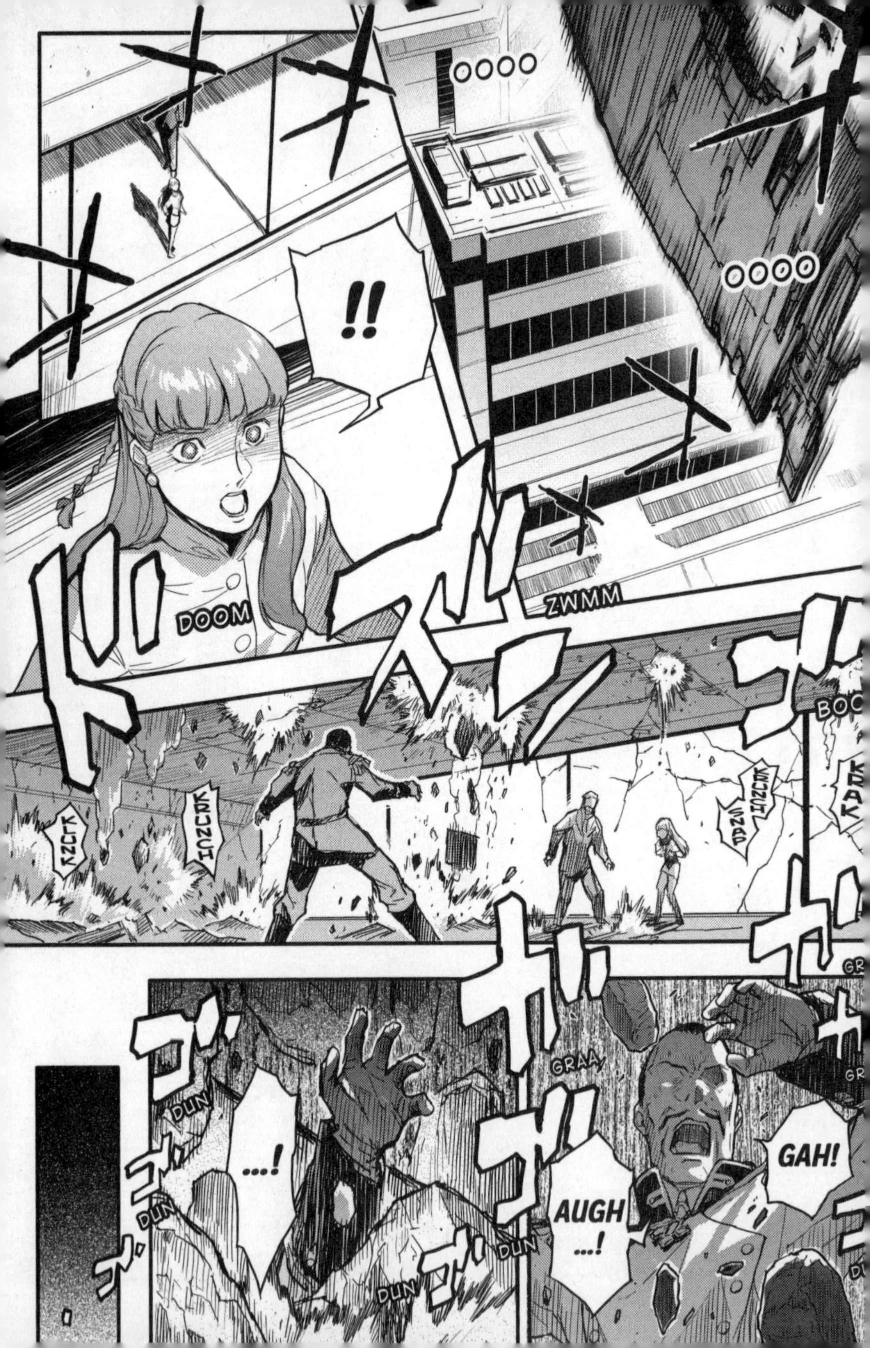
OOOO
OOOO
!!
ZWMM
DOOM
KRAK
KRUNCH
SNAP
KRUNCH
KLUNK
GAH!
AUGH
...!
GRAA
DUN
...!
DUN
DUN
DUN

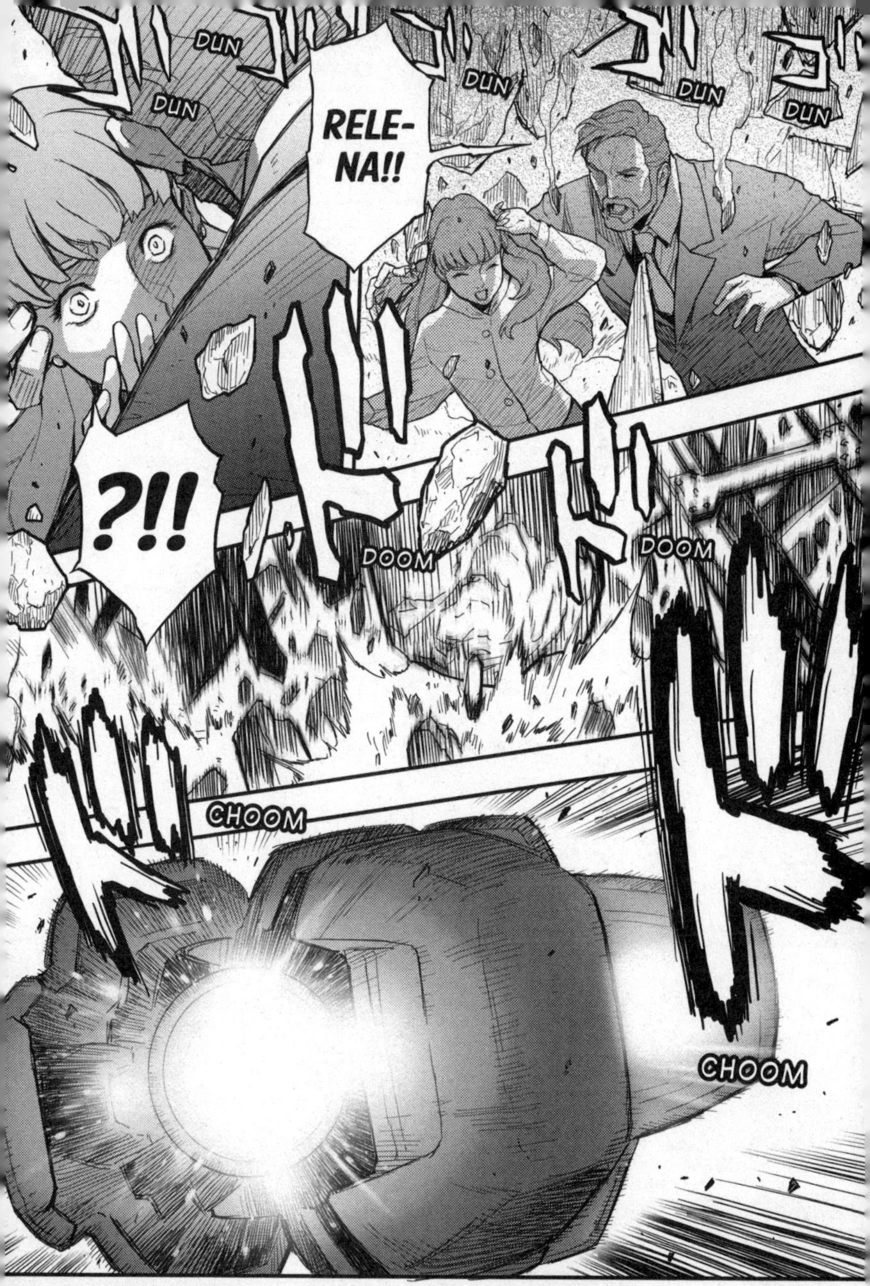
DUN
DUN
DUN
DUN
DUN
RELE-NA!!
?!!
DOOM
DOOM
CHOOM
CHOOM

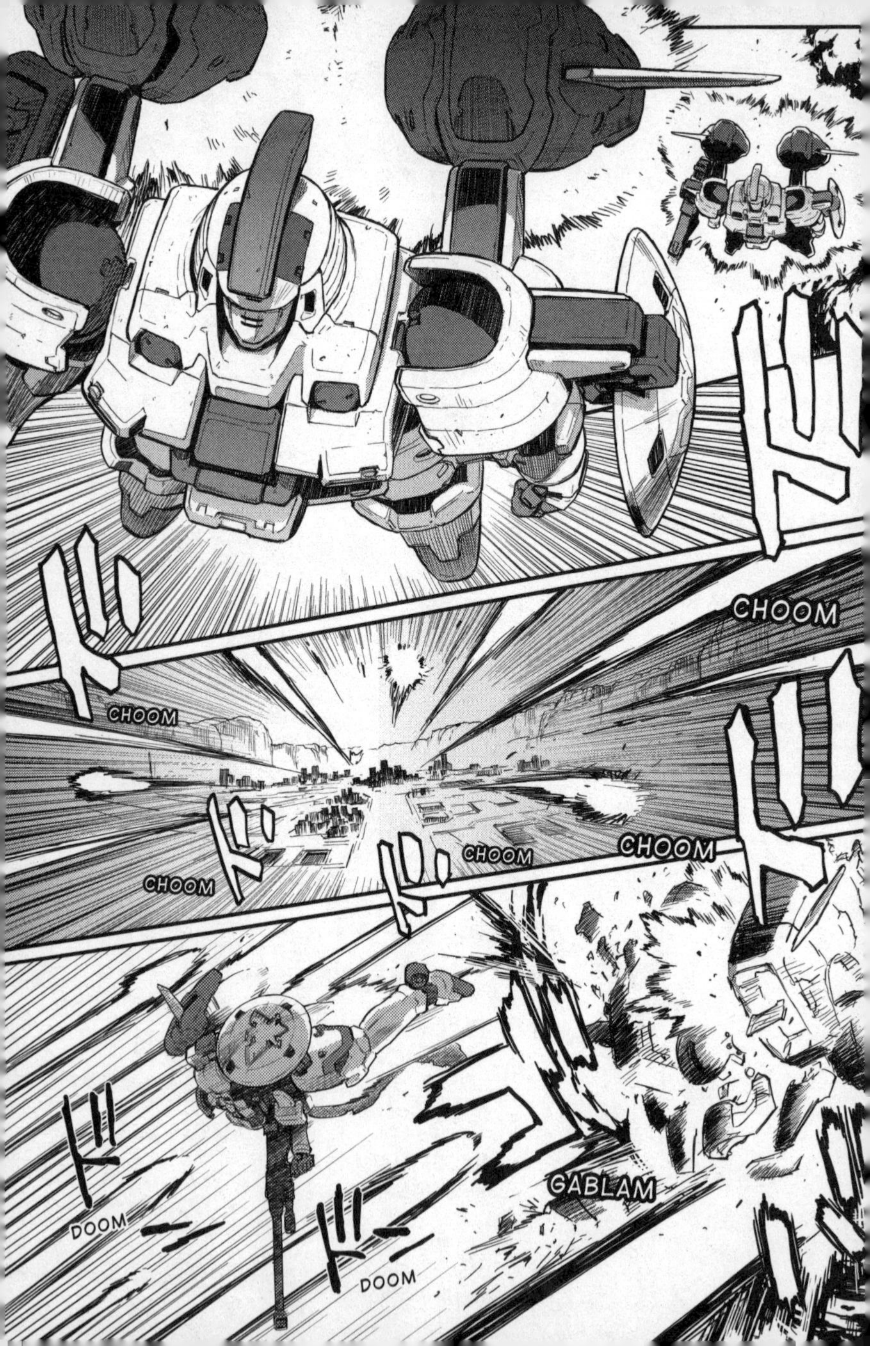
CHOOM
CHOOM
CHOOM
CHOOM
CHOOM
GABLAM
DOOM
DOOM

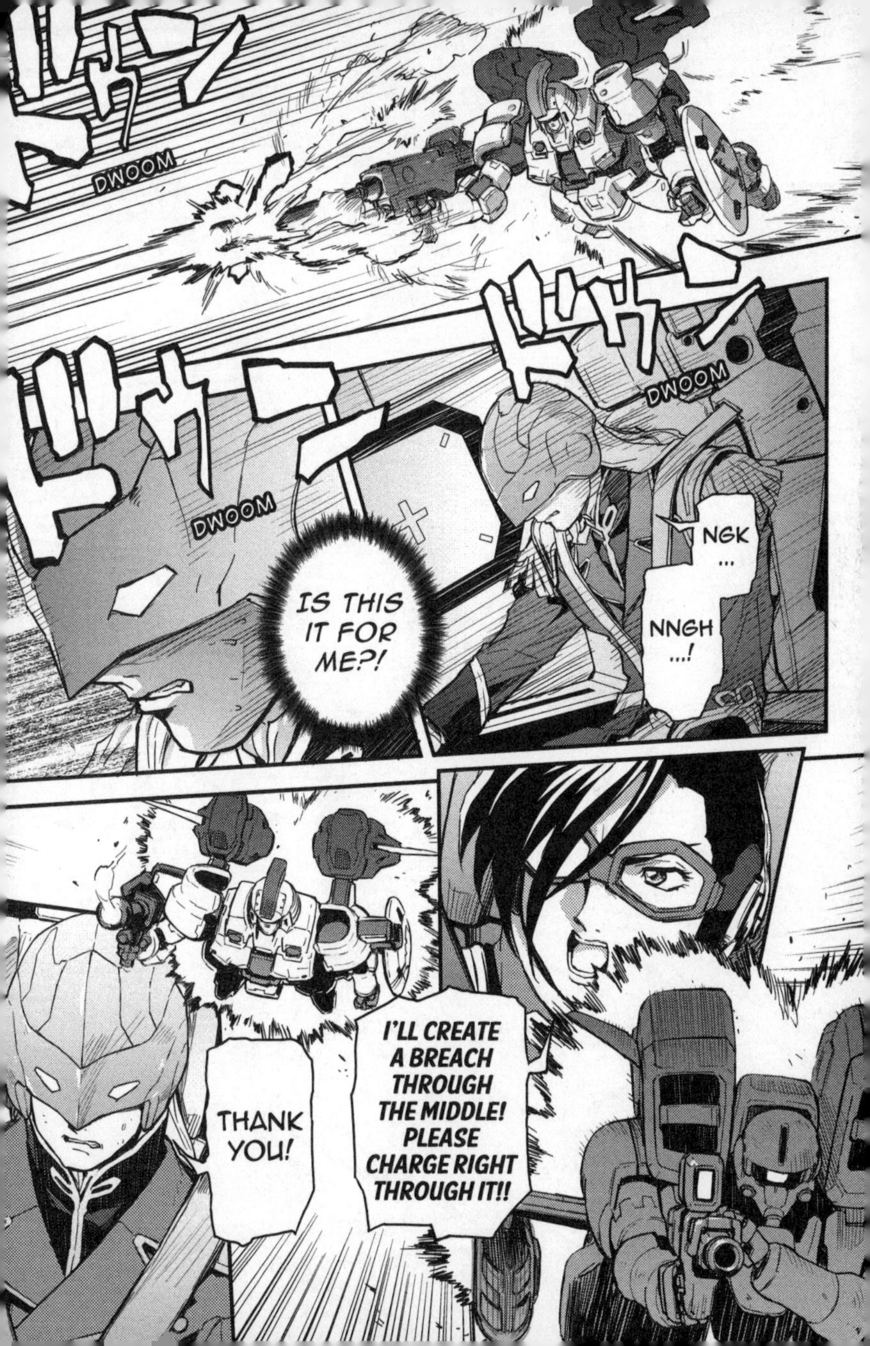
DWOOM
DWOOM
NGK ...
NNGH ...!
DWOOM
IS THIS IT FOR ME?!
I'LL CREATE A BREACH THROUGH THE MIDDLE! PLEASE CHARGE RIGHT THROUGH IT!!
THANK YOU!

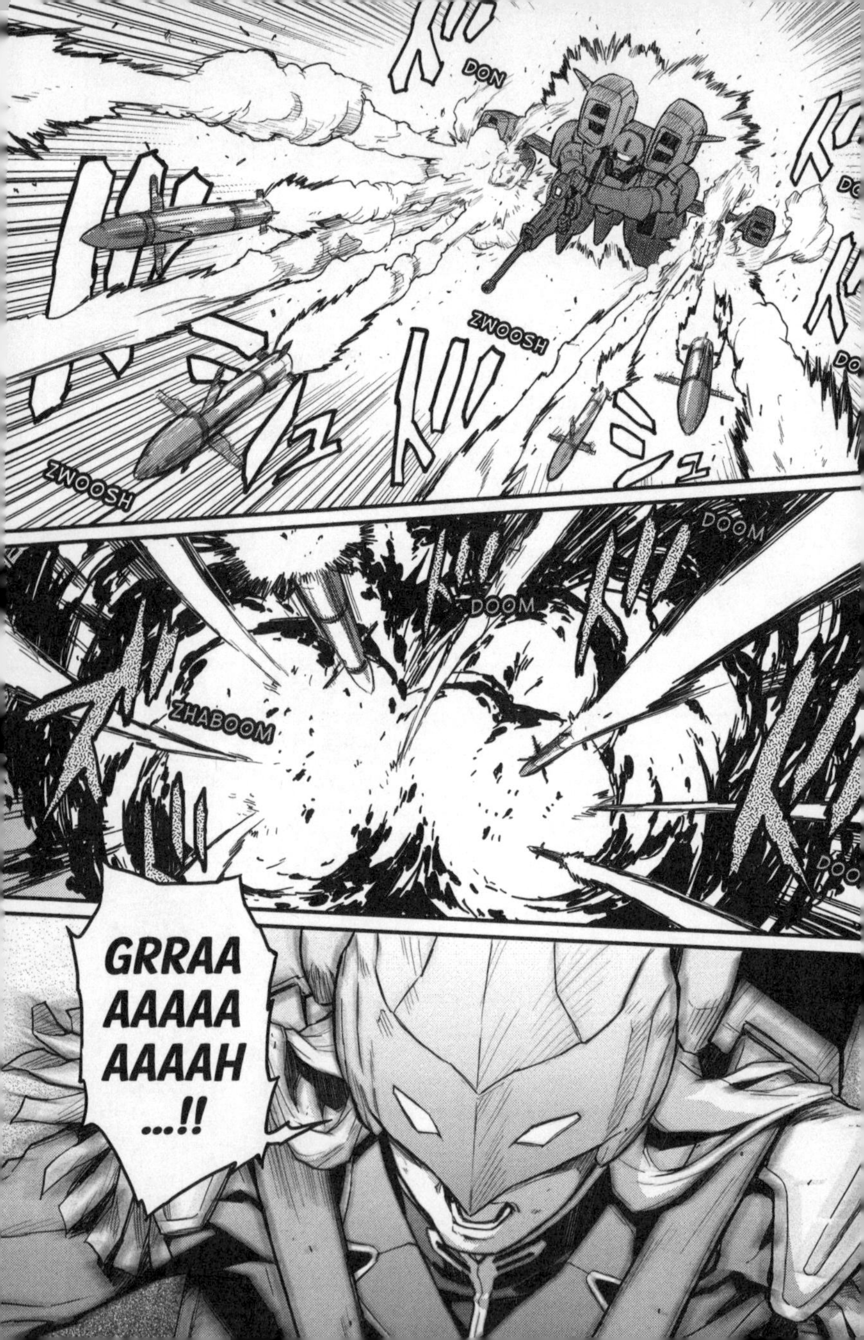
DON
ZWOOSH
ZWOOSH
DOOM
DOOM
ZHABOOM
GRRAA
AAAAA
AAAAH
...!!

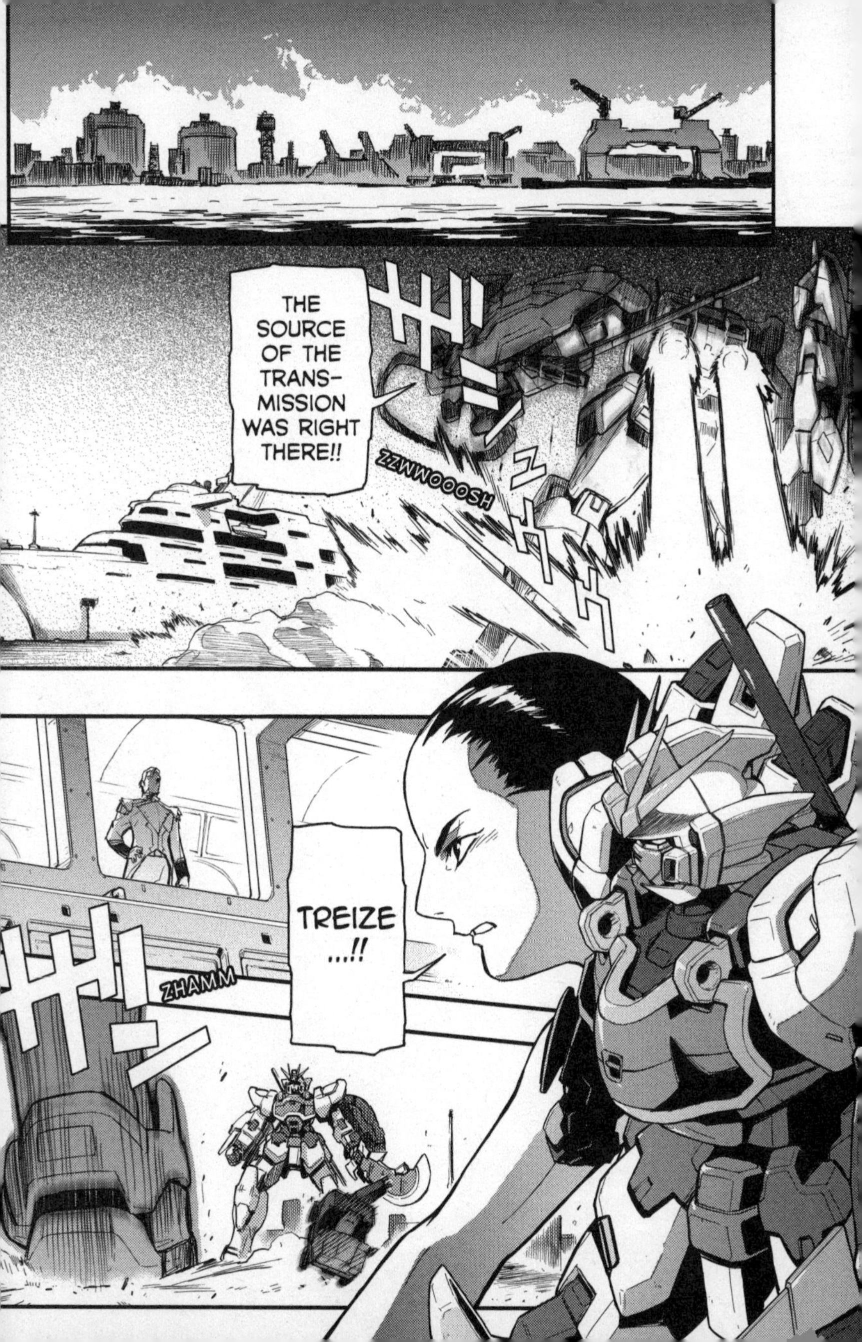
THE SOURCE OF THE TRANS-MISSION WAS RIGHT THERE!!
ZZWWOOOOSH
TREIZE ...!!
ZHAMM

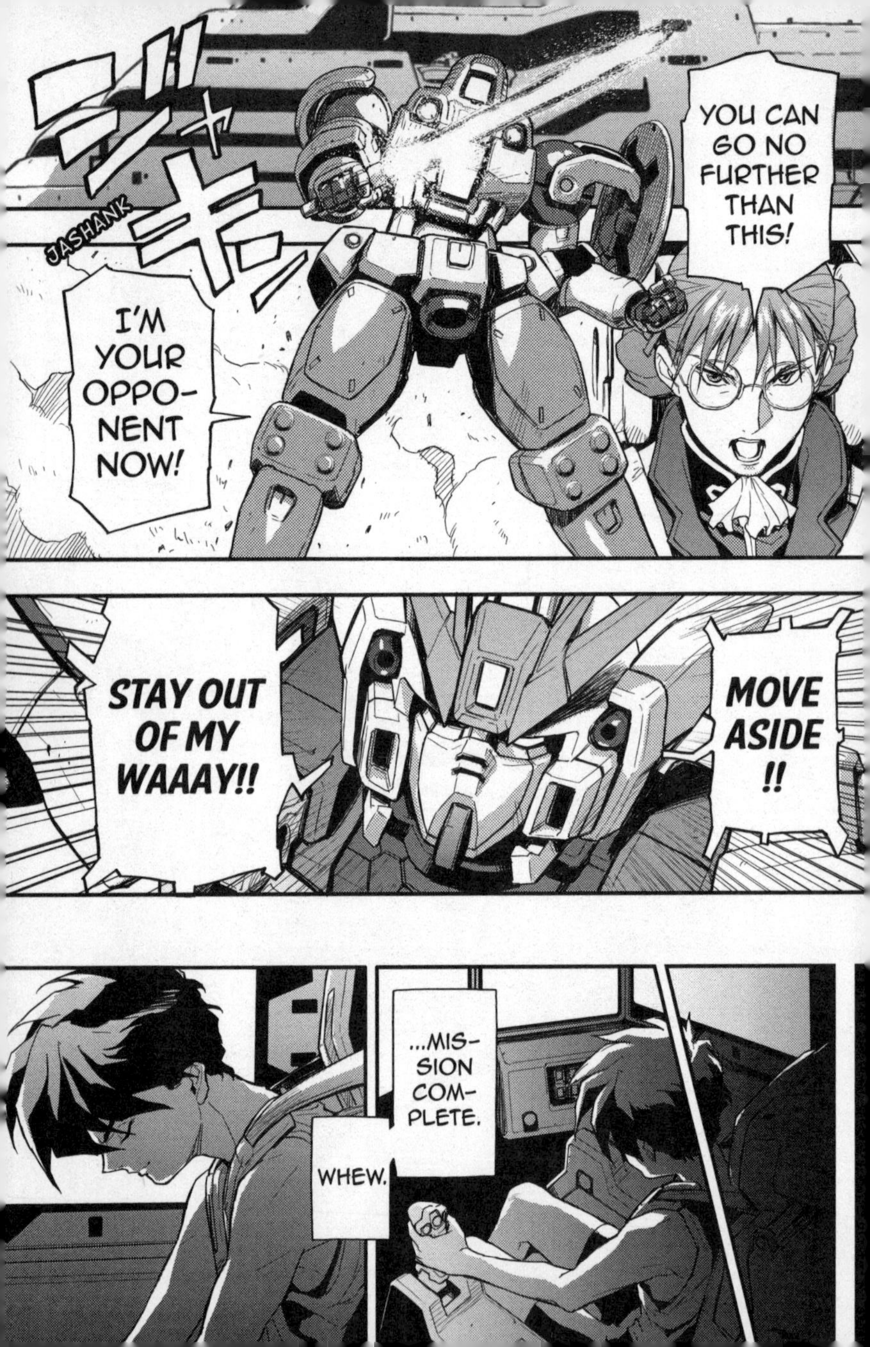
YOU CAN GO NO FURTHER THAN THIS!
JASHANK
I'M YOUR OPPO-NENT NOW!
MOVE ASIDE !!
STAY OUT OF MY WAAAY!!
...MIS-SION COM-PLETE.
WHEW.

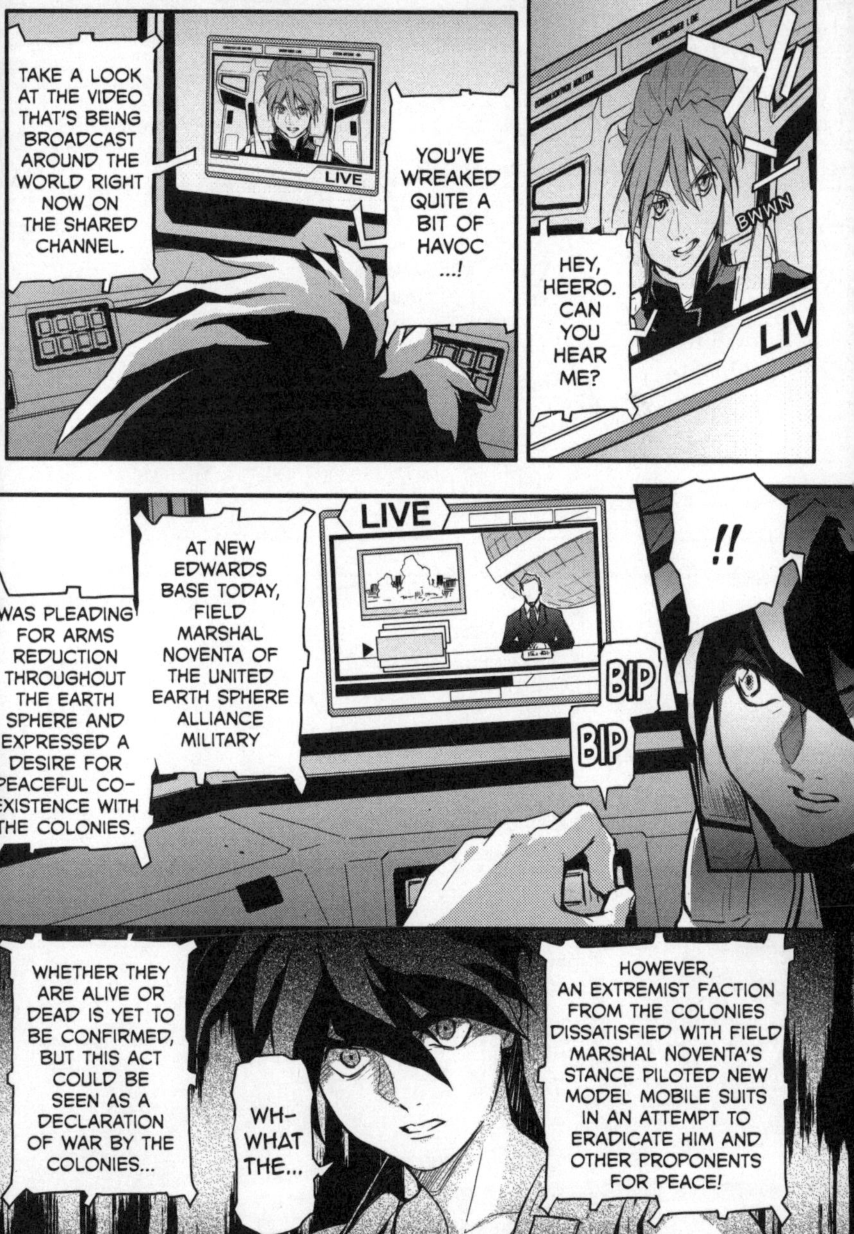
BWWN
HEY, HEERO. CAN YOU HEAR ME?
LIV
TAKE A LOOK AT THE VIDEO THAT'S BEING BROADCAST AROUND THE WORLD RIGHT NOW ON THE SHARED CHANNEL.
LIVE
YOU'VE WREAKED QUITE A BIT OF HAVOC ...!
!!
LIVE
BIP
BIP
AT NEW EDWARDS BASE TODAY, FIELD MARSHAL NOVENTA OF THE UNITED EARTH SPHERE ALLIANCE MILITARY
WAS PLEADING FOR ARMS REDUCTION THROUGHOUT THE EARTH SPHERE AND EXPRESSED A DESIRE FOR PEACEFUL CO-EXISTENCE WITH THE COLONIES.
HOWEVER, AN EXTREMIST FACTION FROM THE COLONIES DISSATISFIED WITH FIELD MARSHAL NOVENTA'S STANCE PILOTED NEW MODEL MOBILE SUITS IN AN ATTEMPT TO ERADICATE HIM AND OTHER PROPONENTS FOR PEACE!
WH- WHAT THE...
WHETHER THEY ARE ALIVE OR DEAD IS YET TO BE CONFIRMED, BUT THIS ACT COULD BE SEEN AS A DECLARATION OF WAR BY THE COLONIES...

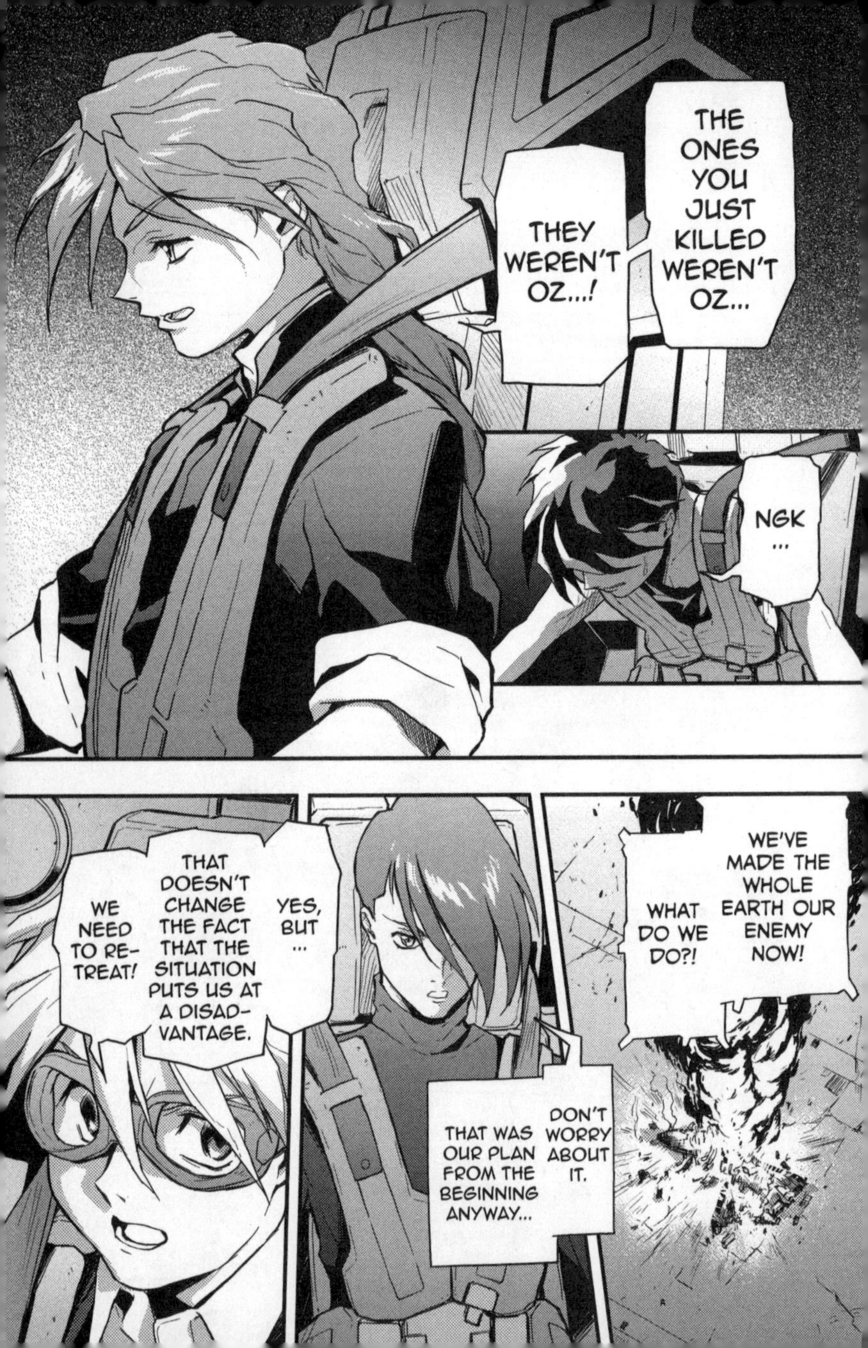
THE ONES YOU JUST KILLED WEREN'T OZ...
THEY WEREN'T OZ...!
NGK ...
WE'VE MADE THE WHOLE EARTH OUR ENEMY NOW!
WHAT DO WE DO?!
YES, BUT ...
THAT DOESN'T CHANGE THE FACT THAT THE SITUATION PUTS US AT A DISAD-VANTAGE.
WE NEED TO RE-TREAT!
DON'T WORRY ABOUT IT.
THAT WAS OUR PLAN FROM THE BEGINNING ANYWAY...

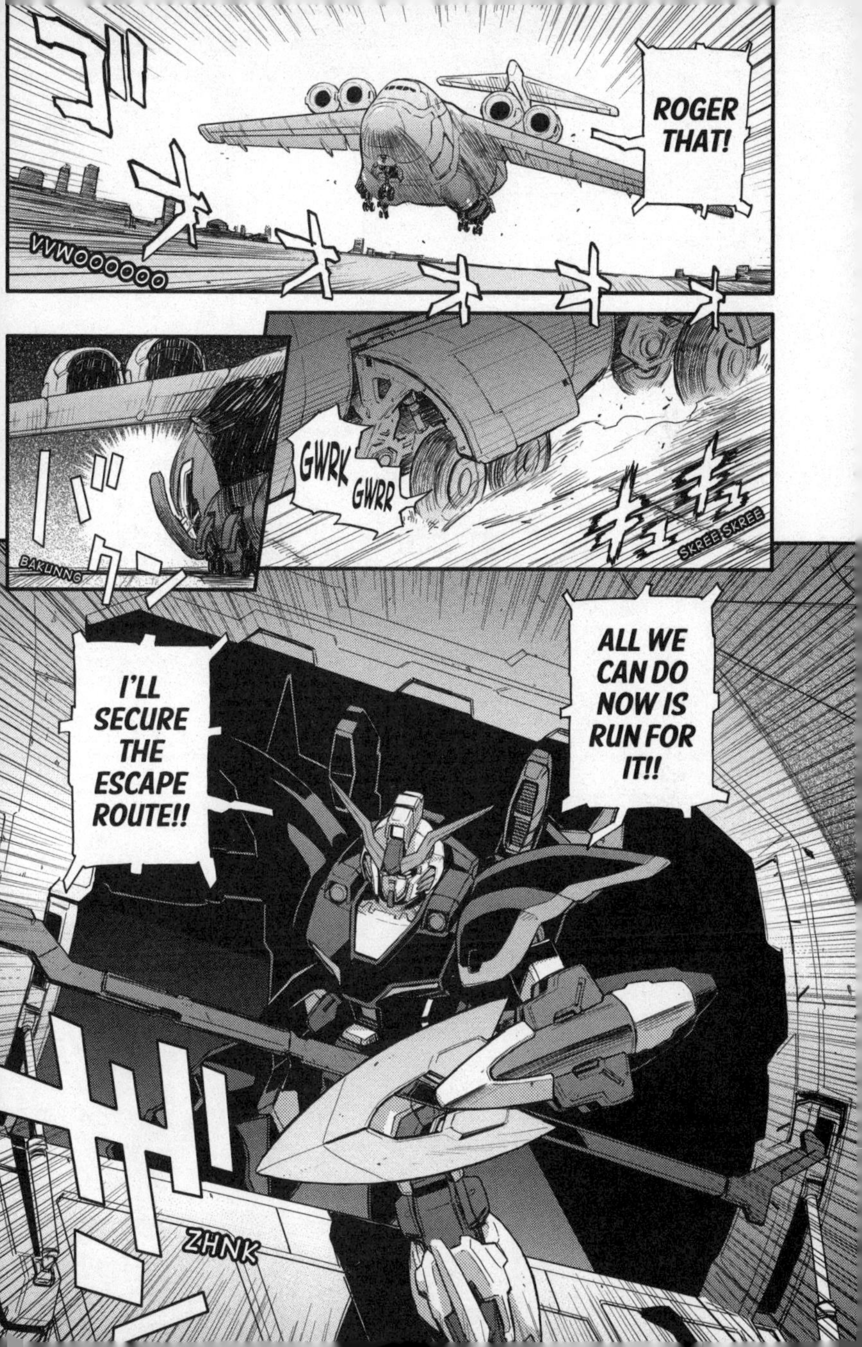
ROGER THAT!
VVWOOOOOO
GWRK GWRR
SKREE SKREE
BAKUNNG
ALL WE CAN DO NOW IS RUN FOR IT!!
I'LL SECURE THE ESCAPE ROUTE!!
ZHNK

SLEEVE NOTES:
Endless Waltz

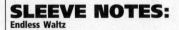

XXXG-01SR
GUNDAM SANDROCK
Armadillo Rigging

Additional armor with support booster rigging. The shields attached to the armor that covers each shoulder are modifications of Maganac rigging. It also adds boosters to strengthen thrust. The armor can be purged if necessary, even mid-battle.

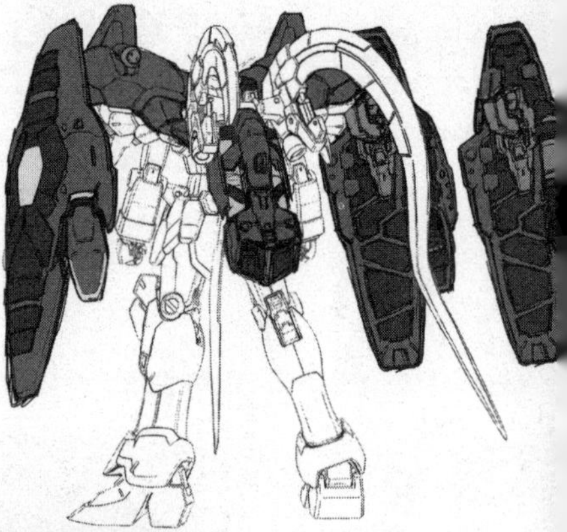

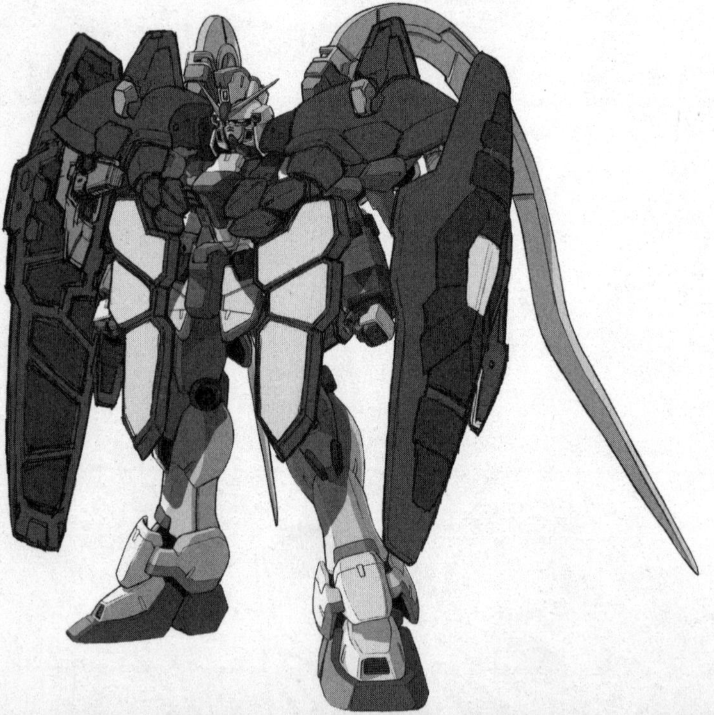

Chapter 16: "A Banquet for the Pleiades" Part 5

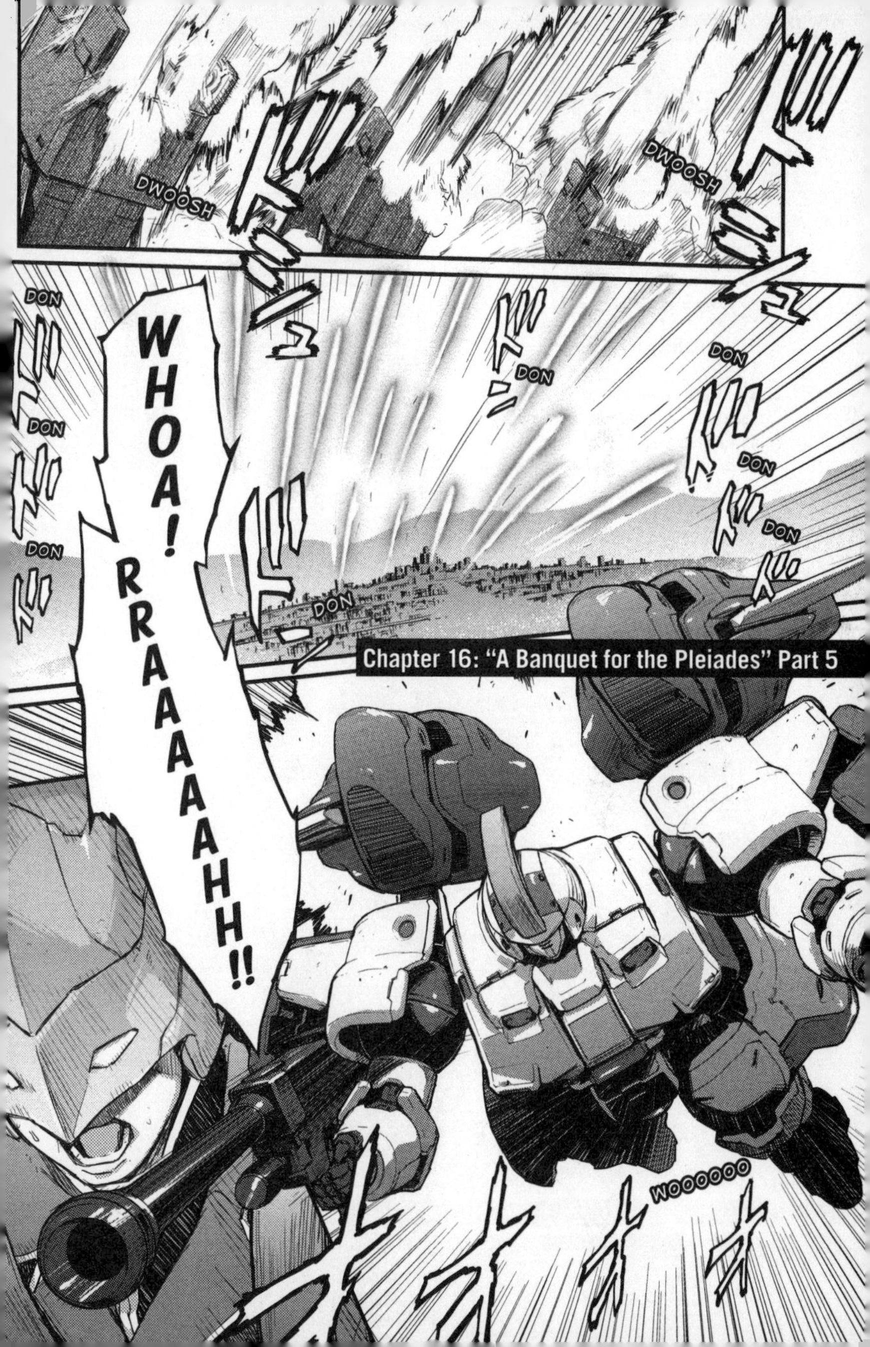
DWOOSH
DWOOSH
DON
DON
DON
DON
DON
DON
DON
DON
WHOA! RRAAAAAAHH!!
WOOOOOO

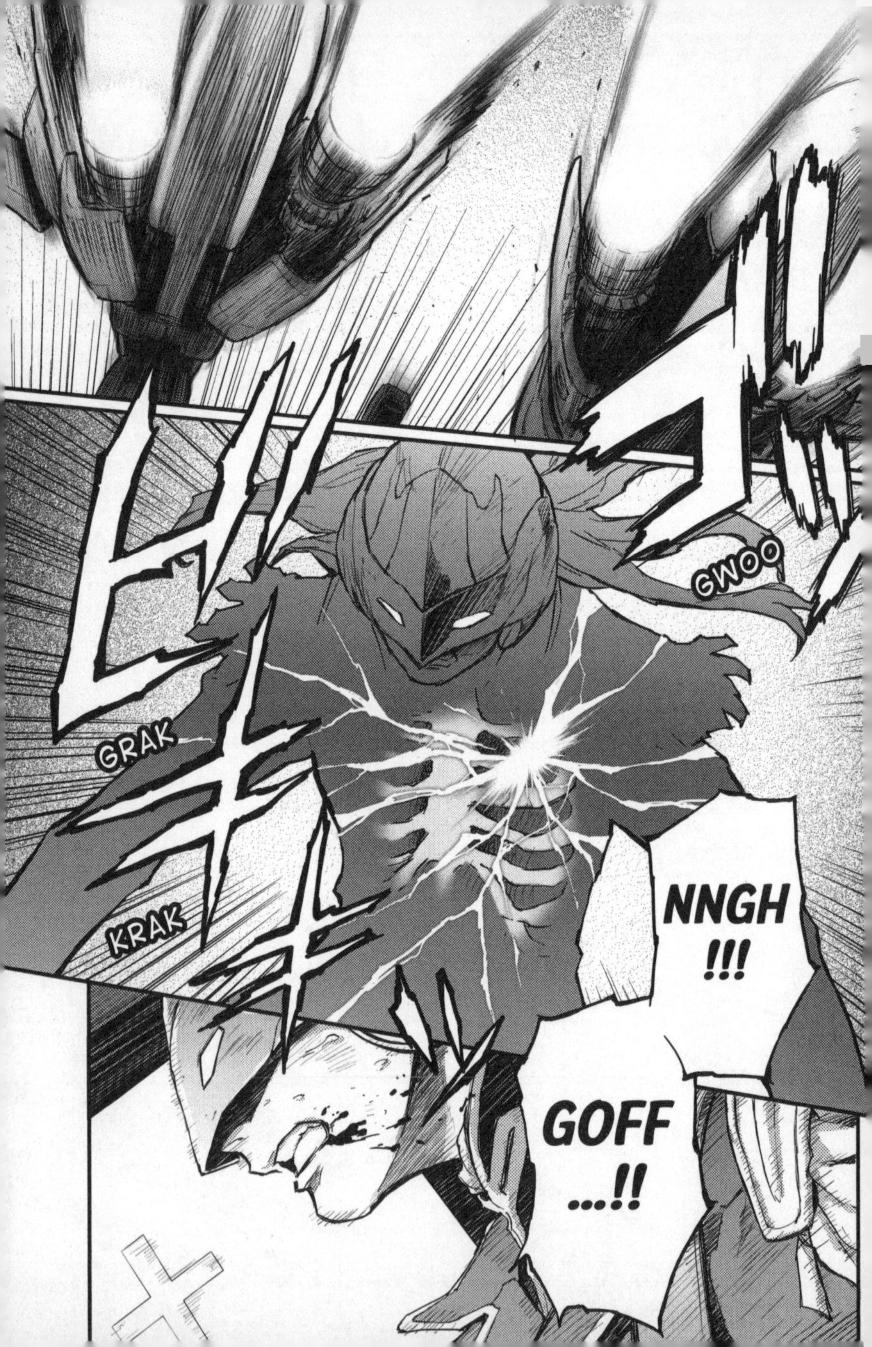
GWOO
GRAK
KRAK
NNGH!!!
GOFF ...!!

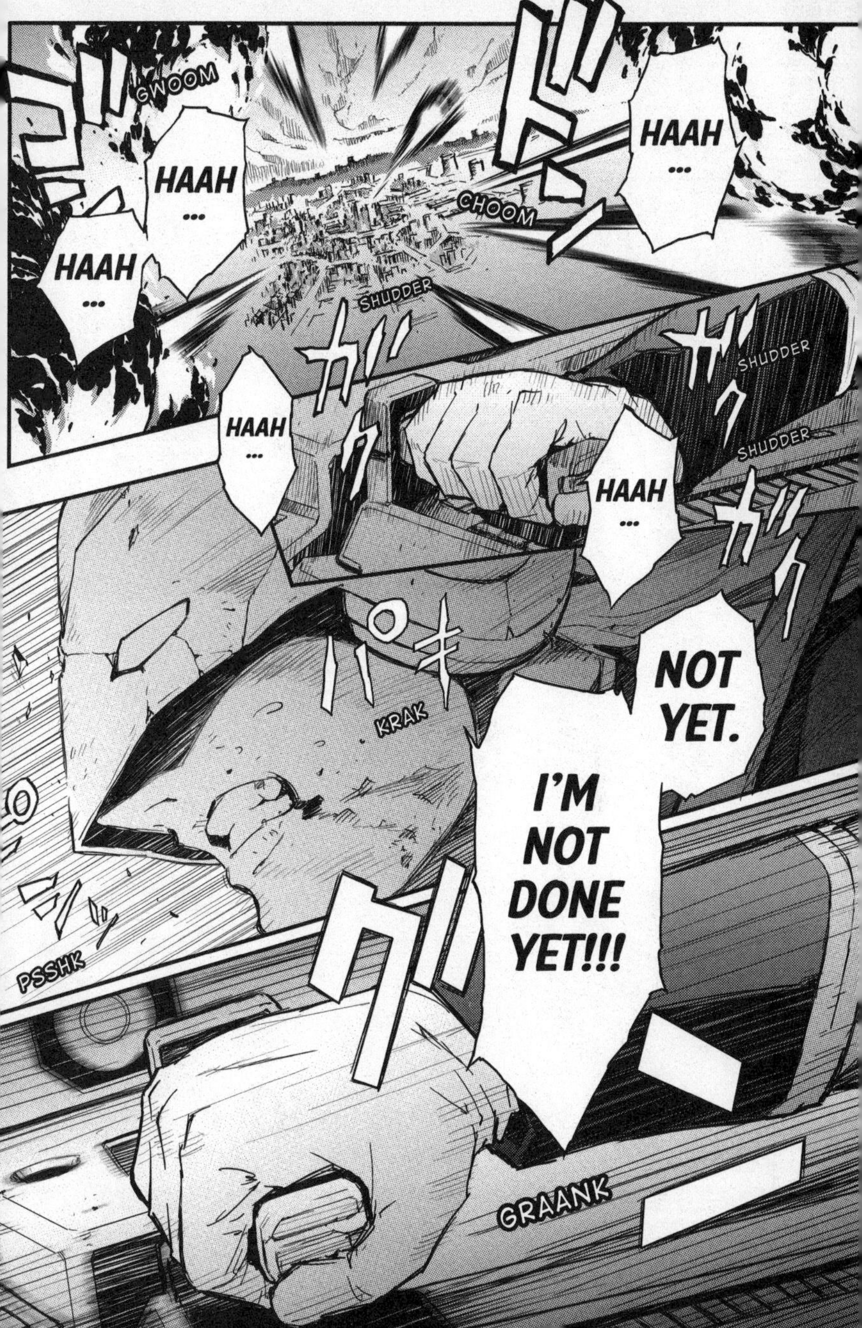
HAAH ...
CHOOM
GWOOM
HAAH ...
HAAH ...
SHUDDER
SHUDDER
SHUDDER
HAAH ...
HAAH ...
KRAK
NOT YET.
I'M NOT DONE YET!!!
PSSHK
GRAANK

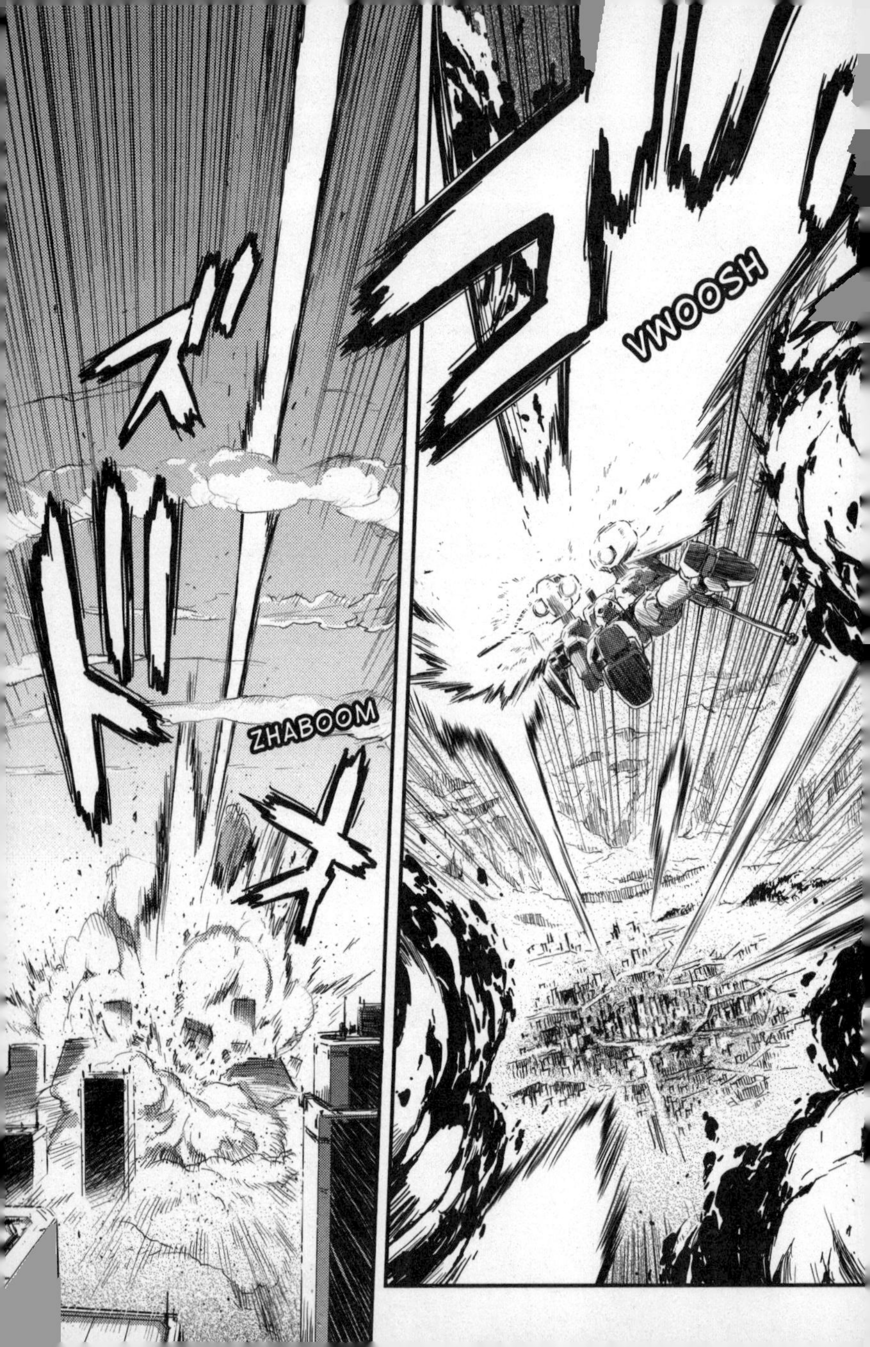
VWOOSH
ZHABOOM

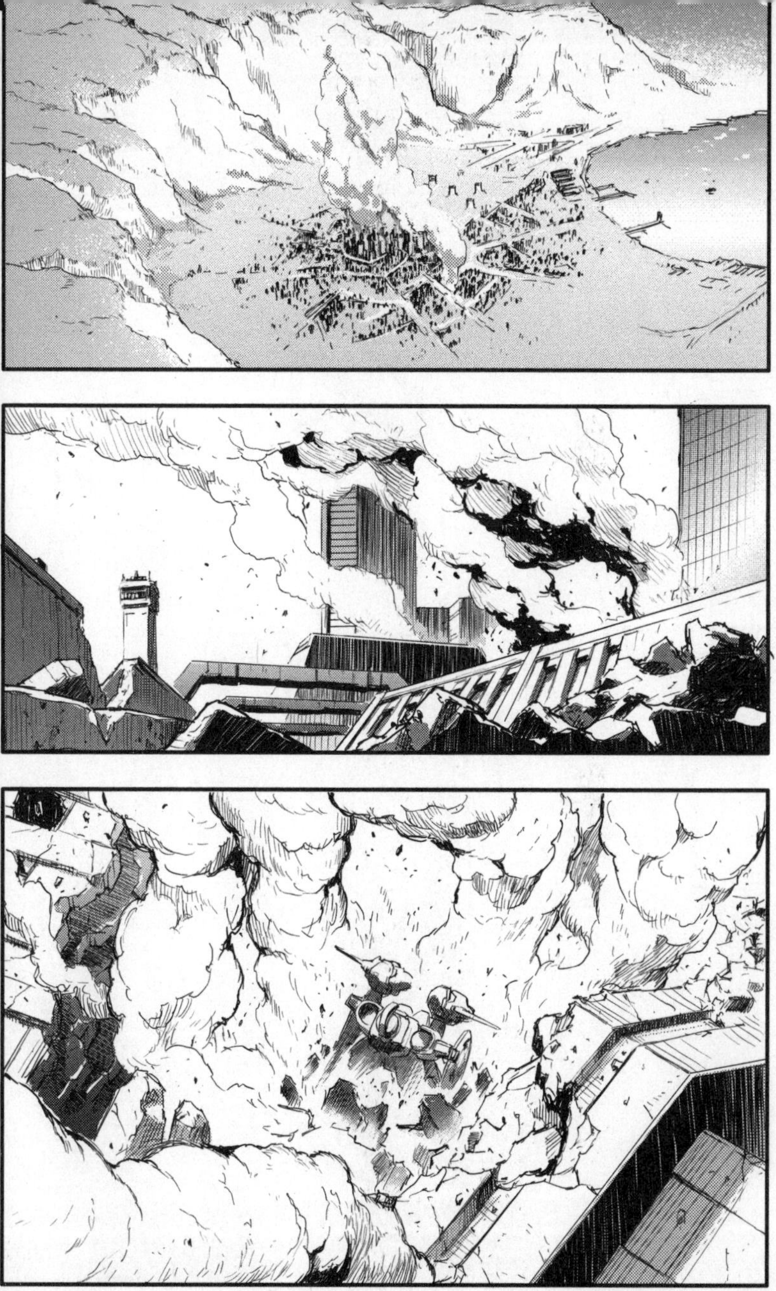

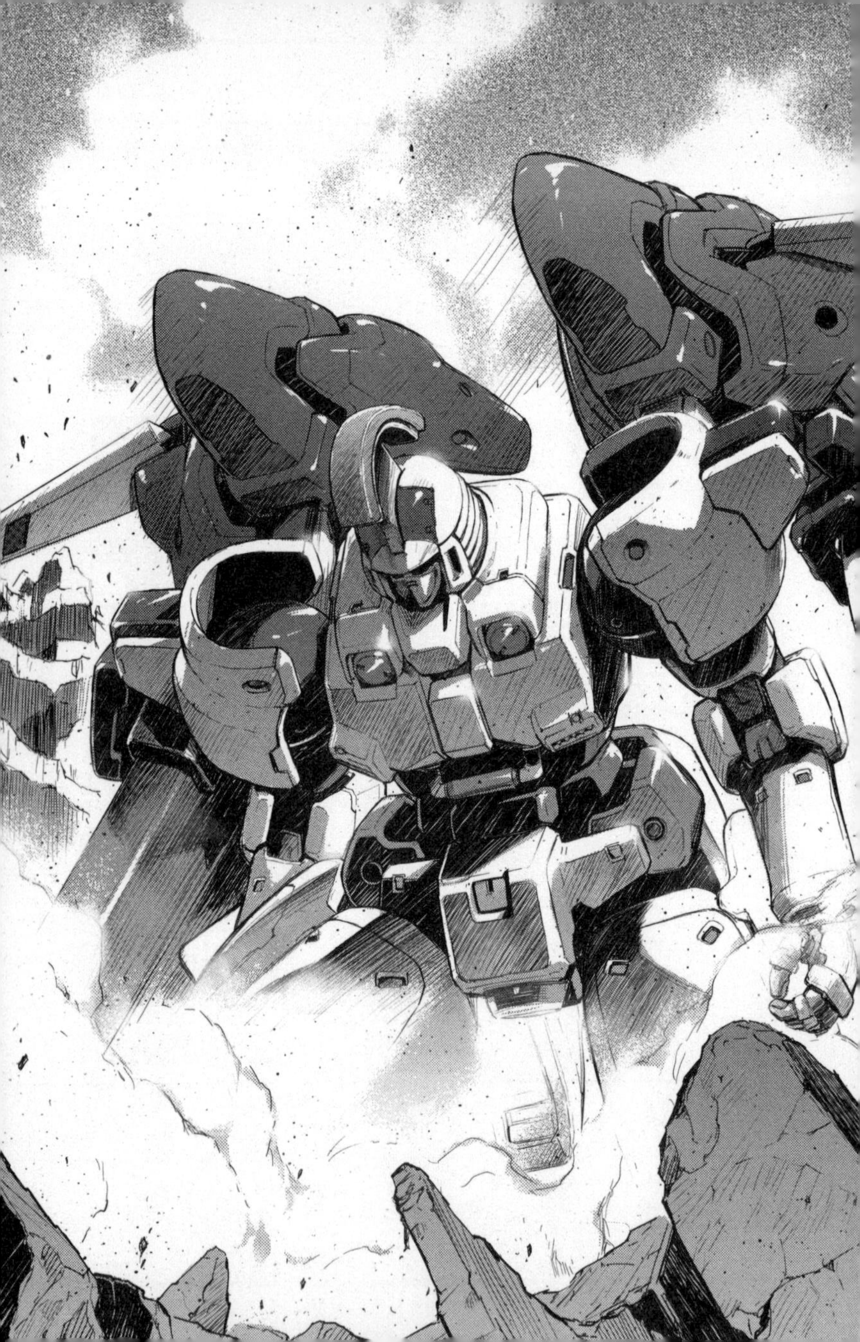

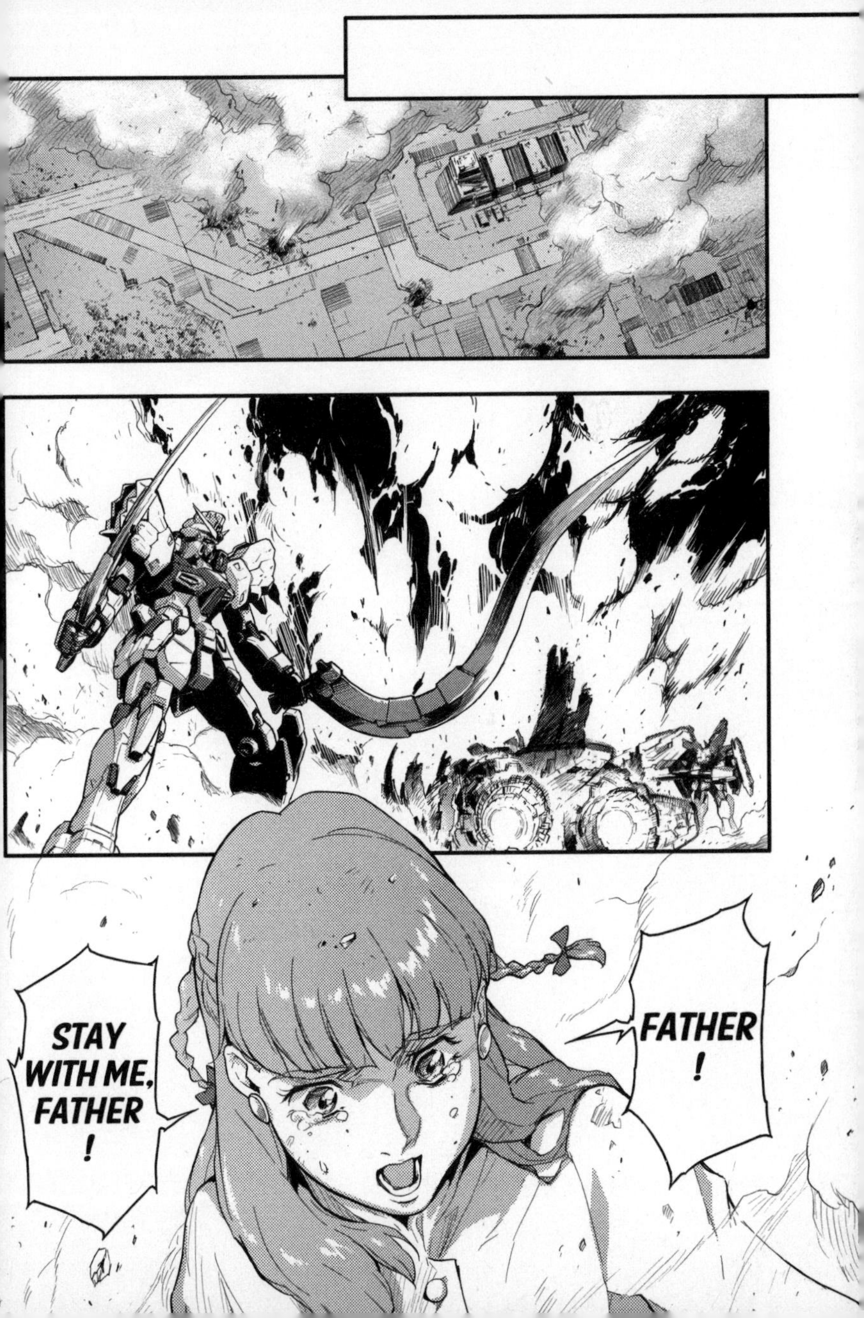
FATHER!
STAY WITH ME, FATHER!

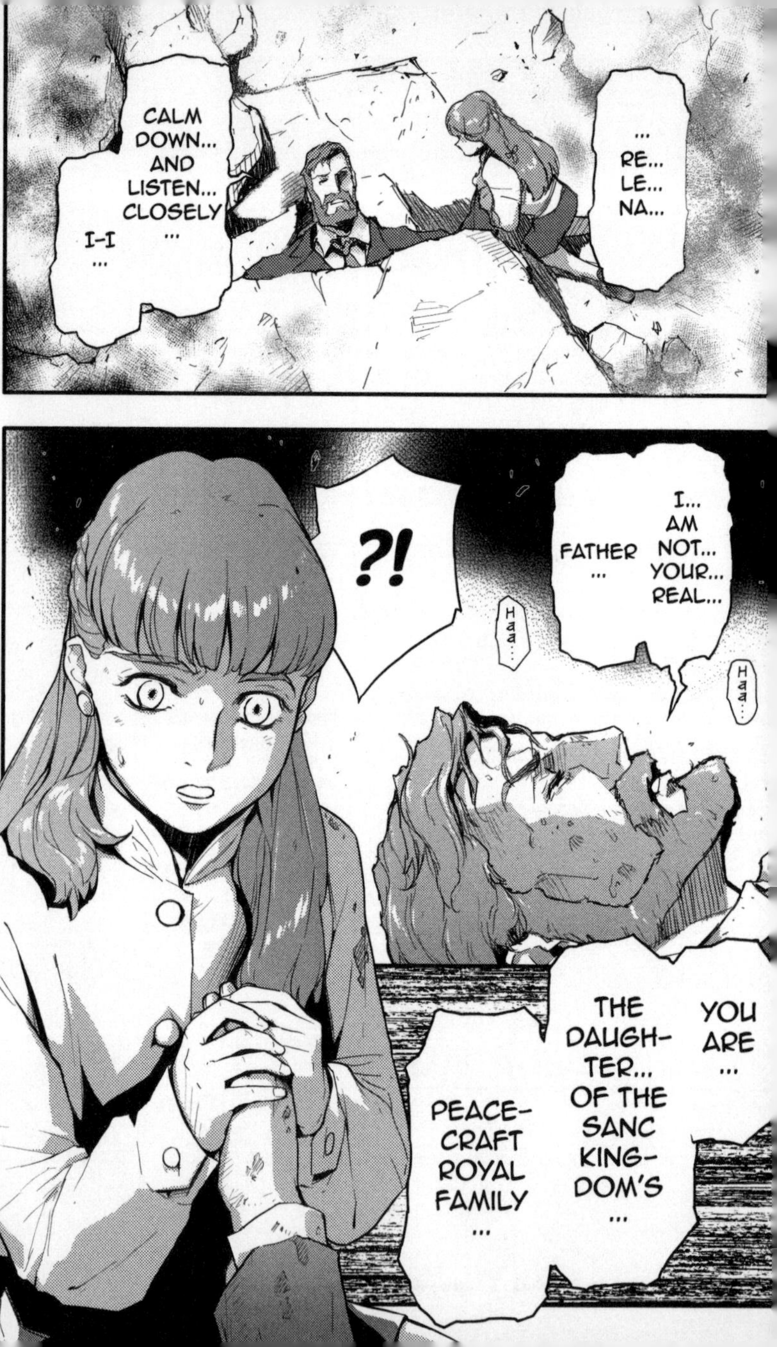
... RE... LE... NA...
CALM DOWN... AND LISTEN... CLOSELY ...
I-I ...
Haa...
I... AM NOT... YOUR... REAL...
FATHER ...
Haa...
?!
YOU ARE ...
THE DAUGHTER... OF THE SANC KINGDOM'S ...
PEACECRAFT ROYAL FAMILY ...

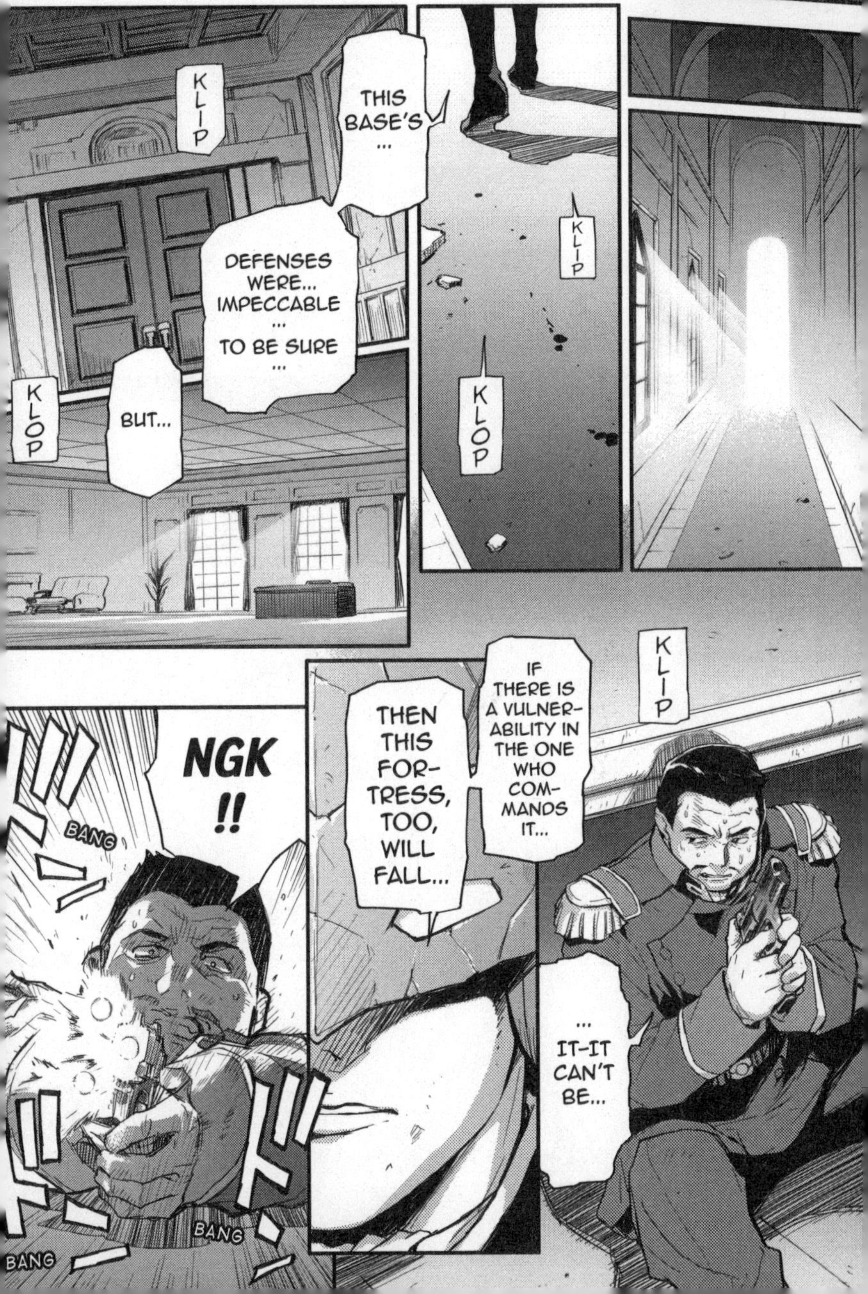

KLIP
KLOP
THIS BASE'S ...
KLIP
DEFENSES WERE... IMPECCABLE ... TO BE SURE ...
BUT...
KLOP
KLIP
IF THERE IS A VULNER-ABILITY IN THE ONE WHO COM-MANDS IT...
THEN THIS FOR-TRESS, TOO, WILL FALL...
... IT-IT CAN'T BE...
NGK !!
BANG
BANG
BANG

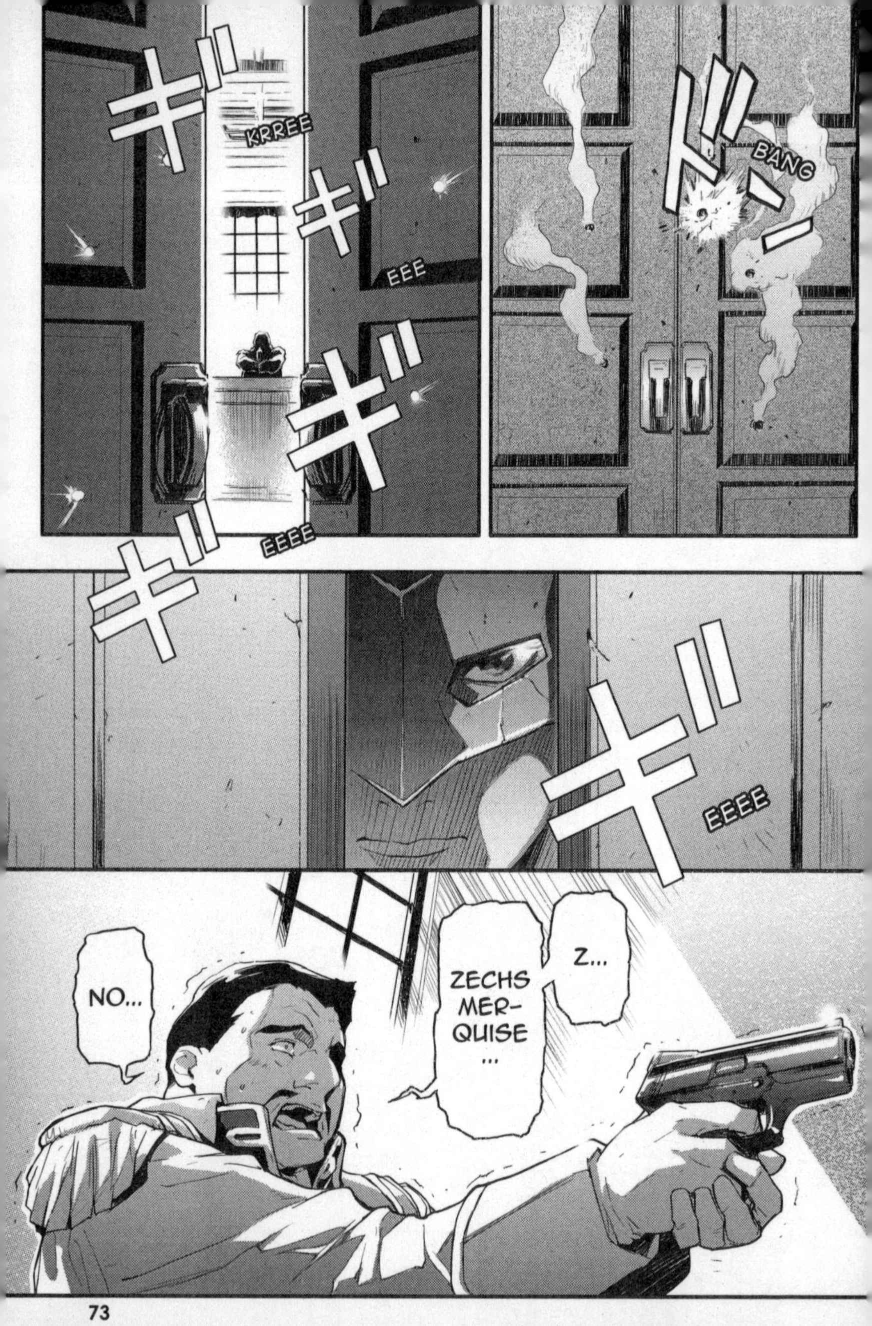
BANG
KRREE
EEE
EEEE
EEEE
Z...
ZECHS MERQUISE ...
NO...

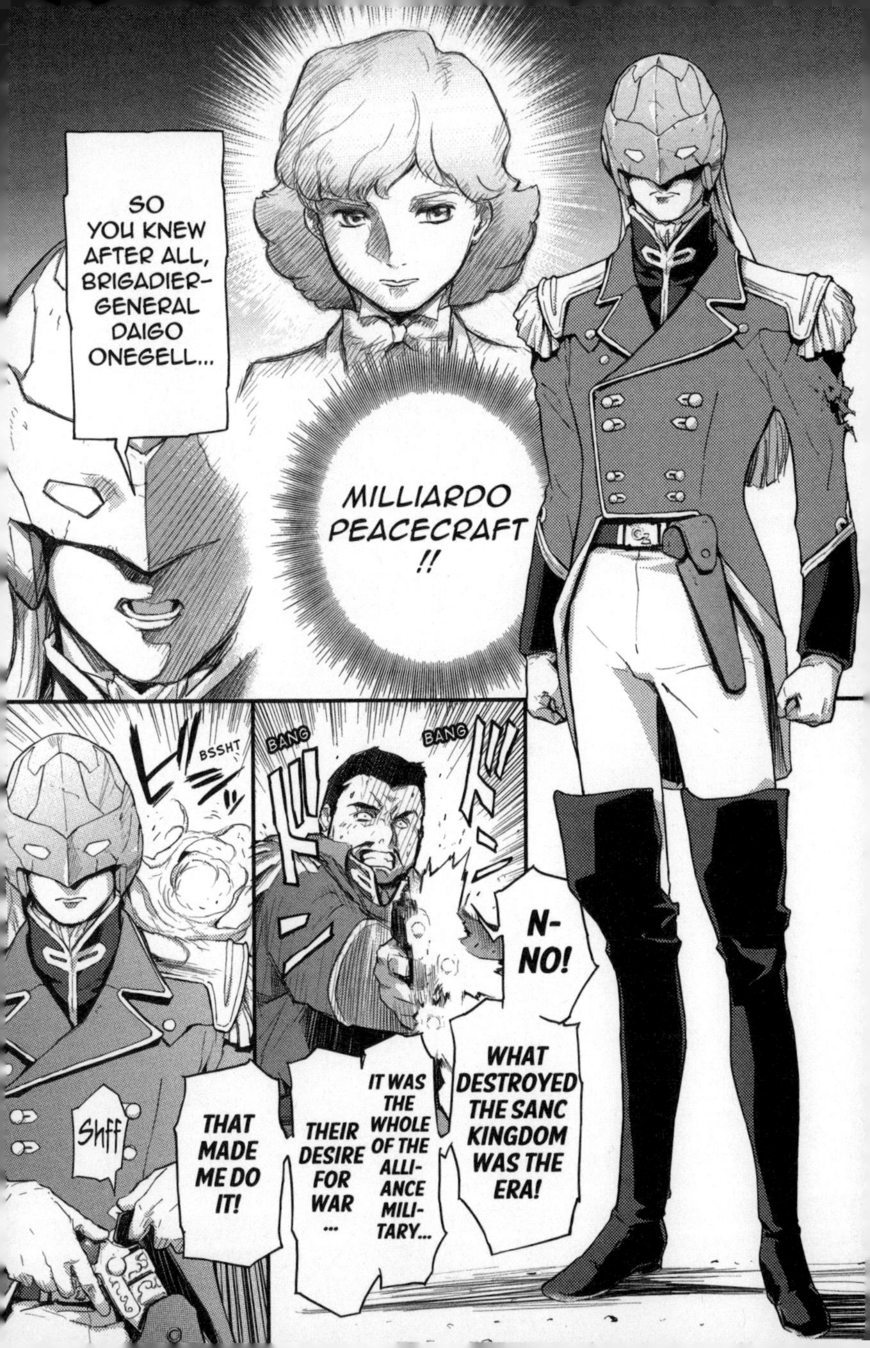
SO YOU KNEW AFTER ALL, BRIGADIER-GENERAL DAIGO ONEGELL...
MILLIARDO PEACECRAFT !!
BANG
BANG
N-NO!
WHAT DESTROYED THE SANC KINGDOM WAS THE ERA!
IT WAS THE WHOLE OF THE ALLI-ANCE MILI-TARY...
THEIR DESIRE FOR WAR ...
THAT MADE ME DO IT!
BSSHT
Shff

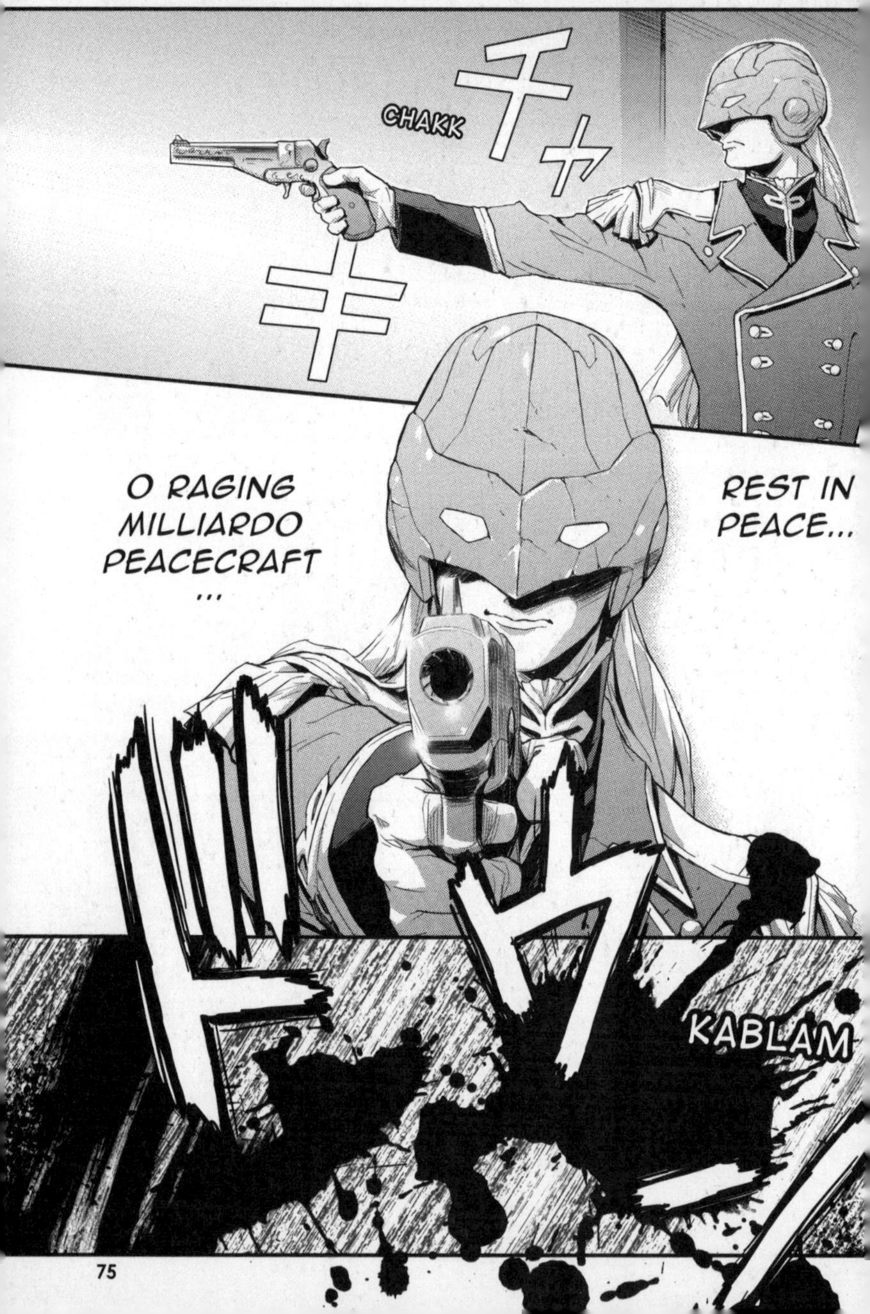
CHAKK
チャキ
REST IN PEACE...
O RAGING MILLIARDO PEACECRAFT ...
KABLAM

New Edwards Base Integrated Headquarters

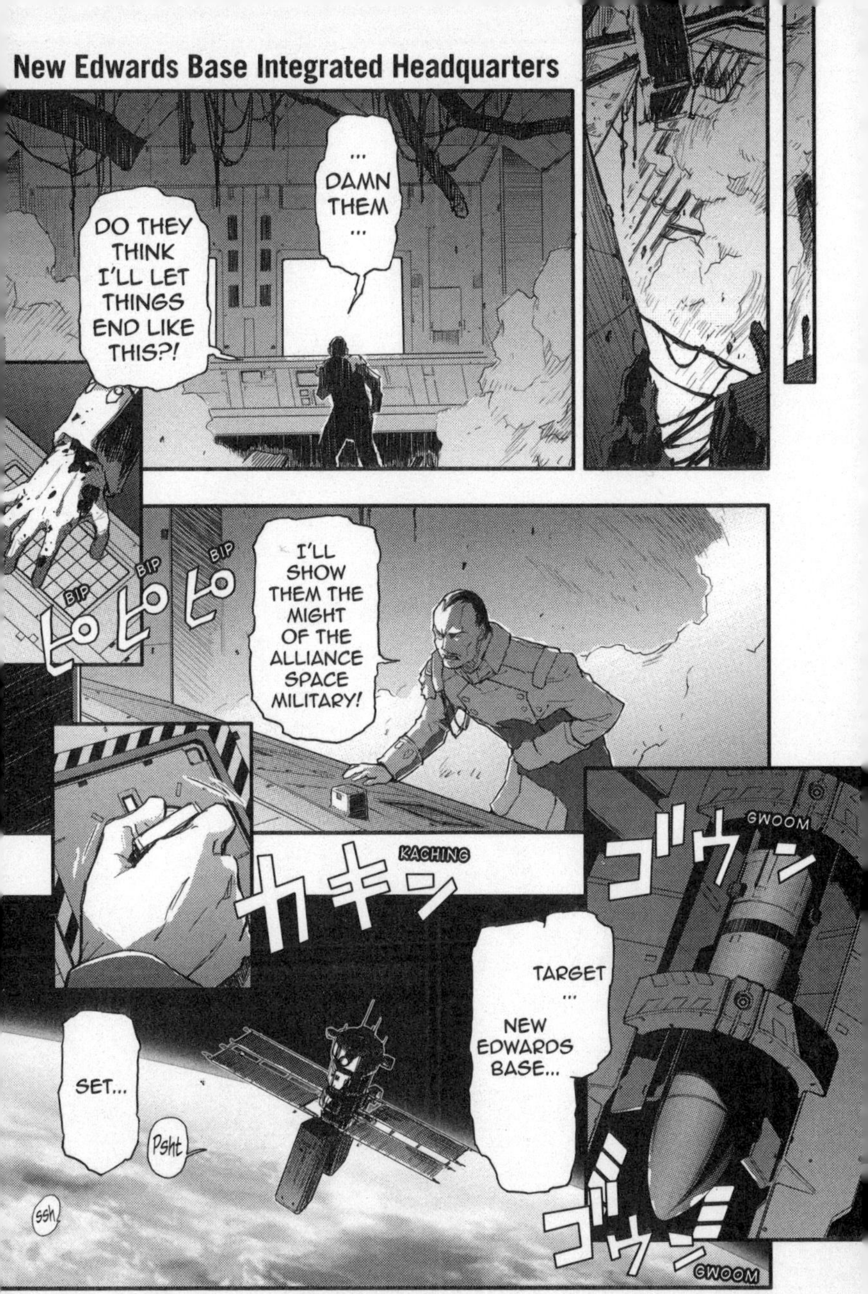

... DAMN THEM ...
DO THEY THINK I'LL LET THINGS END LIKE THIS?!
I'LL SHOW THEM THE MIGHT OF THE ALLIANCE SPACE MILITARY!
ピピピ
BIP BIP BIP
ゴウン
GWOOM
カキン
KACHING
TARGET ... NEW EDWARDS BASE...
ゴウン
GWOOM
SET...
Psht
ssh

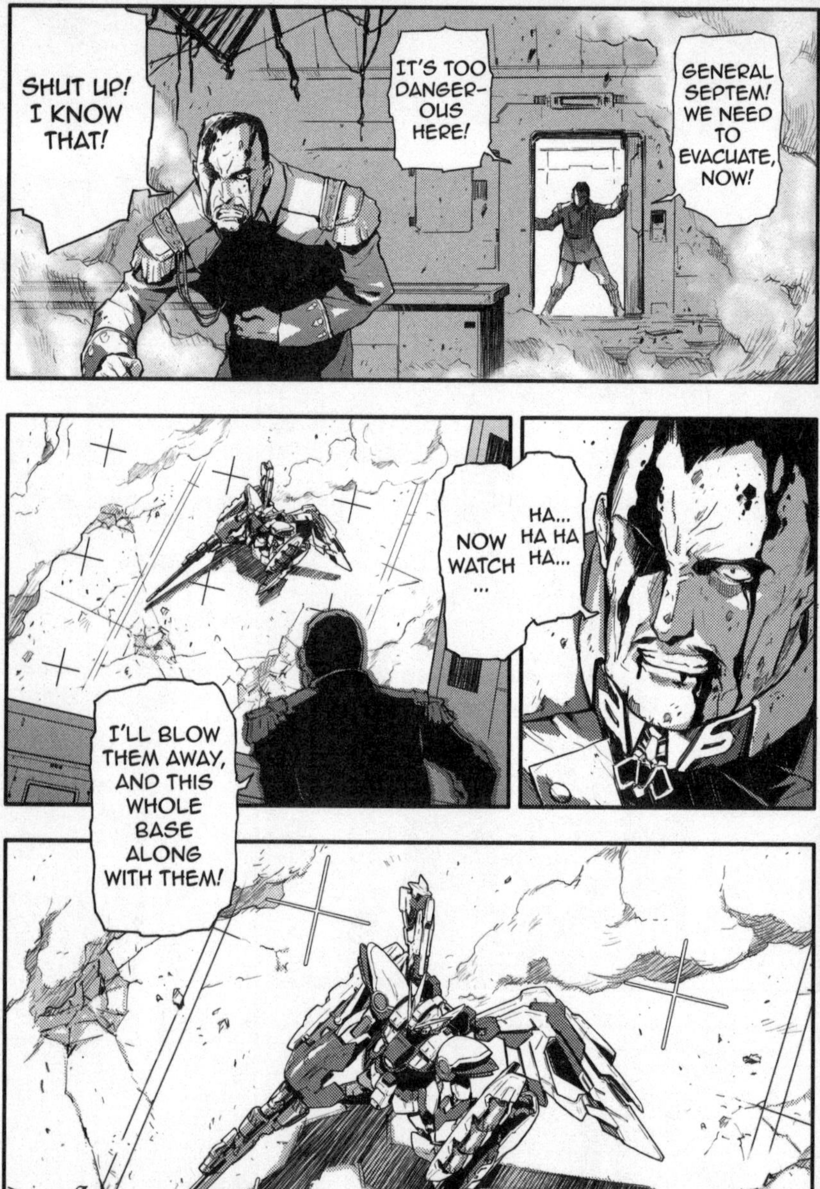
GENERAL SEPTEM! WE NEED TO EVACUATE, NOW!
IT'S TOO DANGER-OUS HERE!
SHUT UP! I KNOW THAT!
HA... HA HA HA...
NOW WATCH ...
I'LL BLOW THEM AWAY, AND THIS WHOLE BASE ALONG WITH THEM!

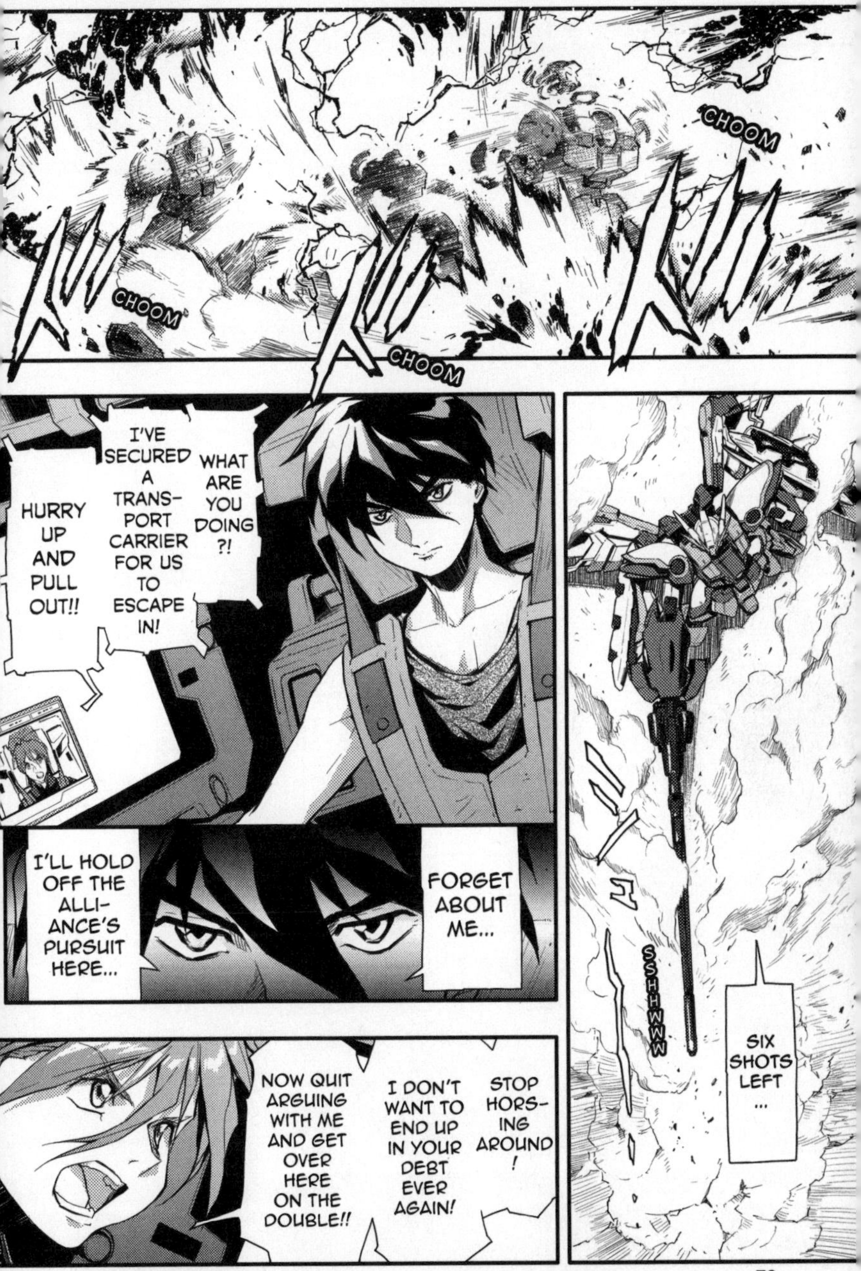
CHOOM
CHOOM
CHOOM
SSHHWWW
SIX SHOTS LEFT ...
WHAT ARE YOU DOING?!
I'VE SECURED A TRANSPORT CARRIER FOR US TO ESCAPE IN!
HURRY UP AND PULL OUT!!
FORGET ABOUT ME...
I'LL HOLD OFF THE ALLIANCE'S PURSUIT HERE...
STOP HORSING AROUND!
I DON'T WANT TO END UP IN YOUR DEBT EVER AGAIN!
NOW QUIT ARGUING WITH ME AND GET OVER HERE ON THE DOUBLE!!

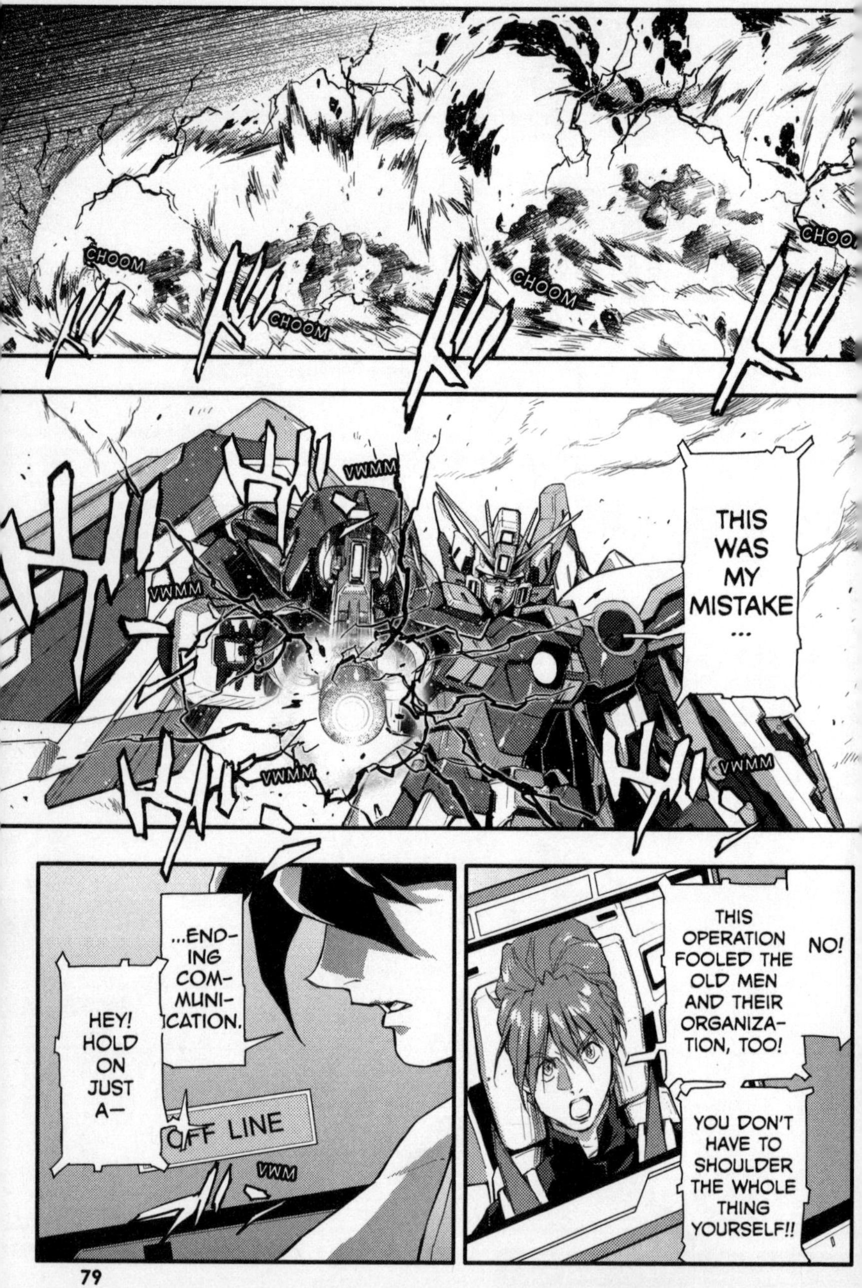
CHOOO
CHOOM
CHOOM
CHOOM
THIS WAS MY MISTAKE ...
VWMM
VWMM
VWMM
VWMM
NO!
THIS OPERATION FOOLED THE OLD MEN AND THEIR ORGANIZA-TION, TOO!
YOU DON'T HAVE TO SHOULDER THE WHOLE THING YOURSELF!!
...END-ING COM-MUNI-CATION.
HEY! HOLD ON JUST A—
OFF LINE
VWM

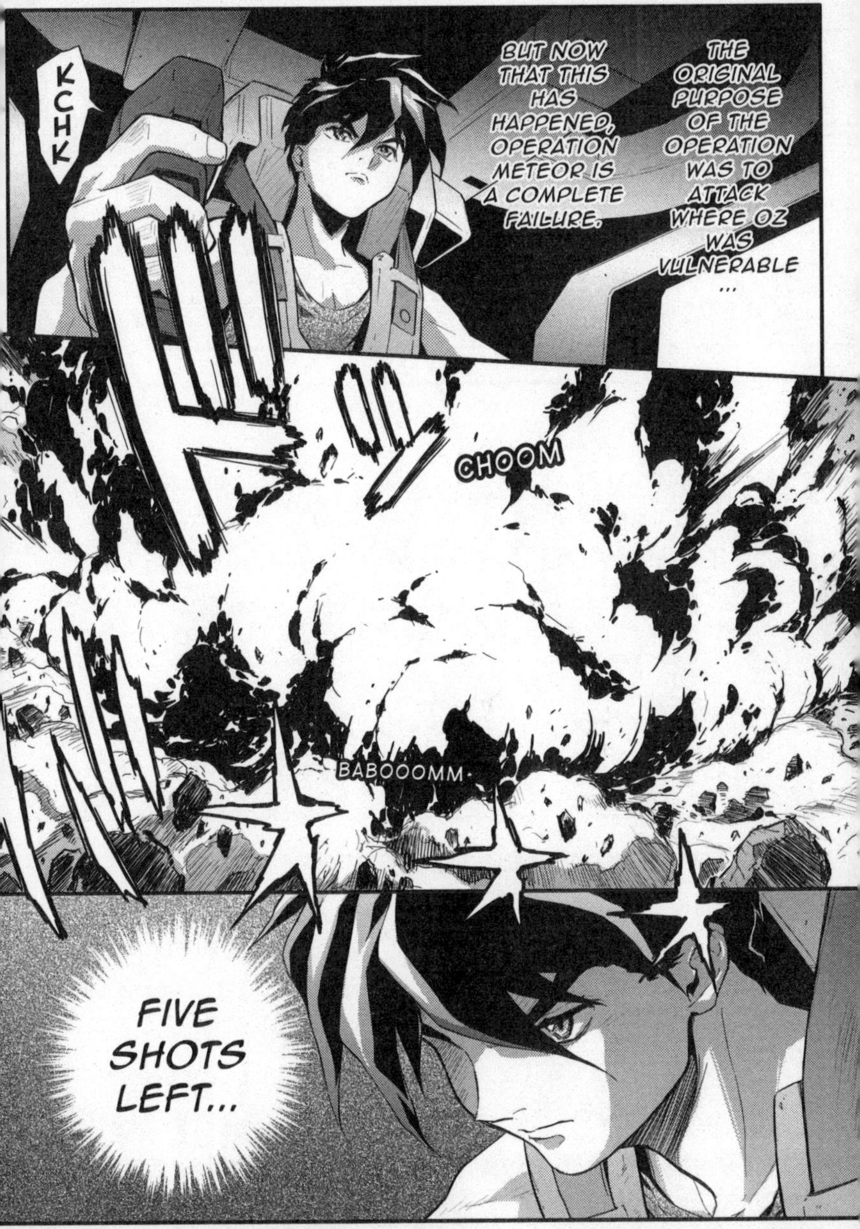
THE ORIGINAL PURPOSE OF THE OPERATION WAS TO ATTACK WHERE OZ WAS VULNERABLE ...
BUT NOW THAT THIS HAS HAPPENED, OPERATION METEOR IS A COMPLETE FAILURE.
KCHK
CHOOM
BABOOOMM
FIVE SHOTS LEFT...

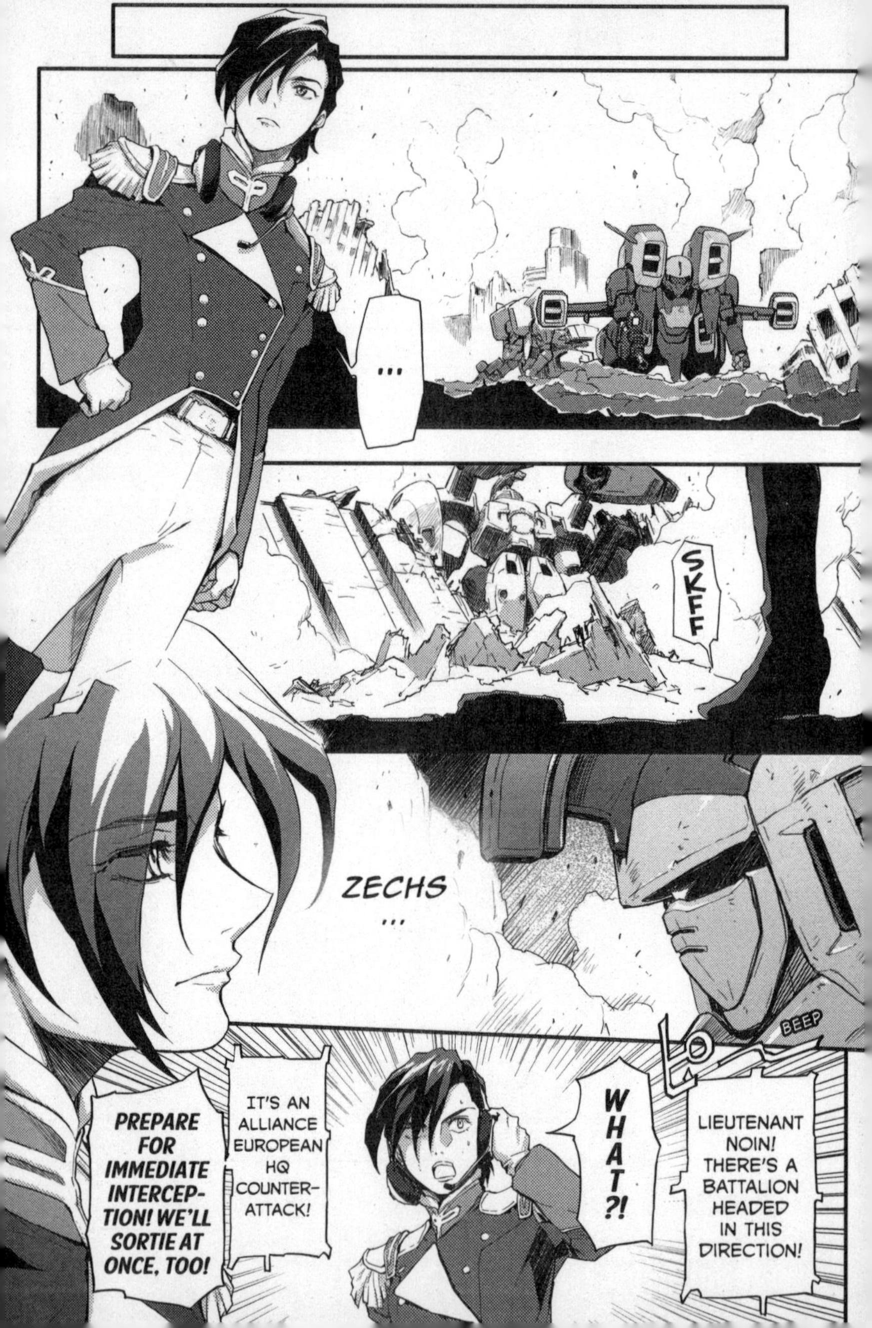
...
SKFF
ZECHS ...
BEEP
LIEUTENANT NOIN! THERE'S A BATTALION HEADED IN THIS DIRECTION!
WHAT?!
IT'S AN ALLIANCE EUROPEAN HQ COUNTER-ATTACK!
PREPARE FOR IMMEDIATE INTERCEP-TION! WE'LL SORTIE AT ONCE, TOO!

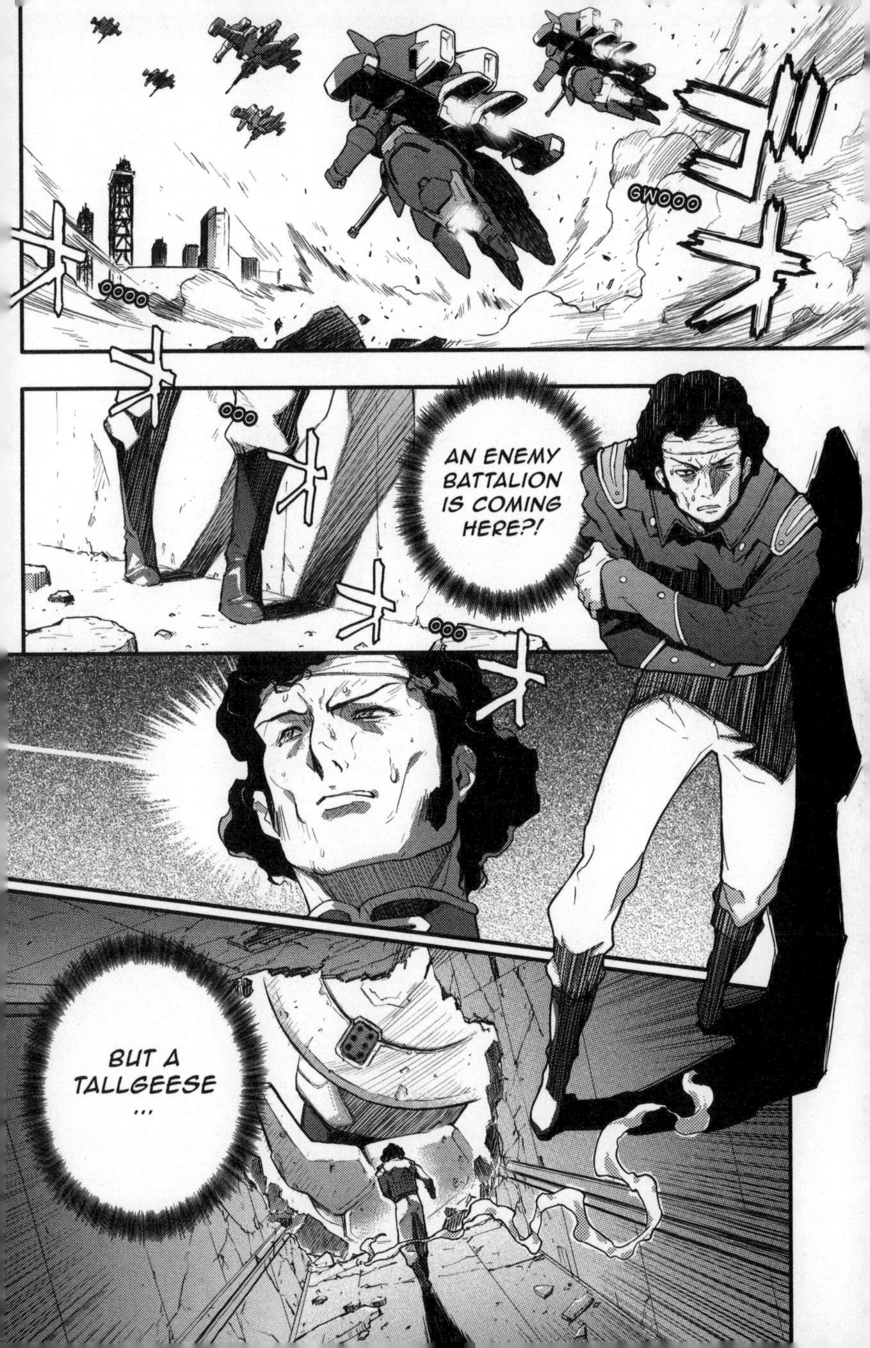
GWOOO
OOOO
AN ENEMY BATTALION IS COMING HERE?!
OOO
OOO
BUT A TALLGEESE ...

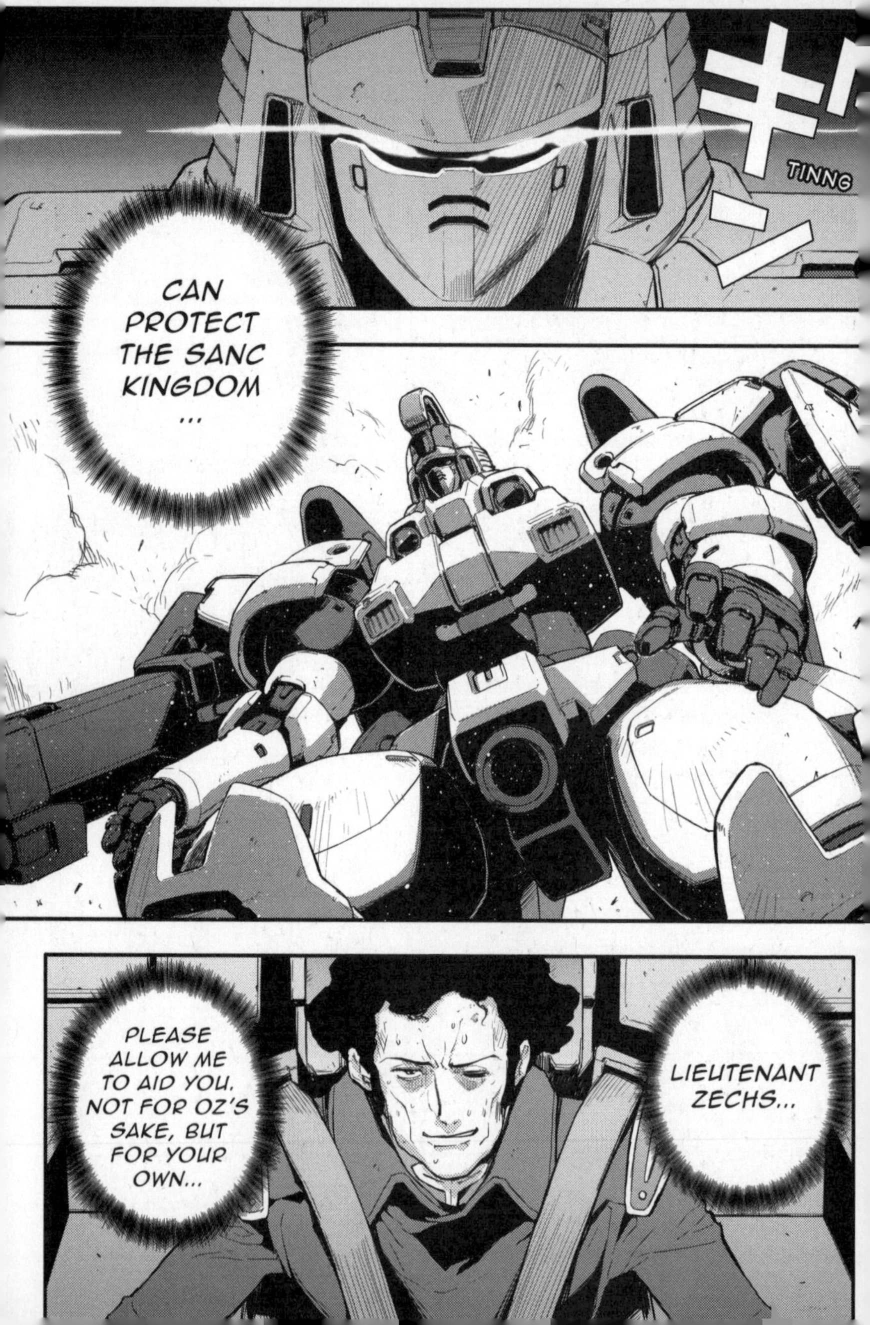
TINNG
CAN PROTECT THE SANC KINGDOM ...
LIEUTENANT ZECHS...
PLEASE ALLOW ME TO AID YOU. NOT FOR OZ'S SAKE, BUT FOR YOUR OWN...

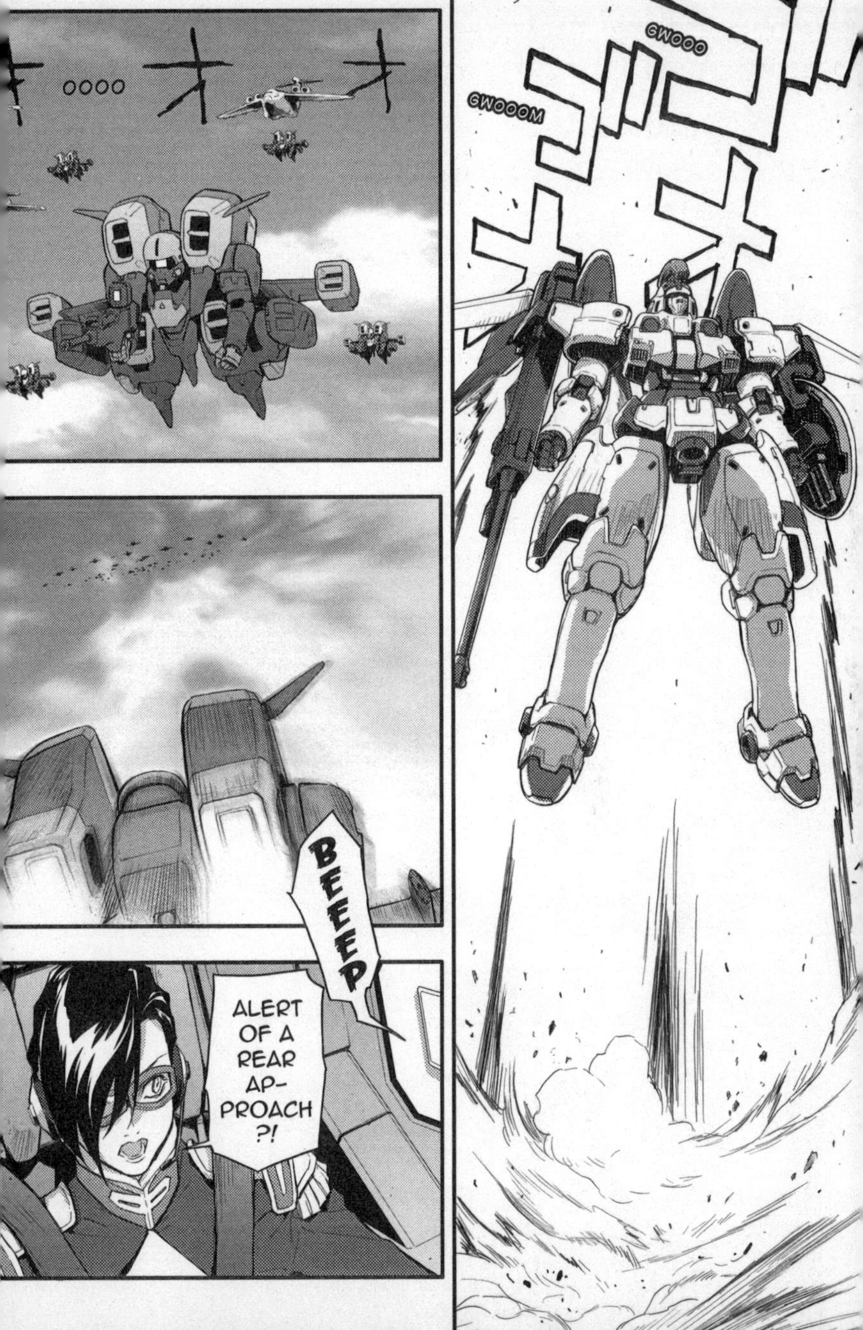
GWOOO
GWOOOM
OOOO
BEEEEP
ALERT OF A REAR AP- PROACH ?!

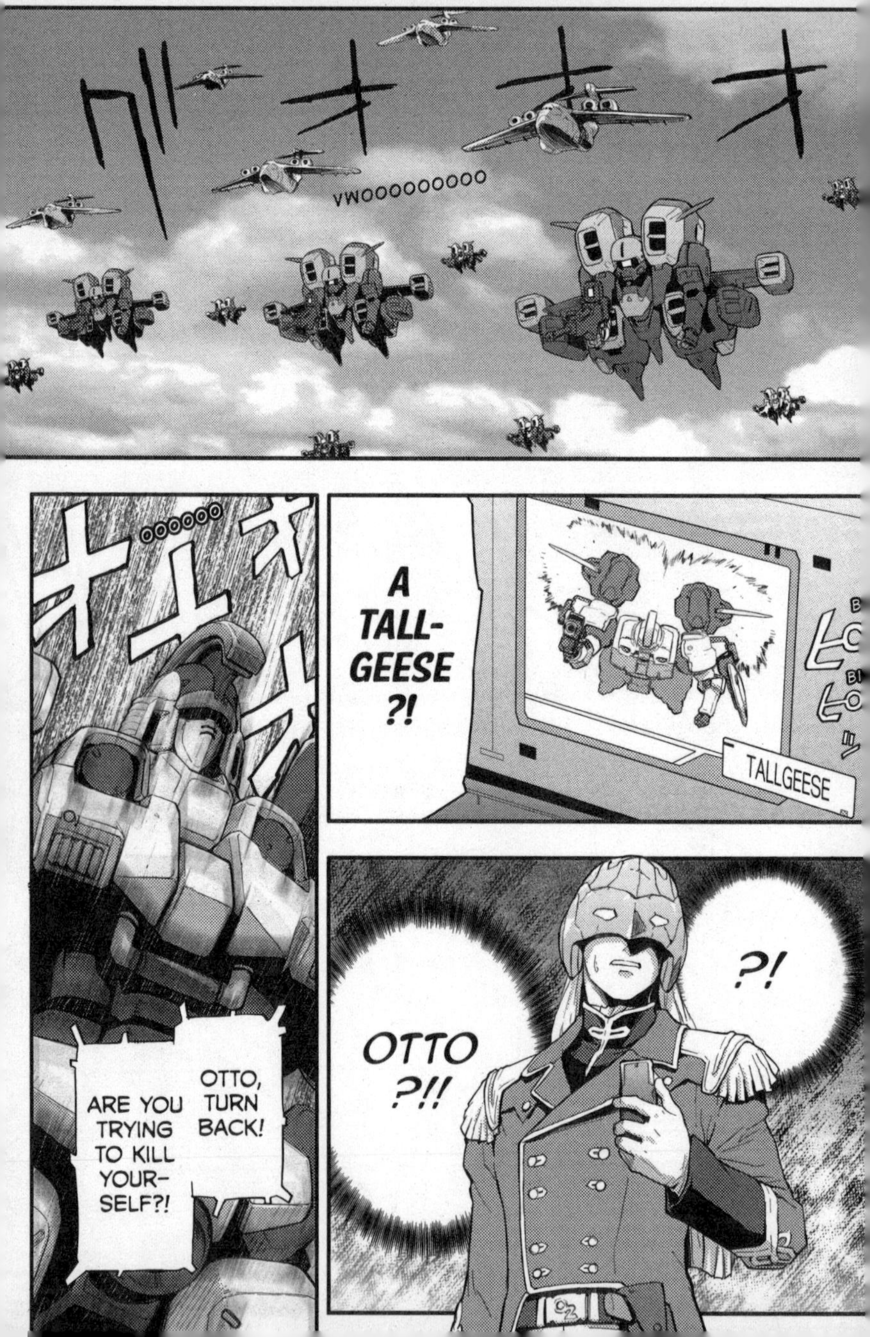
VWOOOOOOOOO
A TALL-GEESE?!
TALLGEESE
B
BI
?!
OTTO?!!
OOOOOO
OTTO, TURN BACK!
ARE YOU TRYING TO KILL YOURSELF?!

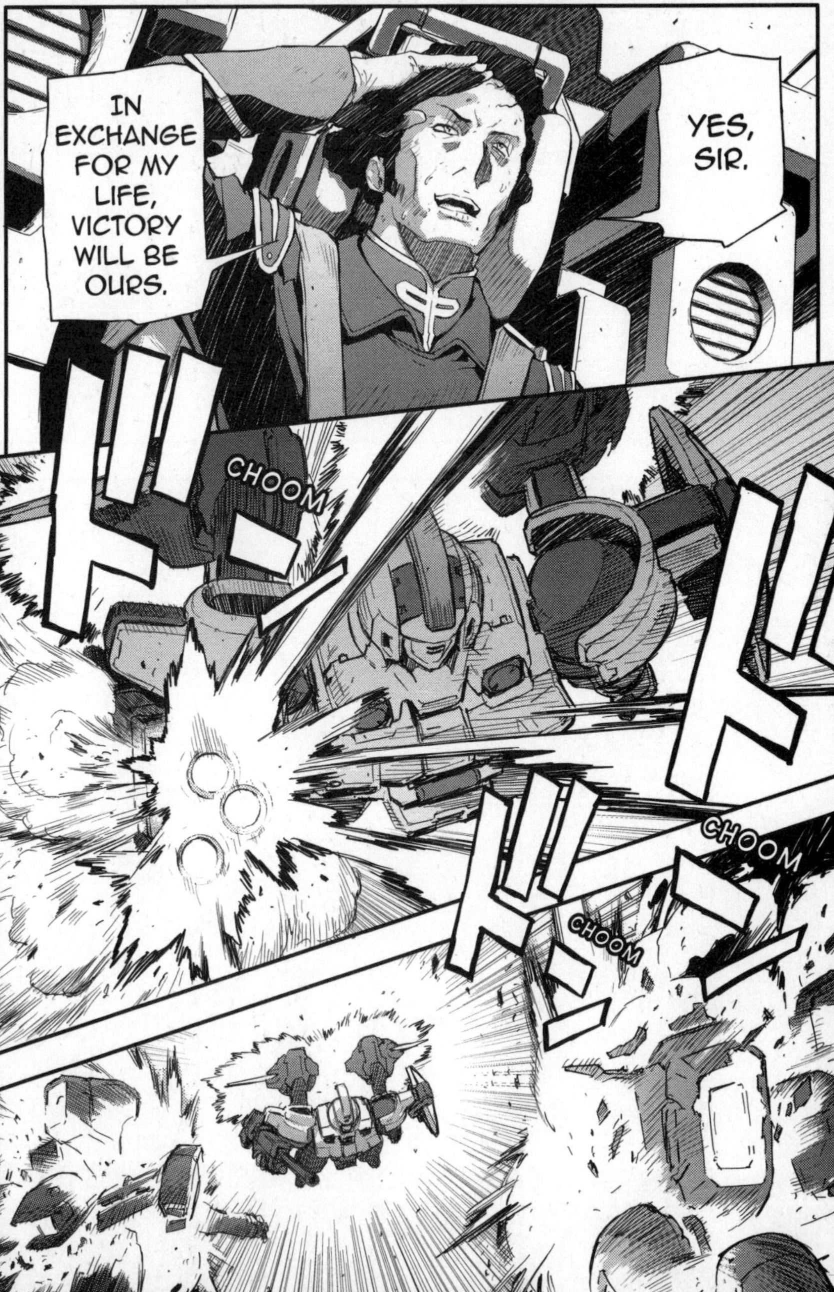
YES, SIR.
IN EXCHANGE FOR MY LIFE, VICTORY WILL BE OURS.
CHOOM
CHOOM
CHOOM

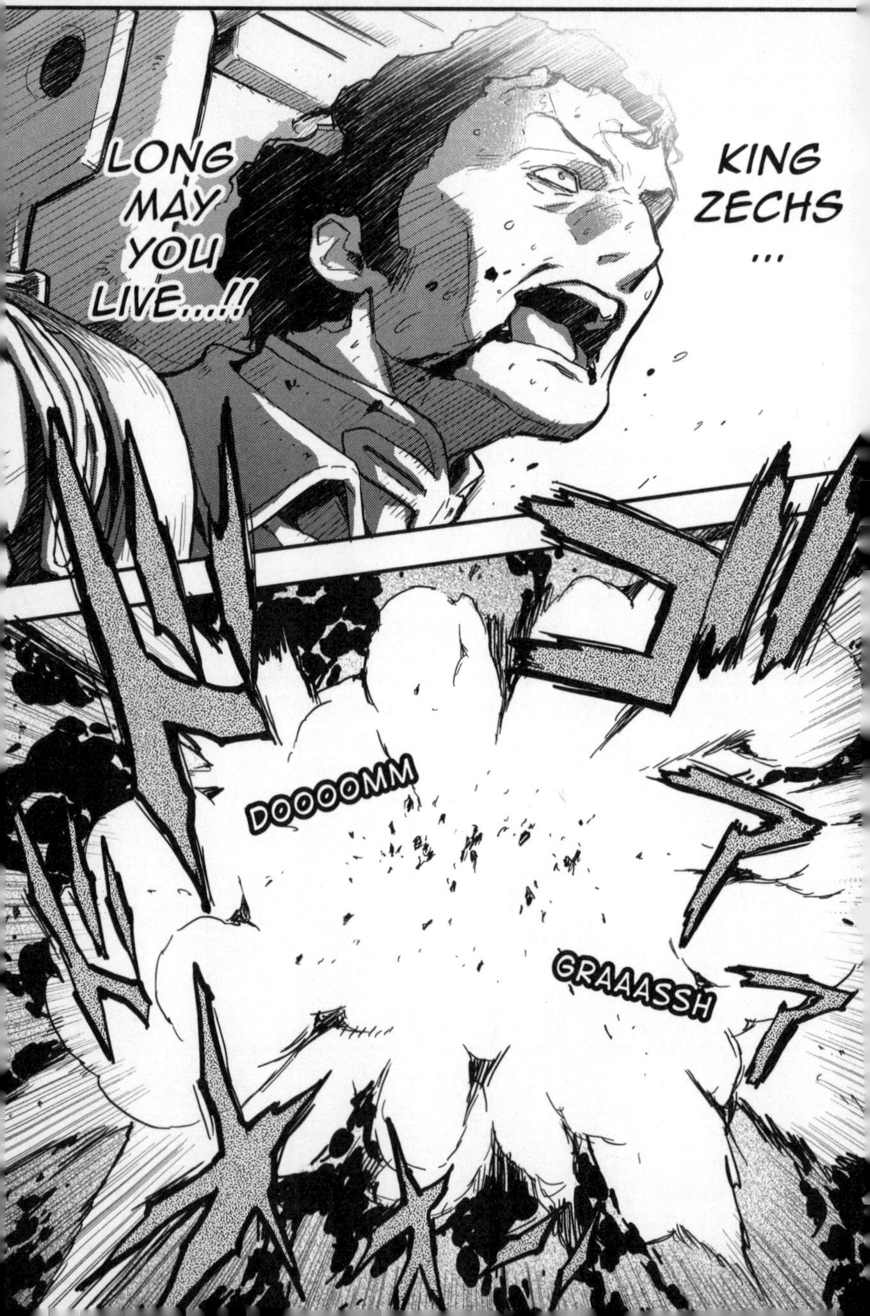
KING ZECHS ...
LONG MAY YOU LIVE...!!
DOOOOMM
GRAAASSH

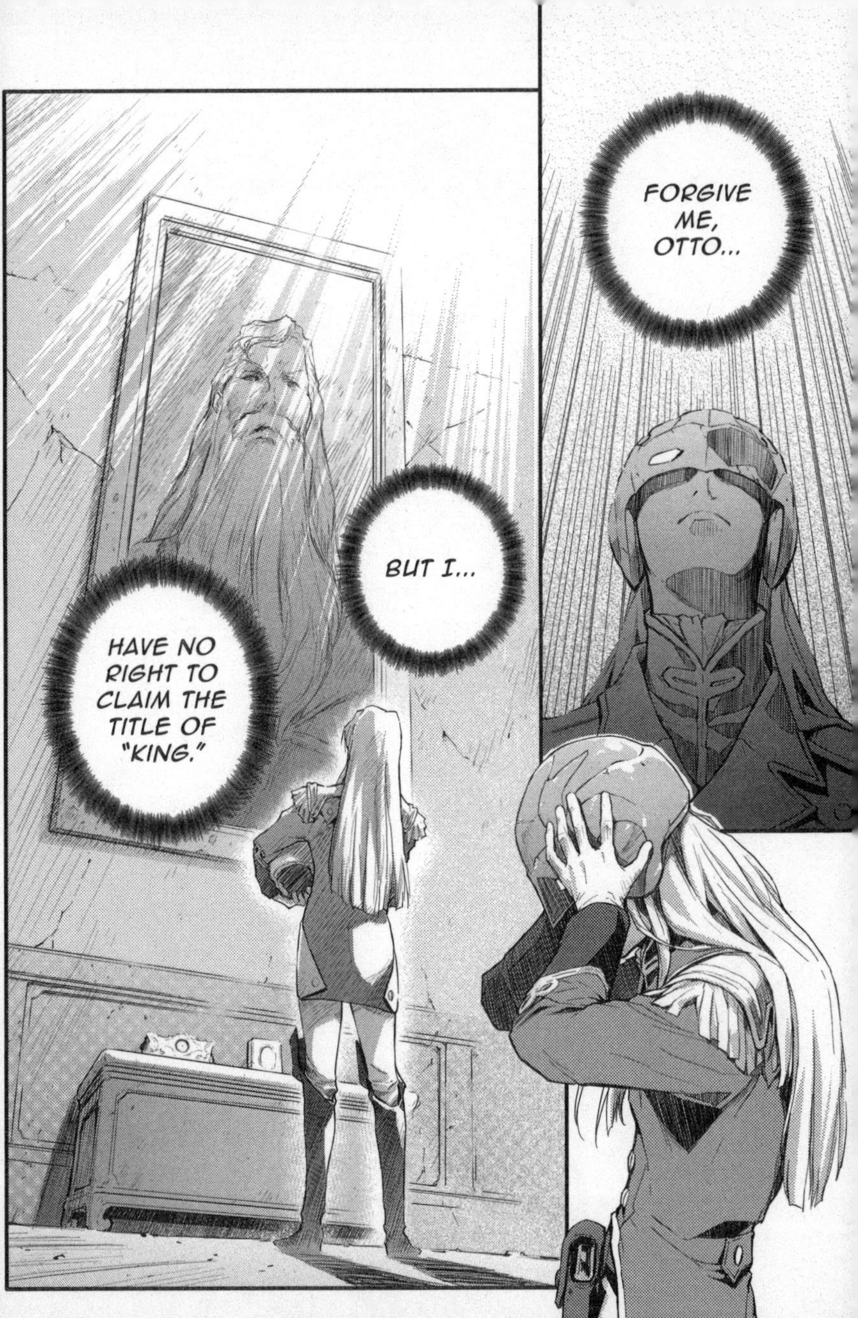
FORGIVE ME, OTTO...
BUT I...
HAVE NO RIGHT TO CLAIM THE TITLE OF "KING."

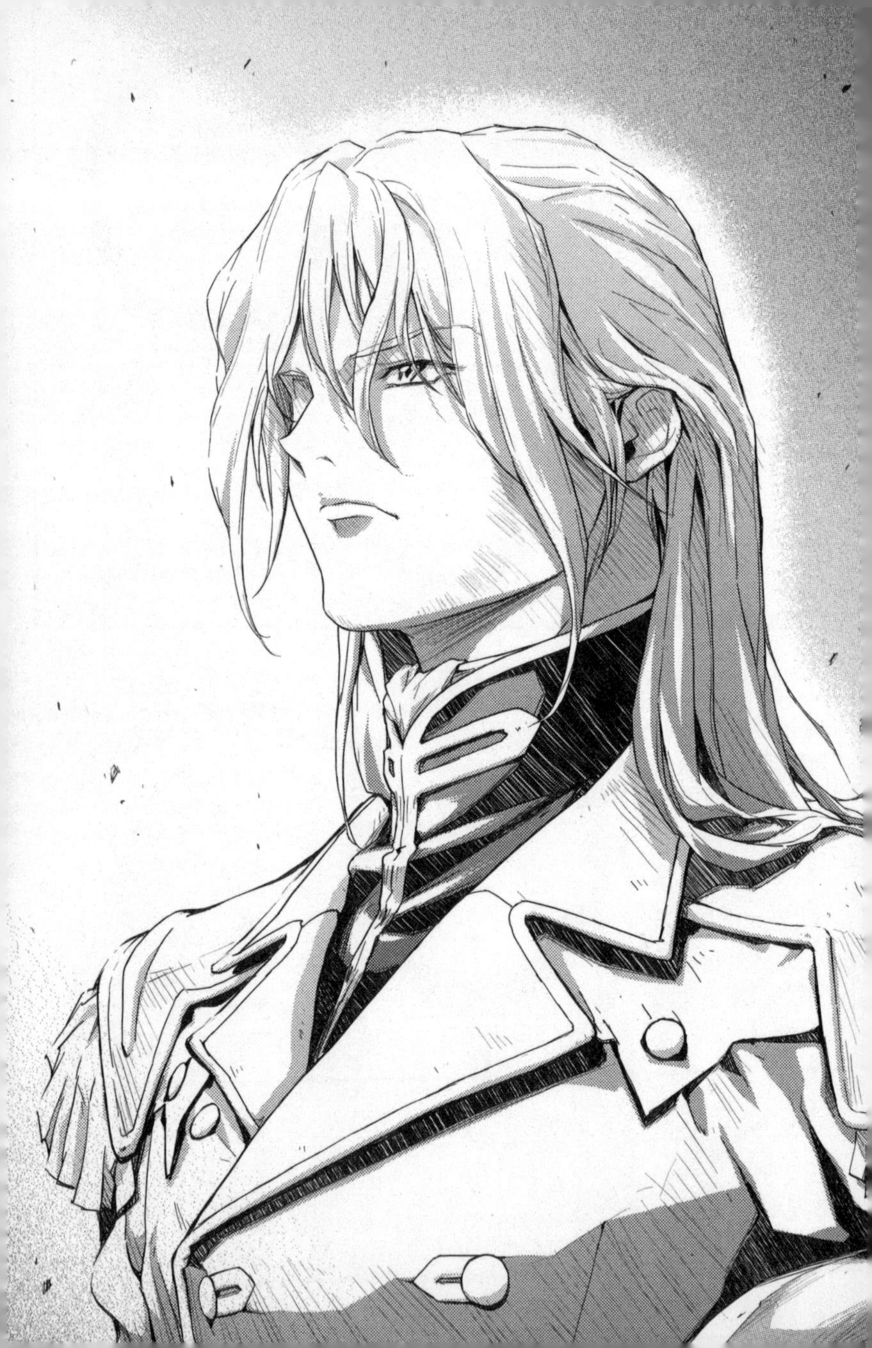

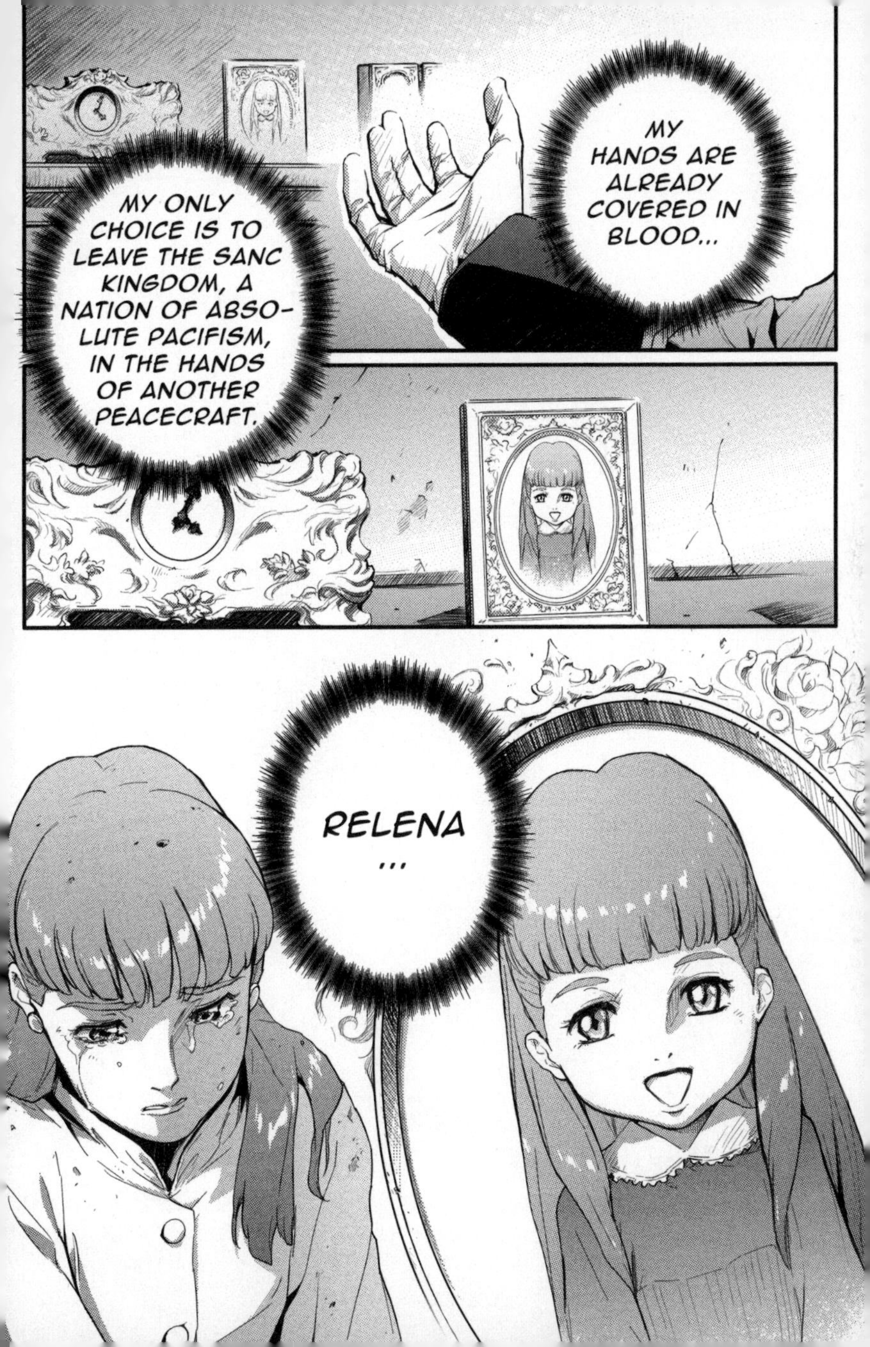
MY HANDS ARE ALREADY COVERED IN BLOOD...
MY ONLY CHOICE IS TO LEAVE THE SANC KINGDOM, A NATION OF ABSO-LUTE PACIFISM, IN THE HANDS OF ANOTHER PEACECRAFT.
RELENA ...

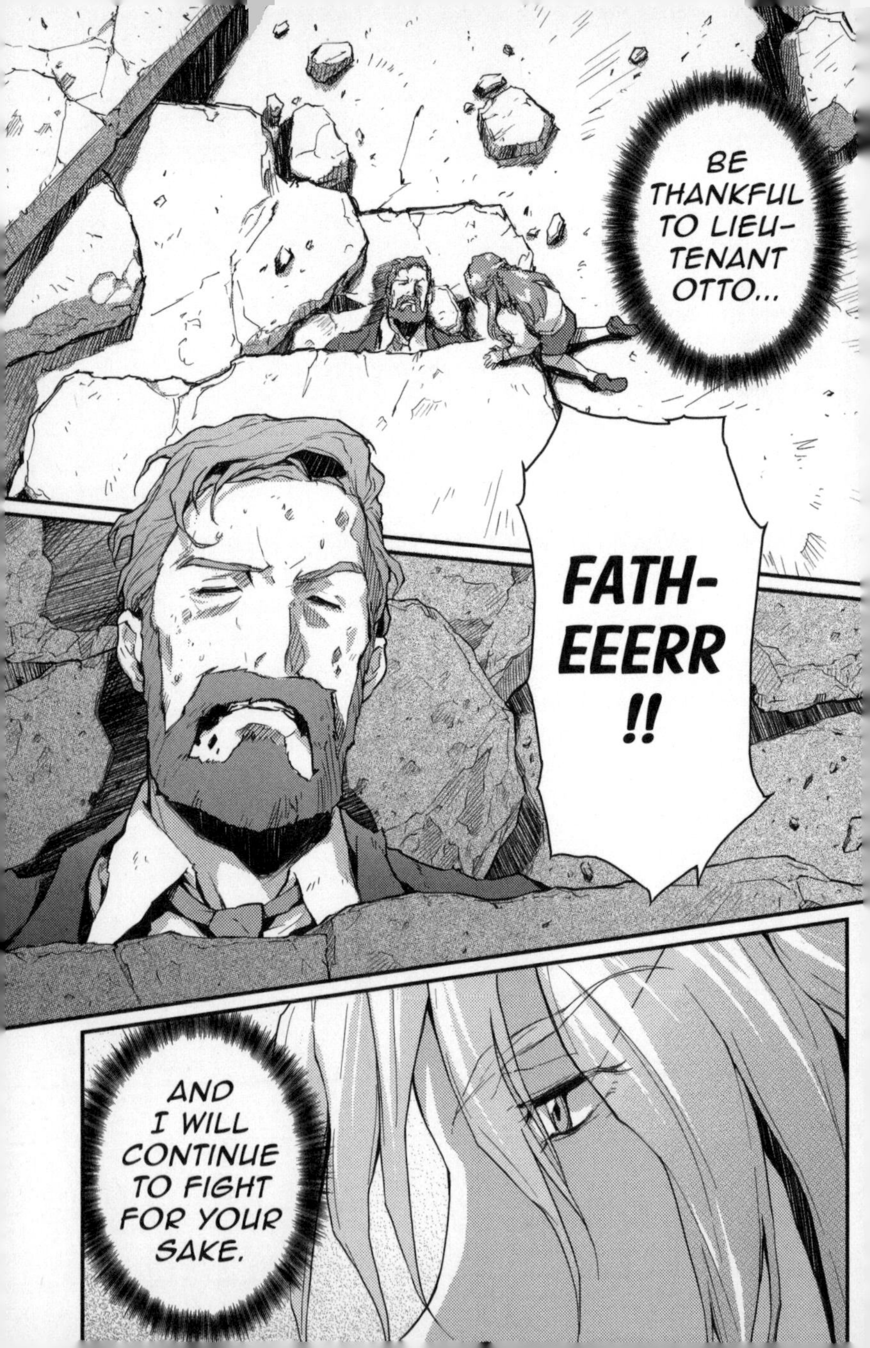
BE THANKFUL TO LIEU-TENANT OTTO...
FATH-EEERR!!
AND I WILL CONTINUE TO FIGHT FOR YOUR SAKE.

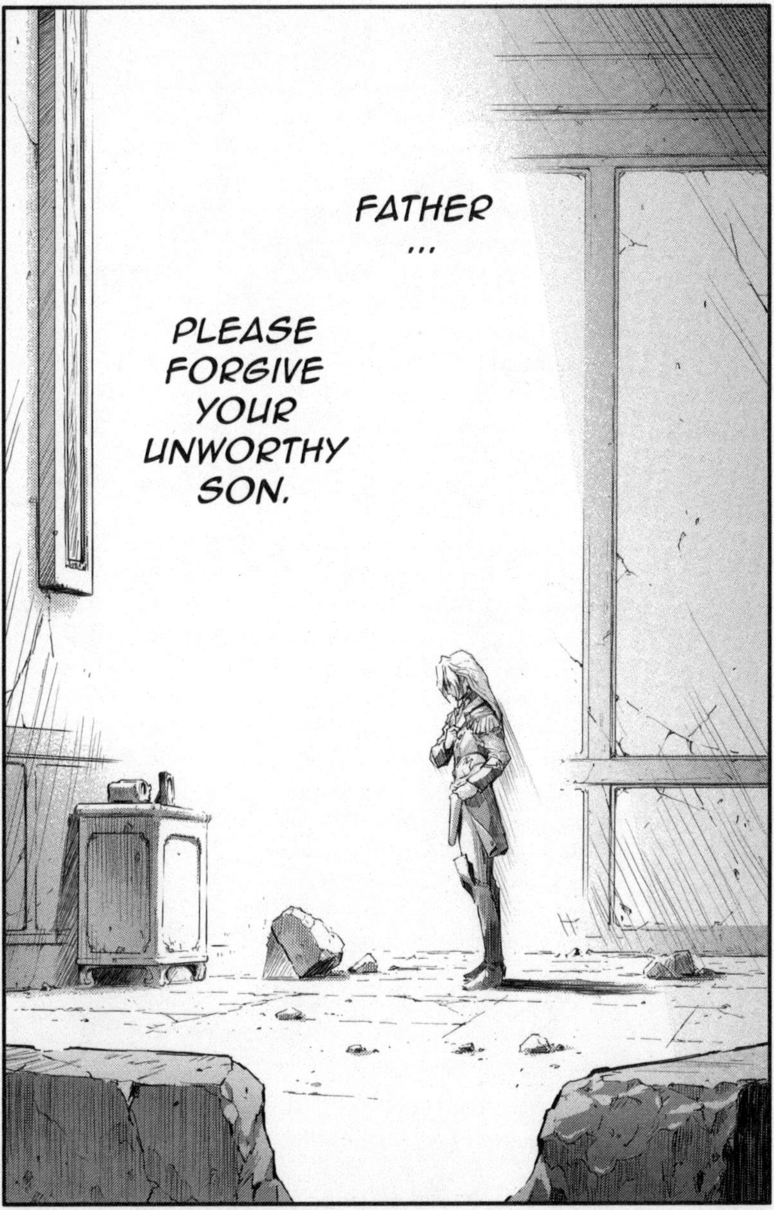
FATHER ...
PLEASE FORGIVE YOUR UNWORTHY SON.

Chang **Wufei**

SLEEVE NOTES:
Endless Waltz

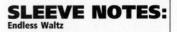

XXXG-01S
SHENLONG GUNDAM
Liaoya Rigging

A sword-style weapon similar to a Chinese broadsword, used for slash attacks. It's connected to the shield by a cable, and it can presumably function in the same way as the Gundam Sandrock's Heat Shotels. It is powerful enough to bisect a Leo in a single blow.

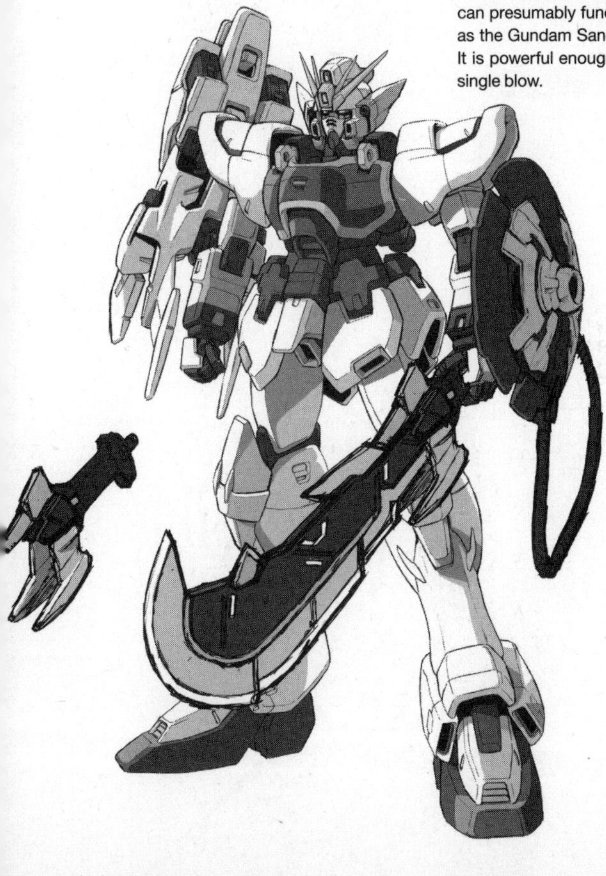

Chapter 17: "A Banquet for the Pleiades" Part 6

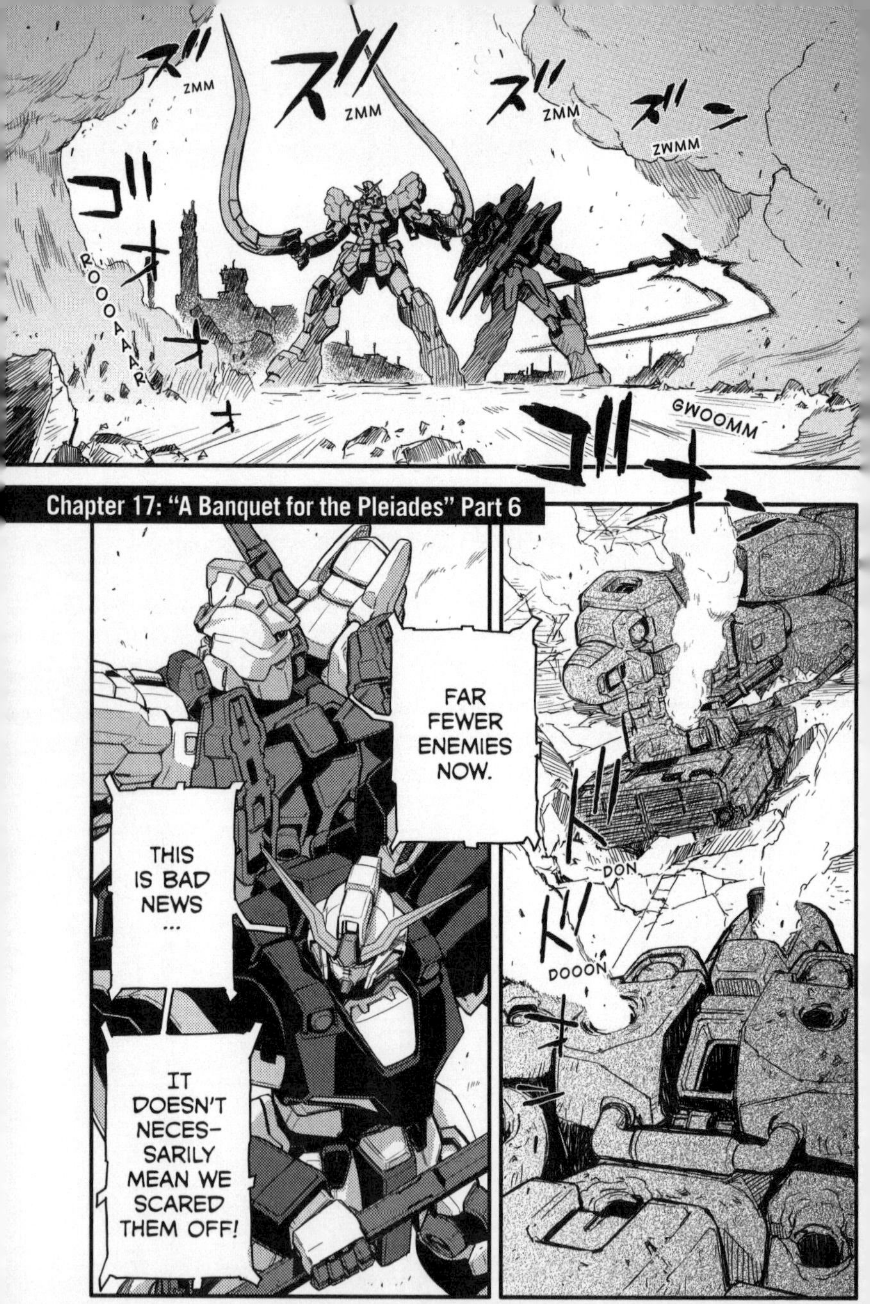
ZWMM
ZMM
ZMM
ZMM
ROOOAAAR
GWOOMM
DON
DOOON
FAR FEWER ENEMIES NOW.
THIS IS BAD NEWS ...
IT DOESN'T NECES-SARILY MEAN WE SCARED THEM OFF!

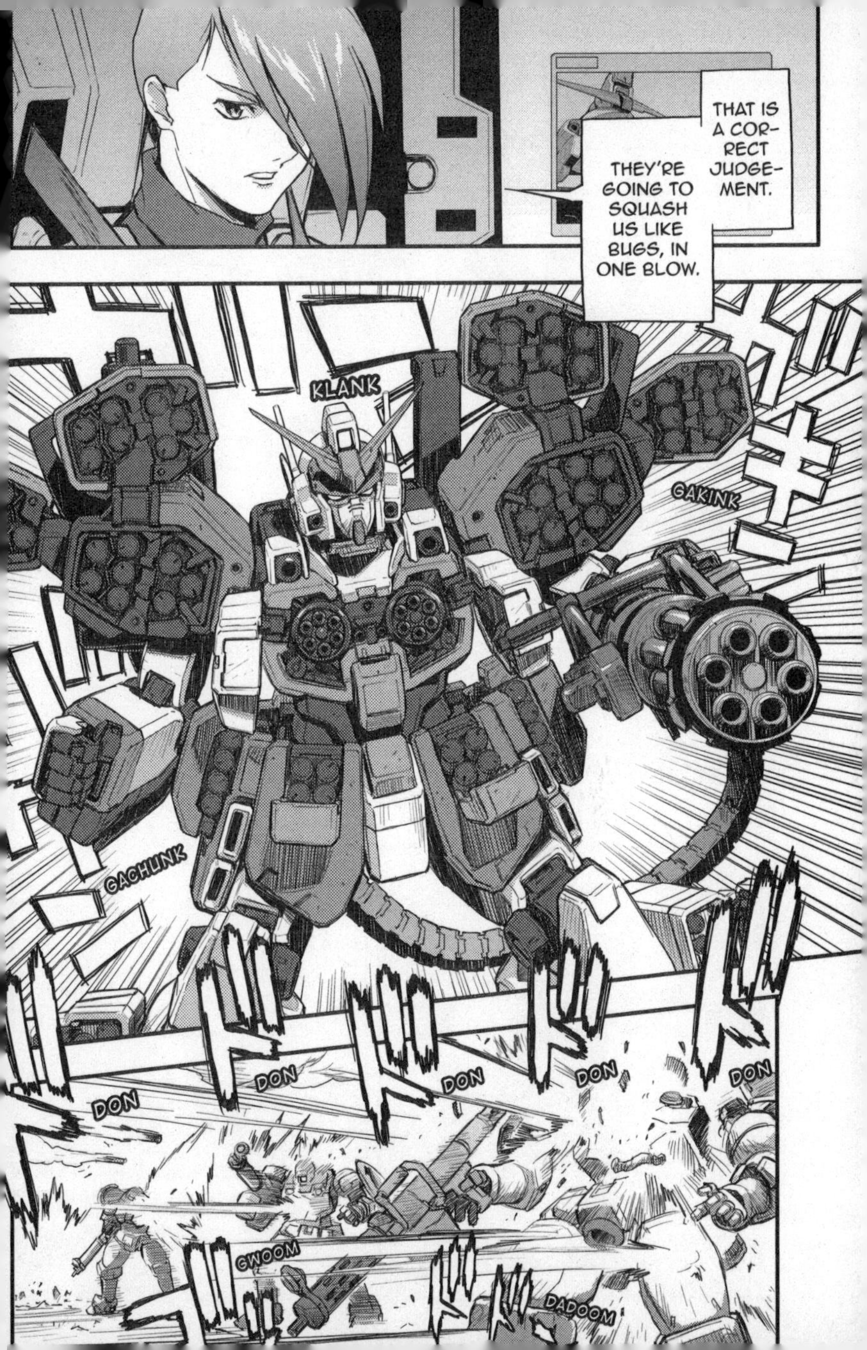
THAT IS A COR-RECT JUDGE-MENT.
THEY'RE GOING TO SQUASH US LIKE BUGS, IN ONE BLOW.
KLANK
GAKINK
GACHLINK
DON
DON
DON
DON
DON
GWOOM
DADOOM

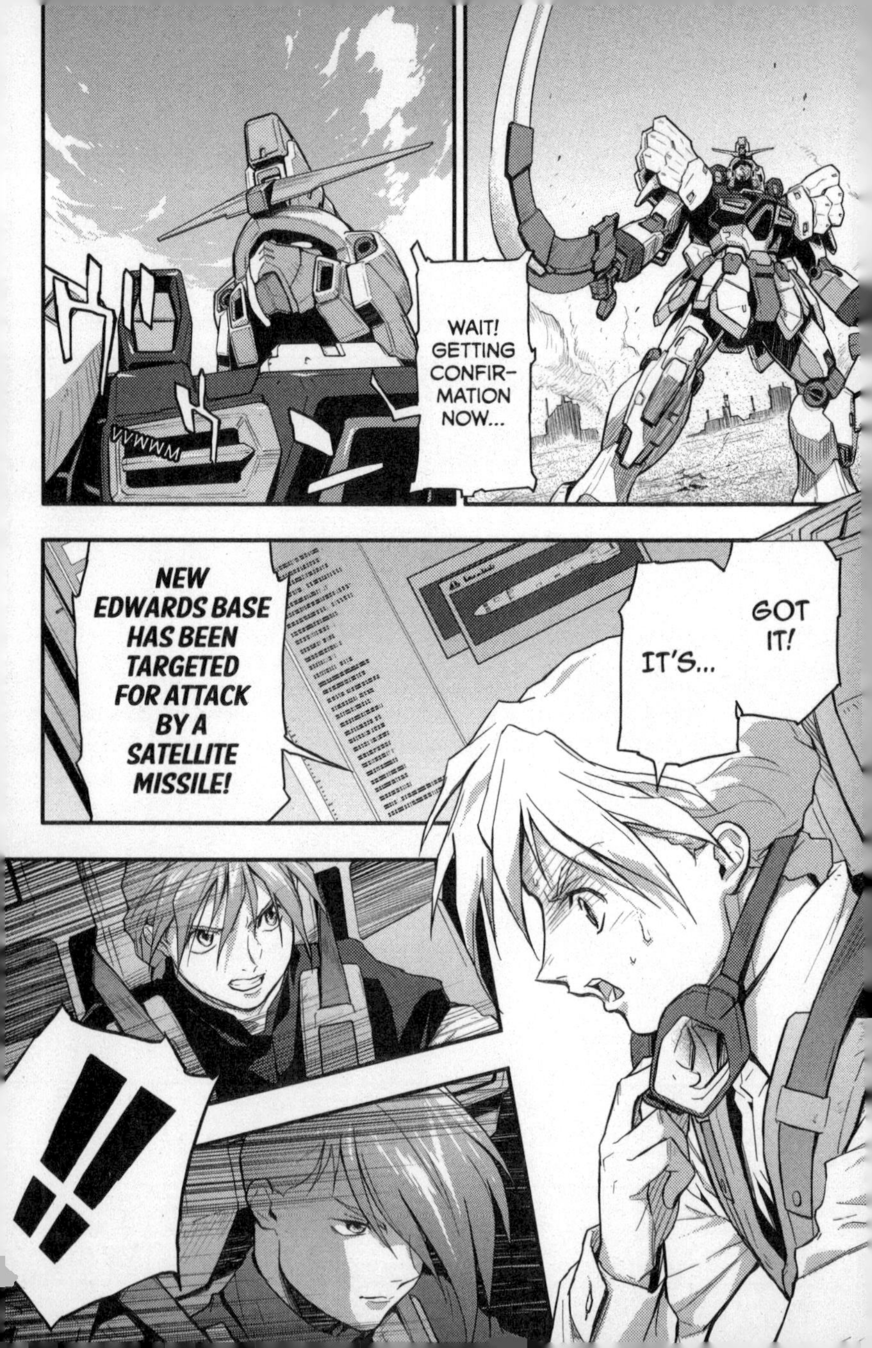
WAIT! GETTING CONFIR-MATION NOW...
VVWWM
GOT IT! IT'S...
NEW EDWARDS BASE HAS BEEN TARGETED FOR ATTACK BY A SATELLITE MISSILE!
!!

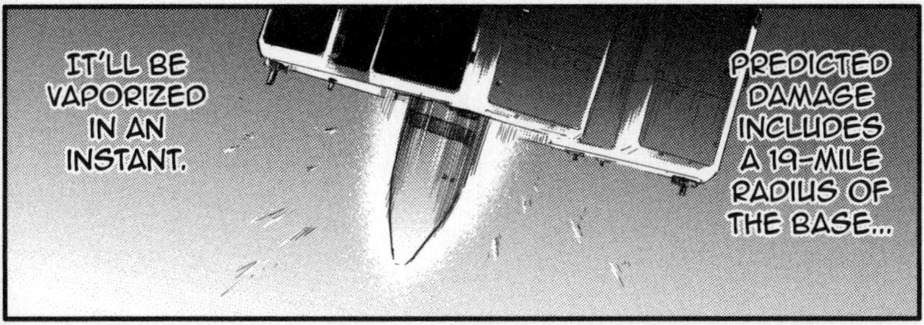
PREDICTED DAMAGE INCLUDES A 19-MILE RADIUS OF THE BASE...
IT'LL BE VAPORIZED IN AN INSTANT.
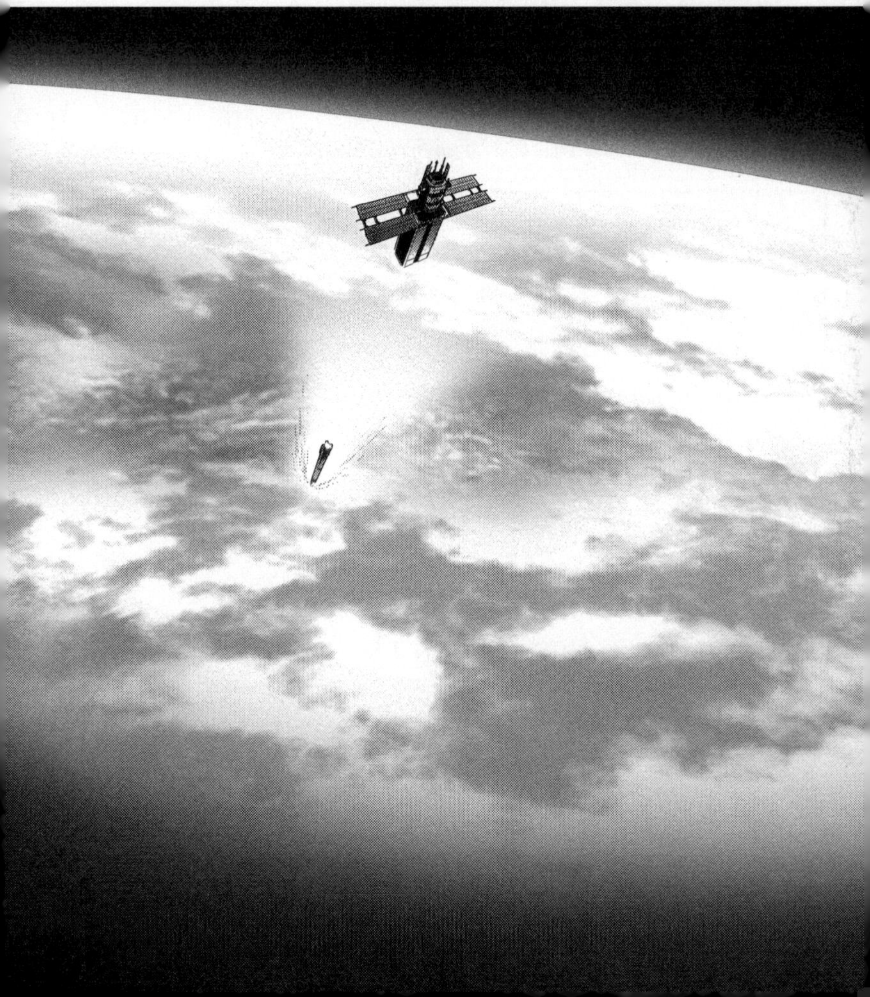

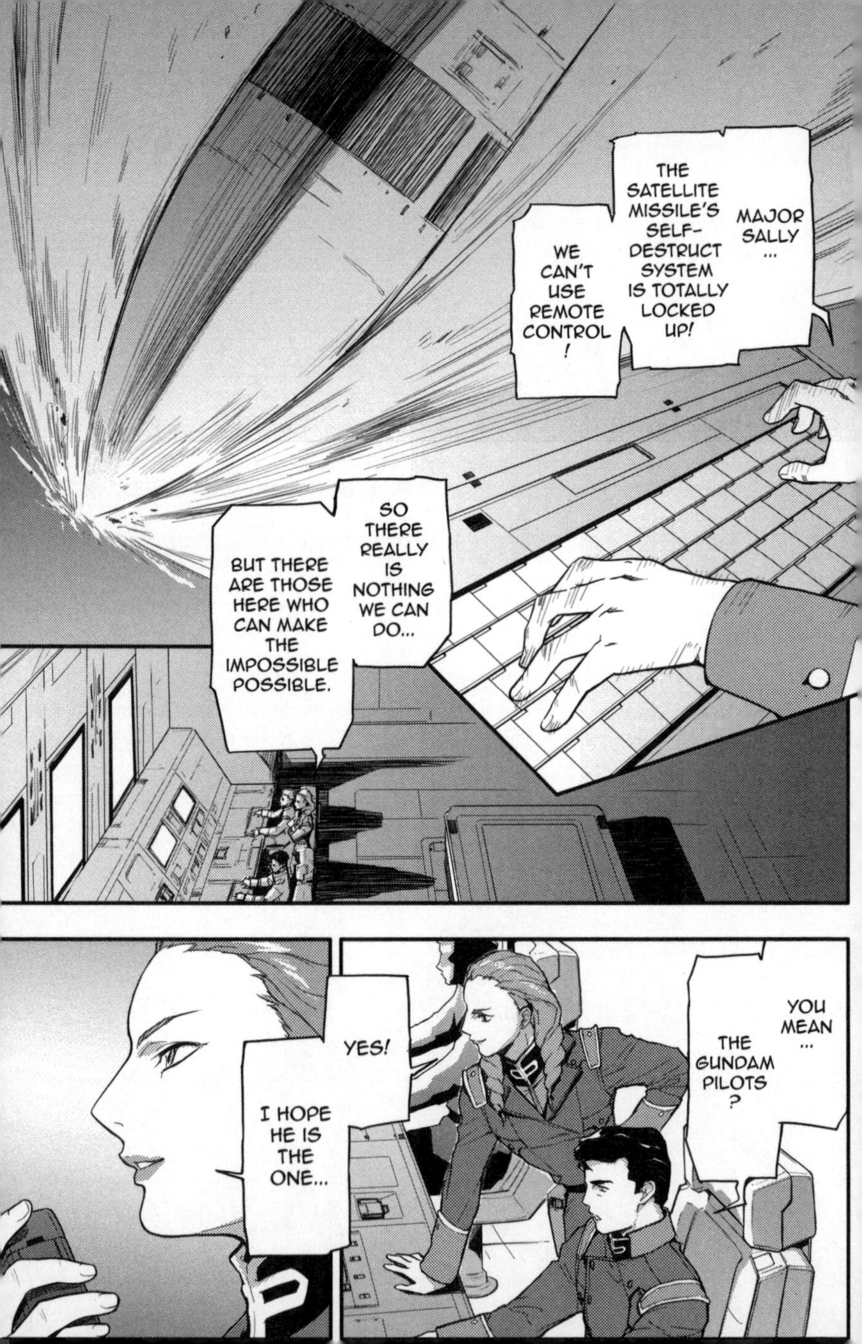
MAJOR SALLY ...
THE SATELLITE MISSILE'S SELF-DESTRUCT SYSTEM IS TOTALLY LOCKED UP!
WE CAN'T USE REMOTE CONTROL!
SO THERE REALLY IS NOTHING WE CAN DO...
BUT THERE ARE THOSE HERE WHO CAN MAKE THE IMPOSSIBLE POSSIBLE.
YOU MEAN ...
THE GUNDAM PILOTS?
YES!
I HOPE HE IS THE ONE...

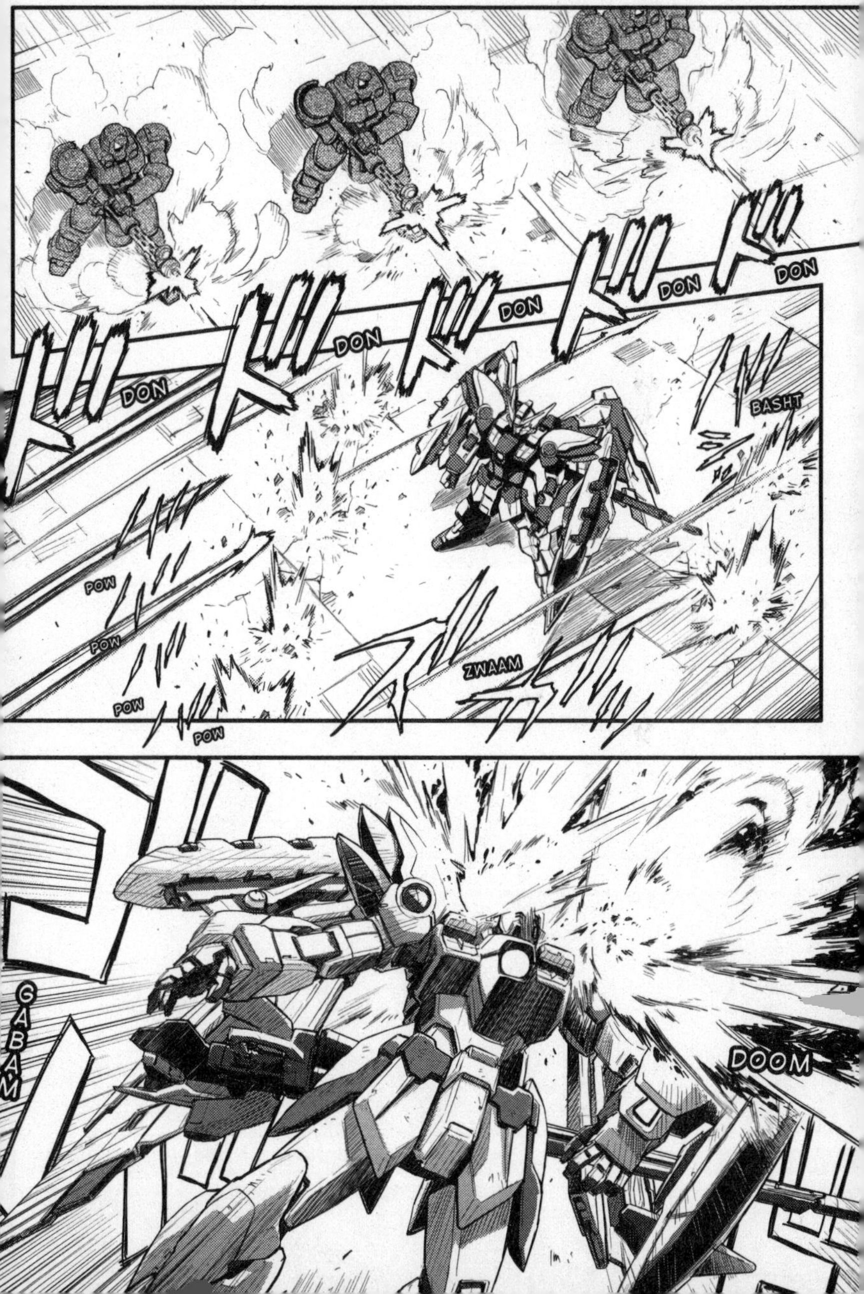
DON
DON
DON
DON
DON
BASHT
ZWAAM
POW
POW
POW
POW
DOOM
GABAM

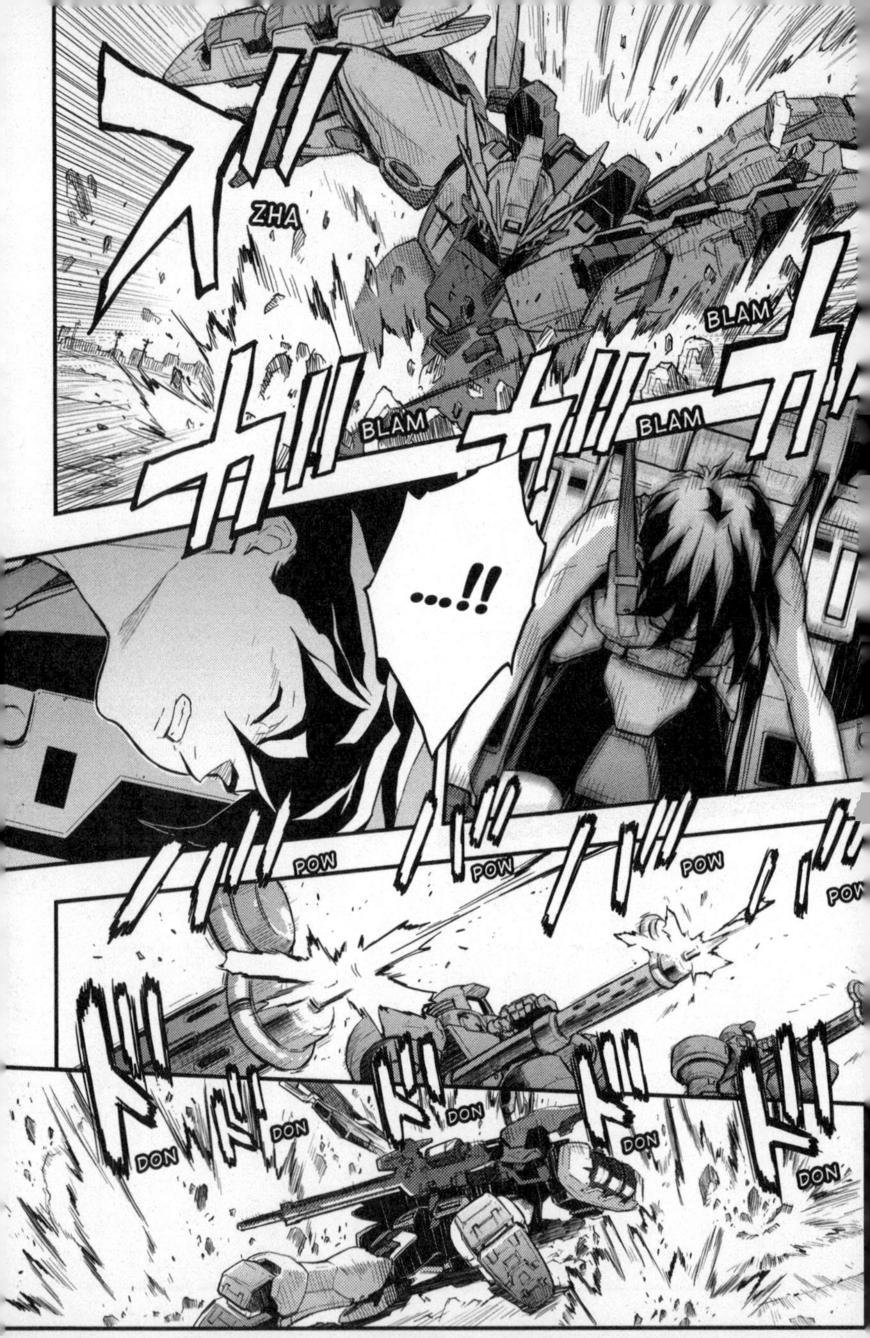
ZHA
BLAM
BLAM
BLAM
...!!
POW
POW
POW
POW
DON
DON
DON
DON
DON

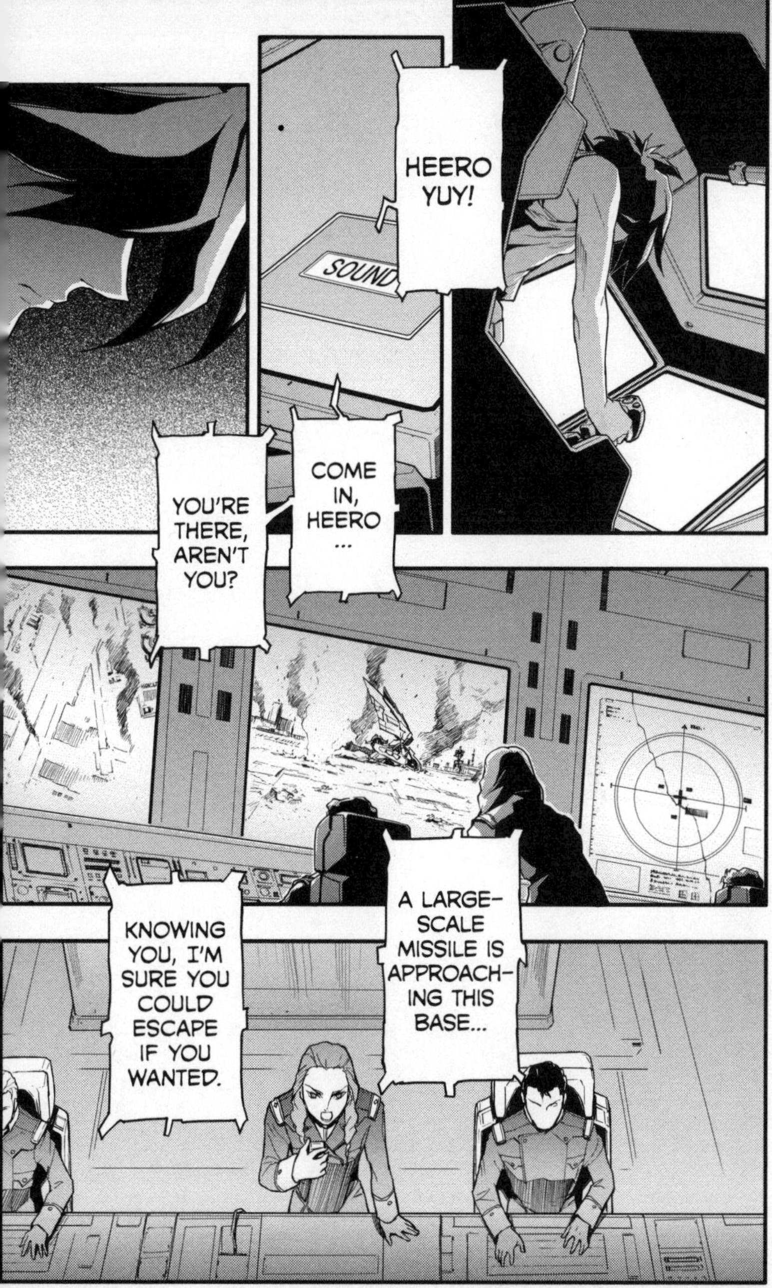
HEERO YUY!
SOUND
COME IN, HEERO...
YOU'RE THERE, AREN'T YOU?
A LARGE-SCALE MISSILE IS APPROACHING THIS BASE...
KNOWING YOU, I'M SURE YOU COULD ESCAPE IF YOU WANTED.

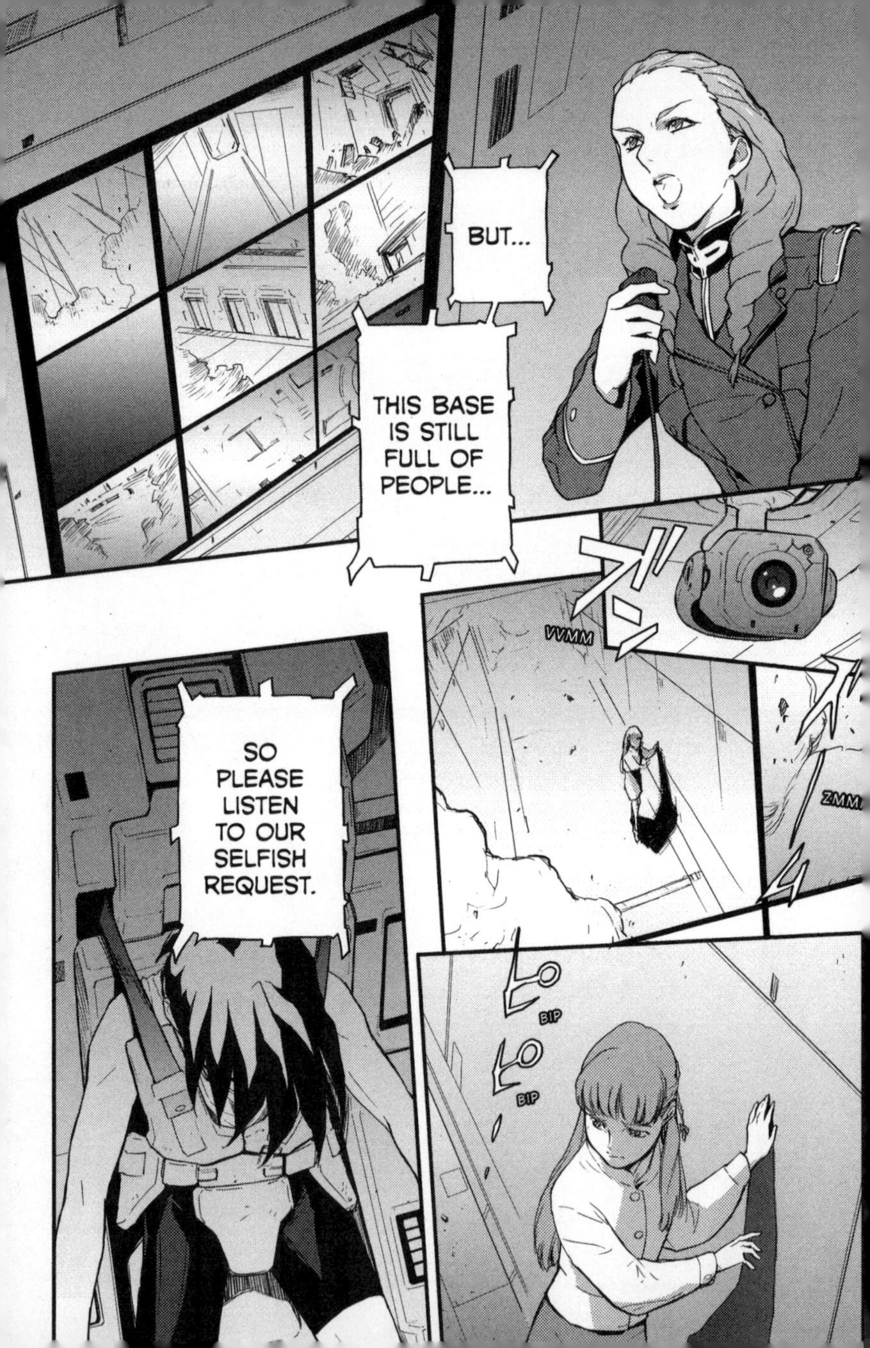
BUT...
THIS BASE IS STILL FULL OF PEOPLE...
VVMM
ZMM
BIP
BIP
SO PLEASE LISTEN TO OUR SELFISH REQUEST.

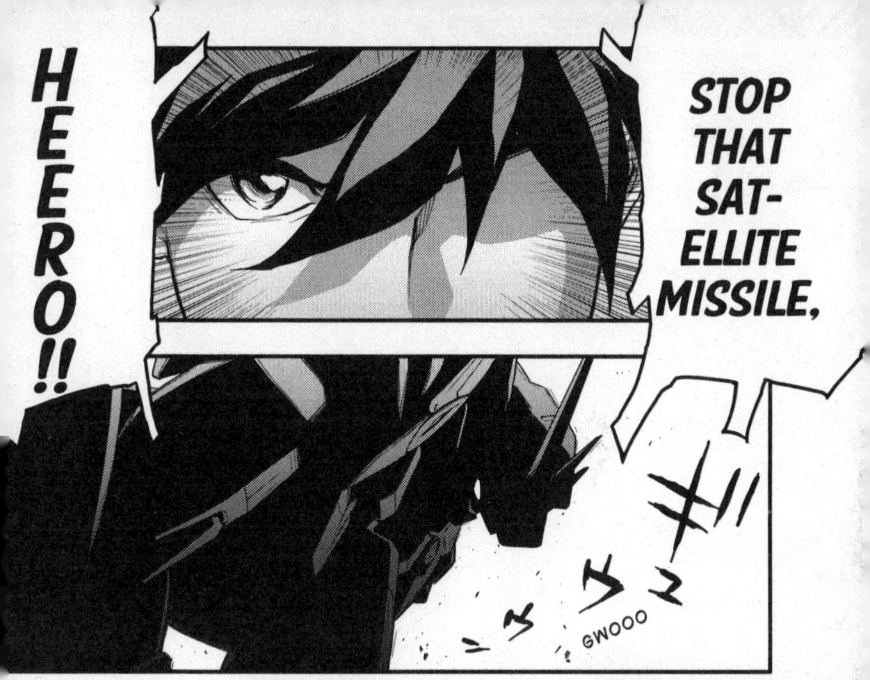
STOP THAT SAT-ELLITE MISSILE,
HEERO!!
GWOOO
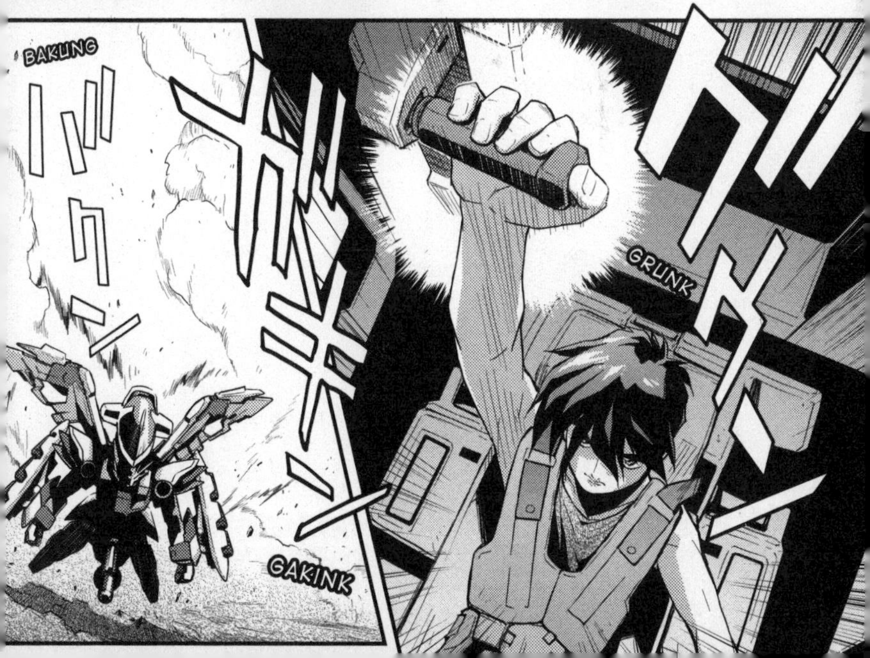
GRUNK
BAKUNG
GAKINK

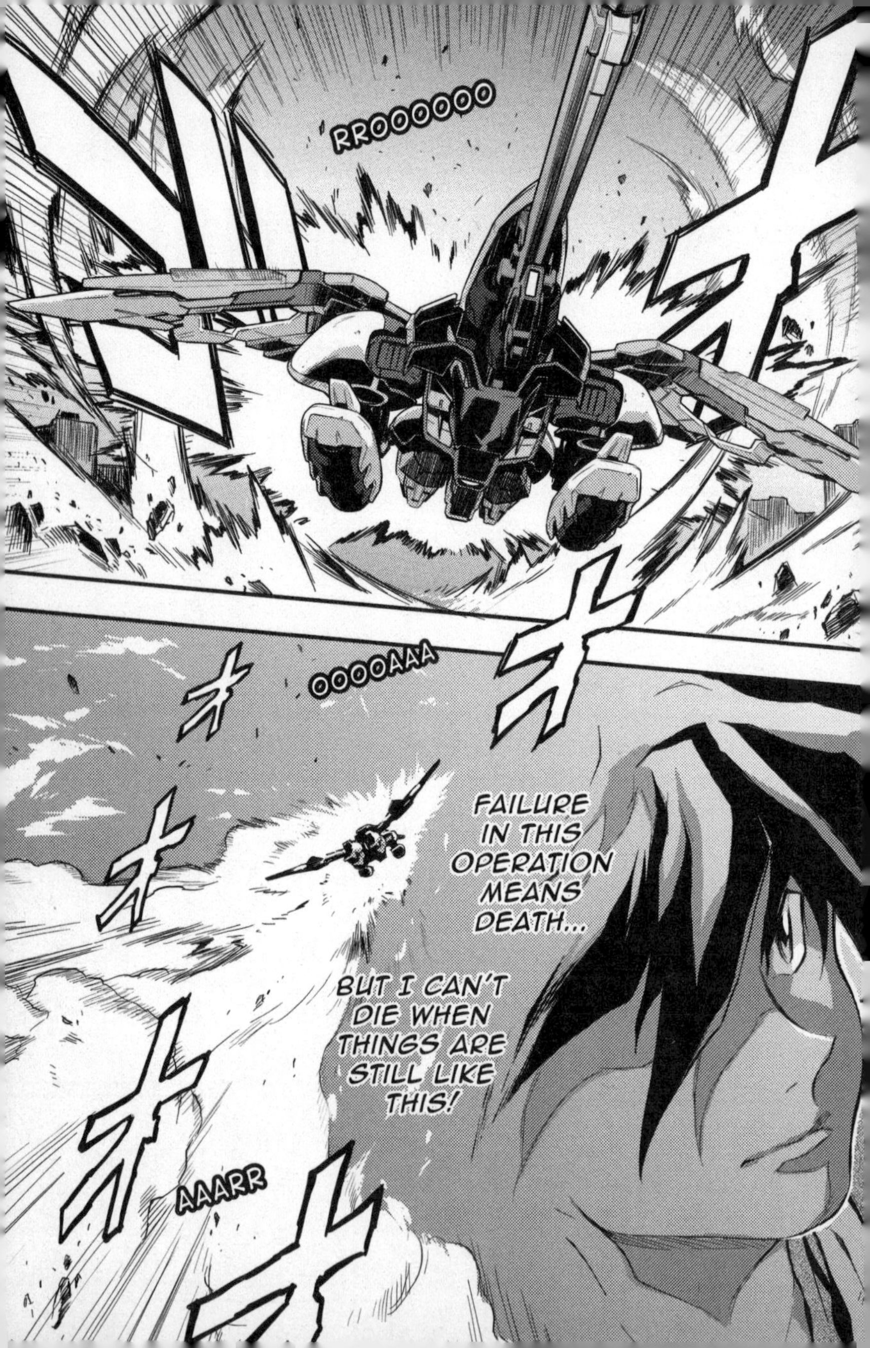
RROOOOOOO
OOOOAAA
FAILURE IN THIS OPERATION MEANS DEATH...
BUT I CAN'T DIE WHEN THINGS ARE STILL LIKE THIS!
AAARR

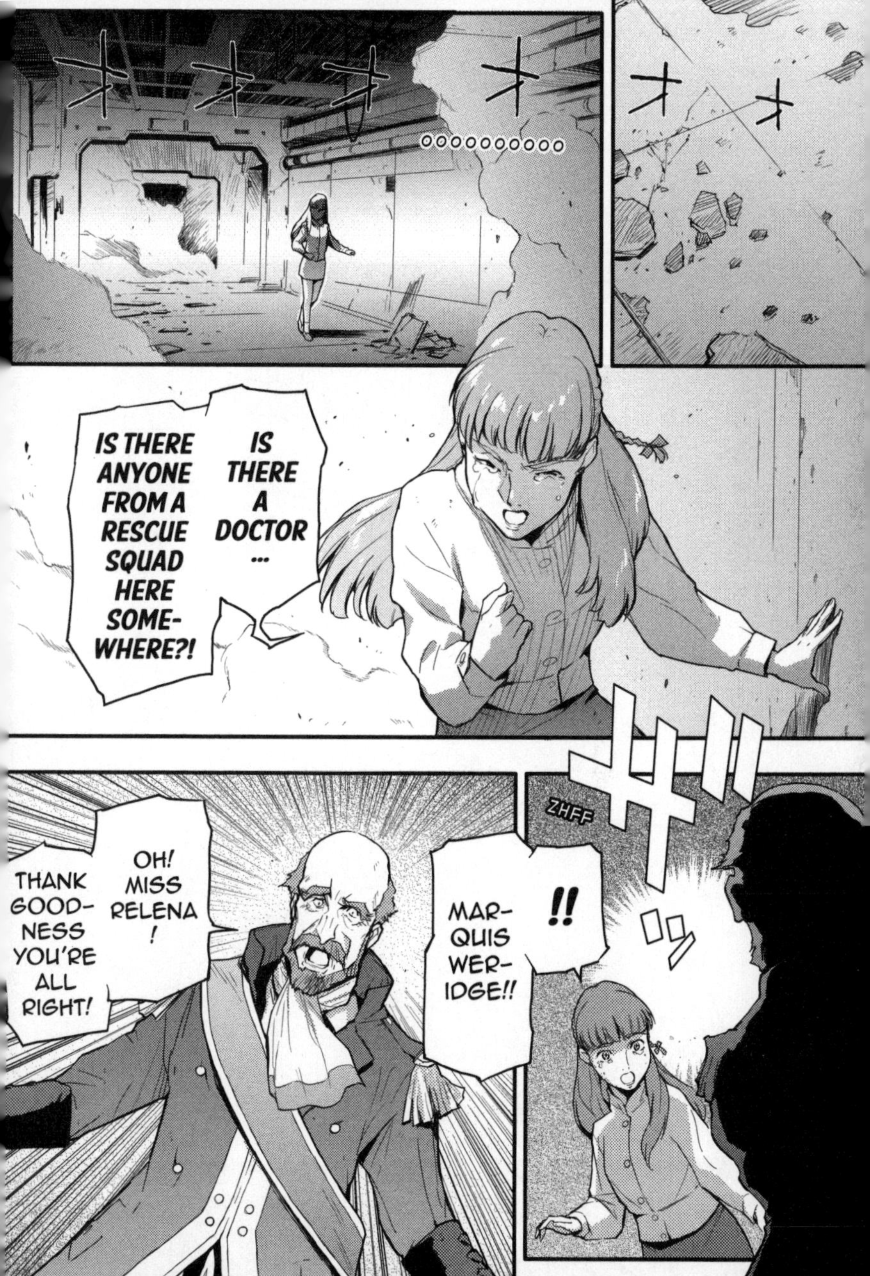
オ オ
オ オ オ オ
OOOOOOOOOO
IS THERE A DOCTOR ...
IS THERE ANYONE FROM A RESCUE SQUAD HERE SOME-WHERE?!
ザッ
ZHFF
!!
MAR-QUIS WER-IDGE!!
OH! MISS RELENA!
THANK GOOD-NESS YOU'RE ALL RIGHT!

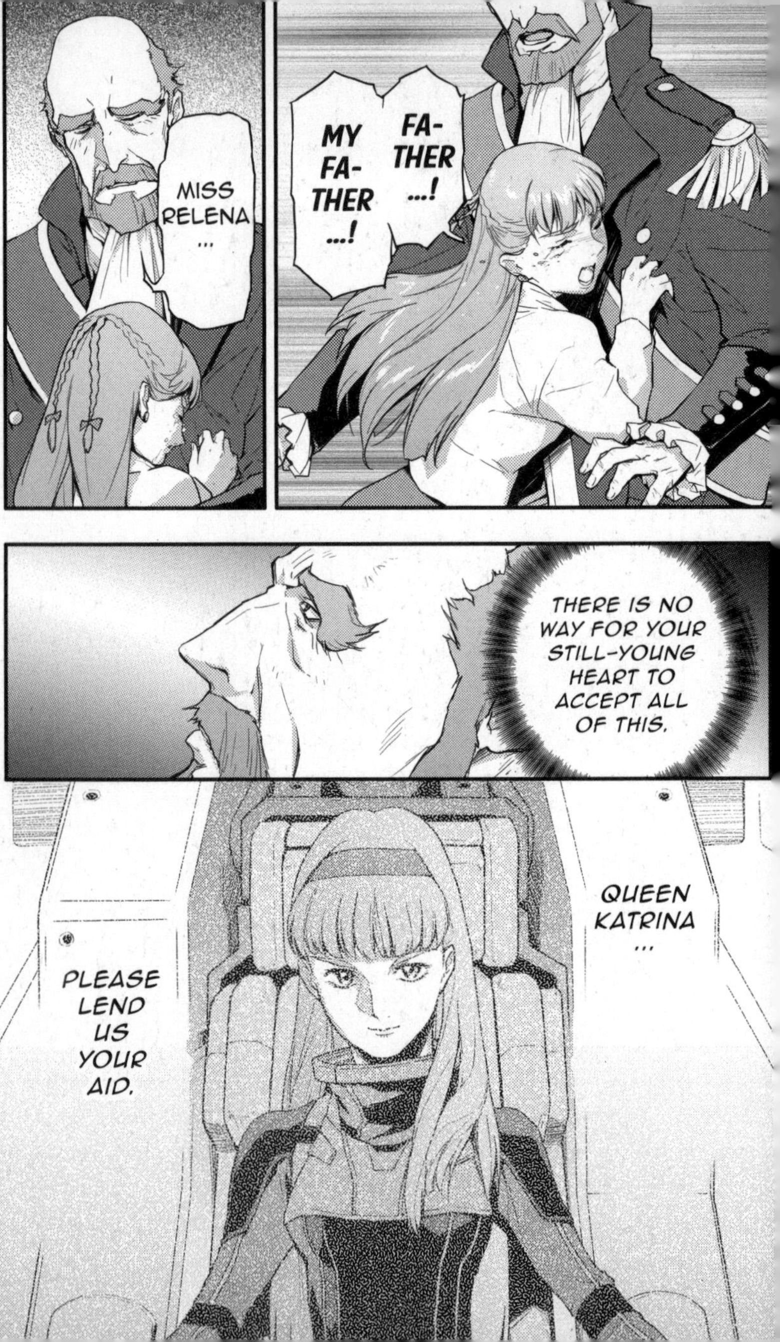
FA-THER ...!
MY FA-THER ...!
MISS RELENA ...
THERE IS NO WAY FOR YOUR STILL-YOUNG HEART TO ACCEPT ALL OF THIS.
QUEEN KATRINA ...
PLEASE LEND US YOUR AID.

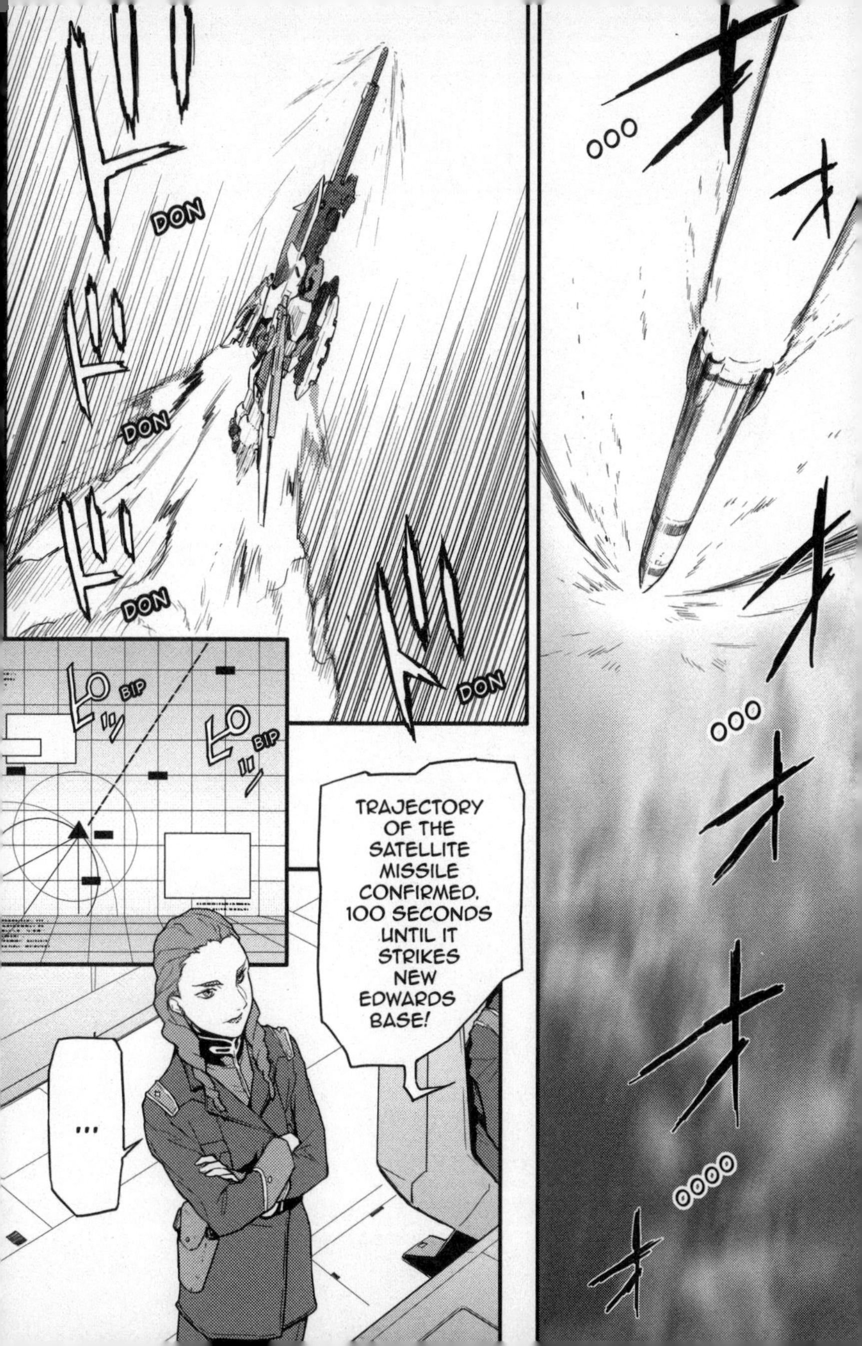
OOO
OOO
OOOO
DON
DON
DON
DON
BIP
BIP
TRAJECTORY OF THE SATELLITE MISSILE CONFIRMED. 100 SECONDS UNTIL IT STRIKES NEW EDWARDS BASE!
...

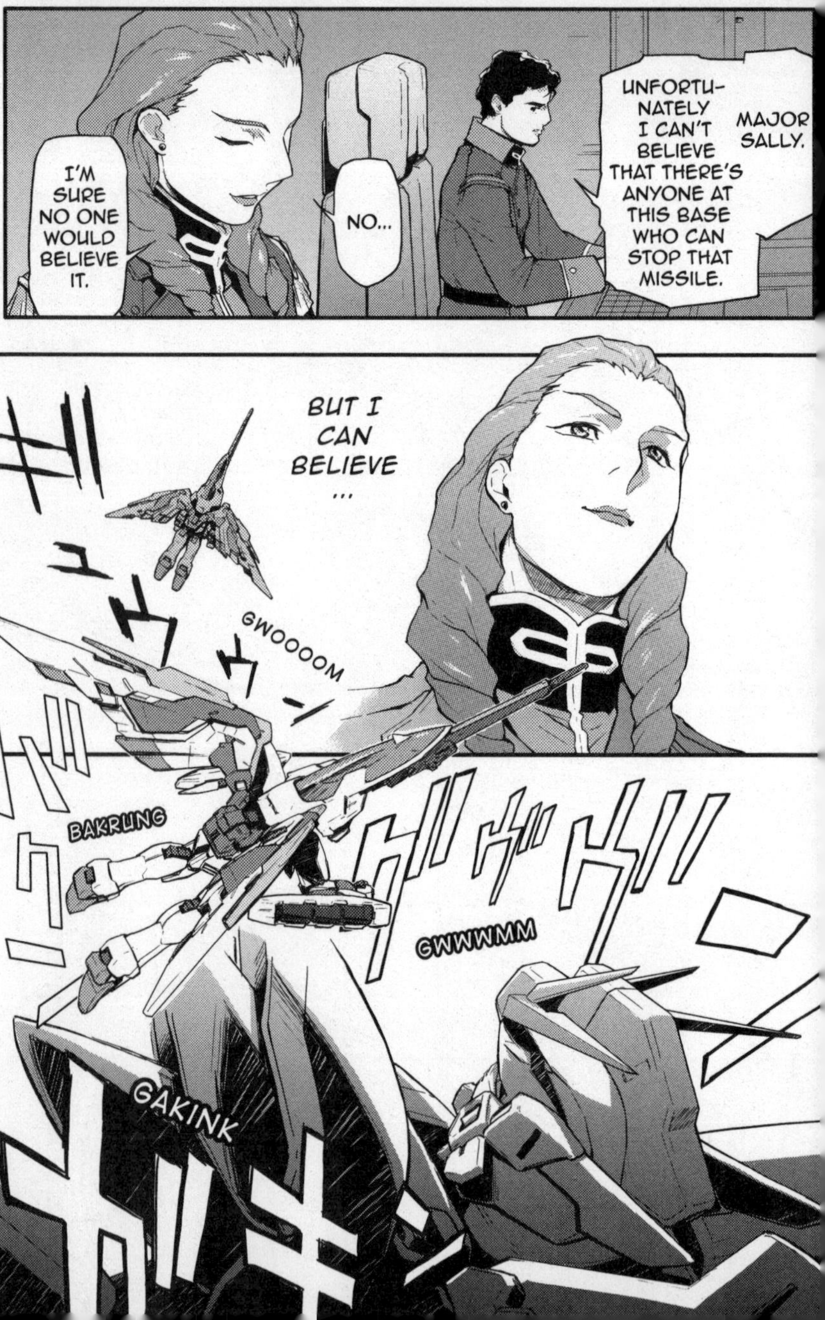
MAJOR SALLY.
UNFORTU-NATELY I CAN'T BELIEVE THAT THERE'S ANYONE AT THIS BASE WHO CAN STOP THAT MISSILE.
NO...
I'M SURE NO ONE WOULD BELIEVE IT.
BUT I CAN BELIEVE ...
GWOOOOM
GWWWMM
BAKRUNG
GAKINK

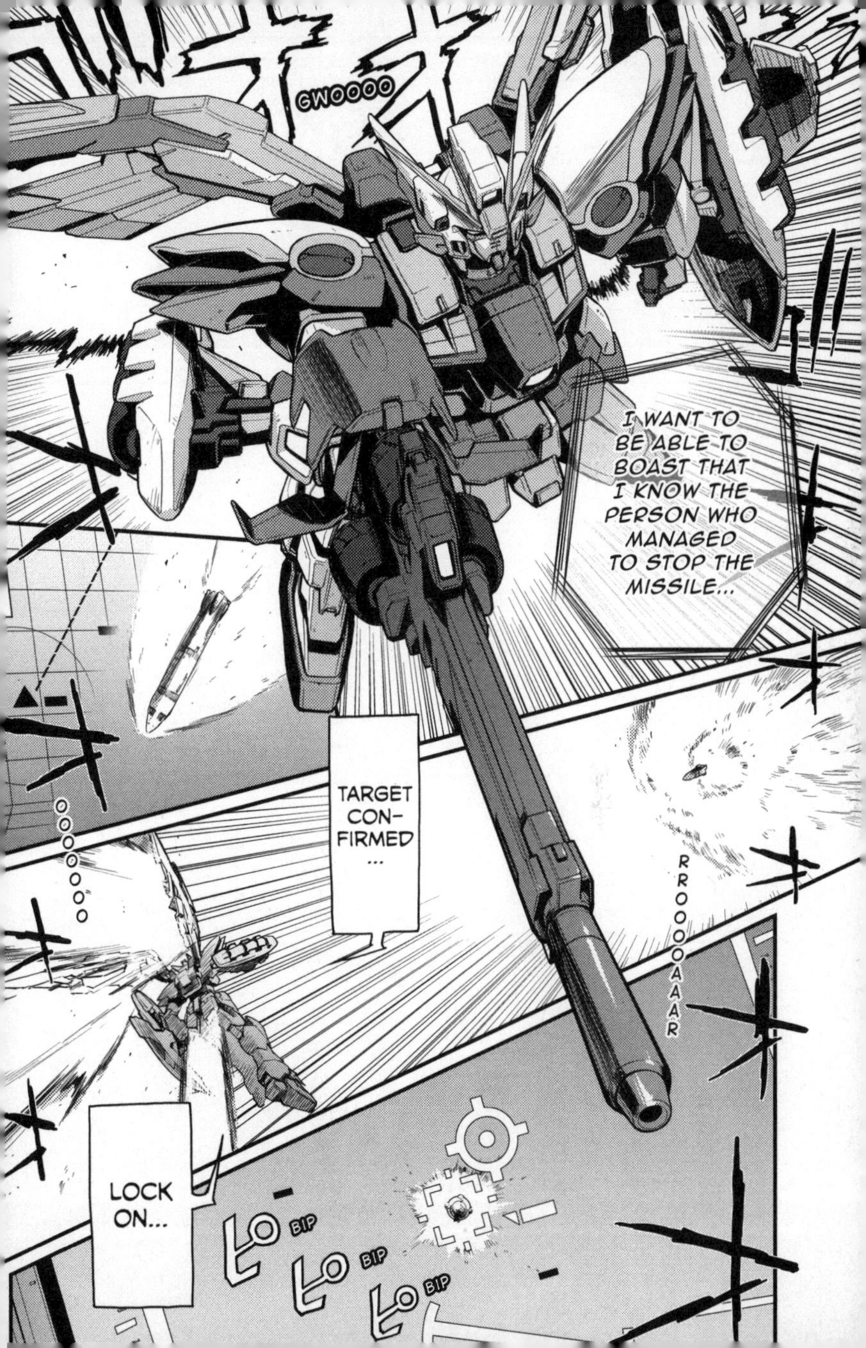
GWOOOO
I WANT TO BE ABLE TO BOAST THAT I KNOW THE PERSON WHO MANAGED TO STOP THE MISSILE...
RROOOOAAAR
TARGET CON-FIRMED ...
OOOOOOOO
LOCK ON...
BIP
BIP
BIP

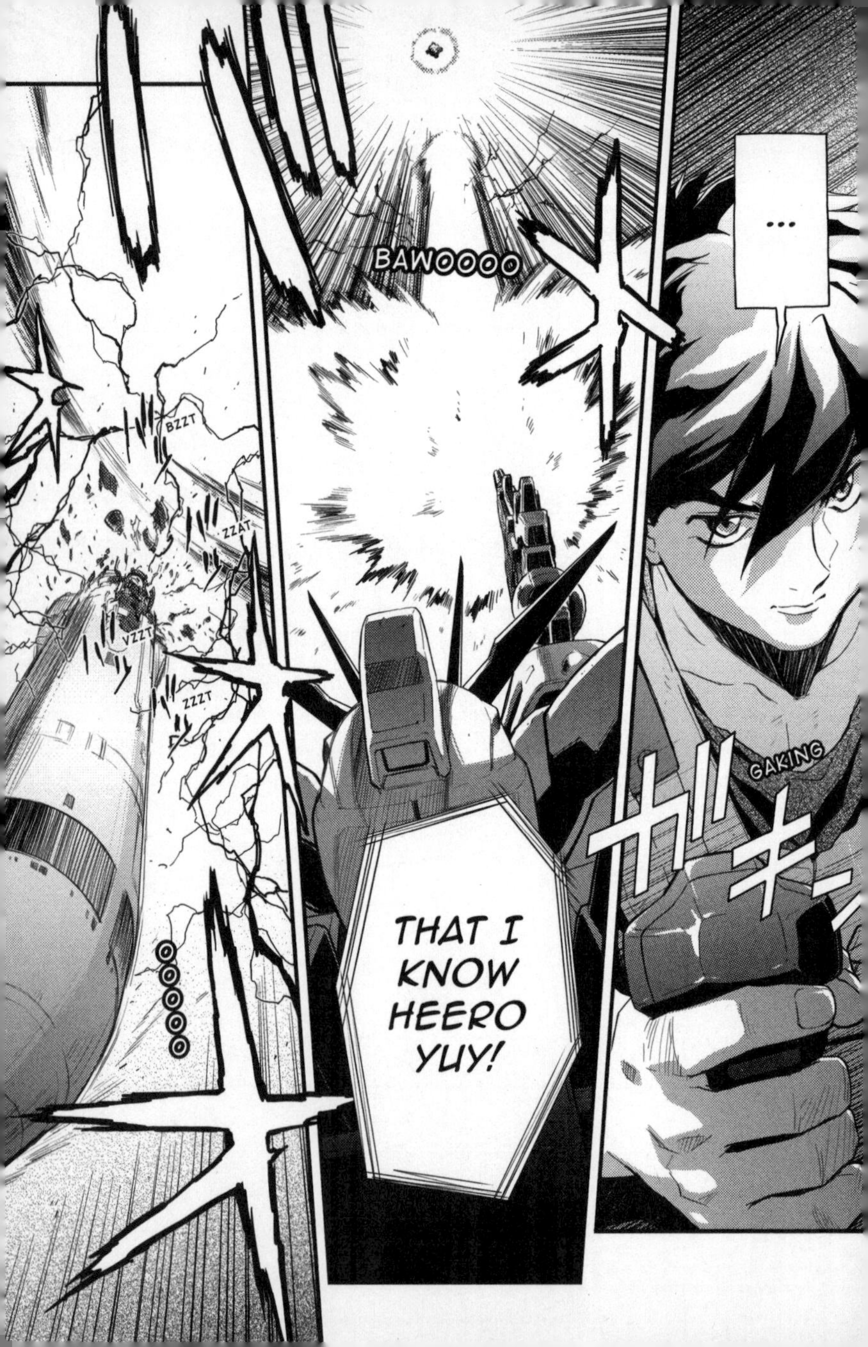
...
GAKING
BAWOOOO
THAT I KNOW HEERO YUY!
BZZT
ZZAT
VZZT
ZZZT
OOOOOO

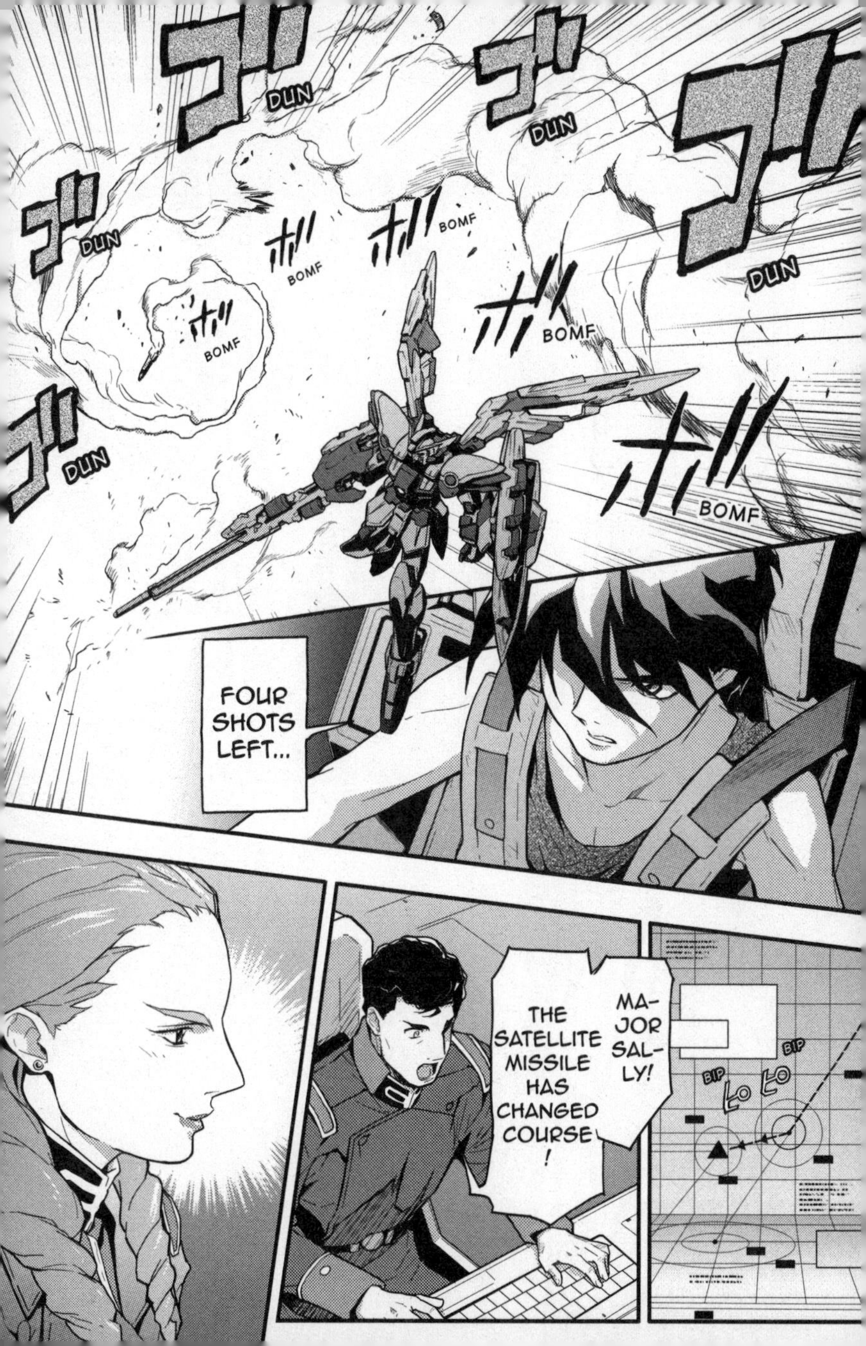
DUN
DUN
DUN
BOMF
BOMF
BOMF
DUN
BOMF
DUN
BOMF
DUN
FOUR SHOTS LEFT...
BIP
BIP
MAJOR SALLY!
THE SATELLITE MISSILE HAS CHANGED COURSE!

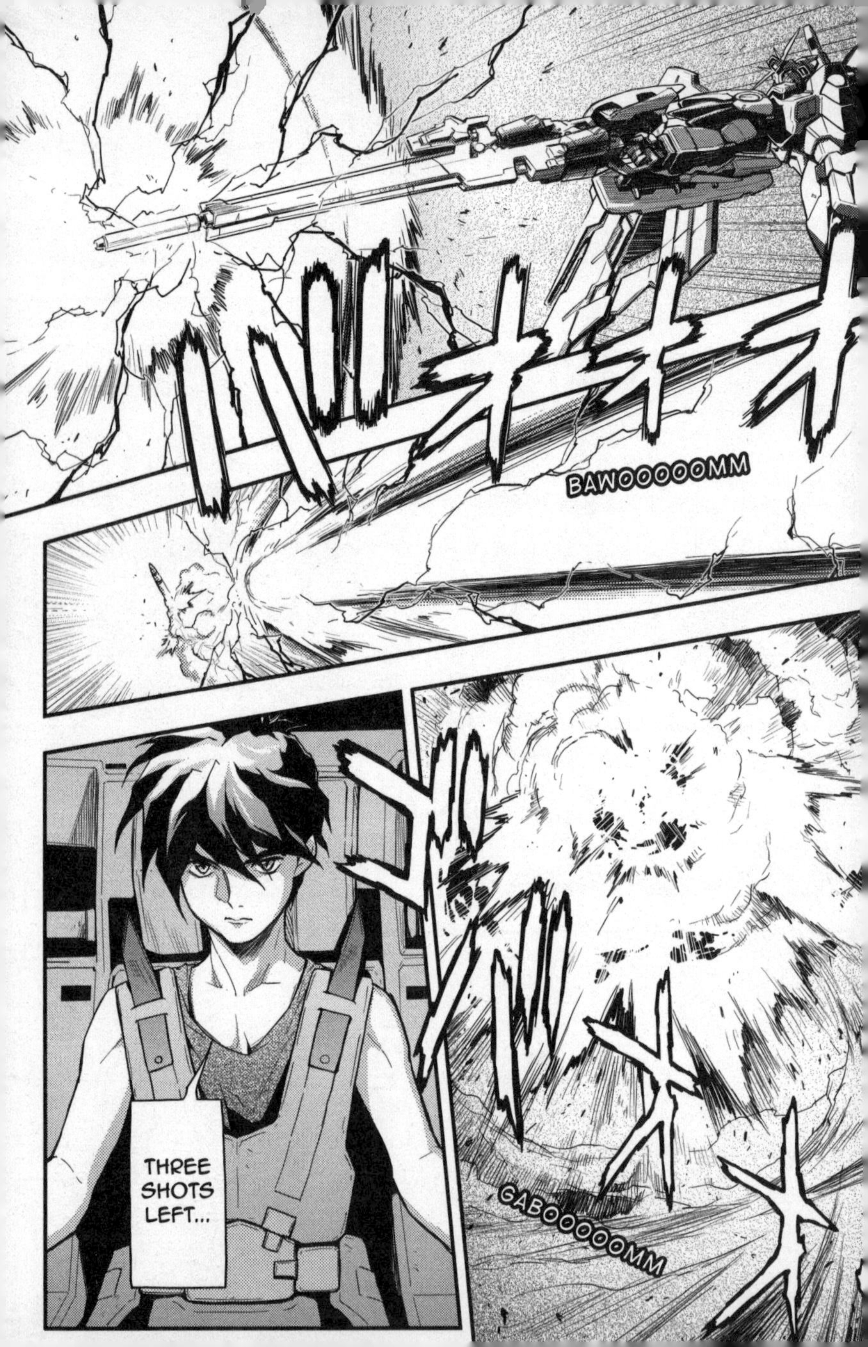
BAWOOOOOOMM
GABOOOOOOMM
THREE SHOTS LEFT...

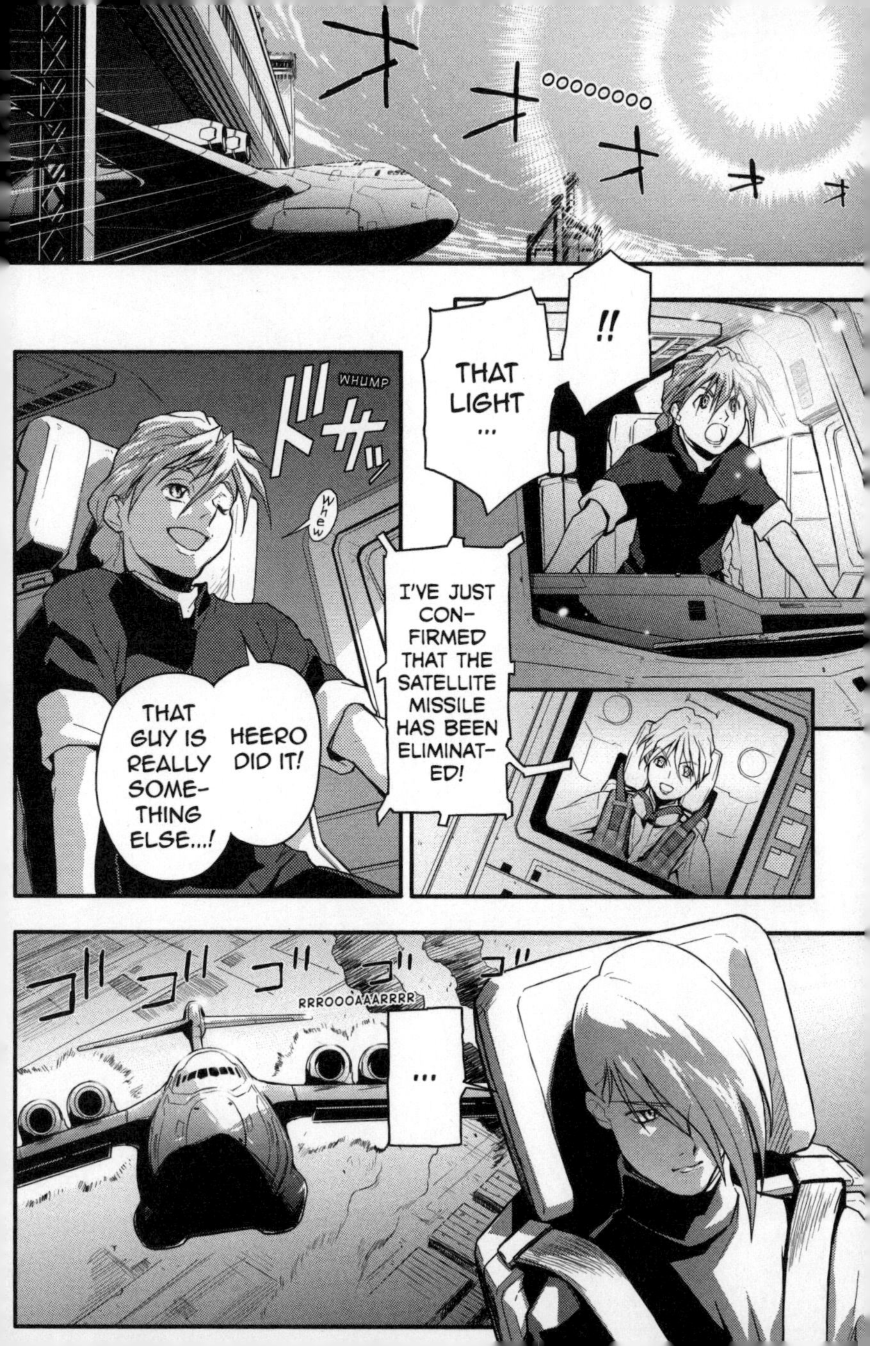
オオオオオ
OOOOOOOO
!!
THAT LIGHT ...
I'VE JUST CONFIRMED THAT THE SATELLITE MISSILE HAS BEEN ELIMINATED!
ドサッ
WHUMP
whew
HEERO DID IT!
THAT GUY IS REALLY SOMETHING ELSE...!
ゴゴゴゴ
RRROOOAAARRRR
...

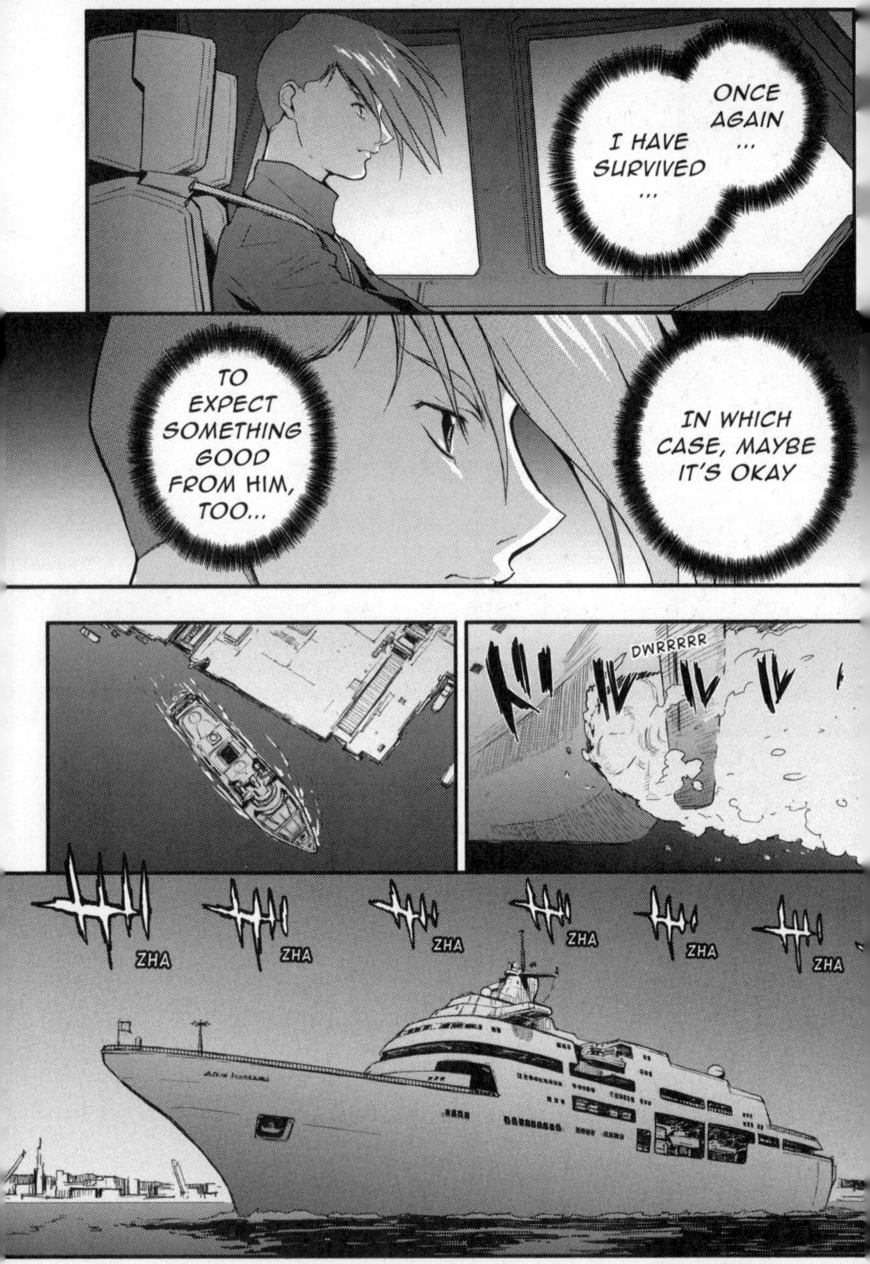
ONCE AGAIN ...
I HAVE SURVIVED ...
IN WHICH CASE, MAYBE IT'S OKAY
TO EXPECT SOMETHING GOOD FROM HIM, TOO...
DWRRRRR
ZHA
ZHA
ZHA
ZHA
ZHA
ZHA

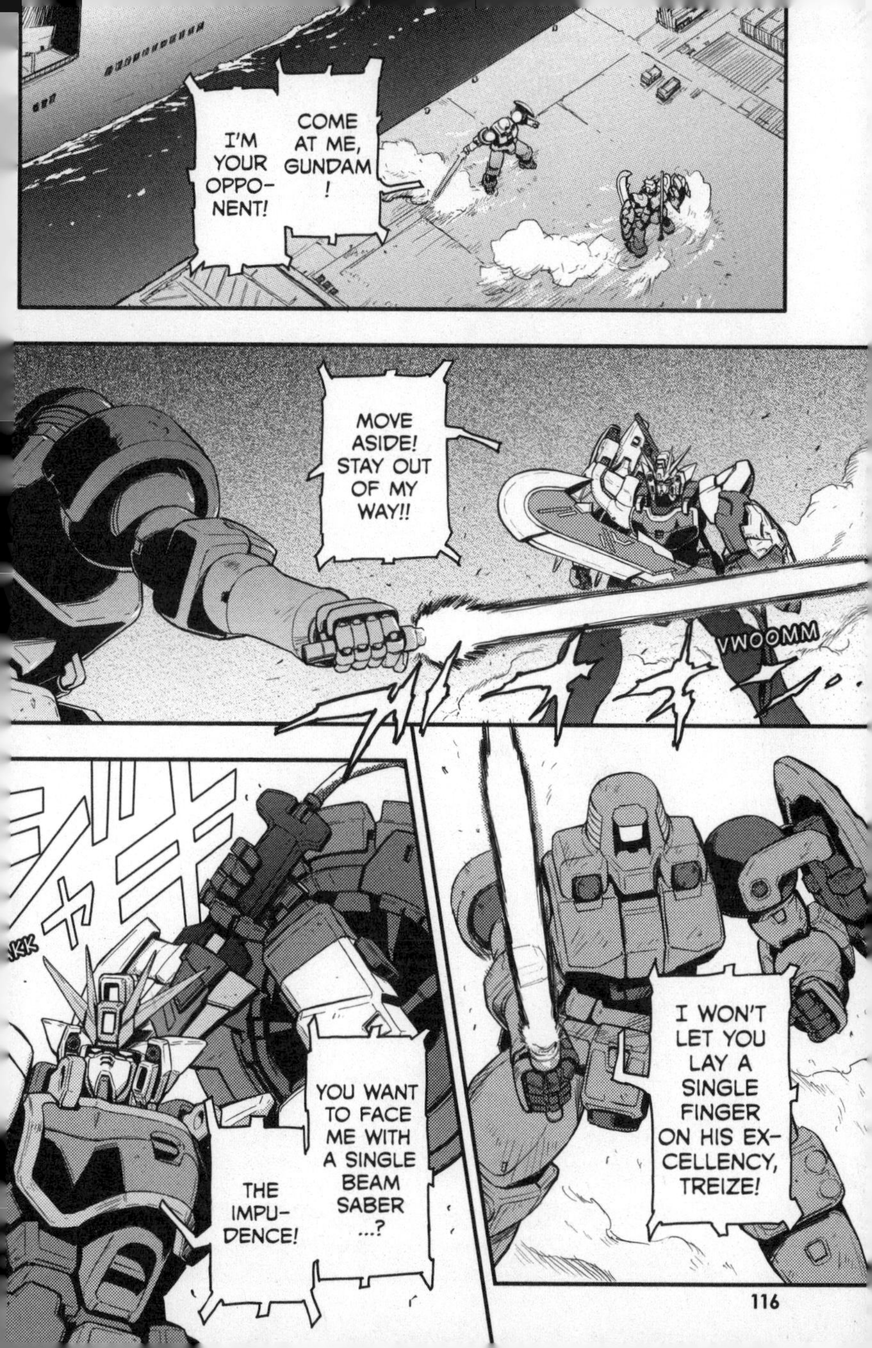
COME AT ME, GUNDAM!
I'M YOUR OPPONENT!
MOVE ASIDE! STAY OUT OF MY WAY!!
VWOOMM
I WON'T LET YOU LAY A SINGLE FINGER ON HIS EXCELLENCY, TREIZE!
YOU WANT TO FACE ME WITH A SINGLE BEAM SABER ...?
THE IMPUDENCE!

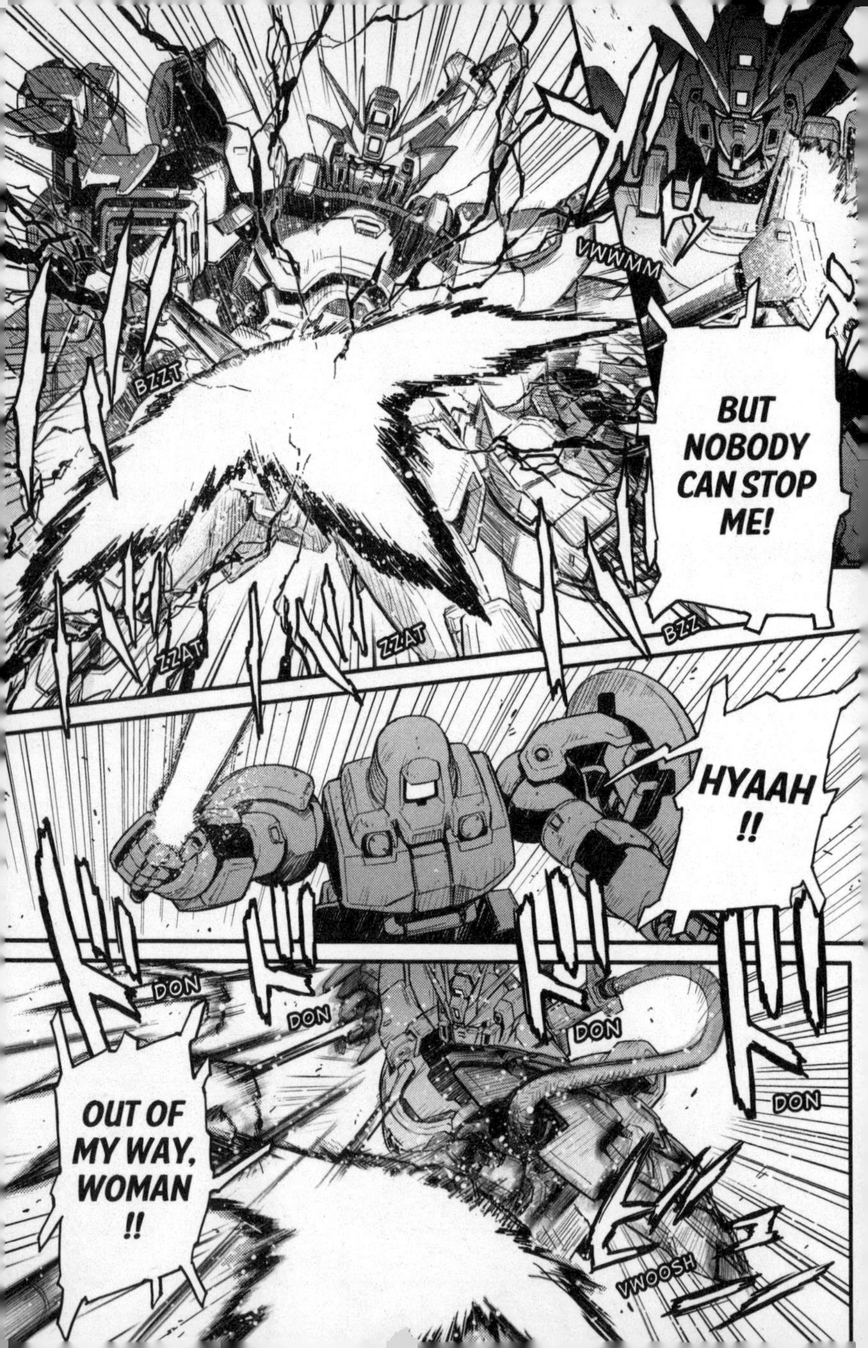
VWWMM
BUT NOBODY CAN STOP ME!
BZZT
BZZ
ZZAT
ZZAT
HYAAH !!
DON
DON
DON
DON
OUT OF MY WAY, WOMAN !!
VWOOSH

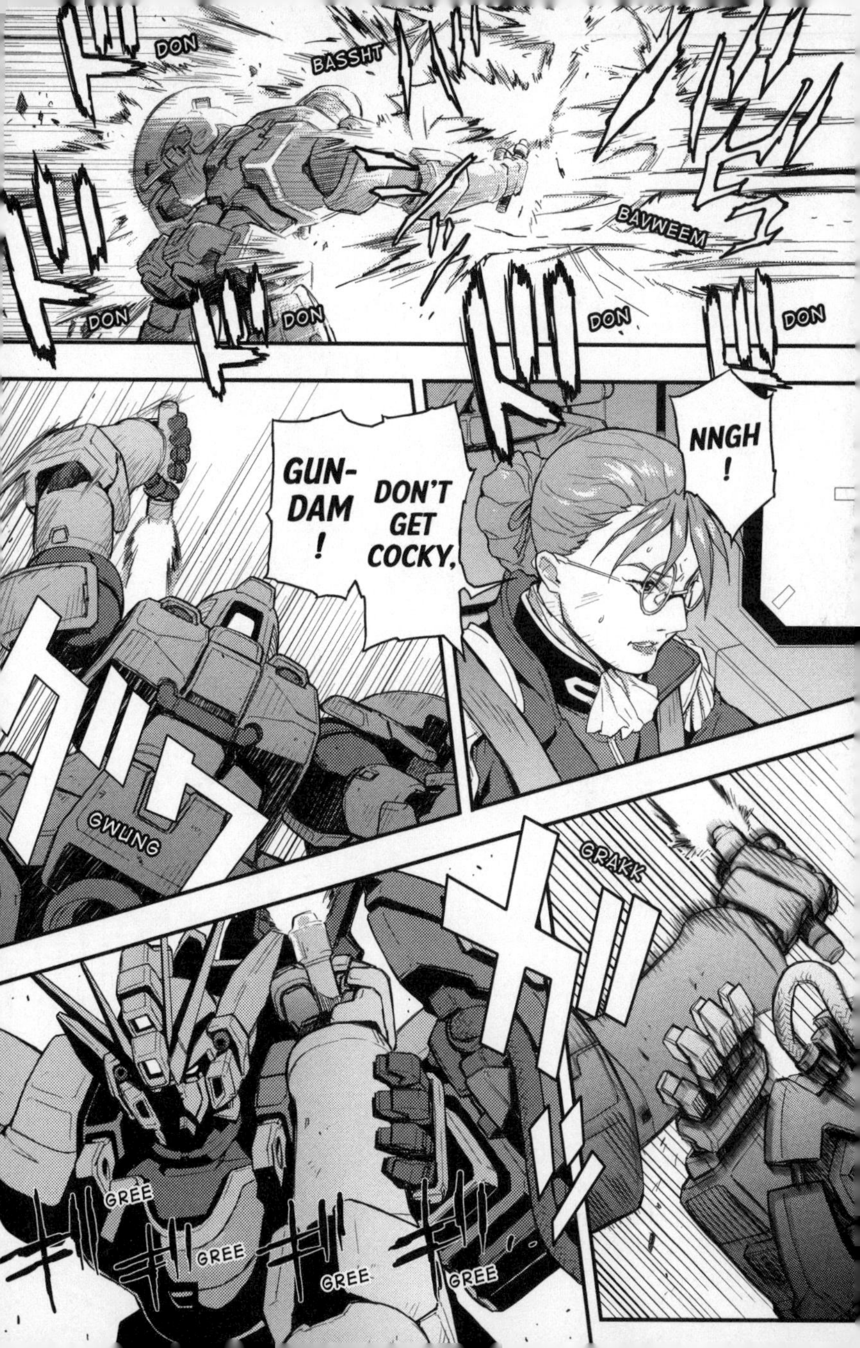
BAVWEEM
BASSHT
DON
DON
DON
DON
DON
NNGH!
DON'T GET COCKY,
GUN-DAM!
GWUNG
GRAKK
GREE
GREE
GREE
GREE

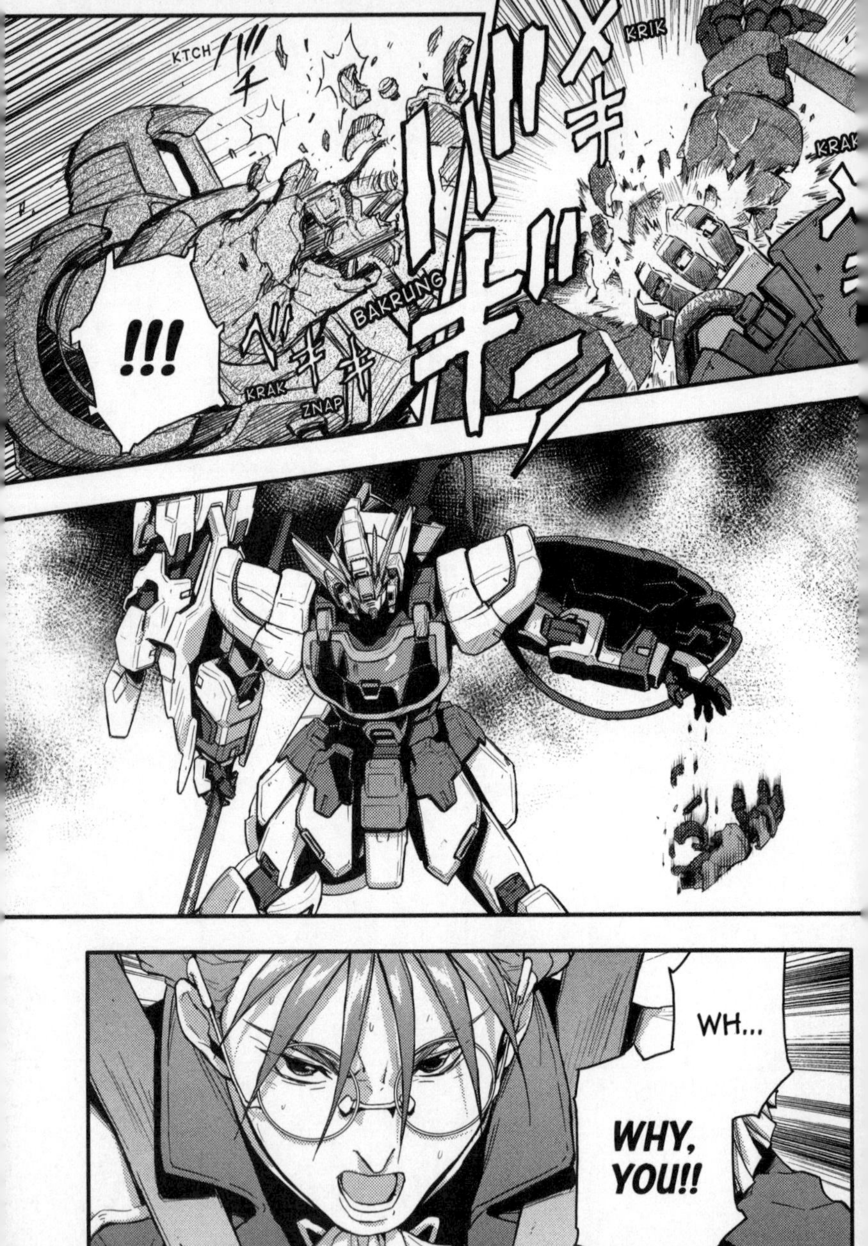
KRIK
KRAK
KTCH
BAKRUNG
!!!
KRAK
ZNAP
WH...
WHY, YOU!!

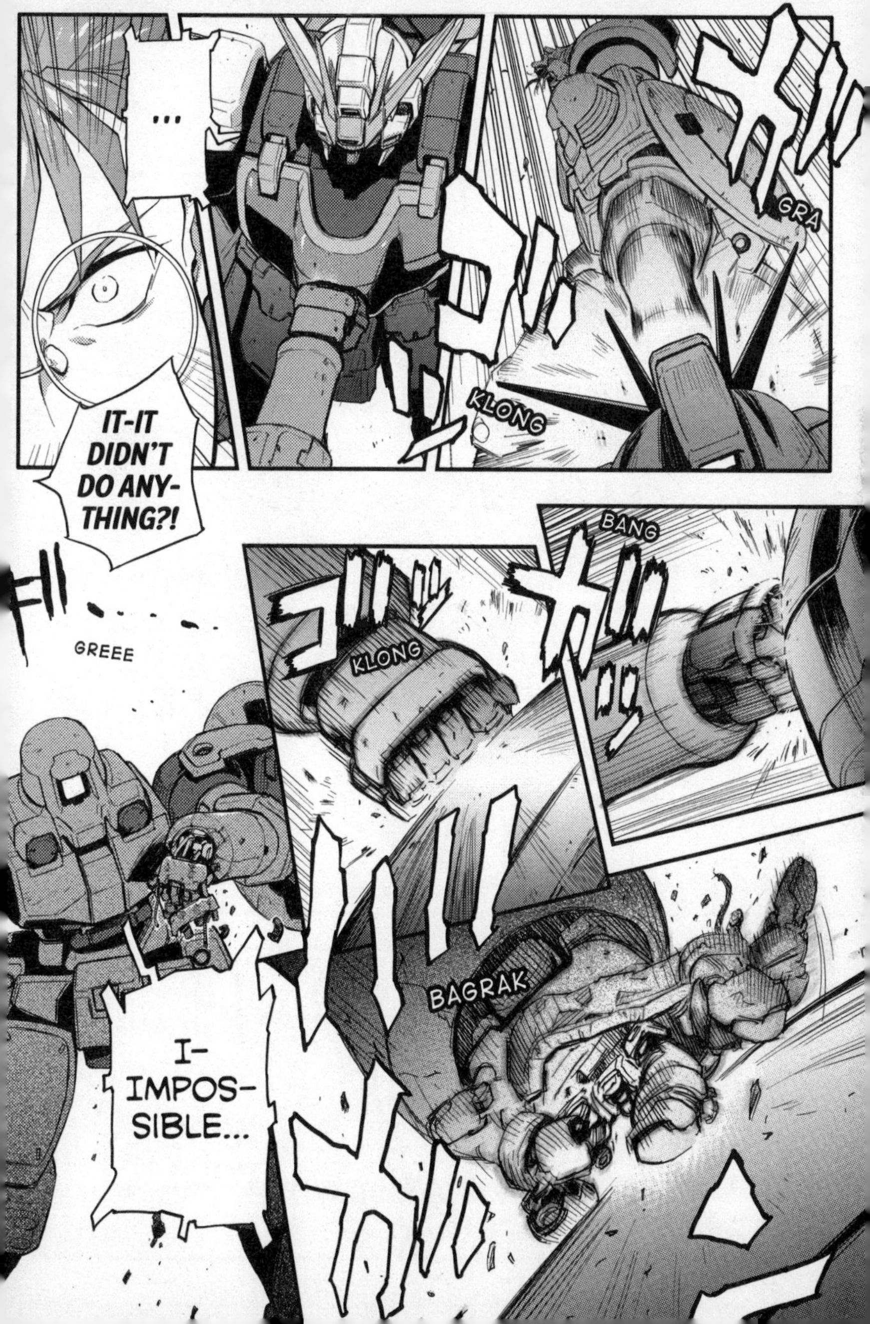
GRA
KLONG
...
IT-IT DIDN'T DO ANYTHING?!
BANG
KLONG
GREEE
BAGRAK
I- IMPOSSIBLE...

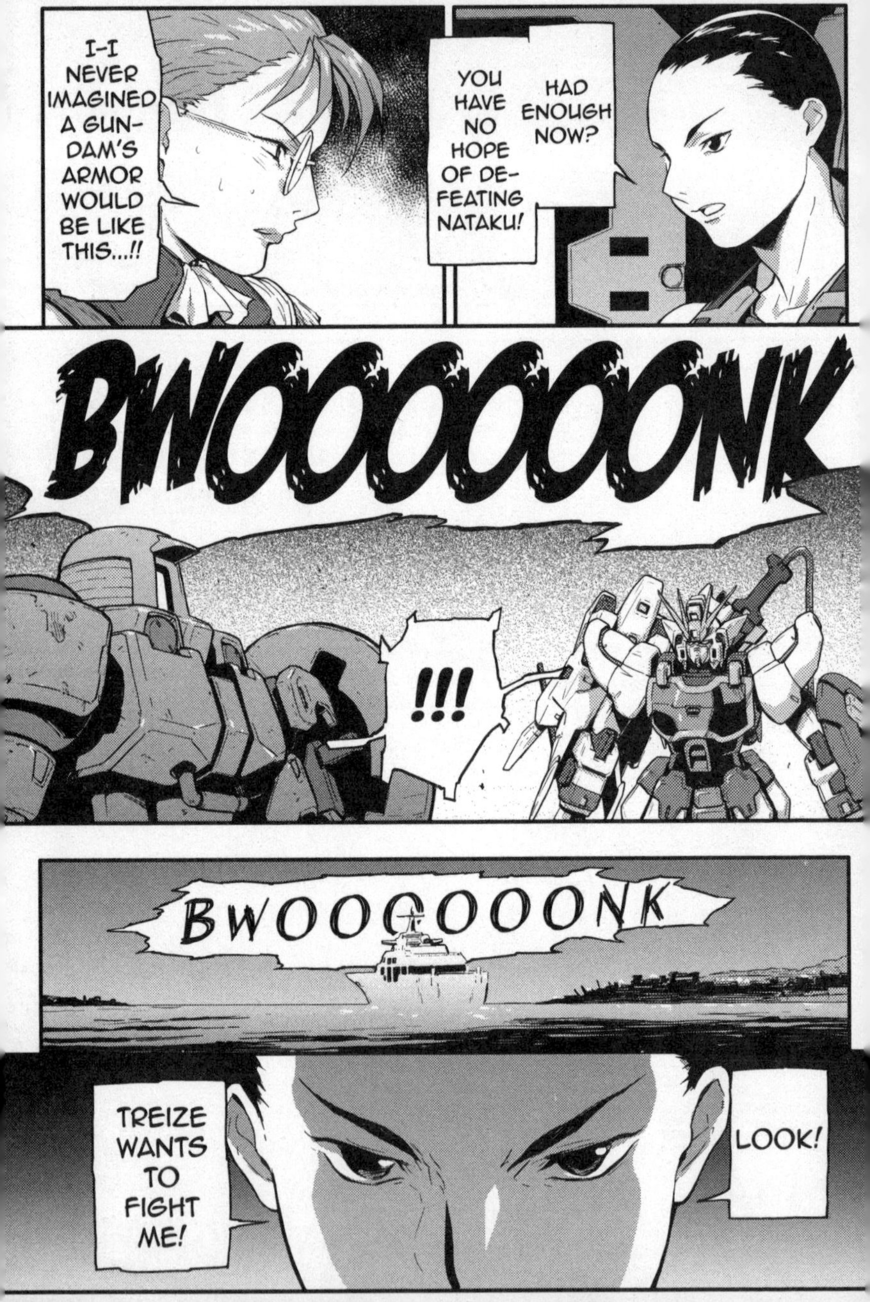

HAD ENOUGH NOW?
YOU HAVE NO HOPE OF DEFEATING NATAKU!
I-I NEVER IMAGINED A GUNDAM'S ARMOR WOULD BE LIKE THIS...!!
BWOOOOOONK
!!!
BWOOOOOONK
LOOK!
TREIZE WANTS TO FIGHT ME!

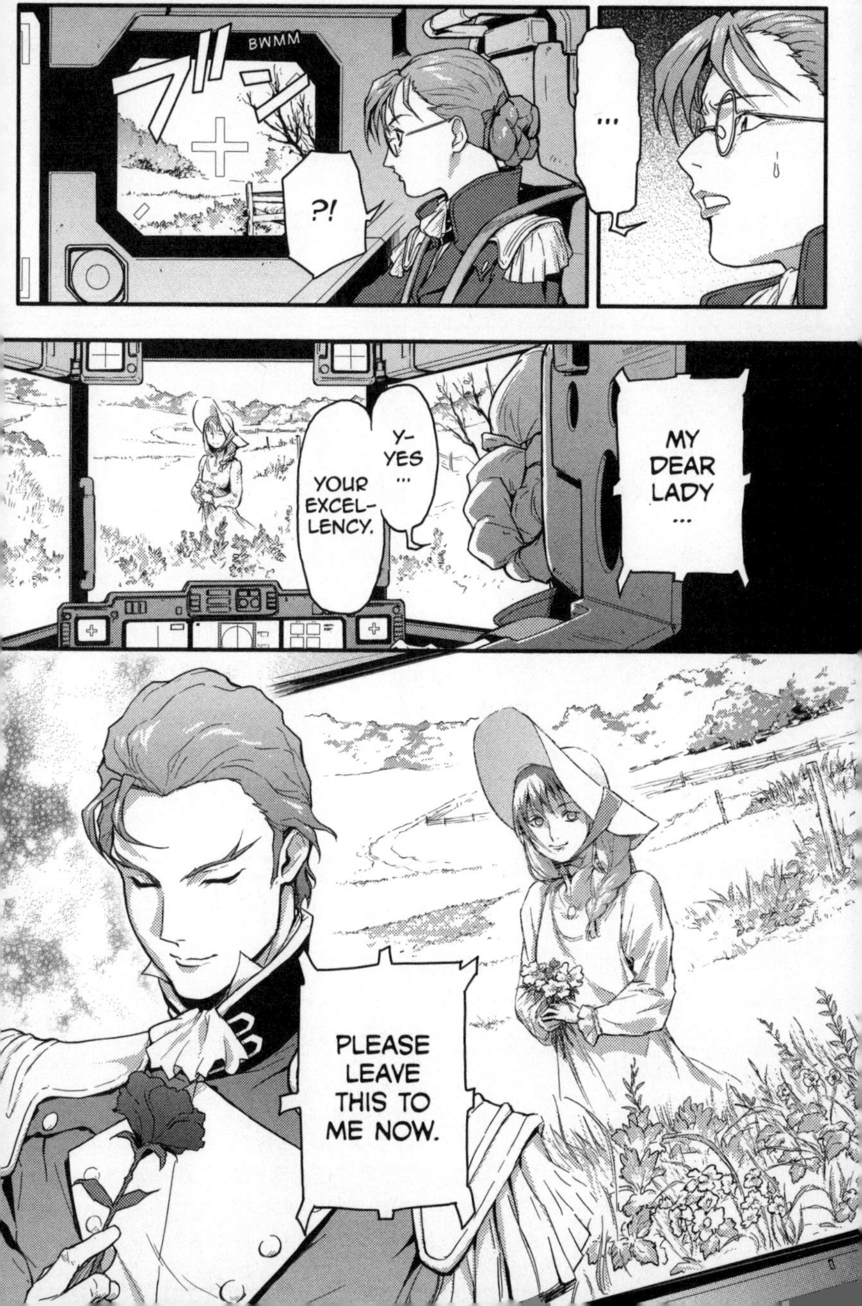
…
BWMM
?!
MY DEAR LADY …
Y-YES …
YOUR EXCELLENCY.
PLEASE LEAVE THIS TO ME NOW.

Zechs *Merquise*

SLEEVE NOTES:
Endless Waltz

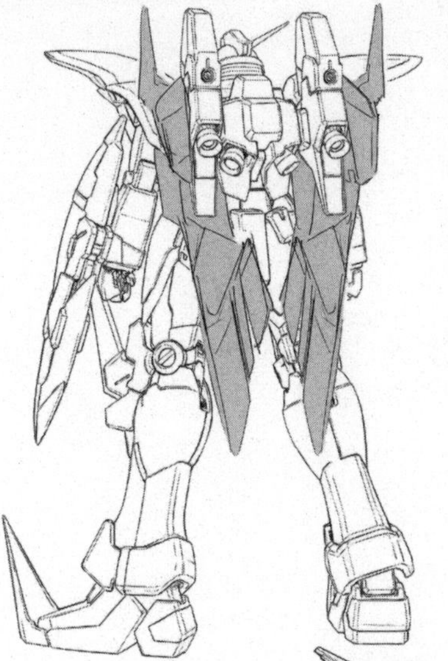

XXXG-01D
GUNDAM DEATHSCYTHE
Rousette Rigging

The Gundam Deathscythe's wing rigging. Set on each side of the backpack, the wings deploy when flying. While slightly smaller, it can give it mobility equal to the Wing Gundam for short periods. On the other hand, using them for cruising might be limited to some degree.

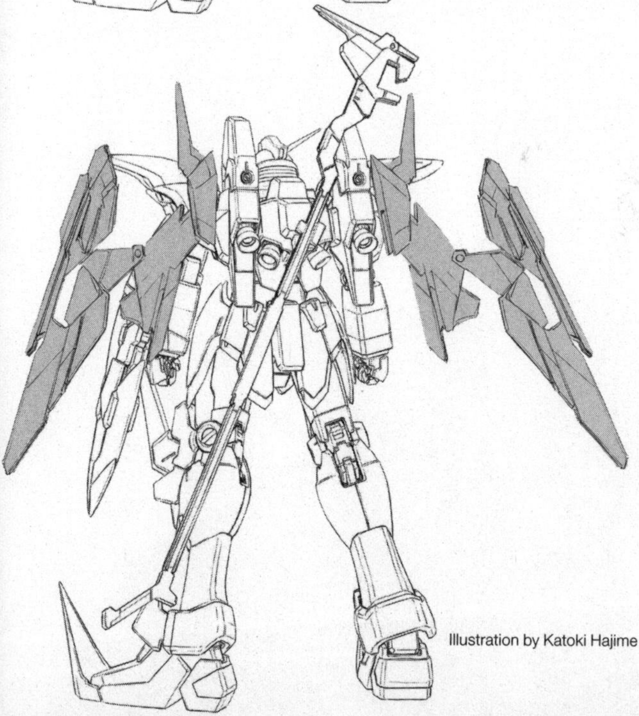

Illustration by Katoki Hajime

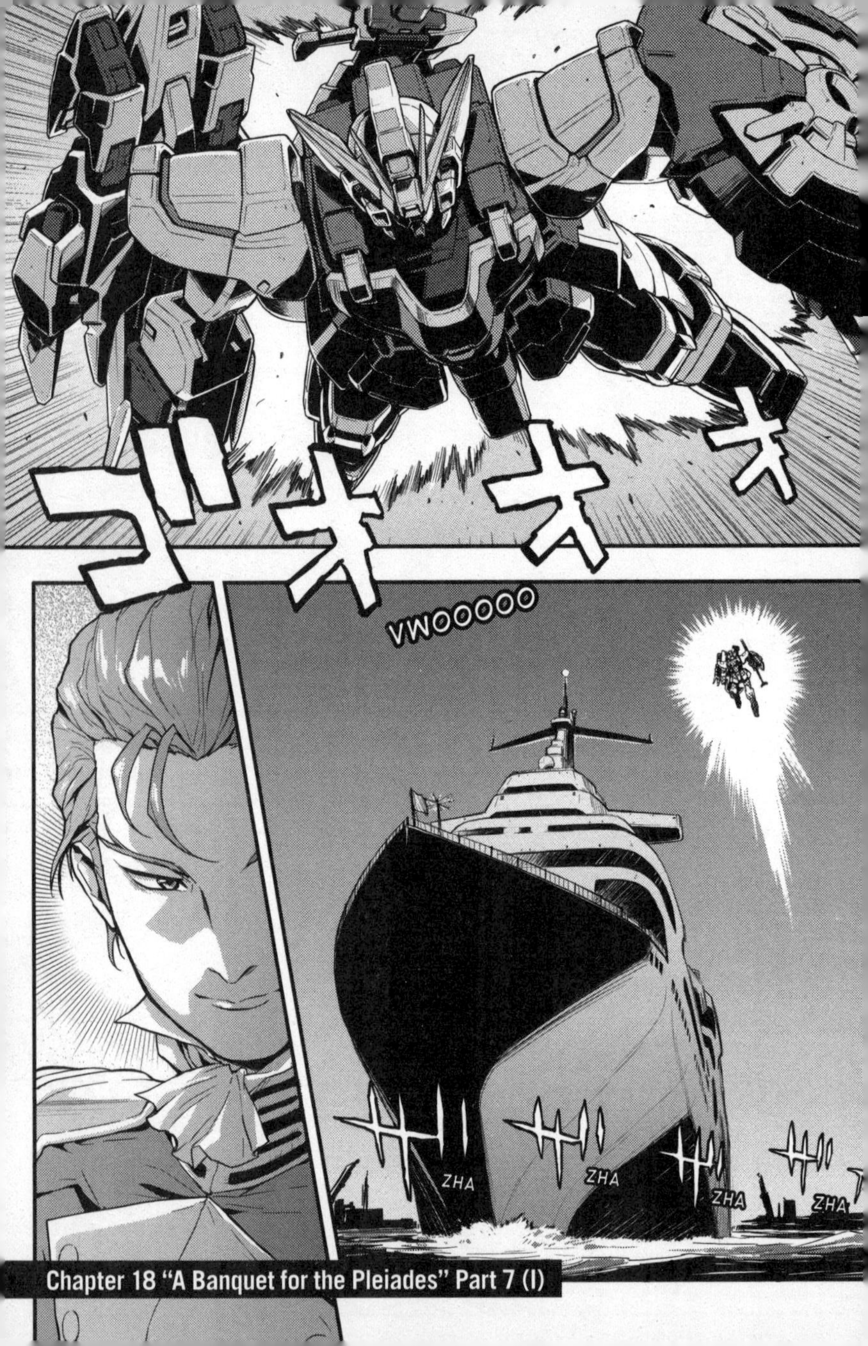
ゴオオオ
VWOOOOO
ZHA
ZHA
ZHA
ZHA

Chapter 18 "A Banquet for the Pleiades" Part 7 (I)

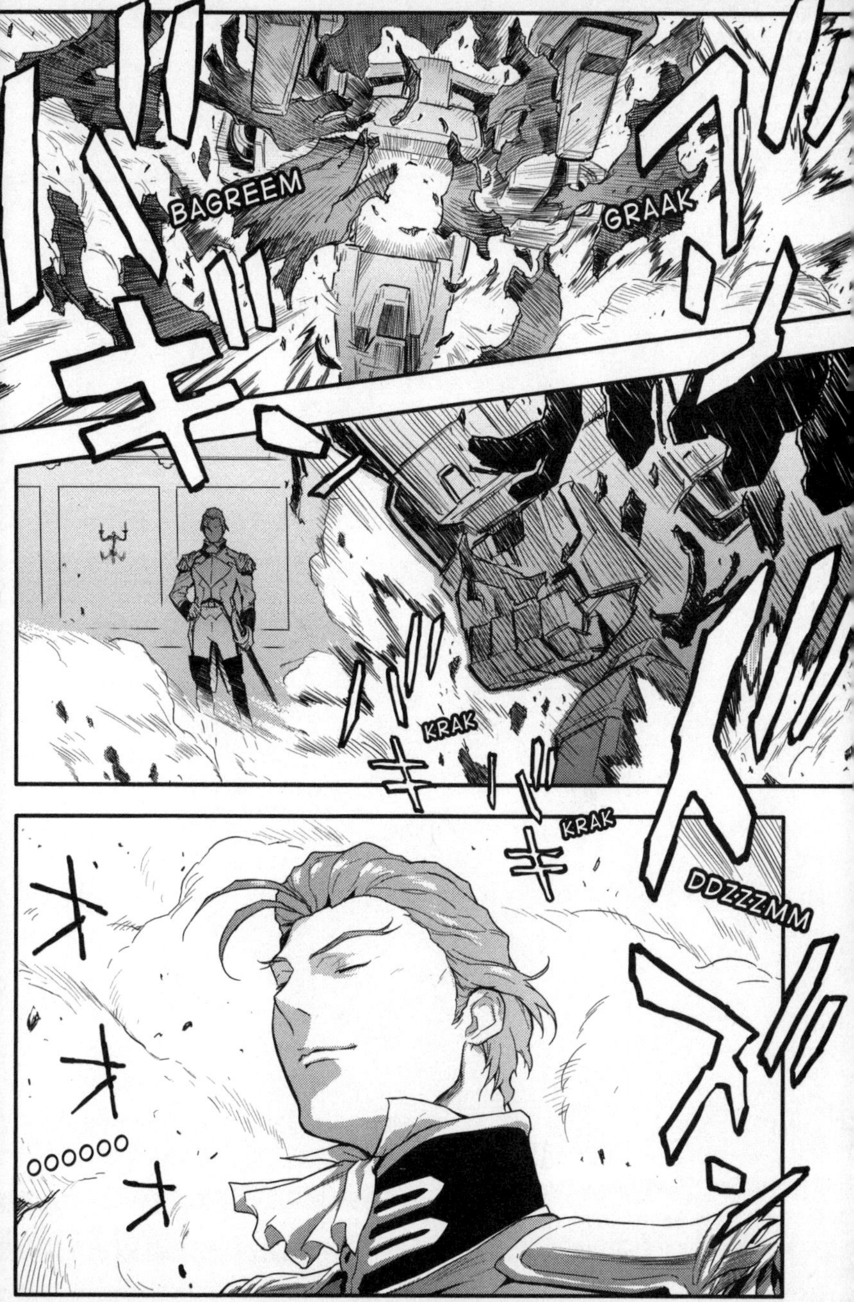
GRAAK
BAGREEM
KRAK
KRAK
DDZ·Z·ZMM
OOOOOO

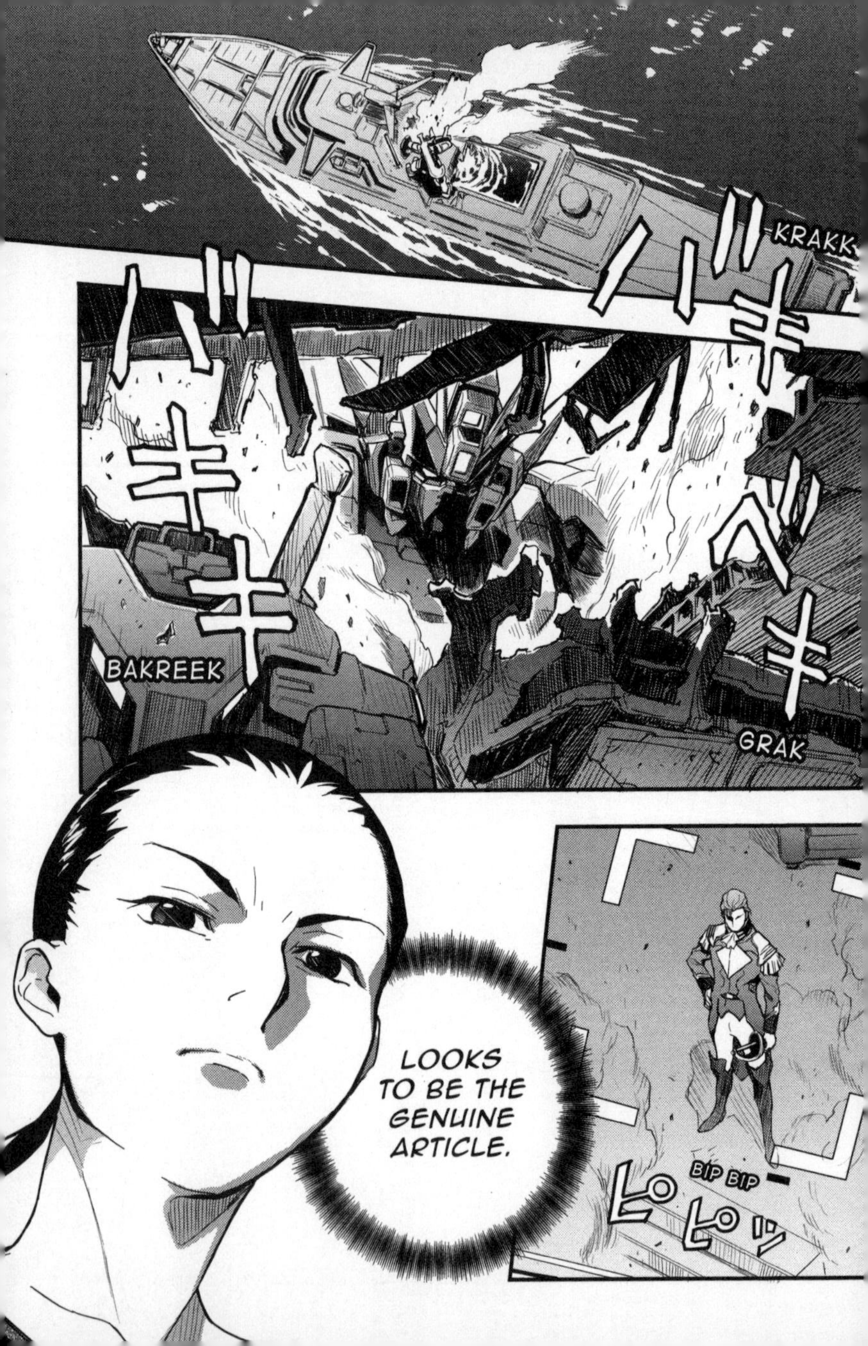
KRAKK
GRAK
BAKREEK
BIP BIP
LOOKS TO BE THE GENUINE ARTICLE.

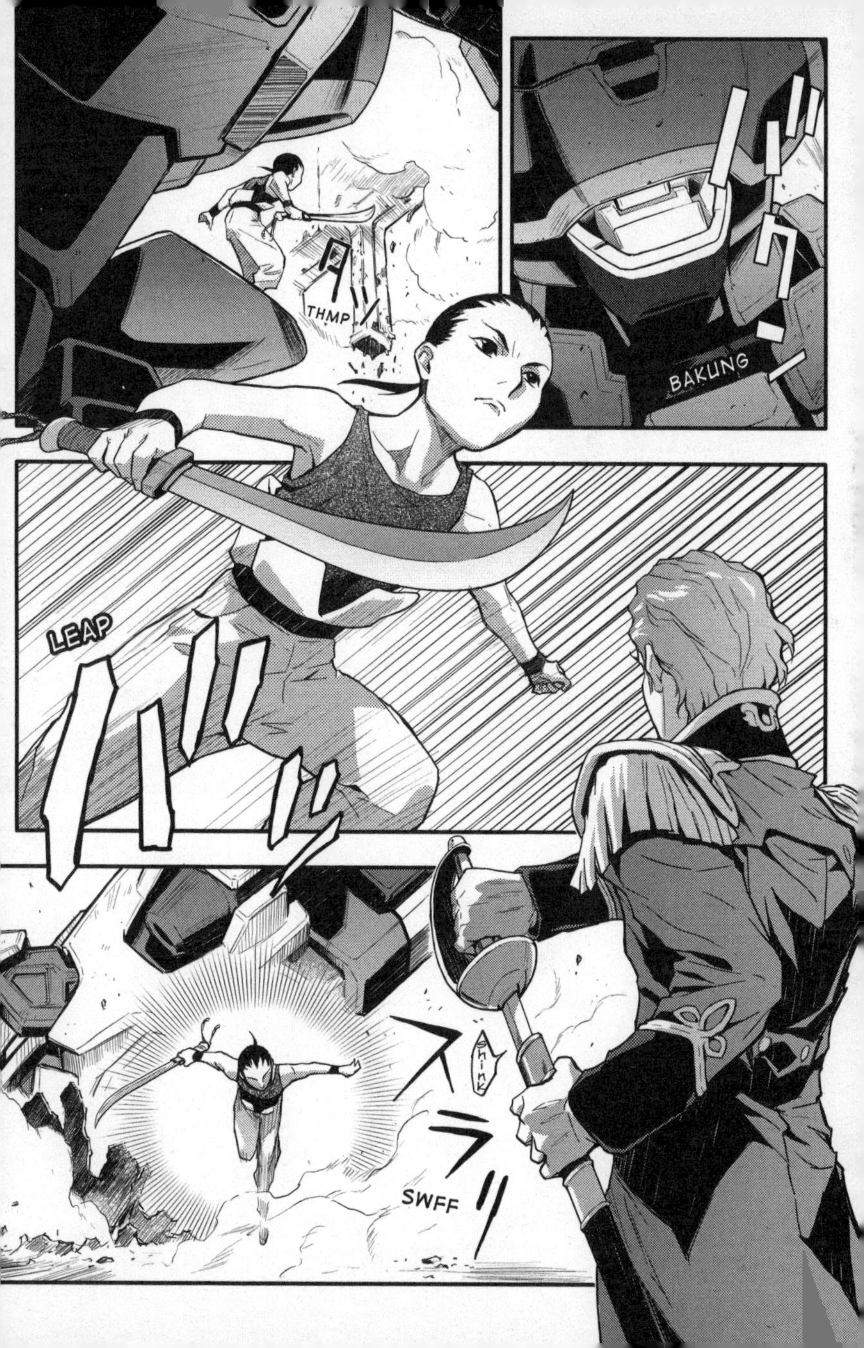
BAKUNG
THMP
LEAP
shink
SWFF

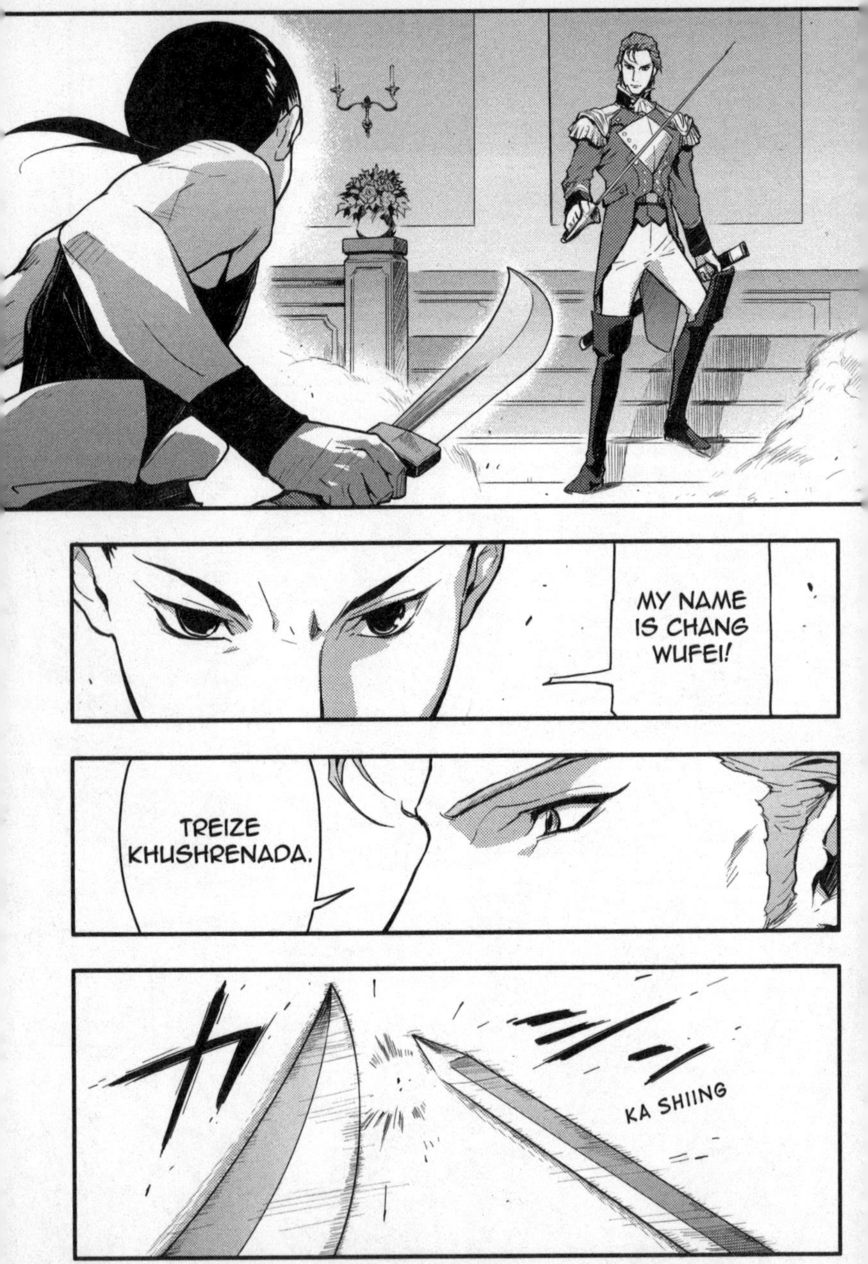
MY NAME IS CHANG WUFEI!
TREIZE KHUSHRENADA.
KA SHIING

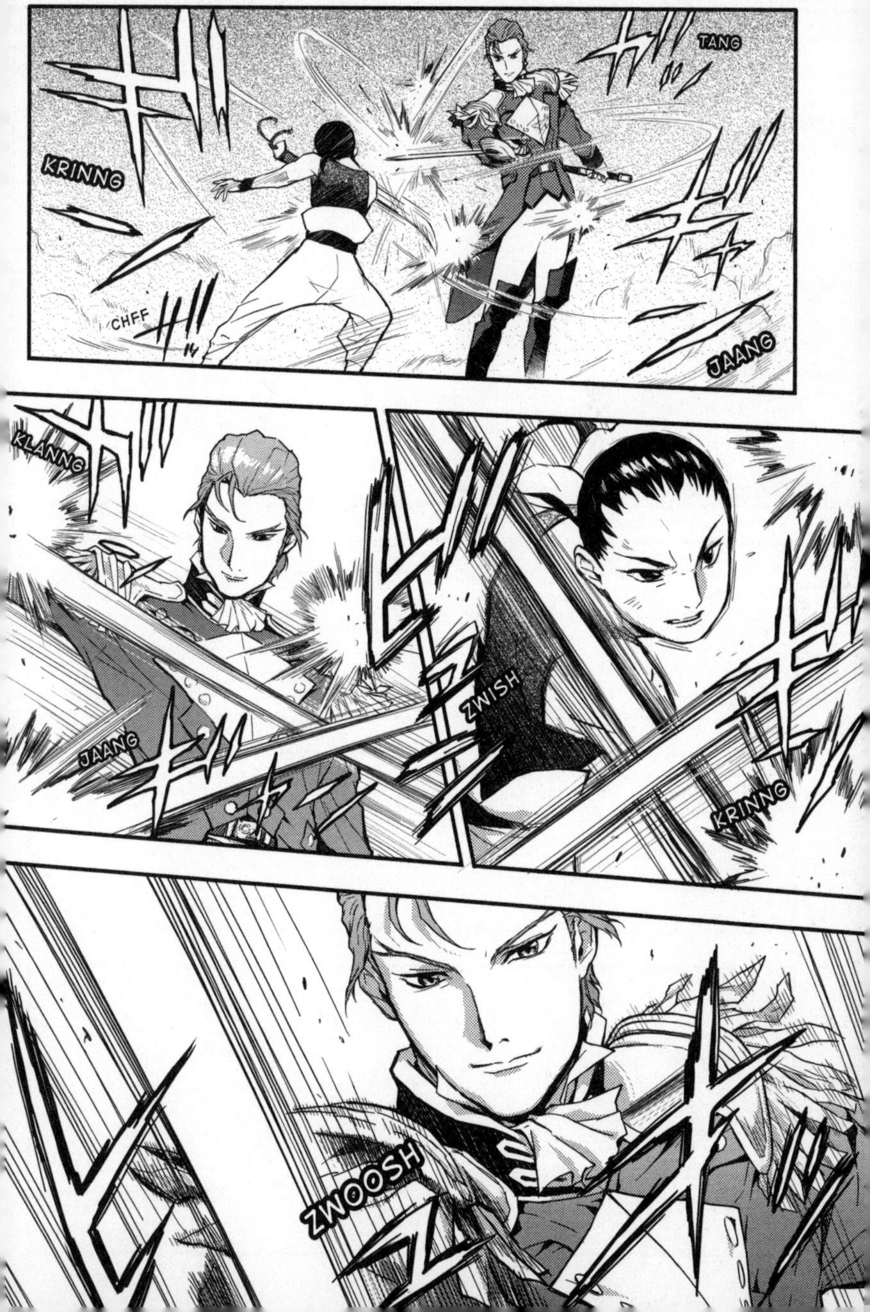
TANG
KRINNG
JAANG
CHFF
ZWISH
KRINNG
KLANNG
JAANG
ZWOOSH

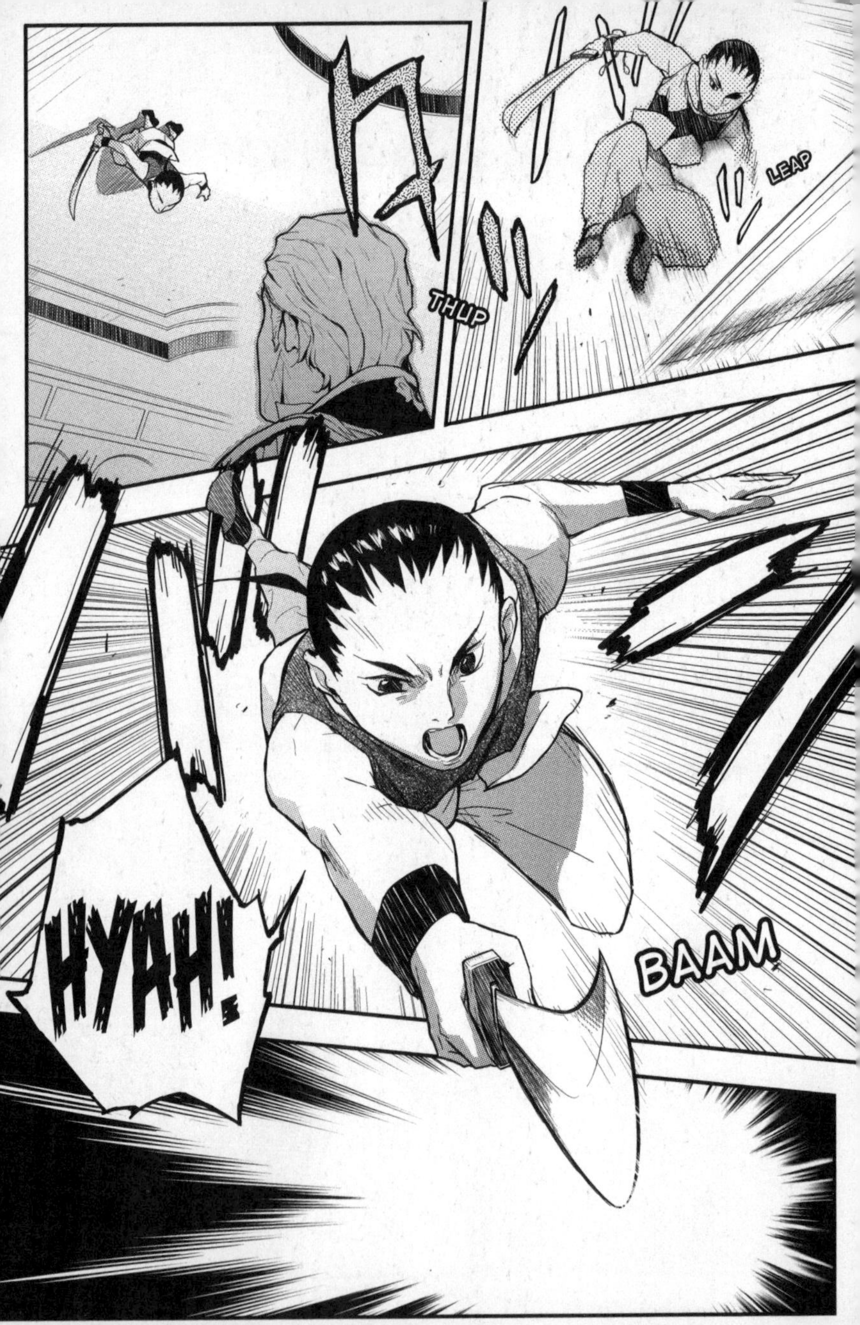
LEAP
THUP
BAAM
HYAH!

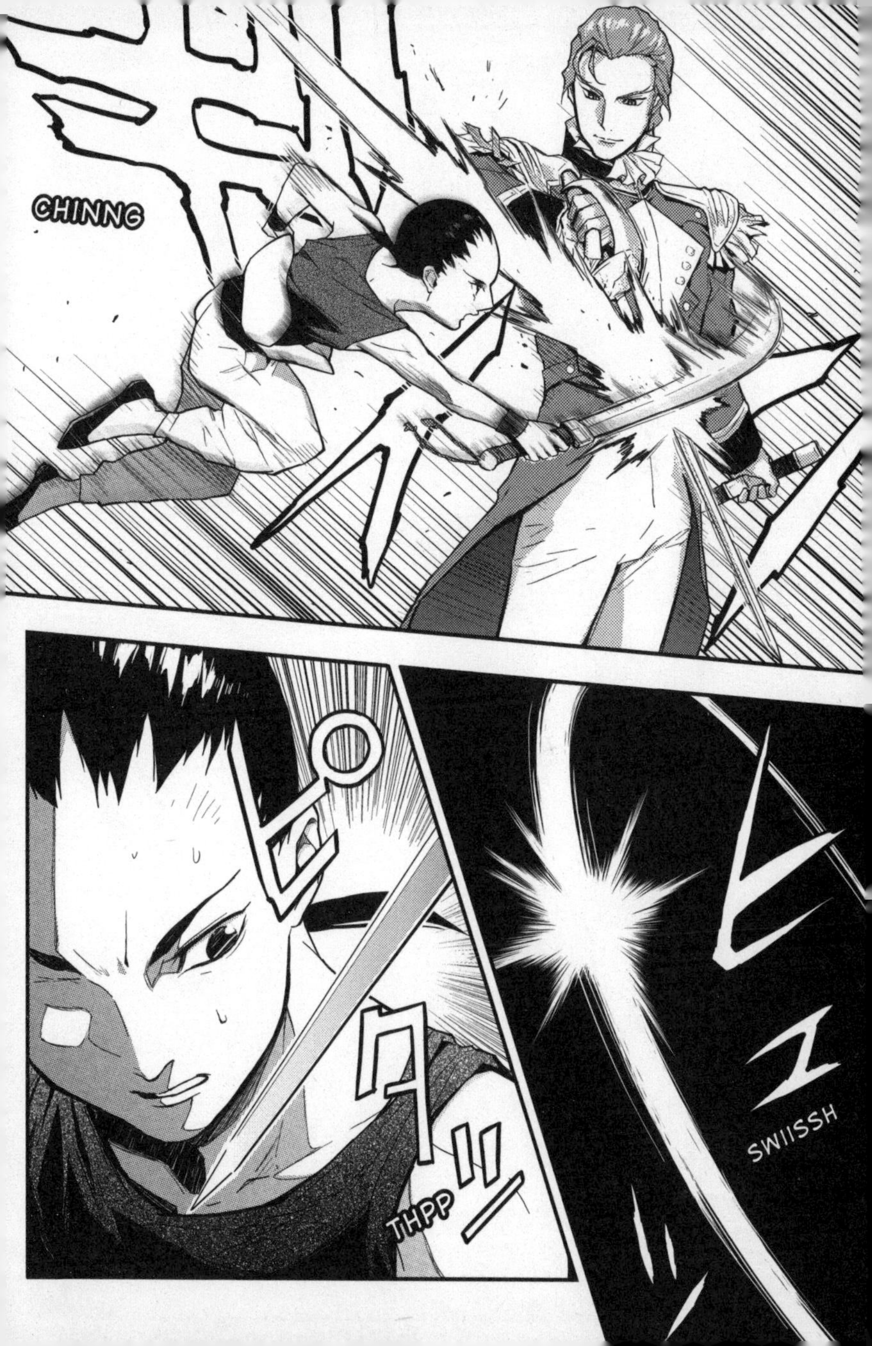
CHINNG
SWIISSH
THPP

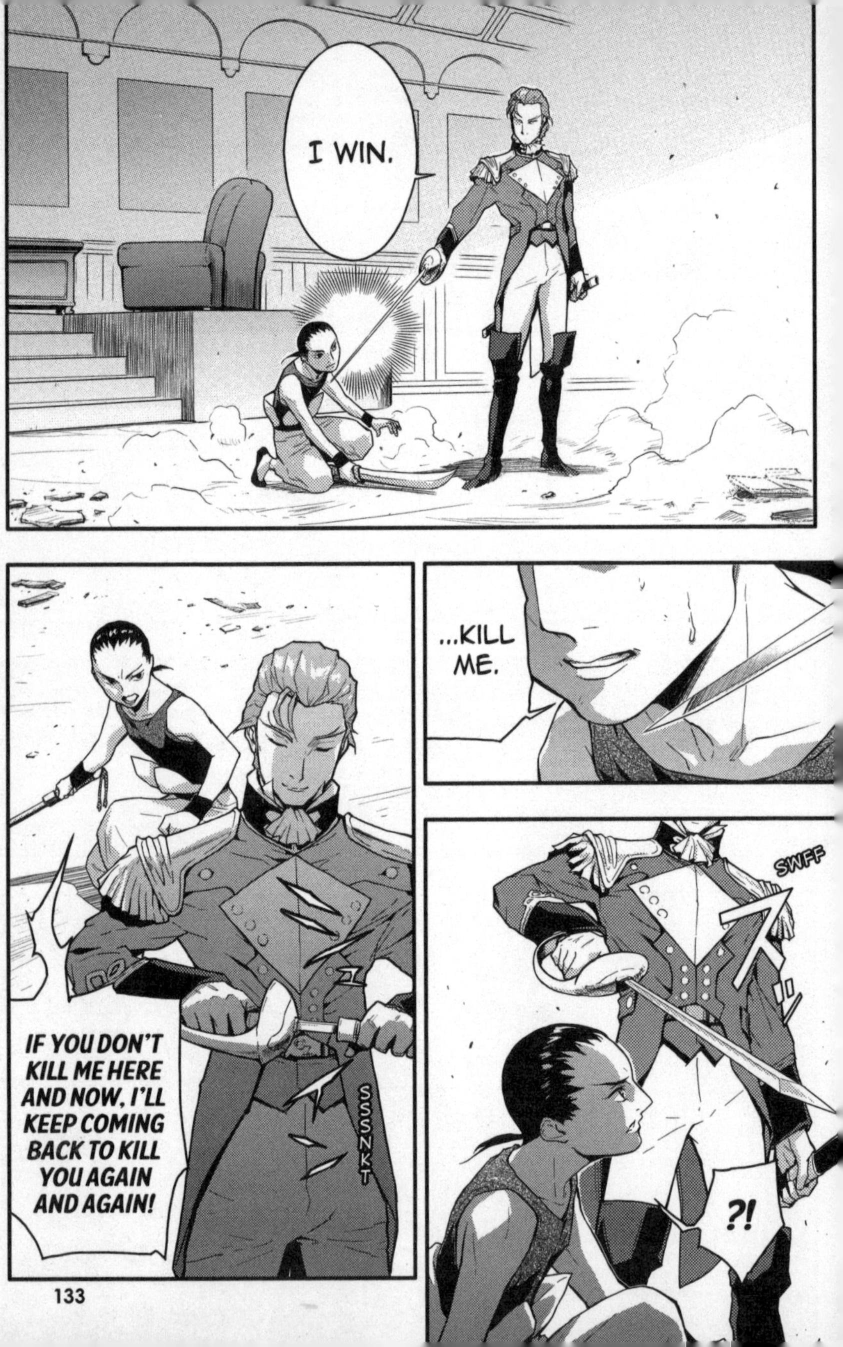
I WIN.
...KILL ME.
SWFF
?!
IF YOU DON'T KILL ME HERE AND NOW, I'LL KEEP COMING BACK TO KILL YOU AGAIN AND AGAIN!
SSSNKT

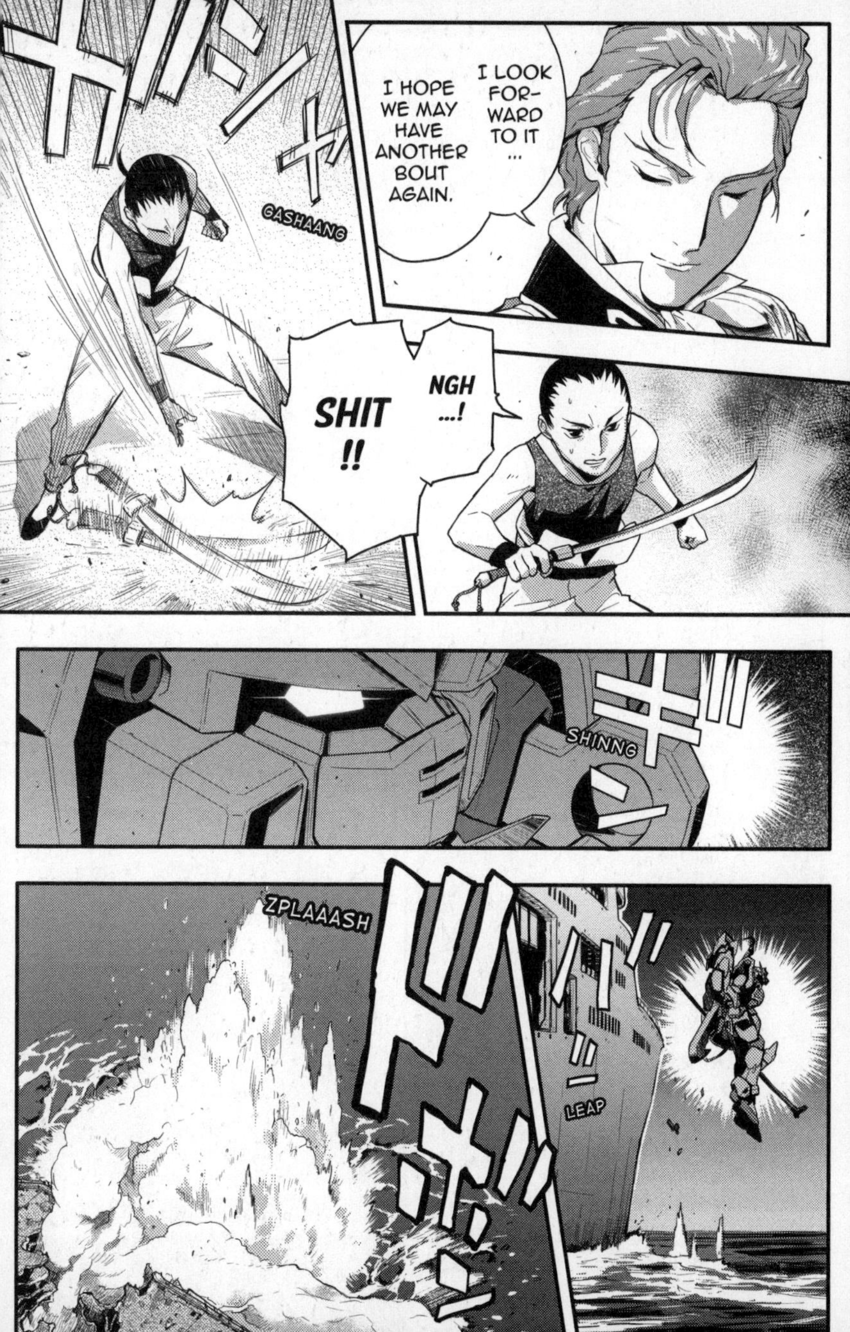
I LOOK FOR-WARD TO IT ...
I HOPE WE MAY HAVE ANOTHER BOUT AGAIN.
NGH ...!
GASHAANG
SHIT !!
SHINNG
ZPLAAASH
LEAP

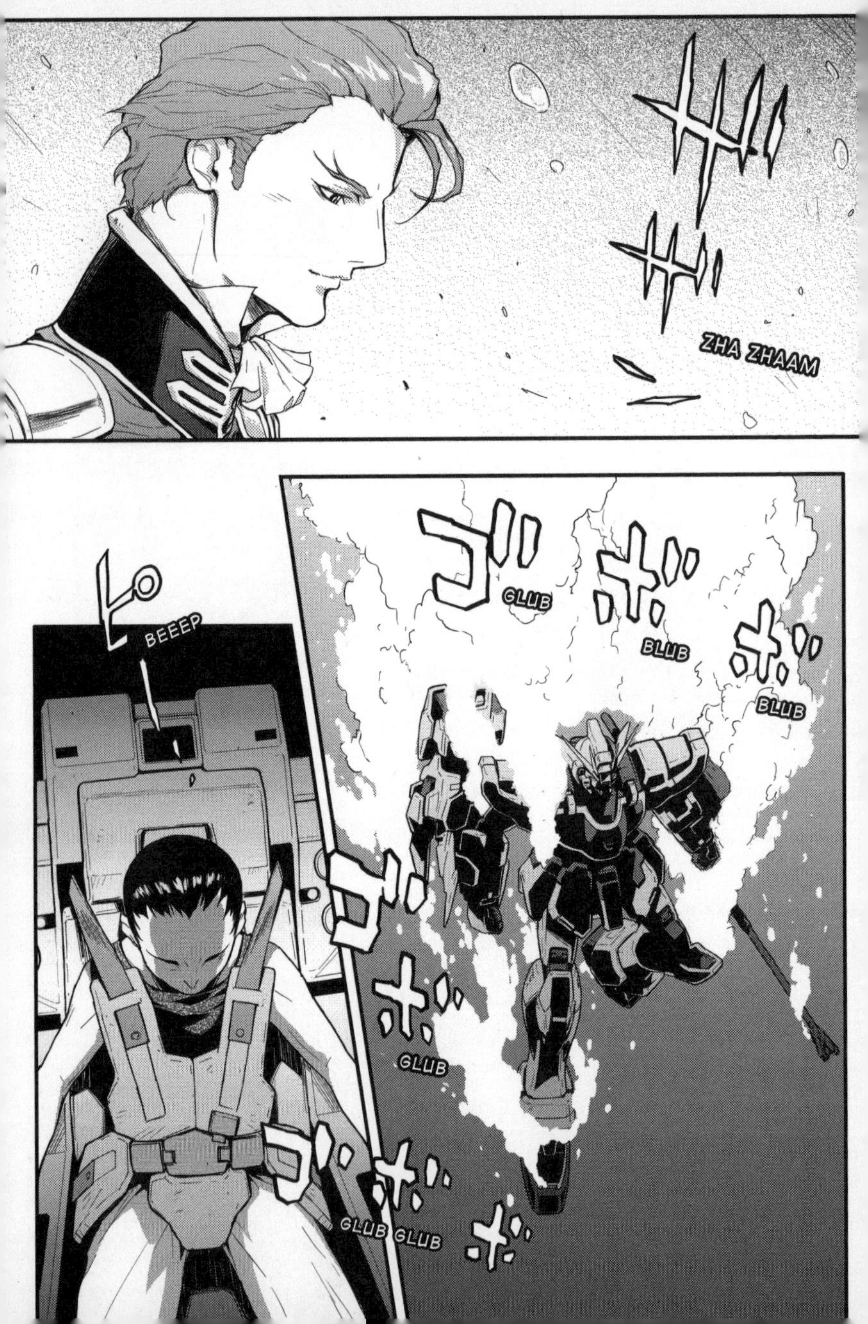
ZHA ZHAAM
GLUB
BLUB
BLUB
GLUB
GLUB GLUB
BEEEP

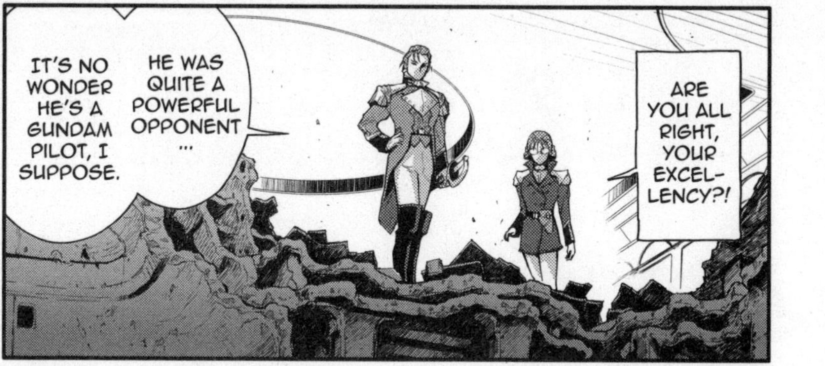
ARE YOU ALL RIGHT, YOUR EXCEL-LENCY?!
HE WAS QUITE A POWERFUL OPPONENT ...
IT'S NO WONDER HE'S A GUNDAM PILOT, I SUPPOSE.
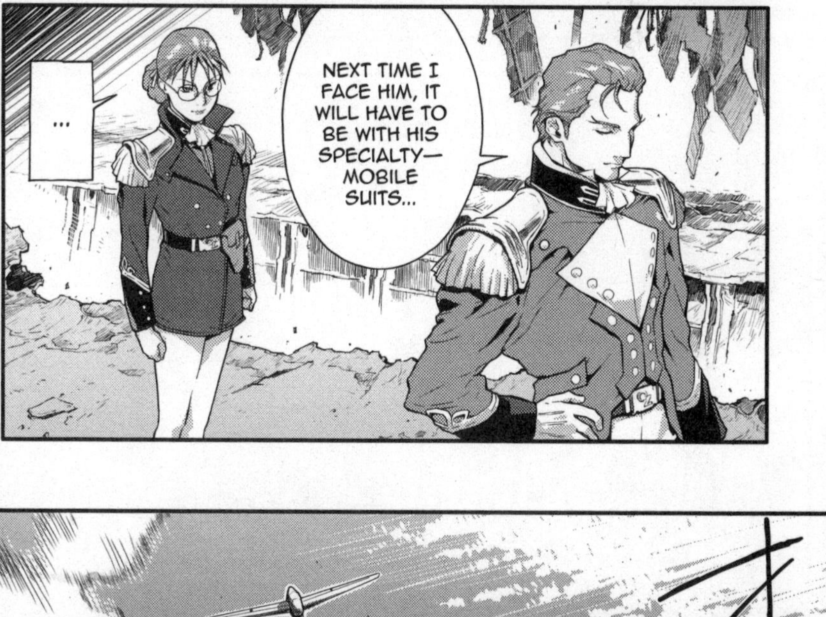
NEXT TIME I FACE HIM, IT WILL HAVE TO BE WITH HIS SPECIALTY— MOBILE SUITS...
...
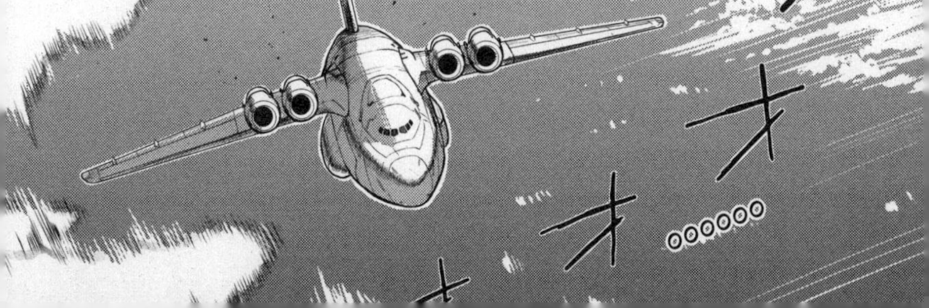
OOOOOO

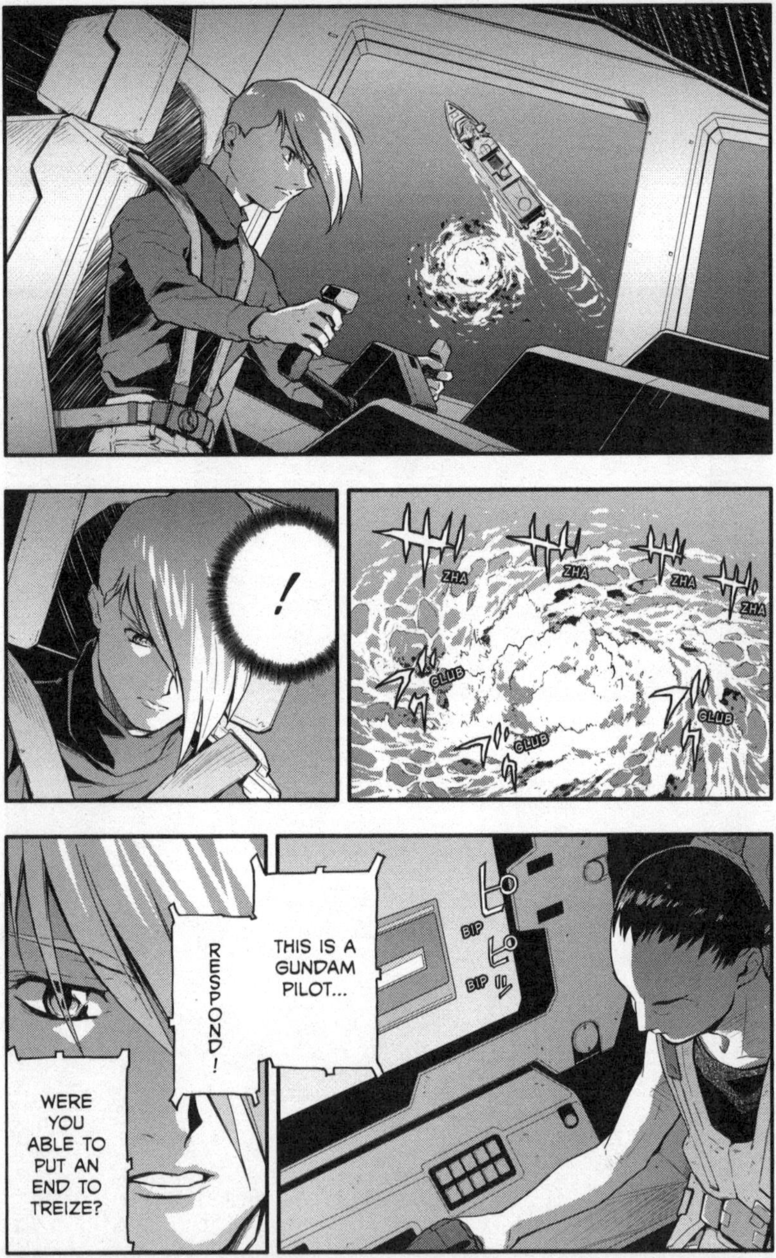
ZHA
ZHA
ZHA
ZHA
GLUB
GLUB
GLUB
!
BIP
BIP
THIS IS A GUNDAM PILOT...
RESPOND!
WERE YOU ABLE TO PUT AN END TO TREIZE?

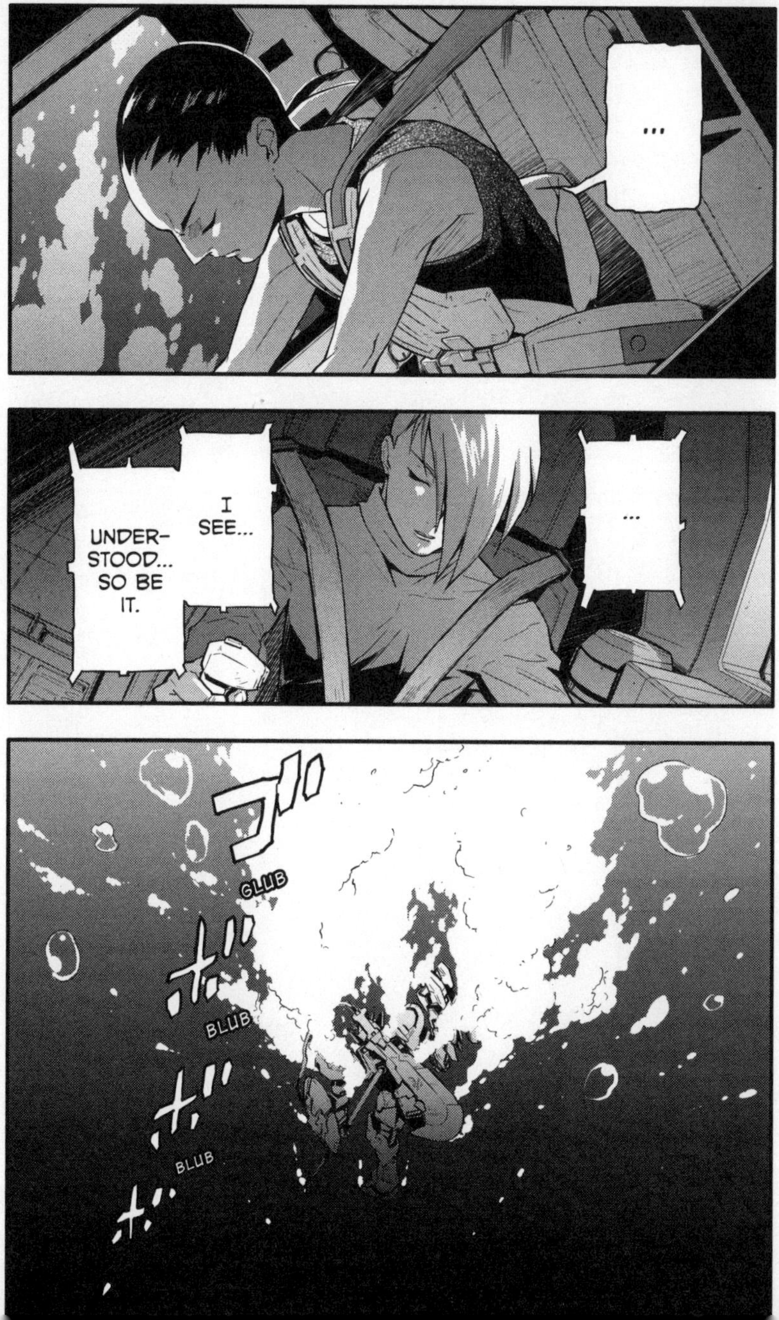
...
...
I SEE...
UNDER-STOOD... SO BE IT.
GLUB
BLUB
BLUB

Heero *Yuy*

Quatre *Raberba Winner*

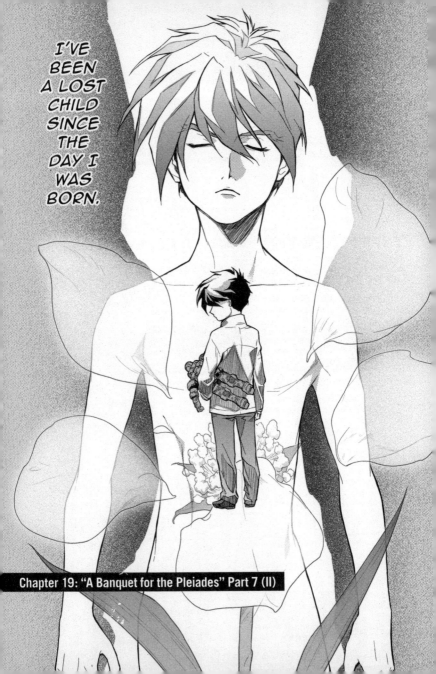

I'VE BEEN A LOST CHILD SINCE THE DAY I WAS BORN.

Chapter 19: "A Banquet for the Pleiades" Part 7 (II)

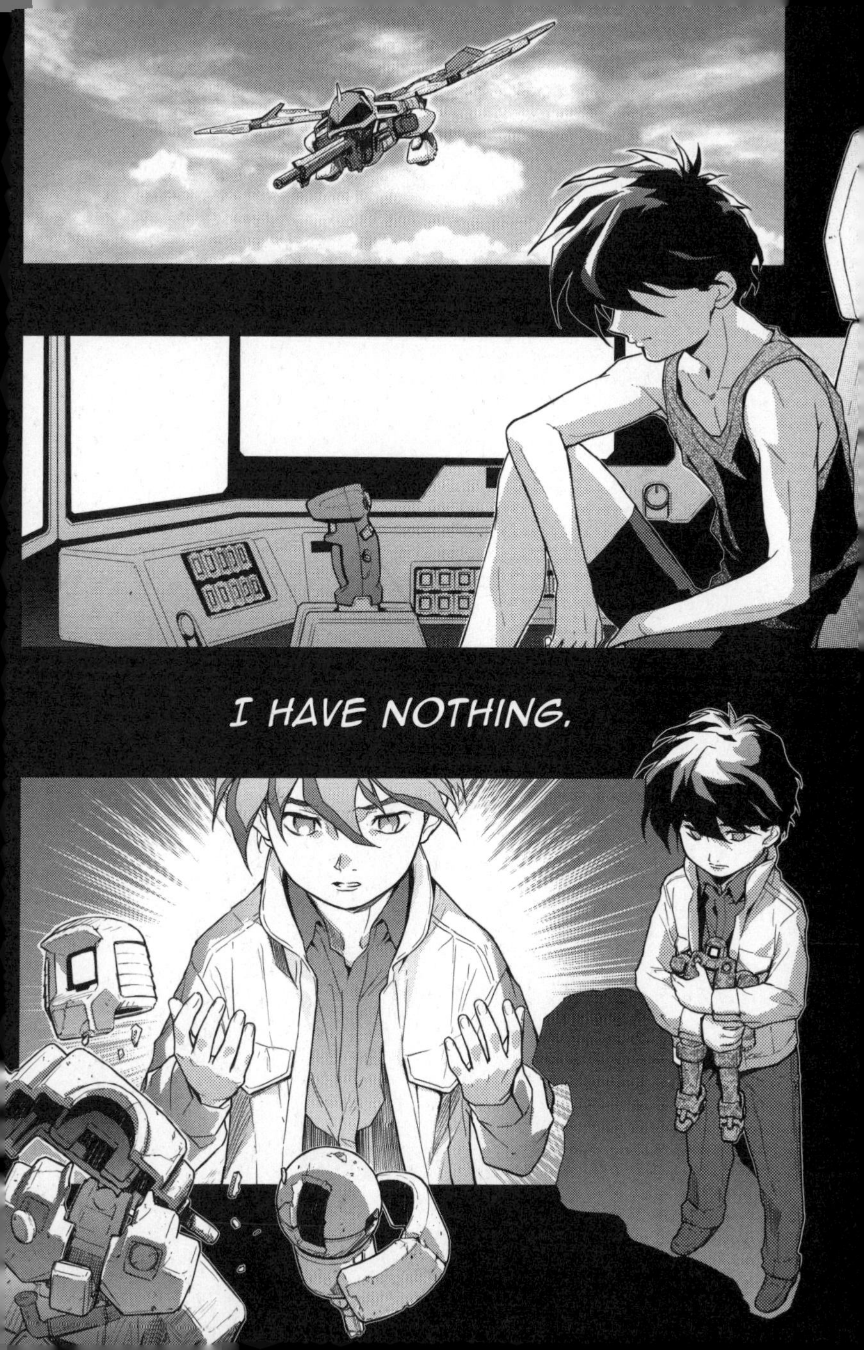
I HAVE NOTHING.

SPACE STOLE EVERY SINGLE THING AWAY FROM ME...

MY PARENTS, MY LEO TOY...

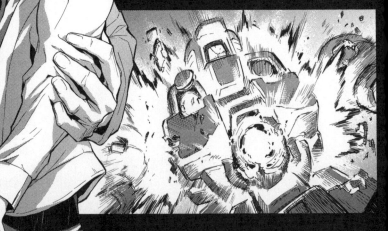

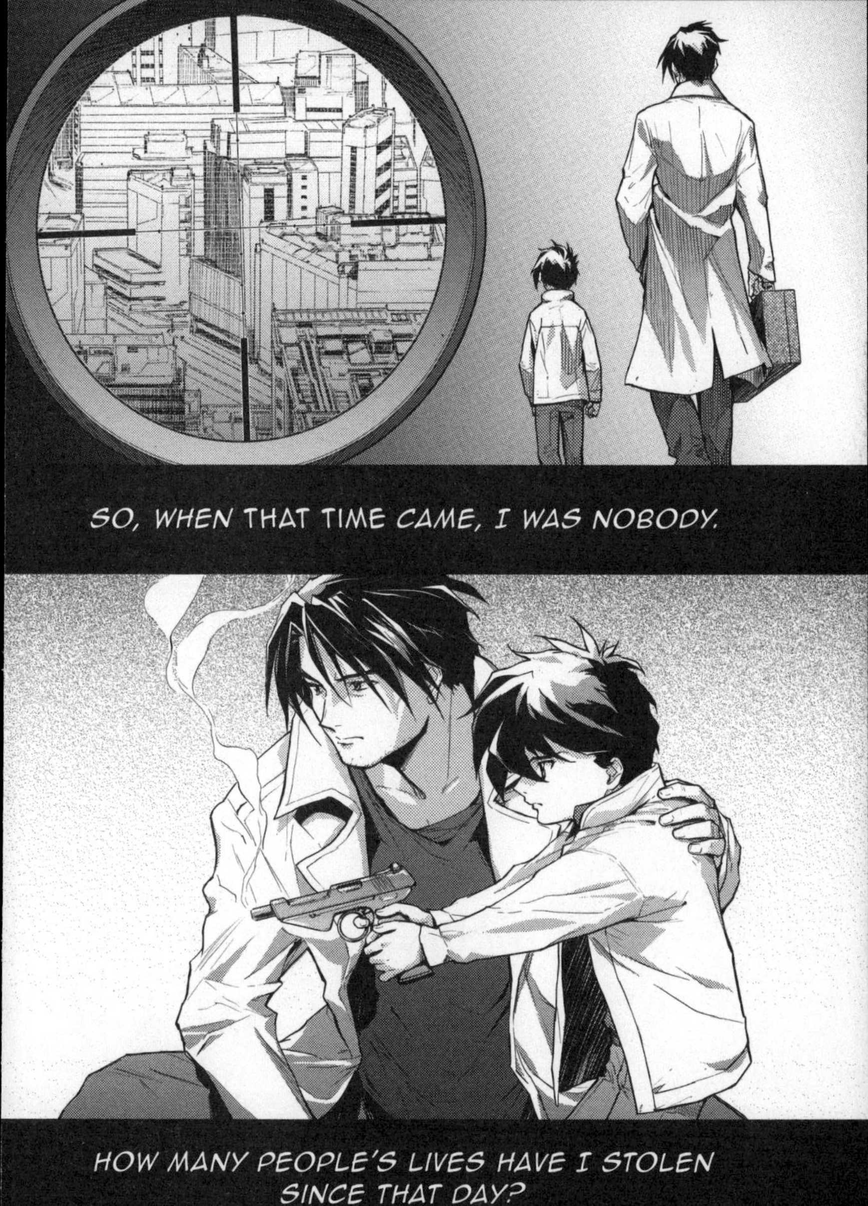
SO, WHEN THAT TIME CAME, I WAS NOBODY.
HOW MANY PEOPLE'S LIVES HAVE I STOLEN SINCE THAT DAY?

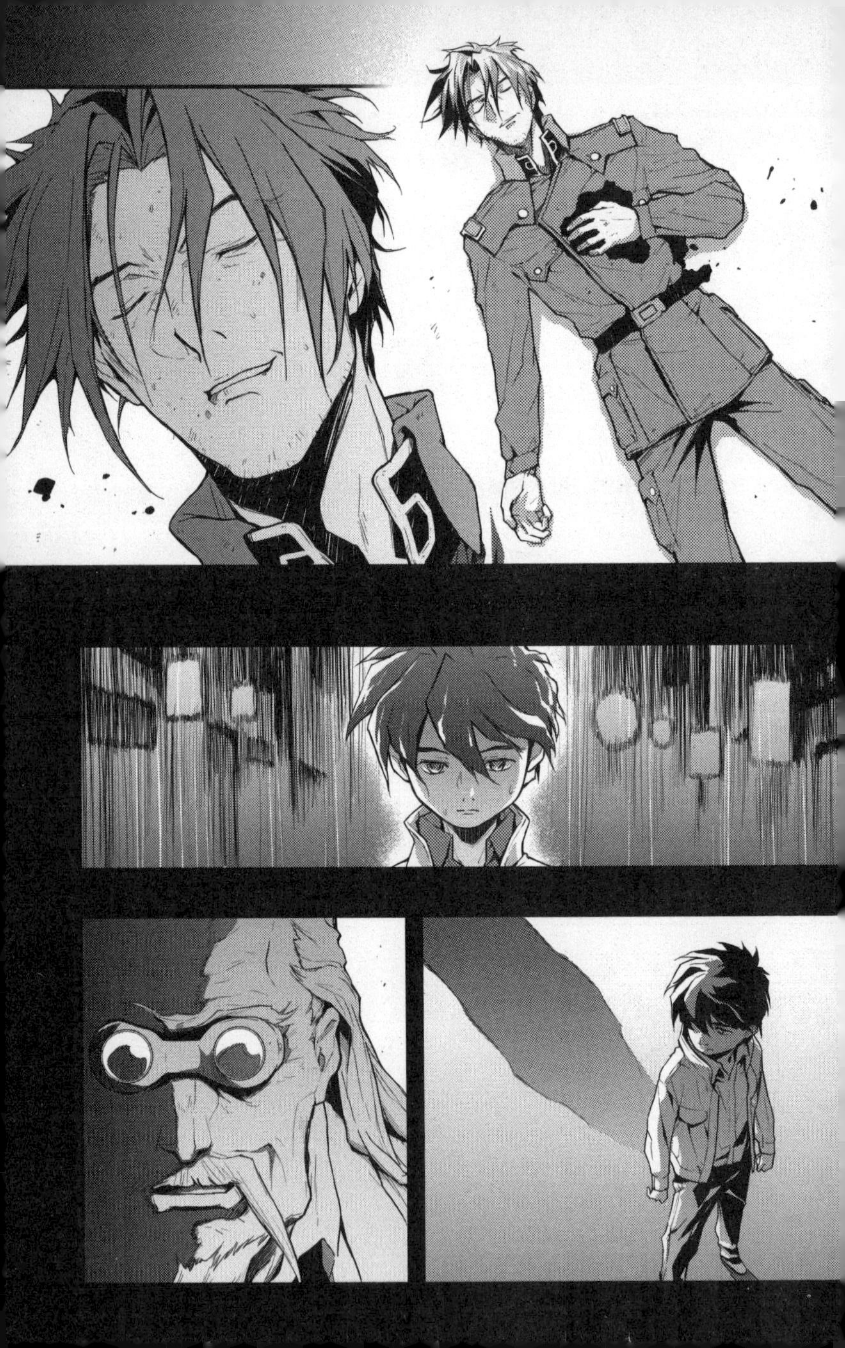

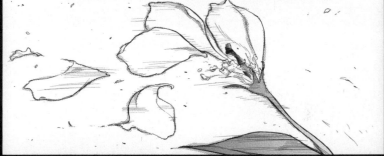

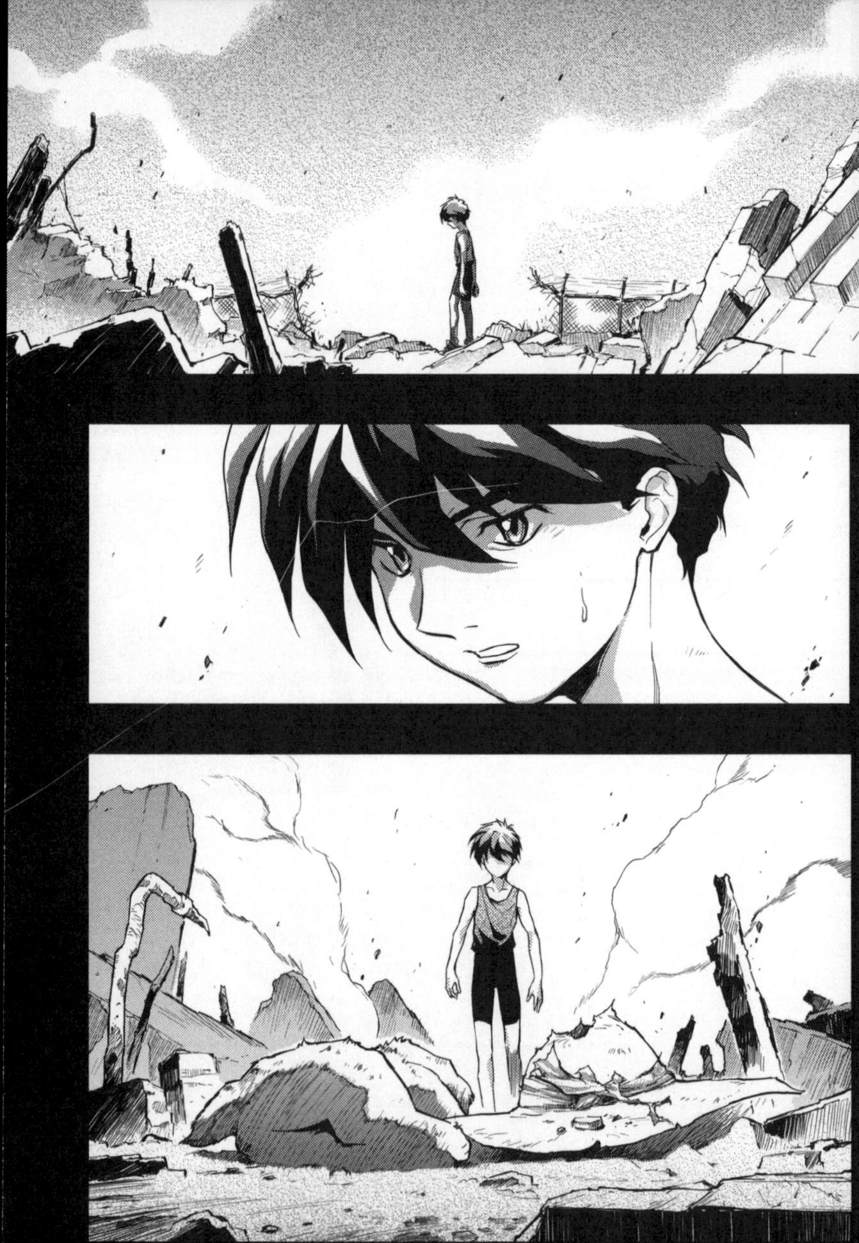

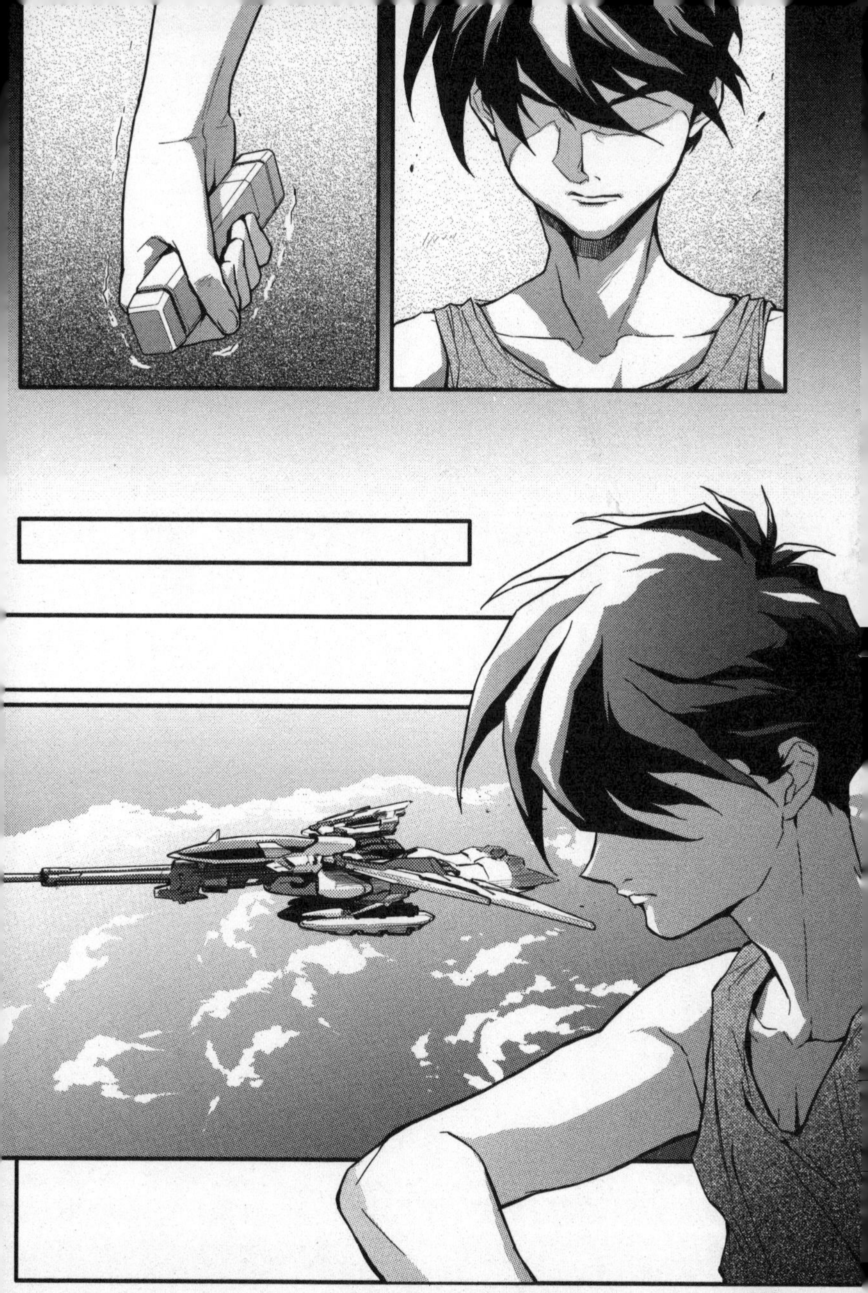

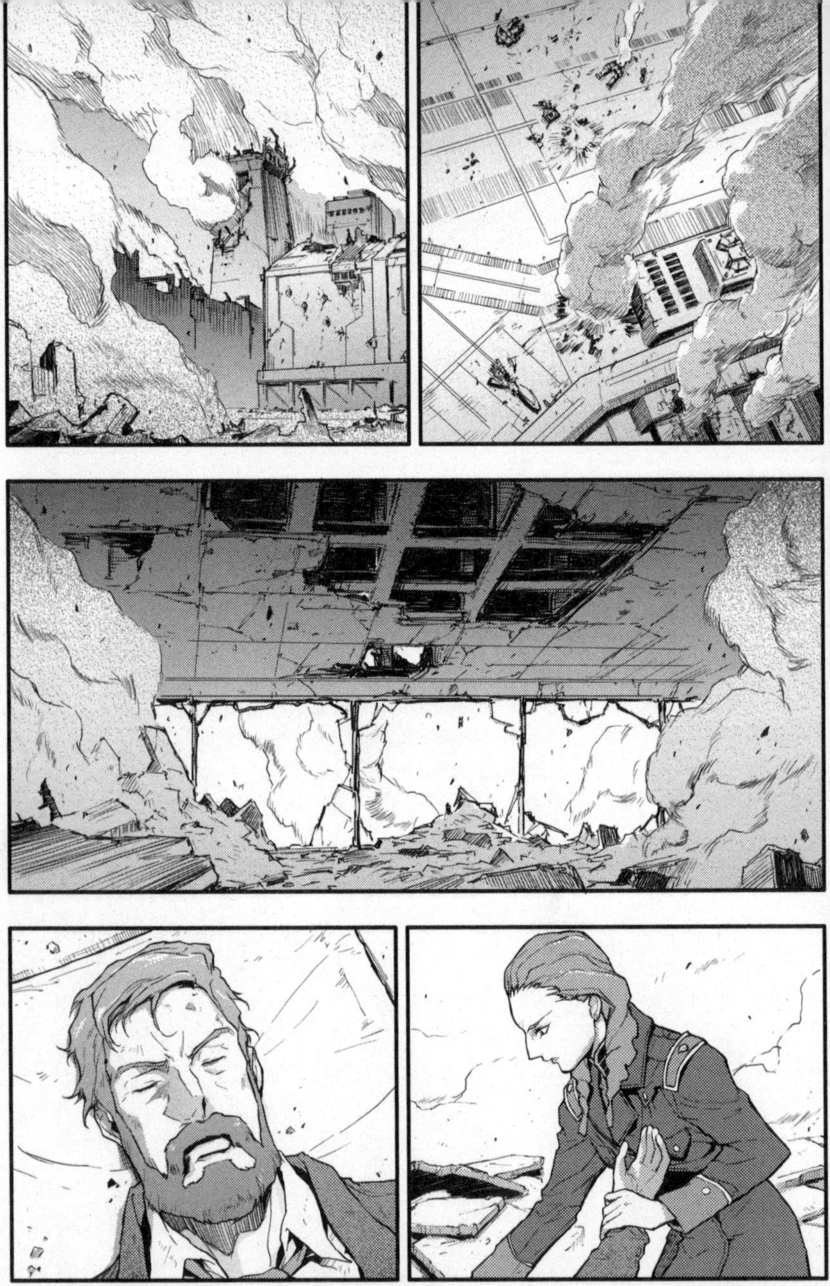

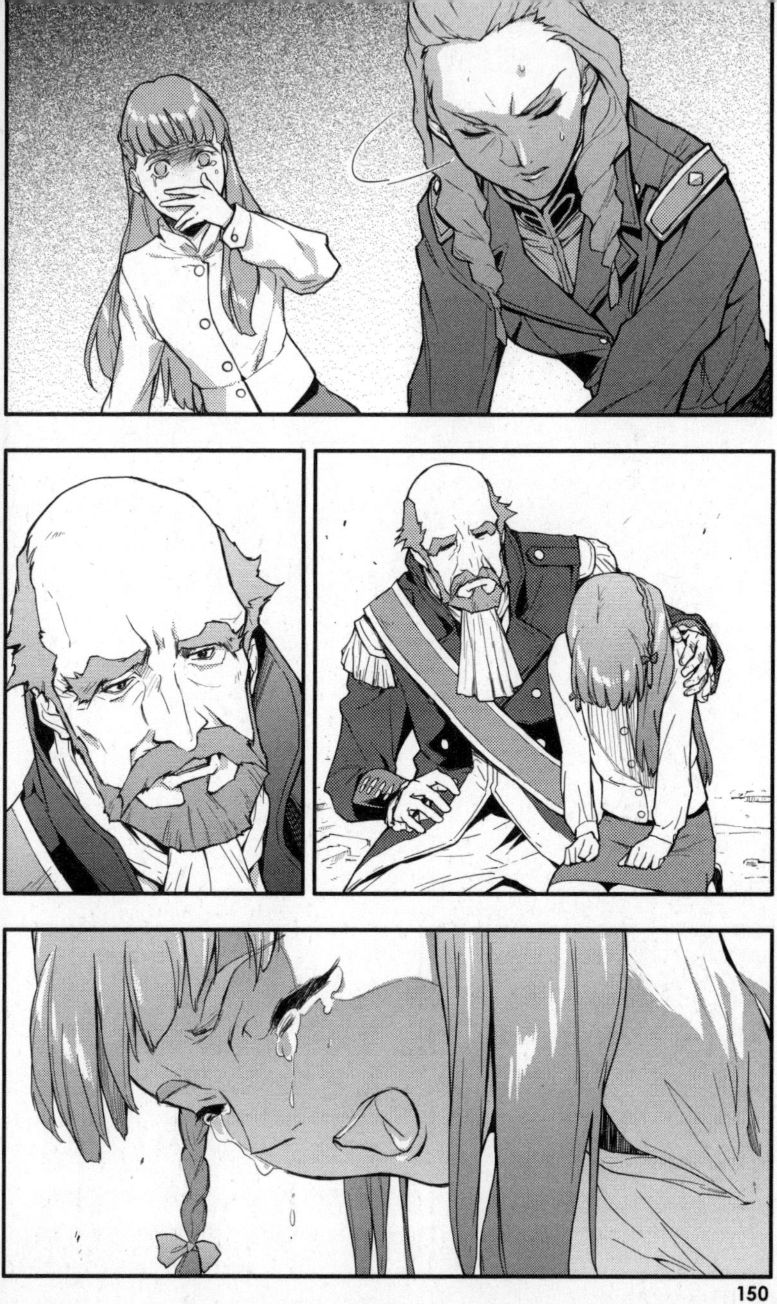

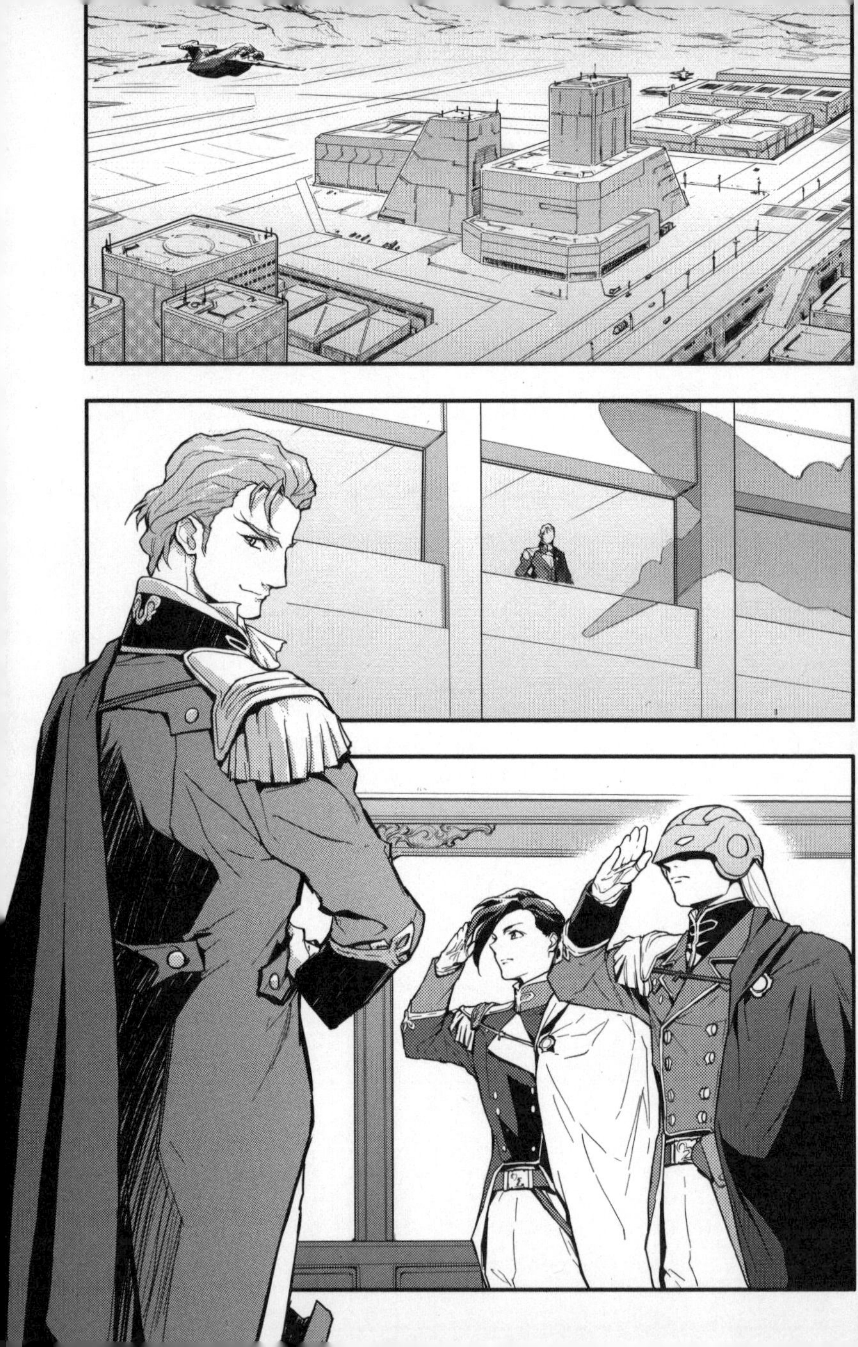

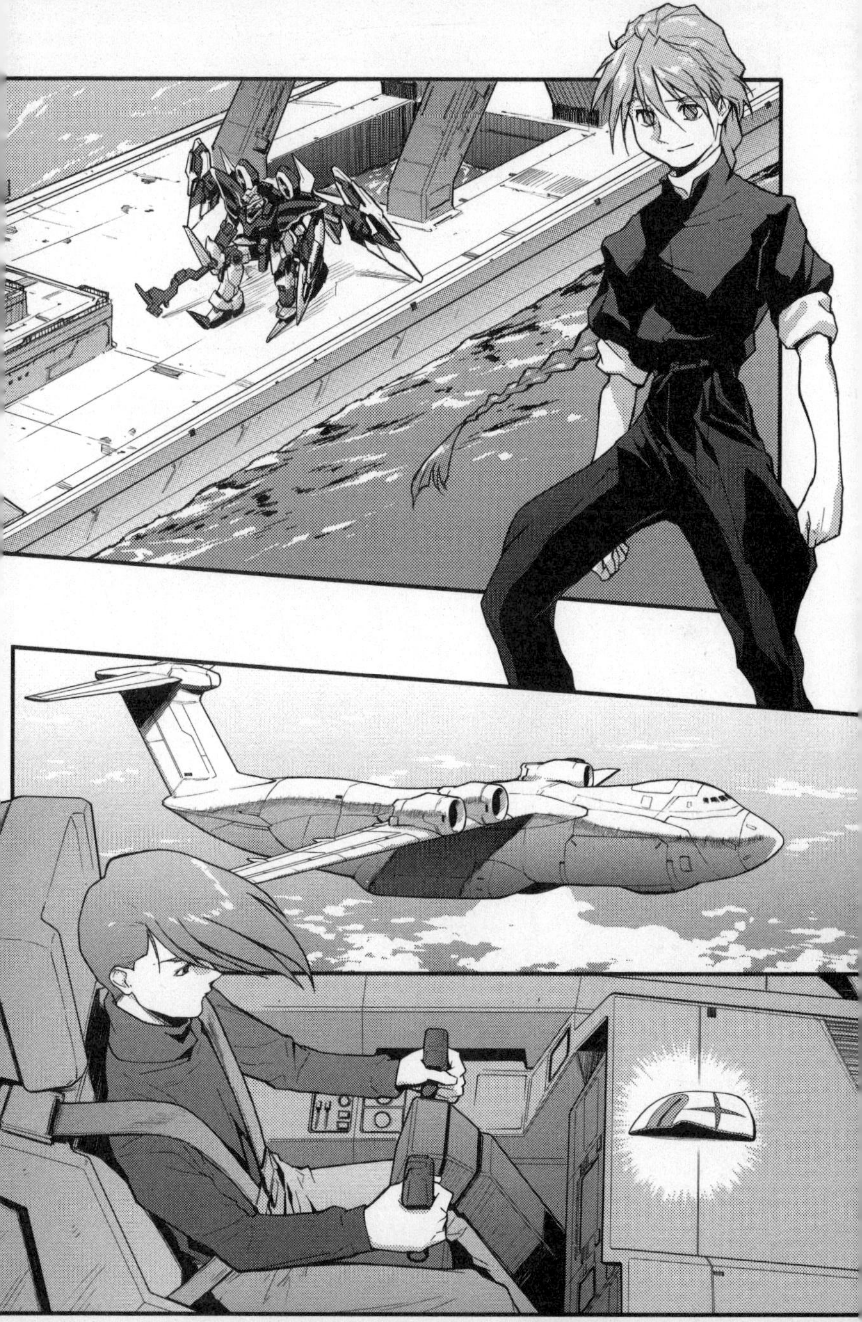

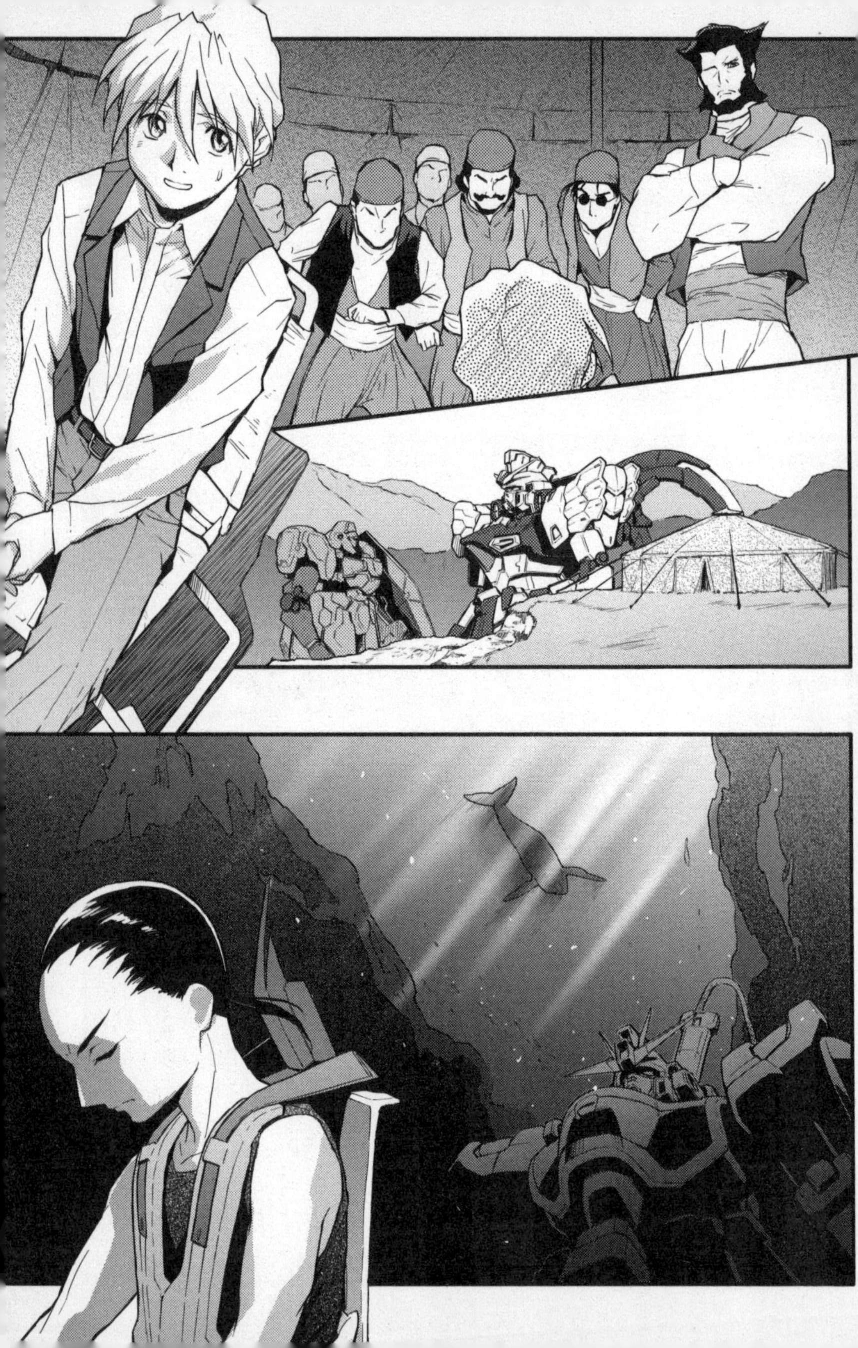

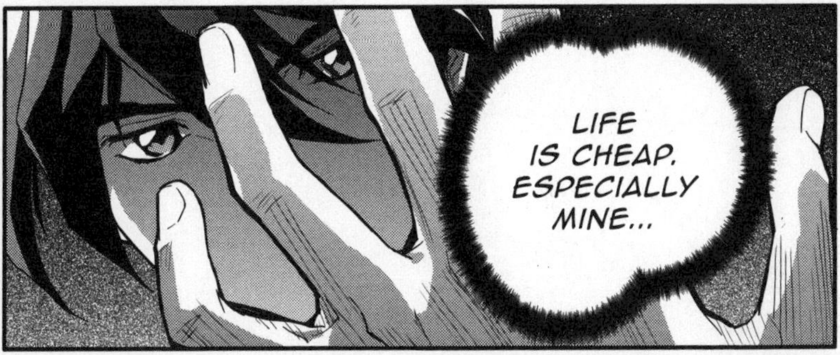
LIFE IS CHEAP. ESPECIALLY MINE...

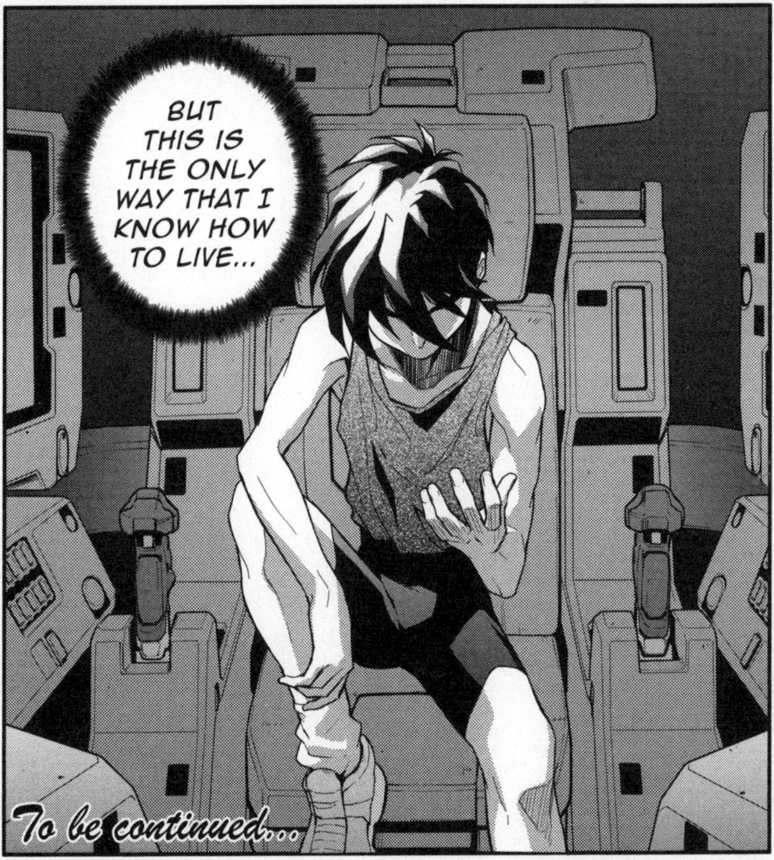
BUT THIS IS THE ONLY WAY THAT I KNOW HOW TO LIVE...
To be continued...

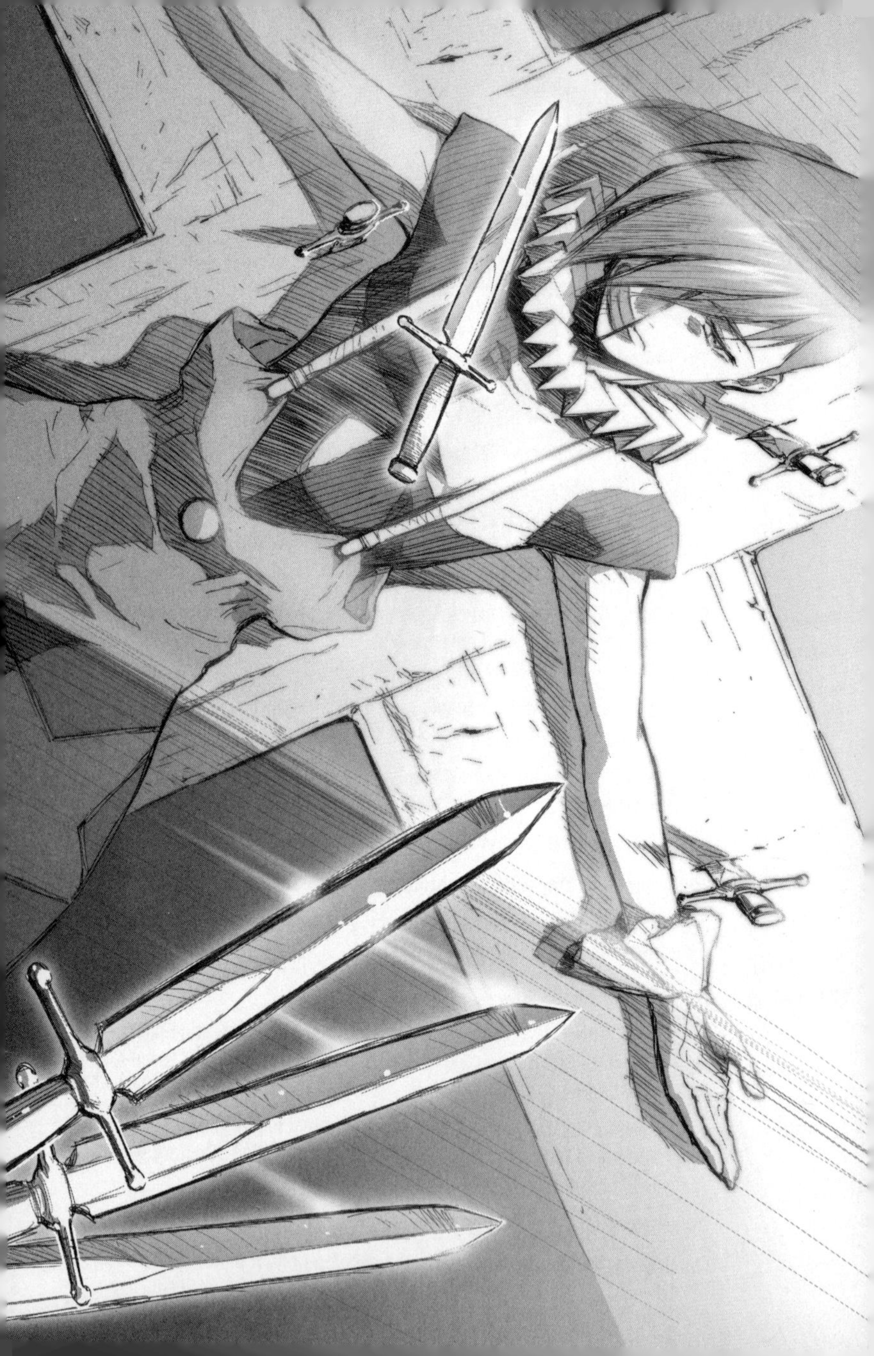

Timeline

Illustrations by Sakura Asagi

Date	Event
A.C. 0001	"After Colony" calendar established. Construction of colonies begins.
102:	Humankind's first space colonies, the L-1 Colonies, are completed.
30 Spring:	Sabrina Peacecraft (who would become Relena's grandmother) and her twin sister Katrina Peacecraft are born in the Sanc Kingdom.
133:	The United Earth Sphere Alliance is established with the aim of resolving conflicts between Earth and the colonies. The Alliance Military is founded.
139:	Colonial self-government is established.
145 Fall:	A delegation ship from Earth is attacked by persons unknown in the L-1 Colony sector. Sabrina was on board and escaped, but is declared dead. Jay Null (later known as Doctor J) develops the "Wyvern" equipped with the "ZERO System."
Nov 27:	Upon learning that the Alliance Military is planning a nuclear attack on the Sanc Kingdom, Katrina stops it in the Wyvern. Afterwards, Katrina comes to be called "The Lightning Queen."
147:	Some colony residents are witnessed committing terrorist acts. The Alliance dispatches the military to the colonies.
149:	The Second Era of Migration arrives. There is a large influx of laborers into the colonies.
150:	Ein Yuy, Treize's father and nephew of colony leader Heero Yuy, is born.
152:	Treize's mother, Angelina Khushrenada, is born.
165:	Colony leader Heero Yuy emerges, and there is a heightened sense of solidarity among the colonies.
171 Fall:	Treize Khushrenada is born.
172:	Duke Cinquante Khushrenada, Treize's grandfather and acting leader of the Romefeller Foundation, passes away. Dermail Catalonia is appointed to take his place.
173:	Leader Heero Yuy calls for independence of the colonies through nonviolence and demilitarization. Two years later the so-called "Declaration of Space's Will" is adopted.
	Treize's brother Vingt Khushrenada is born.
	The Romefeller Foundation initiates the development of Mobile Suits (MS).

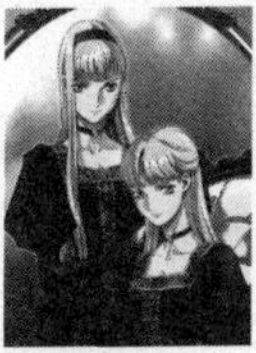

Image from *Frozen Teardrop 5*

Date	Event
174:	The Alliance Space Military begins construction of Space Fortress Bulge. All colony citizens are forced to shoulder the entire cost of the fortress's construction, which gives rise to even further animosity.
175 Apr 7:	Colony leader Heero Yuy is assassinated by a man named Odin Lowe, a sharpshooter affiliated with OZ predecessor "Alliance Special Operations Squad." In a simultaneous terrorist bombing, Treize's father, Ein Yuy, is killed.
	Five scientists working on the development of the MS Tallgeese run away. Development of the Tallgeese is halted.
176:	After the death of colony leader Heero Yuy, armed uprisings break out across the colonies. The Alliance once again dispatches the military to the colonies.
August:	The first model land warfare MS Leo is rolled out. The intermediate range support/indirect assault model MS Tragos begins development.
	Milliardo Peacecraft is born.
177 Apr:	The air warfare MS Aries is rolled out.
180 Apr 8:	Relena Peacecraft is born.
	King Peacecraft of the Sanc Kingdom advocates "absolute pacifism."
	Quatre Raberba Winner is born. His mother Quaterine dies shortly after giving birth.
	Dorothy Catalonia is born.
182:	The Sanc Kingdom is attacked and destroyed by Alliance Military under the command of General Daigo Onegell. Milliardo and Relena go missing.
183:	Treize enters the Alliance Military Academy at age 11.
185 Fall:	Treize is appointed as one of the first teachers at the OZ officer's training school at Lake Victoria Base in the middle of the African continent.
186 Winter:	There is a rebellion in Mogadishu, Africa. An OZ MS squad led by Treize is thrown into actual combat for the first time. Five candidates are selected among the cadets for the battle, and those five include Zechs and Noin.
Spring:	Trieze's brother Vingt is appointed deputy director of the Romefeller Foundation. He becomes a central and essential figure in the foundation.

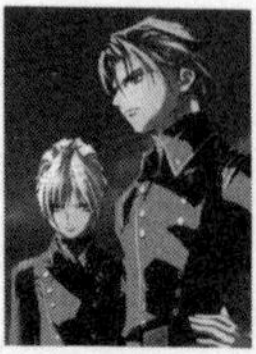

Image from *Frozen Teardrop 1*

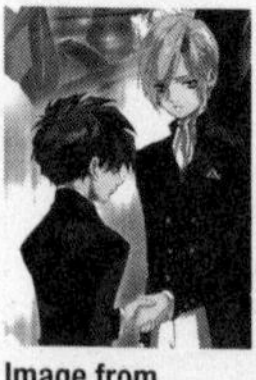

Image from *Frozen Teardrop 2*

Timeline

Date	Event
Summer:	A massive battle between Mobile Suits called "Ocean of Storms War," also known as the "First Moon War," is waged.
	Treize leads a group of just 45 OZ Mobile Suits against 80 anti-Alliance army Mobile Suits, but OZ wins thanks to the state-of-the-art MS Leo Type IV (the Greif).
	Two days after the battle, a massive carrier with 25 Greifs on board goes missing along with cadets Zechs Merquise and Elve Onegell. They were being transported to Space Fortress Bulge.
Oct 26:	Space Fortress Bulge is completed. However, the anti-Alliance army assaults Bulge with the 25 stolen Leo Type IVs that had been painted black (Schwarz Griefs). Treize's OZ Specials are assigned to stamp out the rebel forces and he is successful in expelling them.
187:	Treize's brother and key Romefeller Foundation leader Vingt Khushrenada dies in a terrorist bombing. His mother Angelina Yuy also dies.
	The orphan Duo (age 7) is taken in by the Maxwell Church in the L-2 Colony sector's V08744.
188:	An anti-Alliance coup d'état occurs in Colony V08744. During the incident, coup d'état fighters hole up in the Maxwell Church. More than 240 people are killed. Afterwards, this comes to be known as the "Maxwell Church Tragedy."
	A boy called Odin Lowe Jr. meets Doctor J at Colony X18999. Afterwards, he is given the code name "Heero Yuy."
189:	Treize's daughter Mariemaia is born.
	Leia Barton, Treize's wife and Mariemaia's mother, passes away.
191:	Relena, at age 11, now Vice-Foreign Minister Darlian's daughter, meets a young Zechs (Milliardo).
192:	A massive Peacemillion-class space battleship, the Peacemillion, is completed.
	Duo Maxwell starts working alongside Professor G and his sweeper group.
193:	Treize Khushrenada is appointed OZ commander-in-chief.
	Quatre runs away from his father. On his travels, he meets Rasid and the Maganac Corps.

Date	Event
194:	The boy known as Odin Lowe Jr. blows up an Alliance Military training facility in the L-1 Colonies. During the operation, MS Leos explode, which destroys a civilian facility.
195 Apr 7:	Certain colony residents execute "Operation Meteor."
	Heero and Zechs have their first battle. The Wing Gundam falls into the sea.
	Heero meets Relena.
	The existence of five Gundams is confirmed.
Apr 8:	Duo recovers the Wing Gundam from the sea.
	Vice-Foreign Minister Darlian is assassinated by OZ's Lady Une.
	Through a stratagem by Treize, Field Marshal Noventa and other pacifist Alliance Military leaders gathered at New Edwards Base are wiped out by the Wing Gundam.
May 20:	"Operation Daybreak" is initiated.
	OZ begins to dismantle the United Earth Sphere Alliance. The whole of the Earth is placed under the control of the Romefeller Foundation.
	The colonies are held hostage and the Wing Gundam is set to self-destruct.
	Zechs Merquise and Heero Yuy clash at the South Pole.
	Zechs Merquise is sentenced to be publicly executed for breach of military discipline, but he goes missing.
	Special Envoy Lady Une begins a campaign of reconciliation with each of the colonies.
	"Operation Nova" is carried out.
	On the moon, great numbers of mass-produced Mobile Dolls are sent to Earth. Friction between the Treize faction and the Romefeller Foundation faction in OZ worsens.
	The Gundam Sandrock self-destructs at Singapore Base.
	The Four Gundams take off for space.
	There is internal discord at a Winner family resource satellite. Zayeed, the head of the Winner family, dies.
195:	Quatre builds the Wing Gundam 0, which becomes the prototype for all the other Gundams. He starts attacking the colonies.

Timeline

Date	Event
195:	Treize opposes the use of Mobile Dolls in war and falls from power.
	OZ is reborn with Duke Dermail at its core, and internal conflict with Treize's faction further intensifies.
	Relena restores the Sanc Kingdom.
	Heero receives the Gundam Epyon from Treize, who is under house arrest.
	OZ's Mobile Doll squadrons carry out a campaign to suppress the Sanc Kingdom.
	The Sanc Kingdom is destroyed.
	Relena is appointed as a representative of the Romefeller Foundation. She calls for the formation of a unified world nation.
	Relena is crowned queen.
	The Artemis Revolution is established.
	White Fang rises to action. Milliardo Peacecraft (aka Zechs Merquise) is appointed leader of White Fang.
	The massive battleship Libra is captured by White Fang.
	Milliardo declares war against Earth.
Nov:	Romefeller Foundation VIPs left in space hole up in Space Fortress Bulge.
	White Fang Commander Milliardo Peacecraft takes down Bulge with the Gundam Epyon alone.
	Treize initiates a coup d'état and is reinstated as OZ commander-in-chief.
	Relena is relieved from her position as Romefeller Foundation representative.
Dec 24:	Earth's Treize-led Unified World Nation Army and the colonies' Milliardo-led Revolutionary Army White Fang engage in full-scale clashes. These are later called the "Eve Wars."
	Treize dies in one-on-one combat against Wufei. He was 24.
	A fragment of the massive battleship Libra falls toward the Earth, but Heero manages to stop it.

Date	Event
Dec 24:	In Treize's stead, Lady Une signs a truce accord with White Fang. The Eve Wars are ended.
	The Earth Sphere Unified Nation is born.
196:	A White Fang remnant faction commits terrorist attacks against VIPs. A parallel operation to steal Gundams is carried out.
	The Vulcanus Incident occurs at the automated Mobile Doll production factory satellite Vulcanus.
	The Earth Sphere Unified Nation Intelligence Agency Preventer Sally Po discovers the drifting metal alloy "Neo Titanium."
	Quatre scraps the Wing Gundam 0, Gundam Deathscythe Hell, the upgraded Gundam Heavyarms, and the upgraded Gundam Sandrock by loading them onto a resource satellite and sending them to the sun.
Dec 24:	Vice-Foreign Minister Relena Darlian is abducted at X18999 of the L-3 Colony sector.
	Quatre learns of the Mariemaia Army's movements, and endeavors to recover the four Gundams.
Dec 25:	Mariemaia Khushrenada declares X18999 of the L-3 Colonies to be independent from the Earth Sphere Unified Nation. She declares war at the same time.
	Further, Dekim Barton of the Mariemaia Army executes a plan to drop the L-3 Colony X18999 onto the Earth. This was the true aim of Operation Meteor. However, it is stopped by Heero, Duo, and Trowa.
	The Mariemaia Army sends 470 MS Serpents to Earth.
Dec 26:	The Mariemaia Army takes over the executive office of the president in Brussels, Europe.
	In geostationary orbit, Heero's Wing Gundam 0 and Wufei's Altron Gundam clash.
	The Preventer, Duo, Trowa, and Quatre commence resistance against the Mariemaia Army. They are successful in suppressing them.
	Dekim Barton, mastermind of the Mariemaia Army, dies. The war comes to an end.
M.C. 0022:	Heero Yuy wakens from cryogenic hibernation.

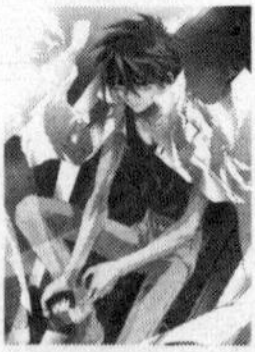

Image from
Frozen Teardrop 1

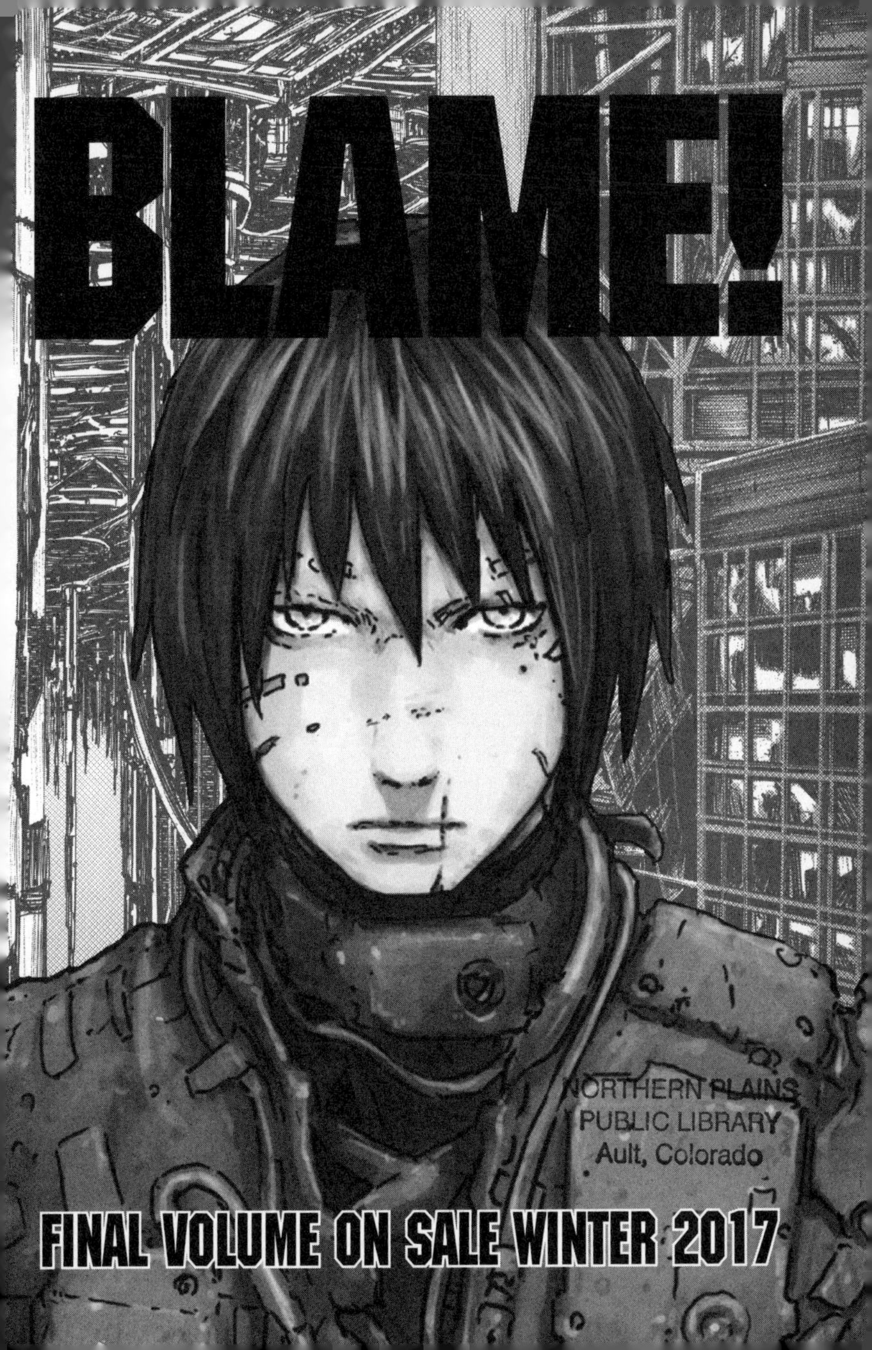
BLAME!
FINAL VOLUME ON SALE WINTER 2017

IN A FUTURE VERSION OF EARTH, THERE IS A CITY GROWN SO CHAOTICALLY MASSIVE THAT ITS INHABITANTS NO LONGER RECALL WHAT "LAND" IS. WITHIN THIS MEGASTRUCTURE THE SILENT, STOIC KYRII IS ON A MISSION TO FIND THE NET TERMINAL GENE—A GENETIC MUTATION THAT ONCE ALLOWED HUMANS TO ACCESS THE CYBERNETIC NETSPHERE. ARMED WITH A POWERFUL GRAVITON BEAM EMITTER, KYRII FENDS OFF WAVES OF ATTACKS FROM FELLOW HUMANS, CYBORGS AND SILICON-BASED LIFEFORMS. ALONG THE WAY, HE ENCOUNTERS A HIGHLY-SKILLED SCIENTIST WHOSE BODY HAS DETERIORATED FROM A LENGTHY IMPRISONMENT WHO PROMISES TO HELP KYRII FIND THE NET TERMINAL GENE, ONCE SHE SETTLES A SCORE FOR HERSELF...

"WHETHER IT BE THE GREAT PACING AND LAYOUTS TO THE FRENETIC ACTION THAT OCCUPIES THE PANELS IN THESE SCENES, EVERY ONE OF THEM ALWAYS PACKS A PUNCH. THESE ARE ALL EMPHASIZED BY SOME GREAT DESIGNS ACROSS THE BOARD."
—THE TURNAROUND BLOG

"NIHEI'S MOODY MASTERPIECE FINALLY RELEASED IN ITS FULL DREADFUL SPLENDOR."
—UK ANIME NETWORK

Mobile Suit GUNDAM WING, Endless Waltz
Glory of the Losers

A Vertical Comics Edition

Translation: Kumar Sivasubramanian
Production: Grace Lu
            Hiroko Mizuno

© Katsuyuki SUMIZAWA 2012
© Tomofumi OGASAWARA 2012   © SOTSU • SUNRISE
First published in Japan in 2012 by KADOKAWA CORPORATION, Tokyo.
English translation rights arranged with KADOKAWA CORPORATION, Tokyo
through TUTTLE-MORI AGENCY, INC., Tokyo.

Translation provided by Vertical Comics, 2017
Published by Vertical Comics, an imprint of Vertical, Inc., New York

Originally published in Japanese as *Shin Kidou Senki Gandamu Wingu Endless
Waltz The Glory of Losers 3* by Kadokawa Shoten, Co., Ltd.
Shin Kidou Senki Gandamu Wingu Endless Waltz The Glory of Losers
first serialized in *Gundam Ace*, Kadokawa Shoten, Co., Ltd., 2010-

This is a work of fiction.

ISBN: 978-1-945054-36-5

Manufactured in the United States of America

First Edition

Vertical, Inc.
451 Park Avenue South
7th Floor
New York, NY 10016
www.vertical-comics.com

Vertical books are distributed through Penguin-Random House Publisher Services.